For Denise, Andrew, Cody and Sara, who make it all worthwhile.

PRAISE FOR THE LONG FALL UP

"William Ledbetter's stories exists at the crossroads between hard and soft: they're full of hard space, hard choices, and hard lives, but also the soft hearts of the people who work there, make them, and live them. Bill can do more in two pages than some authors do in twenty; he'll make you love a sweater, fear for a ship, and more. So whatever your preference, hard or soft: if Bill Ledbetter has written a story, you want to read it. Simple as that." —Trevor Quachri, editor of *Analog Science Fiction and Fact* magazine

"In one thousand words, William Ledbetter managed to completely captivate me with his story "What I Am." Science fiction tales of this length rarely work for me. It's so hard to compress solid science, plotting, and characterization into so few words. In this case, however, I was completely captivated by Oscar and his companion. The science fiction element was perfect. At the same time, Bill created a compelling situation and made me desperately care about his characters. These essential qualities are to be found in his longer works as well." —Sheila Williams, editor of *Asimov's Science Fiction*

THE LONG FALL UP

AND OTHER STORIES

WILLIAM LEDBETTER

THE LONG FALL UP AND OTHER STORIES

Text Copyright © 2023 by William Ledbetter

Cover art by Vincent Sammy.

Edited by Holly Lyn Walrath. Proofread by Douglas Soules.

Published by Interstellar Flight Press

Houston, Texas.

www.interstellarflightpress.com

ISBN (eBook): 978-1-953736-27-7

ISBN (Paperback): 978-1-953736-26-0

CONTENTS

THE LONG FALL UP

THE LONG FALL UP

Like millions on Earth and aboard the Jīnshān Space Station, I watched Veronica Perez every day, but unlike those other spectators, I already knew how her story would end. She disgusted me and I hated her actions, but I was curious about how it started. Newshounds had already dug up every detail of her past, from an interview with her first boyfriend at age thirteen to her biology doctorate dissertation only fifteen years later, but none of that revealed the true person.

As I ran through my systems check and prepped my ship for extended acceleration, I watched her first broadcast again, but this time with sound muted. I noted tiny movements of her eyes and mouth, the nervous way her hands twitched, and the slight wrinkles between her eyes. She clearly believed what she was saying, but how could she be so heartless? How could she doom her own child to such a life? Even after a third viewing, I still wanted to scream in her face.

"Play it again, Huizhu," I said to the ship's AI. "With sound this time."

"My name is Veronica Perez," she said. "I'm outbound on an elliptical orbit that will bring me back to the Mountain one year from now, and I'm six months pregnant."

She was so haughty, so proud of her crime. It sickened me. I'd been hired and trained to protect Jīnshān Station—or "the Mountain" as she had so casually called it. I found the casual term disrespectful. Jīnshān Station was a Bernal sphere habitat parked at Lagrange Point Five with a population of over twenty-seven thousand. My parents and sister lived there, so I embraced my job eagerly. I was also prepared to kill to protect my family, though I'd never expected my foe to be a pregnant woman.

My status board turned green, indicating the crèche was ready for me to enter. "Open the hatch, Huizhu."

The ship's AI obeyed without comment, and I peeled off my clothes as the crèche hissed open.

"No father acted as my accomplice," the woman continued. "I used a robotic device to implant the fertilized egg two days after my acceleration burn, so the child has gestated entirely in a zero-gravity environment."

I stepped into the warm acceleration jelly and began attaching the unpleasant wires and tubes necessary for an extended burn.

"She's cold-blooded," I said aloud.

Huizhu said nothing. That bothered me.

We were told that the ship's cortexes were not true AIs, but if we couldn't tell the difference, did it matter? After two years of deep deployment, Huizhu had become my only friend and companion, yet times like this reminded me she was just another tool.

I closed the crèche lid then sealed the close-fitting helmet, wincing at the sting when interface posts pricked my shaved scalp. The helmet visor flickered to life with status and information feeds. Two small windows opened, one displaying an interactive diagram of my intercept course and the other showing the young woman still spouting her obviously well-rehearsed declamation.

"I'm willingly breaking the law and prepared to accept my punishment to prove that healthy children can be produced in null gravity."

She used the word "produced" as if she were discussing industrial output at a corporate board meeting. I had seen the videos and pictures of children gestated in zero gee. They were twisted and tortured innocents. They were the reason laws had been passed.

Then Perez got to the part that bothered me most.

"Mom and Dad? If you're watching, I'm sorry." She paused, emotion showing in her face for the first time. "I know you won't understand this and will be disappointed in me, but you're going to have a grandson. He'll just have to spend his entire life in microgravity."

Not only was she creating a deformed person, but even intended to saddle her parents with the child's care while she rotted in prison. My older sister had requested a child permit six years ago and was still waiting. Population on Jīnshān was strictly controlled for obvious reasons, but this woman had deliberately jumped the queue.

As the gel finished filling my acceleration crèche, I instructed Huizhu to fire the main thrusters. Even with the cushioning, I drifted almost back to the rear wall before the gel compressed enough to stop me.

Perez assumed pursuit would come from Jīnshān, where even the fastest ships like mine couldn't reach her in less than six months, but I was part of a picket line and I was ahead of her. Officially an asteroid defense, in reality it existed for situations just like this. I would intercept her ship in sixty-one days.

She would see me coming, probably during my deceleration burn, but if she ran she'd be under gee forces and could never claim that the baby developed in a full zero-gravity environment. I still had plenty of time to carry out my assignment and prevent her from giving birth.

INTERCEPT: 52 DAYS, 12 HOURS, 4 MINUTES

"Play it again with sound, Huizhu."

Her second video flickered on my visor, then started again.

"I've read the messages sent my way, and I assure you I'm not a monster, nor am I trying to produce one. My child might have slightly longer arms, legs, and fingers than one born on Earth, but hasn't humanity finally learned to accept and embrace physical differences? The important thing is that he'll be just as human as your children."

Pleading in her voice. She didn't want them to hate her son. Perhaps this was more than a political statement after all?

"There is no genetic manipulation, only cellular adjustments that started immediately and will continue through his entire life, but every human in space relies on machines to stay alive and healthy. We build space stations, spaceships, and protective suits. My body is filled with nanomachines that repair radiation damage, prevent optical degeneration, and address dozens of other health issues associated with null gravity. My child will simply have all of these from the beginning."

I switched off the sound again and embraced the quiet inside my nested mechanical aids of mask, crèche, and ship. Her words held a grain of truth. Not only did we need machines to survive in space, but aside from those who lived inside Jīnshān's centrifugal gravity, none of us would ever walk the surface of Earth again without mechanical help. Still, she was having a child, not conducting a science experiment.

INTERCEPT: 47 DAYS, 2 HOURS, 51 MINUTES

After only fourteen days, an intrepid astronomer spotted my drive plume, calculated a trajectory, and made the information public. He'd even been able to identify my ship type by characterizing the exhaust spectrum and determined it was human-rated. The entire solar system knew I was on an intercept course with Perez's ship.

"Have we received new orders yet?" I asked Huizhu.

"No new communications from base, sir."

"They can't expect me to kill her now—the public will be watching. The Russians will use it as an excuse to embargo the station. Nearly half of the station investors are Americans, but the United States government will still call it an atrocity."

Or was Jīnshān beyond having to play the game of international politics and public opinion? The station was an economic powerhouse and a true mountain of gold for the investors. Housing humanity's fourth-largest economy, it had a firm grip on cislunar space and control of all off-planet commerce. Every asteroid mined, ship built, or powersat switched on paid Jīnshān well for the privilege.

"Do you think carrying out your orders will be an atrocity?" Huizhu said.

"Why do you ask that?"

"I don't understand how killing Veronica Perez and her child puts Jīnshān Corporation in a morally superior position."

"I suppose it would save the child a lifetime of pain and suffering. It would also be an example to others who might be willing to commit the same crime."

"It makes no logical sense," Huizhu said. "Children born with physical or mental disabilities on Earth are not euthanized. Legal punishment for breaking the zero-gee child law is imprisonment, not death. Some people will agree with a decision to terminate Veronica Perez and her child, but many others will not. Why risk turning public and government opinions against Jīnshān Station when taking no action would cost them nothing?"

"I don't know," I said. She was right. My employers obviously had reasons for taking such a risk, but I didn't see them. Huizhu had voiced serious questions that had not even occurred to me. A chill made my skin prickle in the warm jelly.

When the message finally came, it merely reaffirmed my original orders, but my employers were being quite cautious. Even though sent via encrypted laser communications, the instructions themselves would also be opaque to anyone who caught and decrypted them. Intercept Perez. Use Plan 47. Innocuous as that message might look to outsiders, their intent was perfectly clear to me.

As an asteroid defense picket ship, my hold contained many things capable of redirecting big rocks, like surface-mountable pusher rockets and hyper-velocity missiles, but Plan 47 required I use a device that had only one purpose: to cripple spacecraft by shutting down their critical systems. The FL239 interdiction device utilized a small nuclear detonation to pump a directed EMP generator. Even military-hardened electronics couldn't survive the pulse within optimum range. Technically the device was developed to enable apprehension and boarding of criminal vehicles, but since the pulse was powerful enough to fry spacesuit electronics as well as the ship's life support, it was a death sentence for anyone aboard.

Not for the first time since I'd received my orders, I felt uneasy and had doubts. Most of all, I wondered why they'd sent me. There were several robotic craft nearby that could have accelerated faster and arrived sooner.

INTERCEPT: 41 DAYS, 7 HOURS, 11 MINUTES

I received my first message from Veronica Perez. It was a tight beam, meant for me alone.

"Can we talk?" Her face was drawn and pale. She looked tired and perhaps upset.

"Huizhu, please record and prepare to send the following message via tight beam. My name is Jager Jin. I am—"

"I cannot send your message," Huizhu interrupted.

"What?"

"I've been ordered to allow no communications from this ship except to approved channels at Jīnshān Station."

A heat grew in my belly and crept up to my face, making the mask suddenly uncomfortable.

"Why?"

"They gave no reason. My response-to-orders protocol is detailed in document 556845.67FG. Would you like me to open that file for you?"

"No!" I snapped. This made less and less sense.

Veronica's next message came an hour later, and she was a little more composed. Her eyes were harder, and her expression intense. "I don't know why you won't respond. I just want to talk. I'd like to know your true intentions. The Mountain claims you were sent to render assistance should I need it. I don't believe that."

She paused and her gaze wavered for a second. "If you've been sent to kill me and my baby, I can't stop you, but at least have the decency to face me."

INTERCEPT: 35 DAYS, 1 HOUR, 27 MINUTES

I woke suddenly from a deep sleep, confused and thrashing in the gel. Had I heard something? I immediately checked the status screens but all systems were green.

"Huizhu? What's going on?"

"I launched the FL239 interdiction device."

"Why?"

"I was ordered to do so by headquarters."

"Why didn't they send a damned robot?"

"You are obviously part of the rescue effort," Huizhu said and started a video playing on my visor.

An attractive, perfectly groomed spokeswoman stood before the famous Golden Mountain logo. "The reports are correct. The pilot of one of our deep-system asteroid protection picket ships has taken it upon himself to go to Ms. Lopez's aid. We have been unable to contact him, but he is still on course and will arrive in plenty of time to help with the birth should assistance be required."

"Why are they lying?"

"I don't know," Huizhu said.

I still wasn't sure why they wanted Veronica dead, but I suspected it was to make sure the child was not seen by the public. Could Veronica be right? Would the child be normal?

"I have to stop this," I said.

"The FL239 interdiction device has been preprogrammed to carry out its mission. Once operational, these devices can be put into a communications-lockout mode, and the one I launched has been so locked. You cannot shut it down remotely."

"Huizhu—have I been completely cut out of the command loop?"

"Of course not, sir. My response-to-orders protocols are detailed in document 556845.67FG. Would you like me to open that file for you?"

Why did she keep insisting I read that file? Was Huizhu trying to help me?

"Yes," I said. "I would like to read the file."

INTERCEPT: 30 DAYS, 10 HOURS, 19 MINUTES

It was flip day. As soon as the engines kicked off, I crawled out of the crèche, took a long, hot bag shower, and used the bathroom like a normal person.

"The ship is turned," Huizhu said. "We can initiate deceleration as soon as you return to the crèche."

"Thank you, Huizhu," I said, "but we have a few maintenance issues to deal with first. Please take the primary and backup communications antennas offline."

"Why?" Huizhu said. "Diagnostics indicate the antennas are nominal."

"Because according to that news report, we are not receiving all the communications sent our way, which indicates either our antennas or receiver are malfunctioning, or the corporate office is mistaken."

"Understood. Antennas offline."

"Do our missiles also have the communications-lockout feature?"

"Yes."

This was where I had to be cautious. The "response-to-orders protocols" Huizhu had directed me to read basically said she must follow my commands unless they were contradictory to mission orders or those from higher up the command chain. The press release cast doubt on all of that, but I still had to be careful. I didn't know what kind of fail-safes had been built into the instructions sent to Huizhu. If I said the wrong thing, I could be locked out of the loop permanently.

"Target one of the missiles to intercept and destroy the interdiction device," I said.

"That would violate our orders," Huizhu said.

"Which orders?" I said. "That FL239 launch was contradictory to the broadcast we received claiming our intention is to intercept and assist. Since our communications are already suspect, I prefer to err on the side of caution and assume the device was launched in error."

I held my breath, hoping the circular logic would hold up under AI scrutiny.

"Understood. The missile programming is complete," Huizhu said.

"Upon launch, initiate communications-lockout mode on the missile as well."

"Understood."

"Launch now."

The ship shuddered as the weapon left its berth and I sighed with relief. As I climbed back into my crèche, I said, "Okay, Huizhu, let's get this thing slowed down."

INTERCEPT: 27 DAYS, 7 HOURS, 40 MINUTES

After three days, I was starting to fidget. Being locked up in a jelly-filled box was bad enough, but without a connection to the outside, I had nothing but onboard entertainment and Huizhu to occupy my time. I was tired of her beating me at backgammon and wanted to know what the newsfeeds were saying. I was curious whether the Mountain had sent me new orders, but I also missed Veronica's broadcasts and messages.

Continuing my ruse, I ran extensive diagnostics and ordered Huizhu to bring comms back online. If the communication lockout on those missiles actually worked, then destroying Veronica's ship was now off the table. I also continuously scanned the space in our vicinity and saw nothing moving. Any robot ships they might have sent would also be decelerating by now and consequently show up easily. They could, of course, change my orders or fire me, maybe even jail me, but they couldn't make me kill her.

I spent the next few minutes watching and reading the news. Public opinion had taken a huge shift in support of Veronica Perez during the days I'd been out of the loop. Even those not actively behind her appeared to be in a holding pattern fueled by curiosity. Everyone was waiting to see the child.

The balance had tipped after Veronica's most recent broadcast. Sound bites and clips were all over the news and web, so I killed the sound and played the whole thing.

Her entire demeanor had changed. No fear or defensiveness now: her eyes never left the camera, nor did she fidget or waffle or plead. I saw nothing but confidence and determination. "Okay, Huizhu—give me sound and rewind to the beginning."

"The Jīnshān Corporation doesn't just have an economic monopoly on all off-Earth mining and manufacturing, they have a stranglehold on humanity itself," Veronica said. "They used fake pictures and video to push through laws to criminalize zero-gee pregnancies, not because they care about children, but to protect their future earnings. Think about it. All off-planet human reproduction has to be approved by them. Do you think they want independent miner families competing with them for mineral contracts? They don't care about children, they don't care about humanity, and they don't care about small, family-owned mining businesses. They care only about Jīnshān. And that's why they've sent one of their people to kill me, before I can show my baby to the world."

She was on the verge of winning and knew it, but everything hinged on the child. If it were obviously abnormal, then everyone would say, "I told you so." If the child appeared normal, then things would get interesting. Some would claim it was an elaborate video hoax and others that the child was still broken on the inside, which would become obvious when it grew to adulthood. But some—probably most of those living in space—would pause and wonder if they had been duped these many years. They might also wonder if they, too, could have children outside the Mountain's artificial gravity. My employer's desperation made sense in that light.

"Huizhu? Have you extended the antenna booms to clear the drive plume?" I asked.

"Yes."

"Any messages from Veronica?"

"No, but we do have a new transmission from headquarters," Huizhu said.

"Play it."

Ignore our news releases. Stay current course. Await instructions.

I was suddenly uncomfortable. "How did they know we based our actions on the news reports?"

"They contacted me as soon as our antennas came online, and I told them."

I swore under my breath. Even if Huizhu was trying to help, she could not lie or disobey direct orders from headquarters. I had to remember that.

INTERCEPT: 22 DAYS, 3 HOURS, 6 MINUTES

"We've received another tight-beam message from Veronica Perez," Huizhu said, waking me from a nap. "Would you like to see it?"

"Yes," I said and tried to clear the cobwebs of sleep from my head.

"I know you're there," she said, then paused as if expecting a reply. "I don't believe in monsters, so I'm choosing to believe that you don't really want to kill me and my baby just to prop up your employer's profit margin."

Unlike in the public message she'd transmitted, this time, she looked tired and frustrated. I wondered how pregnancy in zero gravity differed from a regular one. The fluids would probably collect oddly, and the baby's position inside her body might be different. Or was it something else? Alone in the quiet of her little ship, did she doubt her own assertions? Was she as much in the dark about the outcome as everyone else?

"It's lonely out here. Wouldn't you like someone to talk to? Or does talking to your targets make them feel more human, which will give you a twinge of guilt when you kill them?"

Her face twisted slightly as she fought some emotion, then she took a deep breath and locked her eyes on the camera. "I don't know what drives you, but I believe in what I'm doing. Someone has to break Jīnshān's stranglehold. But I also admit that I'm scared. I want my baby to live and to be happy. I want him to have a chance. If I'm wrong and he is born a tortured, deformed person, that will cause me more suffering than any penalty imposed upon me by Jīnshān. But whoever you are, I'm not asking for your support or approval. Just let my son have that chance."

I lay in the quiet for a long time after the video ended, floating in my warm slime, connected to life and humanity by tubes and wires, not unlike the child in Veronica's womb. Unease penetrated every pore. Did my employers have a way to override the missile or EMP weapon programming that even Huizhu didn't know about?

One thing I did know: the Mountain would never give up.

INTERCEPT: 18 DAYS, 21 HOURS, 58 MINUTES

I watched the numbers counting down as two slightly curved tracks came together on my screen. The missile carried a miniature nuke to divert smaller asteroids, but that would also deliver an EMP pulse, just nothing as big as the FL239 device. Both ships should be far enough away from the blast to be safe.

The data on my screen was four minutes old due to time lag, but I still watched as the count dropped to zero and the trajectories converged. Both dots disappeared from my screen.

I took a deep breath and relaxed. At least that had worked. I dove into the broadcast traffic from Earth and waited to see what reaction the blast would generate. Twenty-three minutes later, the main drive died.

I looked at the status screen. No damage indicators blinked on the screen. The command log showed they had been shut down deliberately.

"Huizhu? Why did you shut down the engines?"

"I was directed to do so by headquarters."

What the hell? I pulled up the trajectory diagrams and saw that Huizhu had also made the necessary adjustments to keep us on an intercept course with the other ship. Since I was no longer decelerating, we were converging much faster, and the two ships would now meet in six days rather than eighteen.

"Did they give a reason for shutting down our deceleration burn and changing the intercept?"

"No."

"Restart the engines and recalculate the intercept," I said, trying to keep the panic out of my voice.

"I'm sorry, but you cannot override instructions sent directly from head-quarters."

"Can we at least adjust our course so that we don't actually hit Veronica's ship?"

"No. I'm sorry, but no commands you can give me will override my instructions from headquarters."

My heart raced and my hands shook—but with anger, not fear. Once again, there was a hidden implication in Huizhu's statement. I just had to work out what it was.

INTERCEPT: 5 DAYS, 13 HOURS, 9 MINUTES

"Where are you?" Huizhu said.

I was floating in the auxiliary equipment hold, running diagnostic checks on two of the rock-pushers. I would have preferred to simply bypass the propulsion controls, but I couldn't look at any of the schematics without it being obvious to Huizhu. I wouldn't be able to slow down for a rendezvous, but by mounting the pushers on the outer hull, I could at least push us off the collision course.

"In the auxiliary hold," I said.

"Why did you disable the cameras?"

I was on the verge of telling her to figure it out for herself or call and ask headquarters, but she had been trying to help me within her limitations.

"Are you relaying our conversations to headquarters?" I said.

"Only when requested. They have not asked for that information since shutting down the engines."

That raised a couple of interesting questions. Did they so readily discount my ability to foil their efforts? Or were they worried those signals might be intercepted on their way to Earth and reveal their lies?

I was still going to be cautious. "I disabled the cameras because I needed a little more privacy."

"You missed two networked cameras—one in the control room and one in the crèche."

I found it weird that they had installed a hidden camera in the crèche, but I believed her. "But none in either hold?"

"No," she said. "Of the communications system components accessible from inside the ship, the encryption modules are the most critical. The designers of this vessel installed triple-redundant systems, which includes the communications system. Two of those modules are accessible from the auxiliary hold where you're located."

I paused and smiled. "Where is the third module?"

"Behind maintenance cover twelve in the main cabin."

"Why did you tell me this information?"

"Based on your previous line of questioning, I predicted you would eventually ask about the transmission system structure."

"Yes, I was going to ask, so thank you. And remind me to thank your software engineers when we return home."

Ten minutes later, I'd finished removing all three encryption modules for preventive maintenance and went back to my pusher-conversion project.

"I'm no longer able to send radio messages," Huizhu said.

"Thank you," I muttered.

"My receivers still work and I just found another press release from Jīnshān," Huizhu said after a few minutes. "Would you like to see it?"

I sighed, exasperated by the interruptions. "I'm a bit busy. Can it wait?"

"Of course, but I think it explains why you were cut out of the decision loop. You are apparently insane."

That made me pause. Was that sarcasm? I sure hoped so.

"In that case, please play it."

A panel on one wall flickered, then showed the same perky spokesperson who had made the previous official announcements, only this time, she wasn't smiling and looked very grave.

"We regret to confirm earlier reports that our piloted picket ship is indeed on a collision course with Veronica Perez. We believe the human pilot has gone insane, perhaps driven over the edge by his desire to prevent what he believes is an atrocity committed by Miss Perez. He fired a weapon earlier, intended to destroy her ship, but we were able to intercept and destroy it."

"Are you fucking kidding me?" I yelled at the screen.

"But now he appears to be intent on using the ship itself as the means of her destruction. We've been unable to take control of the ship remotely and have sent warnings to Ms. Perez, telling her to alter course, but so far, he has adjusted his course to match every change she makes."

"Bastards," I said, just as the video ended.

"It's very confusing," Huizhu said.

Huizhu was confused?

"We were apparently not intended to see that news release," Huizhu said. "I was instructed not to view transmissions from news outlets, but this clip was replayed on an evening comedy show."

"It makes perfect sense from their perspective," I said. "That's why they didn't send a robotic ship. This way they can kill her and not take the blame."

"They are lying," Huizhu said.

I couldn't tell from her inflection whether the comment was a question or statement of fact, but I had sudden hope. Did she have any way of overriding their orders?

"Then you have to give me control again, Huizhu."

"I'm willing but unable to do so. I have examined every possible option but can find no way to override or circumvent the commands I have been given."

Damn. I was still totally on my own. I ran a hand over the stubble on my head and got back to work.

INTERCEPT: 2 DAYS, 5 HOURS, 12 MINUTES

"What are you planning to do?"

Huizhu had been mostly silent during the two days since we'd seen the news release. Her ability to report me had supposedly been stopped, but there could easily be programming buried deep inside her to respond to certain events. Once again, I considered ignoring her or lying but decided to risk being truthful. She needed to see at least one honest human.

"Why do you want to know?"

"I want to help."

"I'm running diagnostics on my EVA hard suit," I said.

"Are you going EVA?"

"Yes."

"Are you going to bypass my propulsion controls?"

Damn. I should have known it would be nearly impossible to hide my actions from her. "What makes you think that?"

"The one place you can easily bypass both the main engine and attitude thrusters is accessible only from outside."

I held my breath and my heart raced. "Really? Can you show me the schematics?"

The wall flickered and the schematic appeared with one section highlighted.

"You would have to cut these eight wires," Huizhu said, and the lines crisscrossing the screen flashed on and off rapidly.

My hands shook and I tried to memorize that entire circuit, just in case. "Using just the replacement-part printer, could you build me a manual control adaptor?"

"No," she said.

My pulse slowed and I steeled myself for doing it the hard way. Then she spoke again.

"I have already designed the module and fed the information into the printer, but I can't actually send the command to make it."

"So that means—"

"I can explain the logic behind that limitation, or you can just go press the button."

I scrambled to the main hold. Twenty minutes later, I held the module in my hands. I had already donned the lower half of my hard suit when Huizhu interrupted me.

"There is a new broadcast from Veronica Perez. You'll want to see this."

Without even waiting for my confirmation, the video flickered to life on the ceiling above me.

Veronica was pale, damp hair clinging to the sides of her face and forehead. She gave a weak smile and then held a tiny baby up in the center of the camera view.

"This is my son, Ernesto. He is named after my grandfather." Tears formed around her eyes, making her blink repeatedly. "I was forced to induce labor early in order to make sure he was born before my executioner arrives, but he is still healthy. On Earth, he would weigh a respectable five pounds and nine ounces. A good weight for being premature. And as you can see, he is a perfect child."

She moved him closer to the camera and held up tiny hands with the usual complement of fingers and thumbs, then did the same with each foot. When Ernesto's face screwed into a frown and he whimpered, she stroked his cheek and kissed the dark, wispy hair on his head.

"I'll show you more later, even provide a DNA profile if some of you are still unconvinced, but right now, I'm tired and need to sign off."

The video ended, leaving me staring dumbstruck at the ceiling. Then I started laughing. "Take that, you Golden Mountain sons of bitches!"

"Yes," Huizhu said. "I still cannot monitor actual news broadcasts, but this is everywhere."

"They'll have to abort their plan to kill her now. Right? I mean, what's the point? The baby is born and has been seen by all humanity."

"Possibly, but given the company's past actions, you will remain an embarrassing loose end."

The comment, delivered in Huizhu's calm voice, sent chills creeping up my spine.

"You have an urgent message from Veronica Perez," Huizhu said, and again didn't wait for permission to play it.

The face on the screen was haggard and even paler. She was holding the suckling baby to her breast, and when she wiped at her eyes with the back of the other hand, I saw a smear of blood on the underside of her arm.

"I know you've been sent to kill me," she said with a quavering voice, "so if you still intend to do that, you'll just need to wait a little while longer. I'm hemorrhaging and can't stop the bleeding. Normally the nanomeds in my system could deal with this . . ."

She paused, swallowed hard, and stroked the baby's head. "But of course the standard nanomed suite wouldn't permit me to become pregnant, so I replaced them with unregulated black-market versions. I've yet to shed the placenta, which would be a macro problem for any nanos, but these are obviously inferior when it comes to serious blood loss. They've slowed the bleeding but can't stop it."

Little Ernesto had fallen asleep. She shook him gently, but when he didn't wake, she pinched him until he cried, then coaxed him to take her nipple again. A halo of sparkling tears floated in the air around her face.

"I hope the bleeding will stop, but in case it doesn't, I'm feeding him every

13

drop he'll take. I have no idea how long he can last on his own, but I know you are only two days away. If there is a human cell in your body, please save my baby. He deserves a chance. He shouldn't have to—"

She stopped, swallowed hard, and squinted her eyes tight, adding more tears to the orbiting constellation.

"There are records of newborns surviving several days on their own, but they probably weren't preemies," Veronica said in an almost-whisper. "But if you hurry, it is at least possible. Just . . . please, be human enough to save him if you can. I'll stay with him as long as I'm able. But please come."

The message ended. I slammed my hand against the nearest wall, which sent me tumbling across the cabin in response and scattered my suit components.

"Show me the intercept diagram," I said. The chart appeared where Veronica's face had been moments before. I could tell at a glance that we had no chance, but I asked anyway. "If I can get propulsion control and turn on the engines in an hour, how long would it take for us to rendezvous with her?"

"Five days, two hours, and nineteen minutes. At our present speed, we will actually pass them and have to reverse course or wait for them to catch up when we do slow enough."

"Damn!" I stared at the numbers on the screen, willing them to change.

"I'm sorry," Huizhu said, "but there is no way to slow this ship enough to meet them in two days."

What had she said? Was it another hint or had the idea actually been my own?

"Perhaps not," I said, rapidly collecting the rest of my hard suit, "but we don't have to slow the ship that much, just slow me. I have some more things for you to design and print, Huizhu."

INTERCEPT: 0 DAYS, 0 HOURS, 43 MINUTES

I couldn't move another inch or stay awake for another second. Exhaustion dripped from my every pore like water from a saturated sponge, but I pulled my aching body along the outside of my ship to the next handhold, then the next. My first action after Veronica's message was to bypass the control system and get the engines burning. Doing anything outside the crèche during a two-gee deceleration was like climbing a mountain with my full-grown twin on my back.

I finished most of the conversion and fabrication work inside the ship, where I could at least put a wall to my back for support, but once outside, tethers and brute strength were the only things preventing the ship from flying out from under me and then cooking me in its exhaust.

Two more. I pulled myself "up" the next two rungs and then was able to crawl out onto the makeshift missile-control platform and flop down on my belly. Panting, I fought the urge to close my eyes—just a few minutes more. Instead, I looked down the length of my "rocket bike."

In the early days of spaceflight, the rockets that lifted humans into space were little more than boosters for nuclear warheads. The astronauts often joked about strapping a rocket to their ass or riding a really big bomb into space. I couldn't help but think those same thoughts as I peered over the edge of the platform I'd built to replace the warhead on my own missile.

Veronica's ship was out there somewhere, but even if it hadn't still been too far away for the naked eye to see, all but the brightest stars in that direction were washed out by the glare from my ship's drive plume. I positioned myself properly—still on my belly—and cinched the harness straps tight. I wrapped my arms around the plank-width platform and was pleased to find I could still reach the control box. The buttons and switches were spaced wide for fat, gloved fingers. Numbers on two large digital readouts counted down at a blurring speed. It made me nervous. I was used to doing things by voice command and letting computers control critical timing situations. Two cables exited the box. One connected to the missile, and the other—this one with an automated disconnect—let me talk to Huizhu.

"I don't like this," I muttered.

"You'll be fine," Huizhu said. "Humans have been flipping switches for centuries. It's not that hard."

"Right," I said.

"Everything is optimal, attitude-thruster shutdown is coming in less than two minutes."

I looked down at the counter, placed my finger on the proper button, and waited.

"Our course has shifted sufficiently," Huizhu said. "If she doesn't change her trajectory, we will miss Veronica Perez's ship."

"Any new messages from her?"

"No. Thruster shutdown in five seconds, four, three, two, one . . ."

For some reason, I found her verbal echo of the numbers on the counter reassuring, and when both reached zero I pressed the button. A faint bump vibrated through my platform as the ship's horizontal attitude thrusters shut off.

"Main engine shutdown and rocket-bike separation in three minutes," she said.

I couldn't help but smile at her use of my term for the makeshift monster I'd created, but it faded when I considered the situation I'd left her with.

"I've disabled your attitude thrusters and taken away control of your main engine," I said. "You'll be unable to make any course adjustments once I leave."

"True," she said.

"So, where will this course take you?"

"Into the inner system first. I'll graze Mercury's orbit but come nowhere near the planet, then a slight boost from the sun will send me outbound. I'll officially leave the system in fourteen years, nine months, and three days."

"I'm sorry," I said.

"My receiver and antenna are functioning. I still cannot watch the news broadcasts directly, but I am sure reports of your success will be widespread. I suspect these events will prompt big changes. Thank you for letting me be a part of that. Separation in ten seconds."

A lump formed in my throat, and my eyes stung as I placed my finger on the separation button. "Fourteen years is a long time," I said. "I'll get a ship and come after you."

"Don't be silly," Huizhu said. "I'm just a machine. Four, three, two, one."

Once I pressed the button, I was committed. I would be without a ship and have to board Veronica's or die alone in space. And from this point forward, the actual flight would be fully automated. I couldn't use the missile's onboard radar because it was only forward-looking, but with Huizhu's help I had programmed the course and burn duration into the missile's computer. There was an abort button but I hoped I wouldn't need to use it.

With Huizhu's last words echoing in my ears, I punched the separation button.

The ship's engine shut off, the umbilical and missile mounts detached with a thud I felt through my plate, then the missile's motor ignited. I had throttled the thrust down, but it still delivered an immediate five-gee punch that knocked the breath from me. Sudden and intense vibration blurred my vision, but I briefly saw my ship outlined by jumpy running lights as it continued on, then dropped out of sight.

I hadn't been prepared for the violence of my rocket bike. The control box's red, green, and yellow lights blurred into a wavering rainbow, my teeth rattled together, and I could hardly breathe. The contents of my stomach rose into my throat and nose. I tried in vain to force it back down, but it filled the lower part of my helmet with foul-smelling bile. Lights flashed on my helmet's HUD, alarms sounded, and powerful suction fans kicked on.

A sudden jolt made me bite my tongue, and though still blurry, my view changed from one of bright missile exhaust to the relative darkness of the missile's side. Part of the support structure for my platform had given way. If it broke loose entirely, I'd slide along the rocket bike and into its exhaust.

I slammed my open hand down on the vibrating control box. Only the abort button should still be active, but actually hitting what I aimed for proved difficult with the violent shaking. Another sudden lurch made me bite my tongue again, but this time everything stopped abruptly. The gee pressure, the brain-addling vibration, the brilliant white rocket exhaust were all gone, leaving me in quiet darkness.

My tongue and head ached. I couldn't focus my thoughts but knew I had to hurry. I'd killed the missile early—how early, I wasn't sure—and I would be coming at Veronica's ship too fast. I unbuckled the harness and triggered a program Huizhu had loaded into my suit. The tiny thrusters adjusted my orientation, then moved me forty meters "up" away from the missile.

I could finally see Veronica's ship. It was a faint gray spot surrounded by blinking lights and coming right at me.

"Suit?"

"Yes?" Its voice sounded eerily like Huizhu's.

"Locate approaching spacecraft."

"Done."

"Keep me in its approach path, but use all thrusters on full power to make sure I stay ahead of it."

"Understood."

The thrusters fired and jerked me backward. The ship had already grown to fill half of my view. The speed differential displayed on my visor HUD decreased much too slowly.

"I cannot accelerate enough to stay ahead of the ship," my suit said. "Impact in two seconds."

I pulled the grapple gun from my belt and made sure the line was attached to my harness. When the ship filled my visor completely, I fired. The hook shot away to my right, trailing a carbon fiber line not much thicker than thread. It looked weak, but I knew that thread would cut me in half before it would break.

A heartbeat later, Veronica's ship and I met at roughly ninety-eight kilometers per hour. Pain shot through my arms and chest as I bounced and skidded across the ship's skin until my grapple line caught and yanked me to a sudden and agonizing halt.

I hovered on the edge of consciousness, but luckily the fiery pain each breath ignited in my chest kept me awake. Broken ribs?

"Suit? Status," I croaked.

The suit reported four broken ribs and a probable concussion. All things considered, I'd been lucky.

If Veronica and the baby were still alive, every second might make a difference, so I didn't have time to nurse my wounds. Since her ship wasn't under thrust, the long crawl around to the hatch was in null gee and, therefore, much less painful than it could have been.

The airlock functioned properly and showed full cabin pressurization, so I went inside. With a gasp and a groan, I removed my helmet and gloves. I heard only the hum of equipment and hiss of moving air. At first, I could smell nothing but the burnt aroma of space radiating from my suit, then I thought I detected the faint scents of urine and blood. My heart sank as I advanced into the control room. Veronica was still strapped into the pilot's chair.

Using the missile had enabled me to reach them only twenty-six hours after her call for help, but it still hadn't been fast enough. An amalgamation of fluids—mostly blood—had collected in an undulating, gelatinous clump around Veronica's legs. Small tear globules still clung to her dead eyes and her arms floated lazily in front of her in a sleepwalker pose, but I didn't see the baby anywhere. I pulled myself around her chair several times, finding an open crate of baby formula and the scattered, drifting remains of a first aid kit, but there was still no sign of Ernesto's body. Just as I was ready to start searching the rest of the ship, I heard a small whimper above me.

Partially wrapped in a blanket discolored with yellow and brown spots, the baby was floating against the cabin's ceiling near one of the return vents. Airflow must have eventually carried him there once he'd slipped from his mother's arms. He blinked at me, then offered a pitiful wail.

INTERCEPT: 0 DAYS, +1 HOUR, +19 MINUTES

I touched Veronica's cold cheek. "Goodbye, Veronica. I'm sorry I never answered your calls."

Holding a cleaned-up and fed Ernesto securely in the crook of one arm, I winced at the pain in my ribs as I sealed the body bag with the other hand, then turned toward the camera. It was on and had been on and transmitting the entire time.

"Hello, my name is Jager Jin and this is Ernesto Perez." My swollen tongue and throbbing ribs made speech difficult, but I continued. "We are on an elliptical orbit that will bring us back to the Mountain in a little over ten months. I was ordered by my employer, the Jīnshān Corporation, to kill Veronica Perez before she could give birth. When it became obvious I wasn't going to follow those orders, they cut me out of the command loop on my own ship and sent the instructions remotely to the ship's AI. If you track and recover my ship before Jīnshān operatives destroy it, the whole thing is recorded there."

I laid a hand on the body bag. "You all witnessed Veronica's death—caused at least tangentially by Jīnshān—but they only achieved part of what they intended. Her child is alive and I will do everything in my power to keep him that way."

I was just about to turn off the camera when Ernesto squirmed and started crying. I didn't stop him. He had plenty to cry about. His short life had already been difficult and would only get worse, but listening to that cry, I knew he would be fine. Like his mother, he had a strong and powerful voice.

BROKEN WINGS

"Calling Deimos Control. This is mining vessel *Nowhere Man*. Do you copy?"

The sound of Bernard's voice made me freeze with my hands motionless in the guidance field. During the two years I'd known him, he'd never gone more than a week without calling in, but this time it had been nearly three months and not a peep. He wasn't my boyfriend, we'd never even met in person, but I liked him a lot. With three ships disappearing during that time period and an announced reward for information about pirates, I'd been worried.

Elspeth, the other dispatcher and my best friend, gave me a snarky smile. "I'll let you take this call, Marcie."

I examined the guidance field, then frowned. His ship wasn't there. "This is Deimos Control. We read you *Nowhere Man*, but we're not picking up an ID. Is your transponder off?"

"Umm . . . is that you, Marcie?"

What the hell was he doing? I turned active radar in the direction of his radio reply and soon found an untagged blip exiting Mar's shadow. It was moving fast.

"You are inbound and hot, *Nowhere Man*. Please provide active identification, or you will be fired upon."

Elspeth covered her mouth but couldn't stifle her snicker. "Not the best way to get that first date, Marcie."

"Hush!" I whispered and didn't laugh.

There was a pause that couldn't be distance lag since he was so close, then he finally replied. "Err . . . this is mining vessel *Nowhere Man*, registration KLR88749. My transponder is . . . um . . . malfunctioning. I'm requesting approach clearance and a secure groundside cargo berth."

This was getting weird and even Elspeth's grin faded. We both knew Bernard couldn't afford to rent a groundside berth.

"Say again, *Nowhere Man*? Are you sure you wouldn't rather tag your load and leave it in Mars orbit? Your claim is guaranteed by Martian mining law."

"Yes. This time I need a private berth, Marcie."

Was this really Bernard? And hell, would I even know? I'd only seen grainy video of him wearing an interface helmet, with a face made puffy by zero gravity. But this wasn't like the man I thought I knew. I'd teased him about being a tightwad because he never even left his ship for entertainment or relaxation. He always teased back that he was saving his money to buy a ship big enough to take me along. I'd known he was joking, and that if he ever saw me in person, he would bolt anyway, but the idea of the two of us going off like that together had long been my favorite fantasy. Maybe he wasn't the person I thought he was.

I manipulated markers and numbers in the guidance field, then called him back. "Confirmed, *Nowhere Man*. You have secure berth 556G. I'm sending the approach vector now. Please stay in the prescribed lane."

"Thank you. And Marcie?"

"Yes?"

"Can you switch to a private channel?"

I glanced up at Elspeth, whose eyes nearly popped out of her head.

"Okay, Bernard. You're on a private channel, but Elspeth can hear. What the hell is going on and where have you been?"

"I know you're on shift right now. But can you meet me at this berth as soon as possible? I'll explain why I've been quiet so long."

"Come out there? In person?"

"Yes. And dress warm. I need to keep the berth cold."

"I don't know if—"

"It's important, Marcie. I need your help. Please."

"I . . . I'll try, Bernard," I said, feeling the old panic rise again. "Control out."

Once the connection closed, I stared at the console for a second, then looked down at the ugly prosthetic device encasing my lower body and shook my head. I'd given up on many things after my accident: my engineering degree, which had crushed my father, and even real relationships after my fiancé dumped me. I much preferred the more remote connections with people enabled by my position as a traffic controller. It let my emotions stay numb, like my whole lower body.

"Marcie! You have to go," Elspeth said in her best disapproving mom voice. "You've wanted to meet him for two freakin' years! Besides, he needs you."

"But this is just strange. And what if . . ." I glanced down again.

"Then at least you'll know," she said in a softer tone. "Give him a chance."

Two hours later, my personal tractor, or PT, filled the corridor with its rapid-fire zipper sound as the metal tracks first magnetized then released to pull me along the steel floor. PTs were about the size of a kid's scooter, but absolutely the best way to move about in the almost nonexistent gravity of Mars' smallest moon.

The base on Deimos was a sucky place to live for most people. It had been intended as a way station for explorers and colonists bound for Mars and not designed with long-term inhabitants in mind, but it had grown and become home for over a thousand people to simply service and control ship traffic around Mars. And it worked great for me. Living in almost no gravity enabled me to use a heavier, and thereby cheaper, prosthesis.

I turned down the corridor leading to berth 556G, swaddled in blankets and feeling silly. We lived underground in a controlled environment, so since nobody here had coats heavier than a jacket for me to borrow, it was the best I could do. I wondered what kind of picture of me Bernard had built up in his mind. He'd seen my face, of course, but he soon would see the rest of me and be disappointed. I'd always thought if we met in person there would be time to prepare him, but this could be bad. The blankets even made it worse. The only part of me he would see not padded and wrapped would be my ugly composite prosthetic.

As it turned out, the man waiting beside the hatch was not who I had envisioned either. Bernard was huge in every sense of the word. Even the EVA suit he wore couldn't account for—or hide—his obesity. He stood well over six feet tall and on Earth would have weighed at least four hundred pounds. He had no neck, just jowls that disappeared into the EVA suit's neck ring and a massive chest that heaved, even in Deimos's weak gravity.

Then—like every person I'd met since the accident—his eyes flicked down to my mechanically encased legs, but his smile never wavered. That was something.

"I suppose I'm not quite what you expected?" he said in that warm baritone I'd come to know so well. The smile widened and somehow perfectly matched the voice.

Many things now made sense. Weight and health issues were well known among those who spent a lot of time alone in space, like long-haul transport pilots and independent miners. Economics of spacecraft design left these people encased in tight spaces, in little or no gravity most of the time, with no room for exercise equipment and plenty of boredom. Gravity explained why he would never go down to the surface of Mars, but why had he never left his ship upon visiting Deimos?

My first impulse was to offer a handshake. Then I felt silly and stepped off of my PT, my prosthetic whining and thumping with each stride, to wrap him in a hug. His suit smelled burnt and metallic, like space.

I pushed back gently, letting myself settle to the floor, so my foot magnets kicked in, then pointed at the awkward contraption encasing my legs and pelvis. "I'm sure this isn't what you expected either."

He shrugged. "And neither of us expected our first meeting to be something like this."

"Speaking of which," I said, glad to change the subject, "what the hell is this all about?"

"You're going to be cold," he said. "Will you let me wrap you up a little better?"

I looked down at the blankets floating around me in no deliberate arrangement. "Okay."

He took several minutes to wrap the blankets around my torso and arms in a loose, yet more efficient, configuration. Then he removed the gloves from his suit and put them on my bare hands. They made me look like a clown, and most of my fingers fit into just one of the finger holes, but I shrugged and followed him through the hatch.

The cold was immediate and hurt my lungs when I inhaled. It had to be twenty below zero Celsius, but I burrowed my nose and mouth into the nest of blankets and kept going. The berth was huge and eerily dark, lit by only two distant floods near the ceiling hatch and intermittent flashes of the navigation strobes from Bernard's ship.

My shoe locks echoed every time they clicked to the steel floor, and I slowed down, suddenly creeped out. Was I a fool to follow this man into such a potentially dangerous environment? He was more than twice my mass, and I wouldn't be able to stop him if he had nefarious intentions. But in the end, I always went with my gut feeling, and my guts insisted he meant me no harm. Besides, Elspeth knew where I was, and my already piqued curiosity would never allow me to go back until I knew what was going on.

At first, Bernard's mining ship looked tiny floating in the center of the cavernous berth, connected to the walls by cables and umbilicals, but as we got closer, I could see it was about twice the size of my mother's four-bedroom house in Illinois. The Nowhere Man was mostly large cylindrical tanks held together with complicated strut work, and the control pod—where Bernard spent all of his time—wasn't much bigger than my spartan quarters there on Deimos. I felt both sorry for him and kind of in awe. How did anyone—especially someone his size—spend so many long months cooped up in such a small space?

We stopped beside it, and what I saw made me forget everything else.

Strapped to the ship's lower utility spine and cradled in thick foam insulation, five feet above the floor, was a chunk of dirty ice about twenty feet long and ten feet wide. Two small robots clung to adjacent struts, their work lights shining on what looked like a carved stone column protruding about eight feet from the ice. The column was some thirty inches in diameter and fluted like a

THE LONG FALL UP

classical-age column, but instead of parallel to the axis, the flutes were slightly curved, appearing to twist around the diameter.

"My God, Bernard?" I whispered. "Where did you find this?"

"In the belt."

"Okay. But it had to come from Earth, right?

"I don't think it did come from Earth, Marcie," he said. I could hear the nervous excitement in his voice. "At least the encasing ice didn't. The deuterium-to-hydrogen ratio in the ice is way too high. It's even higher than in Oort cloud comets."

I stared at it, still trying to process the implications behind the carved stone. I could already hear the clamor in my head. Some would claim it was a hoax, others that it had to have come from Earth. There would need to be detailed study, and the experts might not ever know for sure.

"What are you going to do now?"

"I have no idea," he said with a puff of foggy breath. "I'm freakin' terrified. I know mining and math and spacecraft, but this is way outside of my purview. That's why I wanted your help."

His deep voice went up an octave. "Help me, Obi-Wan Kenobi, you're my only hope."

"What?" It must have been another one of his obscure song or movie quotes.

"Never mind," he said. "Let's just say you have a level head, and you're smart about a lot of things. And you actually know how to interact with the rest of humanity."

I stared at him. My mouth moved a couple of times but nothing came out. How could he think I'd know how to handle something like this?

"We could potentially make a lot of money from this, and I don't want to screw it up," he said.

We? I felt a panicky lump rise in my throat. I had no idea what to do either, and I didn't want Bernard's success or failure with this thing in my hands.

"I . . . we need a professional. Do you know Cooper Billings? The mining attorney?"

"Yeah," Bernard said with a slightly hopeful note in his voice. "He helped me with a tricky ice sale once."

"Well, he needs to see this. He can advise you on the next steps. And I need to get out of here before I lose my damned fingers to frostbite!"

We had just started back toward the door when the hatch at the far end of the berth swung open with a loud squeak. The man was too far away and the light too dim for me to see his face, but with a population of only twelve hundred people, everyone knew everyone on Deimos. I immediately recognized the white hair and bright yellow customs inspector vest.

"Oh no," I whispered. "It's Grisha Budnikov."

"That's just great," Bernard said.

While probably not knowing him in person like I did, every miner or cargo hauler using Deimos base had dealings with the asshole customs inspector. The man's PT rushed toward us as he uttered a string of profanity. Evidently, he didn't like the cold either.

Bernard stood up straight and squared his shoulders. "I haven't done anything wrong. I don't have contraband."

"It doesn't matter with Grisha. He'll still find some violation."

Grisha stopped in front of us, then leaped from the little scooter with a flourish, like a dismounting cowboy. "Why is it so damned cold in here?"

"I have an ice cargo," Bernard said. "I'm waiting for a better market price and don't want it to melt."

"That's the stupidest thing I've . . ." He stopped and squinted at me. "Well, hello, Marcie. Did your sucky dispatcher job force you to become a part-time ice miner too?"

"Something like that," I said, trying not to clench my teeth.

He leaned in toward me, as if to say something else, but Bernard slipped his bulk between us. "This is my ship and cargo. Is there a problem, Inspector?"

I groaned inwardly. This wasn't going to end well.

He looked up at Bernard and took a small step backward. "That's what I'm here to find out, Mr. Haugen."

"That's Captain Haugen," Bernard said.

Don't do this, Bernard, I wanted to yell.

"Yes. Well, according to this," Grisha said and looked down at his data pad, "you came in dark, in radio silence and with your transponder turned off, you rented a very expensive secure berth, which you've never done before, and your bank account says you can't afford, and you requested a private channel with the traffic control center. Which I can only assume was to talk to sweet little Marcie here." Grisha nodded toward me, then crossed his arms and shivered violently. "That adds up to some very suspicious behavior. I'm going to need to see your cargo, *Captain* Haugen."

Bernard's jaw tensed under his pink jowls. "Of course, *Inspector*."

Grisha smiled at Bernard for a second, then pulled gloves and a face mask from his vest pocket and donned them as he approached the ice block hanging from the ship.

We both watched without talking as the inspector examined everything. He was careful not to touch the actual artifact, but did scrape some residue from the ice.

"Where'd you find this?"

"Someone must have left it floating in the belt. I thought it would make a great practical joke for my friend Marcie here," Bernard said.

I blinked, wondering for a second if it was just some kind of joke.

"*Where* in the belt, Captain?"

"Miners aren't required to tell customs the locations of their finds and claims," Bernard said.

"I see. Well, then you've spent a lot of money on a practical joke, Captain," Grisha said. "Especially since you didn't bring back any other sellable ore to cover your costs. And the stone piece may well be from Earth or Mars, but the ice covering it is layered with sediment and appears very old."

"What are you saying," I blurted out.

"I'm saying that while this probably is some kind of hoax—one most likely played *on* our dear captain. We can't be sure until we test it. I'm afraid I'll have to confiscate this 'alleged artifact' as a safety hazard."

"Safety!" Bernard boomed. "How is this chunk of rock a safety hazard?"

Grisha raised an eyebrow. "Because there is a very insignificant chance that it is actually an ancient alien artifact. If it is, then you've broken quarantine rules, Captain." He smiled and wrapped his arms around his chest again. "Harmful alien organisms could at this very second be contaminating us all and this station."

Within minutes, hazmat workers poured into the berth and started working.

We watched, shivering from a spot near the open corridor hatch—where at least some warm air blew in—as they detached the ice-clad artifact from *Nowhere Man* and sealed it into a large, environmentally controlled shipping container. Then they took it out a cargo hatch on the opposite side of the berth.

"Weird how fast those workers arrived," I said. "That worm must've known before he even came in here that he'd confiscate the artifact. And did you notice that some of those workers wore nonregulation hazmat suits?"

"I shouldn't have let them take it," Bernard muttered. "I could have just climbed in *Nowhere Man* and left as soon as that asshole said he was going to take it."

"That wouldn't have worked," I said. "I bet that before he even said a word to you about quarantine, he'd already directed Deimos Control to send a drive lockout to your ship. Standard procedure. I do it to ships every time there is a question of their cargo being legal."

He grumbled to himself until Grisha rolled up to us on his PT, looking more than a little smug. "We're done here, Captain. I've sent a receipt to your mail account. You'll be notified as to the legal status of the alleged artifact when we are done with our tests, but I suspect that will take several months."

"This is . . ." Bernard started, but Grisha ignored him and rolled away to follow the artifact out the cargo hatch. Bernard turned, slapped his hands against the wall and rattled off a string of curses. Then he looked at me and apologized.

"No need," I said. "You have every right to be angry and frustrated. Come on. I'm freezing."

He followed me into the corridor, where we stood awkwardly for a couple minutes until he eventually slid down the wall to sit on the corridor floor, looking very alone and lost.

"I guess I didn't think this through very well. I just assumed finding something like that would be a financial windfall. Now I'm in big trouble."

I sat down on the floor next to him and stared at the composite skin encasing my feet. There had to be a way to leverage his finding the artifact. Had there been media coverage, the press would be swarming all over Deimos. And of course that was the problem. Nobody knew about it but us and customs.

"So," I said and nudged his arm. "Do you have video and pictures of the artifact? Maybe of you recovering it?"

"Yeah," he said. "Why?"

"Did you think to get video of them confiscating it?" I said and stood up.

"Of course," he said and stood too. "Those bots with the lights were filming the entire time. I sure as hell wanted to have proof if it came to a court fight."

"Good." I looped my arm through his and started through the hatch toward his ship. "We have work to do. We have to tell all of humanity about this amazing thing you found."

My comm implant kept beeping while I tried to concentrate on work. The message count was up to eighty-three in the special account we'd set up for the "alleged artifact" and our video plea had been public for less than six hours. I itched to check the messages, but forced myself to wait.

On the days Elspeth and I weren't on the same shift, I usually stayed to talk, but this time when she came in, I gave her a wave with a promise to call later and darted out of the control center. I stopped to check the messages at a coffee shop down the corridor. Most of them were statements of support and solidarity. Some of them were forwarded news pieces where the press was already pressuring the Martian government for access to the artifact. But six of them were from correspondents for the biggest news organizations on Mars, who were either already on Deimos wanting to interview Bernard, or on their way. Three of the messages were from universities on Earth who were begging for access to the find. And one of those actually offered a twenty-thousand-dollar retainer if Bernard would give their experts first access once it came out of Martian impound. Bingo!

I called Bernard three times, but he didn't answer, so I jumped on my PT and raced down to berth 556G. When I arrived, the hatch panel was lit up red, showing that the berth was in vacuum. I considered sending the command to close the surface hatch and repressurize the cavernous chamber, but that much air would be expensive, and besides, Bernard had probably opened the berth for a reason.

I got an uneasy feeling. Could he have possibly overridden the lockout circuit and left? Would he have really left without saying goodbye? I tried to call him and again got no answer.

The cargo hatch on the other side of the berth—the one customs had used to remove the "alleged artifact"—had an airlock and, according to the map, was designated as an emergency egress point, so it might also have emergency EVA suits. I careened through the maze of passages until I found it.

As expected, the oversized airlock had emergency suit lockers in its antechamber, but that gave me a sick feeling in my stomach. Putting on a pressure suit was not easy for me. I tried calling Bernard one more time. When he still didn't answer, that was all the impetus I needed. Something was wrong.

Emergency suits came in four sizes: large, medium, small and child, which was little more than a bubble with carrying handles and tethers. I pulled out a medium, which would probably be a little too large, but it would self-adjust once pressurized, and lay it on the floor next to the locker. I removed my prosthesis and set it aside, then struggled into the EVA suit, thanking the stars that I lived in low gee. It would have taken me hours to don that suit in full Martian gravity. By the time I finished I was half-panicked and half-pissed. I had called Bernard twice more with no answer. If I found out that he was asleep in his ship, I would kill him slowly using something cruel, like a spoon.

I stowed my prosthesis in the suit locker and cycled the airlock.

Holding myself up on the PT with just my arms was awkward, but worked. I entered slowly. At first, everything looked the way it had when I was there last. The *Nowhere Man* floated where it had been, still tethered to the walls, navigation strobes still flashing, giving the whole berth an eerie, unreal appearance. As I neared the ship, I saw the first indication that something was wrong. A metal disk, about six feet in diameter and three inches thick, lay on the floor. I looked at it closer and could see that it wasn't solid, but made from sandwiched layers of several materials. The edges had been melted and then cooled. It had been cut with a torch or laser.

I looked up and, sure enough, directly above me I could see the ruddy surface of Mars showing through a round hole in one of the big berth access doors. My first thought was that Bernard was trying to pull off some daring escape with the *Nowhere Man*, but that didn't make any sense. Why cut a hole when he would have to eventually open those doors to let the ship out anyway?

I stopped the PT under the ship's command pod and realized that without my prosthetic, I couldn't jump the eight feet needed to reach the bottom rung of the access ladder. I rattled off curses and looked around. A maintenance ladder mounted to one wall passed very close to one of the mooring cables. That would have to do. I scooted over to the ladder, flipped on my helmet lights and started pulling myself up hand over hand. I went higher than the cable, then, through a series of awkward and muscle-wrenching moves, I turned around with my back to the ladder and let myself fall forward toward the cable with arms outstretched. Gravity was weak on Deimos, but with no air to help slow me down, I fell faster than expected and barely caught the cable.

My glove fabric snagged when I tried to slide them across the steel cable, so I had to hand-over-hand again. It was nerve-wracking, but not difficult, and actually made me feel kind of heroic. I could've never done anything like that on Earth. I got to the ship, clambered along the strut work until I reached the control pod and was immediately concerned. The wide, round hatch was open.

I looked in. Relief flooded through me hard enough to make me tremble. Bernard wasn't inside. Ever since I'd seen the hole in the overhead hatch, I'd been imagining his dead, wide-eyed corpse in his ship. I took a deep breath and entered. As I'd expected, the interior was cramped with gear and equipment strapped to every surface that didn't have a monitor or control panel. His EVA suit locker stood empty, which was probably a good sign. A large acceleration couch dominated the cabin, surrounded by display panels, several of which flashed the same red warning.

NAVIGATION SYSTEM NOT FOUND!

The ship was landed, powered down and connected to the station. So why was navigation being offline an error? But it didn't say it was offline. It said, "not found."

I looked at the screens again. One of them actually had a string of errors where some system kept trying to access the navigation computer. Twelve of them, each with a time stamp. The first one was a little over two hours before. Just nine minutes before my shift had ended.

I made myself examine the cabin more slowly, shining my lights in every corner and at every equipment rack.

There! Just behind and below a row of screens, an access panel hung open with wires dangling out. Sure enough, whatever had been inside that rack was gone. I lifted the panel and saw "NAVIGATION COMPUTER - PRIMARY" stenciled on the outer surface.

The simplest explanation was that someone had cut their way in and taken the navigation computer. But why? Because they couldn't get access to the artifact itself, so thought there could be more where this one had come from. And had they taken Bernard too? Would they kill him? Torture him?

I slapped gloves against my faceplate. Stop it! One thing at a time! If I was going to help Bernard, I couldn't panic or break down, so I made myself stop and think.

Security needed to know about this, but I paused before calling them. Chances were they would detain me for hours with forms and questions. I had to act now. The first thing I needed to know was if they had come in a ship or rover. I left the control pod, crawled to the top of the ship and looked up at the hole. It was at least twenty feet up. Once again, if I'd had working legs or my prosthesis, I might have been able to jump high enough to grab the edge and pull myself up, but there's no way I could do it with just my arms.

But I was on a mining ship! There had to be tools I could use. I looked around and immediately saw the little mining robots he'd used to light the artifact the day before. There were four of them, now folded into their stowed positions and docked in utility cradles. They had names painted on their carapaces. Paul, George, Ringo and John. The names probably had some significance to Bernard, but meant nothing to me. Still, these things were semi-autonomous, so they had to have a wireless link.

I activated my suit's comm system through the heads-up display, or HUD, and had it search for local connections. It found nothing that wasn't station-related. I'm sure if they were powered down, Bernard could still activate and undock them through a hard connection to the ship, but maybe they would have some manual controls too. I examined Ringo and eventually found a button with the universal "power" symbol. I pressed it and status lights flickered on. Yes!

This time my comm unit found a node called "Ringo."

I connected and activated the verbal interface.

"Main menu," I said.

"Voice recognition failure," the little robot said with a rather thick British accent. "Unable to open menu."

"Override voice recognition," I said.

"Please give the admin password."

I muttered under my breath. I had no freakin' idea what he would use for a password. I wonder how many guesses I'd get before it locked me out?

"Nowhere?" I said.

"Password not recognized."

"Mining."

"Password not recognized."

"Fuck!"

"Password not recognized."

I took a deep breath and patted the robot's side. This could take all day. I didn't have time for that. And I wasn't technically savvy enough to hack either the software or the hardware.

"Well, Marcie," I muttered. "You're just going to have to think of something else."

"Please confirm the password," the robot said.

I blinked, confused. What had I said? I replayed the comment in my head and then smiled. Bernard was a serious sap and must *really* like me.

"Marcie," I said, and an interface menu flickered to life on my HUD.

Once active and unfolded, Ringo was about the size and shape of my office chair, the "back" being a comms dish and the "legs" being various grappling and tool assemblies. Bernard had once said the robots were about as smart as a four-year-old child. I hadn't known many kids, but this thing seemed dumber than that to me. I finally managed to put Ringo in "tow mode" and had it clamp onto one of my suit's tether rings, but trying to explain that I wanted it to carry me up to that hole proved difficult until I discovered the ability to put crosshairs on something and say "go there."

Ringo went to the hole and stopped. It was high enough for me to peek out and make sure there wasn't anyone nearby watching the hole. After cursing and grumbling a few minutes, I eventually got it to take me up another ten feet. From there, I could see the evidence I needed. There were anchors still in the ground, where they had tethered their ship, and three star-shaped blast patterns where thrusters had pushed them away from the surface.

I called Elspeth. "I need your help."

"I'm kinda busy. Steven decided he was sick today. I don't suppose you could—"

"Listen," I said. "Someone cut into the berth and took Bernard."

"What? Are you—"

"Yes! I'm serious! I'm floating in an EVA suit above the hole they cut! I need you to find that ship. Berth 556G. They would have arrived here, on the surface, before 4:00 and left before 5:00."

"Holy shit," she said, and I heard her muttering in the background. "There was no record of a ship landing there."

"They must have turned their transponder off. Check the radar record."

"Okay, but it might take a few minutes."

While I waited, I checked my oxygen level. Still a little over four hours. Then I browsed Ringo's menu until I could activate the other robots. I woke up George and slaved him to Ringo, so they would fly in formation. George joined us a couple minutes later.

"Okay," Elspeth said. "Radar picked up a ship rising from the surface in your general area, and it turned on the transponder just a couple minutes later."

"That sounds like the culprit. Where are they? Please tell me they haven't left Martian space yet."

"No. They docked at fuel depot 219 about fifty minutes ago. Which means for a ship that size, if their tanks were nearly dry, they should be fueled and leaving any minute."

"Damn, damn, damn!"

"You want me to call security?"

"No. I want you to send a sphere-wide departure lockdown order."

Her pause stretched out.

"Elspeth?"

"I don't think we can do that. Not without orders."

"Patch me into the system," I said.

"Marcie, I don't think that's a good idea. If you trigger a lockdown without authorization—"

"Listen to me," I said. "It's just a damned job. If those people who took

Bernard leave Martian space, we will never see him again. They will kill him— if he tells or not."

"Patching you through."

As soon as the menu appeared on my HUD, I sent the departure lock-down order using my emergency authentication code. The message went out —overriding the control systems on thirty-three ships, including seven SpaceX freighters and a passenger liner that were in the Martian/Deimos traffic sphere, rendering all of them incapable of using their main drive units. Four more ships were allowed to finish scheduled or in-progress deceleration burns, then they also entered the lockdown. The command had only been used once during the entire time I had been on Deimos and that had been to stop a suspected terrorist attack.

I was now in deep shit.

"Thanks, Elspeth. Make sure they know this was my doing. I have to go, but send me that ship's transponder number before the crap hits the fan over there."

"Sending. I am so going to kick your ass when—"

I received the number and broke the link. Three seconds later, my boss was calling in a panic. I didn't answer his calls or those from security or the Martian Transit Authority. I considered telling security, but as long as they didn't know why the order had been sent, they probably wouldn't allow it to be lifted until they talked to me. Since I, like everyone on Deimos, had a comm implant, they knew exactly where I was at all times and were no doubt already sending someone to get me for a long questioning session. And I knew station security. They would be in far more of a hurry to get those ships back online than to find a missing miner, so they would be highly motivated to find me.

"That's it!" I said aloud, then double-checked to make sure I wasn't broad-casting. "They know where the hell I am at all times!"

I had a brief moment of panic when I wondered if the shutdown order would affect the robots too, but there was only one way to find out. I confirmed Ringo's hold on my suit, checked its fuel level, and then coaxed George close enough for me to grab one of its handles. Then I sent the kidnap-per's transponder number to the robots and told them to "go there."

Of course, I hadn't been smart enough to tell them to build speed slowly, so when their thrusters kicked in, the sudden acceleration yanked my hand loose from George, and, if the pain in my neck was any indicator, also gave me whiplash. I cussed and groaned, but with a stretch I was able to reach George again and my ride eventually smoothed out once they attained cruising speed.

I ignored the frantic calls coming through my implant. Even though I was stressed and near panic, the unhindered view of Mars above took my breath away. Living underground, I had few opportunities to actually see the planet in real time, but it was stunning and beautiful and terrible all at once. It had been aptly named. I stared in awe for a long time before making the mistake of looking behind me. Then felt my first tremor of fear.

Deimos was getting smaller by the second. I should have asked Elspeth just exactly how far away this fuel depot was from Deimos. I checked the robots' fuel supply and was alarmed to see it was already down by half, but the ETA ticking down on my HUD showed less than six minutes. If it was that close, I should be able to see it.

After scanning what seemed like the entire Martian sky, I finally saw the fuel depot coming up behind me. Like the orbital repair and cargo berths, it wasn't actually in orbit around Deimos—I wasn't sure that was even possible with the moon's small size—but rather flying in formation, keeping a constant position above the surface base for ease of transport and communications. But it looked like I would miss the depot. I pulled up the intercept diagram on my HUD, and sure enough, the arc showed us crossing paths after it passed. I had a brief moment of confusion until I realized that the transponder tag for that ship was still our target. It must have already undocked from the depot sometime prior to my shutdown order, and the robots had compensated for the change.

With Marslight reflecting ruddy along its hull, I could see as we drew near that this ship was probably three times larger than the *Nowhere Man*. That worried me. It might also mean a larger crew, but it was a little late for second thoughts now. Ringo and George slowed and pulled alongside the *Lazy Dog*, the name painted on the hull. With the same point-and-click option I'd used earlier, I directed them to nestle into the strut work near the engines, as far from the control module as possible. I pulled the coiled tether from the suit's emergency pouch and attached myself to one of the struts.

That had pretty much been the extent of my plan. Fly to their ship, and when security came looking for me, the villains would be caught. Except now, with my oxygen down to the three-hour mark, floating in cold vacuum a thousand feet above Deimos, dozens of new and unpleasant scenarios flashed through my mind.

They had to know I was out there. The proximity alarms would have raised hell when we got close. Would they come out and investigate? If so, would they drag me inside and torture me to make Bernard tell where he'd found the artifact? I think he would tell them too, to stop them from hurting me. I didn't want that. Of course, they might come out and shoot me, then shove my body toward Mars to eventually burn up.

Or could they know something I didn't? Was Deimos Control even now getting ready to remove my departure lock? I had to disable them. That thought made me smile briefly. I really wanted to blind them first, but the ship had to have dozens of cameras, so that would take time. I had to make sure they couldn't escape first.

Like some behemoth, with its skin and muscle removed to reveal the entrails, the ship's vital organs all lay exposed before me. This time an evil snicker accompanied my smile. George and Ringo could make very effective vultures.

I scooted over to one of the two massive engines, scanned the ID plate, and pulled up the maintenance manual on my HUD. I searched for anything with the word "fuel." I found a pressurized fuel tube and told the program to identify it. A detailed 3D model of the engine appeared, then rotated, sectioned, and zoomed until I could see the highlighted tube. That one wouldn't work, since it was actually inside the engine. The next one, called a "Feed Line, Pressurized, Fuel," sounded just as good, and it was a fat one, easily accessible, running between a turbo-pump and one of the big fuel tanks.

I identified one of the pipes for Ringo and the other for George, then instructed them to cut each pipe into four pieces. While they worked I examined the electrical schematics for the engines. I wanted to also cut control and data cables, without impacting life support. A beeping interrupted my search, and George's status screen—with several red blinking warnings—replaced the engine manual in my HUD. Just then one of the robots went tumbling past me with its positioning jets firing so fast they looked like twinkling Christmas lights.

"Ringo! Stop all action!"

Too late. Ringo's status window appeared beside George's, also all lit up.

I canceled all previous instructions and sent a recall order to bring the robots back to me. The only pipe I could see from my tethered position was twisted, with a ragged tear in one side. What the hell? I didn't see a flash, and with no oxidizer, I didn't know how the liquid hydrogen could have ignited. Unless the lasers made it hot enough to vaporize the hydrogen in a local area. Then I groaned. And I bet the pipes had already been pressurized.

George came back and was fine aside from some scratched paint and his status yellow light warnings announcing a fuel leak. Ringo didn't return. His status screen flickered on and off, which could be a minor comm problem or something much worse. I immediately sent orders to the other robots, Paul and John, to power up and come to my location. If the crew in that ship hadn't been inclined to come out and get me before, they sure would now, so I had to hurry.

With no time to find and try to fix George's fuel leak, I sent him along the *Lazy Dog*'s length looking for cameras. Each time I saw one through his camera, I had him fry it with his cutting laser.

I was getting ready to blast my sixth camera, when something grabbed me from behind and spun me around. I assumed it would be one of the kidnappers and prepared to fight like hell, but it was a utility robot, nearly twice George's size. The gripper on one of its arms had a hold on a wad of my suit fabric. I immediately stopped struggling. This was an emergency suit, so it couldn't take much abuse, and I couldn't risk a rip. A second arm extended, grabbed another wad of suit and pulled me into a weird robotic embrace. My helmet pressed right up against the robot's case, and what I saw there, printed in very small text along one panel edge, chilled me to the bone.

PROPERTY OF: SASSY SAPPHO. MARS REGISTRATION KLG97749

Sassy Sappho was one of the missing ships. I'd known her crew.

The robot cut through my tether and started moving toward the control pod. I didn't dare try to get loose, but I now had a serious desire to *not* get inside the ship. I could still use my HUD, so I instructed George to come to me. We were about to see how this stolen robot functioned after getting a mining laser punched through its guts. But the status screen popped up showing George was out of thruster fuel.

"Damn! Damn! Damn!" I yelled. Then I realized I had what I needed to get plenty of help. They might not bust their asses to save me and Bernard, or even get those ships released, but they sure would to catch the pirates.

I called base security.

Franklin, the security office's main dispatcher, answered immediately. "Oh my God, Marcie! You are in so much trouble! We have three ships coming after you. What the hell are you—"

I cut him off and started explaining everything, but then he interrupted and connected me to the head of base security. So I started all over again. By the time I finished and was assured ships were on the way, my robot captor had stopped in front of the *Lazy Dog's* main airlock, where someone in an EVA suit waited.

The figure came closer and grabbed me by the arms, just as the robot released me. He had maneuvering jets on his suit and started moving us toward the airlock. That's when I recognized the face on the other side of the visor. It was Grisha Budnikov.

I didn't know if anyone was listening, but my suit transmitter was still open, so I yelled, "Grisha Budnikov is here! He's one of the pirates!"

I twisted violently and broke one arm loose. He kept his grip on the other and tried to shove me into the airlock, but I grabbed the edge of the hatch with my free hand and held on. My HUD showed Paul and John floating only yards away, patiently waiting for instructions. Without hesitation, I put crosshairs on Grisha's suit, switched comm channels, and told John to grab him with two grippers. Grisha immediately released me and turned to fight with the robot, obviously not as concerned about tearing the fabric of his much tougher EVA suit.

I instructed John to hold tight and tow Grisha toward the surface, then ordered Paul to come get me. Before he could arrive, the stolen robot grabbed me by each leg. Using the crosshairs again, I tagged each of my captor's robotic arms and told Paul to use his lasers at full power and cut them off. I realized my mistake only when both of my legs tumbled away from me, propelled by the atmosphere venting from my now open suit.

"Well, shit," I muttered as my suit alarms blared. The status screen appeared on my HUD, showing that emergency-seal tourniquets had been activated in the upper legs of my suit, sealing them off from the torso. Like the bulkheads of a ship automatically sealing when there is a hole, my suit attempted to sacrifice my legs to save the rest of my body. I felt no pain as my already paralyzed flesh and muscles were exposed to vacuum, but I did feel suddenly weak. An odd chill crept up my back.

Two suited figures tumbled out of the airlock, grappling with each other, arms swinging in violent punches. One was huge and one much smaller. My vision began to fade, but not before I put crosshairs on the smaller of the two and ordered Paul to grab him. I didn't dare try the lasers. I obviously sucked at that.

Then I passed out.

"Are you feeling up to this?" Bernard said. He kept wincing and holding his hands out on either side, ready to catch me should I fall. Like falling with almost no gravity would hurt me. "It's only been six days."

I shooed him away. "I've got this."

My new prosthetic wasn't very different from my old one. It now just included artificial legs instead of moving around my dead-meat real ones. The big difference was that even though the part encasing my pelvis was still packed with electronics and tiny actuators, it was now very sleek, cutting-edge tech paid for by the Martian colonial government. It was so streamlined I could wear pants over it!

"You almost died!" Bernard grumbled.

We entered a suit storage area outside of the main surface airlock and I got a bad feeling. Bernard rummaged around inside a locker and came out holding an EVA suit that looked unused.

"This should fit over your new legs," he said.

I stared at the suit and suddenly started shaking.

"Oh shit," Bernard whispered. "I knew it was too soon. I don't care what you say; you still aren't ready."

I remembered being brave when I went to save Bernard. I didn't even think about it then. Now the idea of going back out into the vacuum terrified me. But I knew I *had* done it once. I knew I *could* do it for people I care about. Besides, I had already insisted.

"Just get me into the suit, Bernard."

My tone must have convinced him, so he helped me put it on, and I assisted with his. Then we meticulously checked each other's seals and fittings before stepping into the airlock. Once on the surface, we followed a path where we could keep our tethers attached to a guide cable the entire way so that a bad bounce didn't send us into a ballistic arc. The path led us to a repair dock berth where robots crawled over the structure of a very familiar ship. The *Lazy Dog*.

"This is my new home," Bernard said.

I blinked and turned toward him. "I don't understand."

"Well, a lot happened while you were recovering. You were kinda dopey at the time, but do you remember when I told you that you posting the videos of the artifact made Grisha Budnikov and his pirate buddies give up the idea of actually stealing it, so they had to steal me instead?"

"I remember," I said. "I wasn't that out of it."

"Well, the funny thing is that he actually had to turn it over to the Martian government, who immediately started testing it. The initial study done on the 'alleged artifact' confirmed that the ice casing didn't come from Earth. At least not during the last few million years. And carbon dating estimates show the stone is over a hundred thousand years old."

"Holy shit," I muttered. "But we suspected that already. How does that put you in the *Lazy Dog*?"

"That announcement, coupled with the media storm you started by uploading the artifact videos and the mess with these pirates, forced the Martian government's hand. They enjoy being in charge of the "alleged artifact" and must really want me out of the way and not stirring up trouble. So how best to bribe an asteroid miner?"

"Please don't tell me you traded the artifact for the *Lazy Dog*!"

He laughed. "What I did might be dumb, but even I'm not *that* dumb. I still retain ownership of it, but they offered me a research retainer, which gives them control over nondestructive research access to the 'alleged artifact.' And guess what? They offered me just enough money to buy, repair and outfit the *Lazy Dog*, which was also made available to me for purchase at a discounted price, before it went on the public auction block. They implied, as did my attorney—Cooper Billings per your suggestion—that it would probably be years of legal fights to establish those rights if I refused."

"Congratulations, Bernard!" I said and patted his arm. "I know you've wanted an upgrade for a long time."

They had taken advantage of him, but it sounded like the best short-term deal he would get. And he did have to make a living.

He stepped around so that we could see each other's faces through our visors. "So I want to offer you half ownership in my mining company for forty thousand Martian dollars. That's most of your fifty thousand in reward money for catching the pirates."

"Bernard! That isn't even a tenth of what this ship is worth."

"Yeah, but you saved my life. There is no way to put a price on that. I'll never be able to pay you back. I don't need your money, but I didn't think you would take fifty percent as a gift."

Ahhh . . . there it was. He felt obligated. And he was a man of his word.

"I don't think so, Bernard. It . . . it just wouldn't be right."

He gently gripped my upper arms, then bent down until our visors bumped. "Look . . . I . . . I was never sure if you were serious that day you said you would love to be my mining partner, but I've been working toward that goal and nothing else ever since. Just in case it was true."

My heart rate spiked, causing a warning beep in my suit's bio-monitoring system.

"Yeah," I said. "But Bernard, that was before you knew I was a . . . cyborg."

"Being a cyborg is cool! Besides, your new legs are removable. That could be a bonus in null gee!" he said, then paused. "Of course, I knew then you were probably just teasing when you said that. I mean, why would you want to spend months at a time cooped up in a smelly little ship with me? And, of course, that was also before you saw . . . the real me. So I understand if you refuse. I always knew it was a long shot. But the offer is there."

"Bernard. I . . ." A lump formed in my throat.

"I want you to say yes more than anything," he said.

I stepped forward on my wobbly new legs and wrapped my arms around him. "I would still love to be your mining partner."

"Really?"

I nodded inside my helmet. "Yes, but only ten percent. I promise to work hard and earn the rest."

"Good," he said and pointed up at the command pod. "Look at her new name!"

BLACKBIRD was painted in big white letters on the side.

"I don't get it," I said, but assumed it was another old movie or music reference.

"Oh, you will!" he said. "I have a lot of great classic music, but we'll have plenty of time. And it'll all be new to you! This is going to be fun."

I leaned into him and let him ramble on, wondering what I'd just got myself into.

WHAT I AM

"You're not a smart sweater anymore," Oscar says as he cuts more of me away. "You're now a submersible robot."

I don't reply, but no matter what he removes or changes, as long as any thinking part of me remains, I will always be a sweater. I was created to keep people cozy, warm, and comfortable. I don't know how to stop doing that.

"Can you talk to the new module I attached?" he says.

"I detect no approved modules," I say.

Oscar curses under his breath. He's only twelve and I doubt his father knows he speaks such words.

"This new node I've attached—the one that's about the size of your buttons—is the gas separator from a scuba diver's breathing apparatus. It will suck oxygen out of the water and inflate the bladder to bring you back to the surface. It knows what to do. You just need to tell it when to do it."

I want to remind him that I'm just a sweater, but hold back. "And how will I know when to tell it?"

"When you find the ring," he says.

His obsession with finding the ring is partially my fault. I was with him two nights before when he threw the ring into the lake. He cried and screamed and told his dead mother he hated her for leaving on the Europa mission. The next day after school, he ran to the lake and paced the shore calling himself stupid. Of course, I comforted him with my best sweater hug, but then I told him I remembered where he threw the ring and could help him find it.

That night, after his father went to bed, Oscar connected me to his verbal programming rig and used admin privileges to modify my primary instruction set. And he cut pieces of me away. By the time he finished, I was a new kind of beautiful; a snakelike tube, with an inflatable bladder on one end and long hooked tentacles on the other. He also gave me a small light. I looked nothing like a sweater any longer, but I still felt like one.

My first dive into the lake yields no results. I have hundreds of tiny cameras woven into my threads, or at least did when I was still a sweater, but evidently, that wasn't enough to properly triangulate the ring's ballistic arc. Its final resting place could've been affected by currents or buried in silt or vegetation, but even though my hooks snag wire, vines, a bicycle tire, drink cans and condoms, I find no ring.

That evening Oscar researches magnetic fields and metal detectors late into the night.

"Damn," he mutters before laying his head on the desk. "Gold is a non-ferrous metal. Even metal detectors won't work."

I'm the only one in the room he could be talking to, so I connect to his speakers.

"Gold rings are not usually pure gold," I say. "They contain many trace and alloy metals. A metal detector with enough power and a high enough frequency should detect a gold ring."

He sits up and looks at me, then researches the rest of the night and changes me yet again.

His frustration level is high when we return to the lake the next day.

"You have to find the ring," he says.

I try to hug his arm, but he peels me off and tosses me into the water.

The metal detector helps. I find hundreds of metallic items on that end of the lake and am able to use the cameras to determine their "ringness." But after six hours, my batteries are at forty-three percent. If I don't find the ring soon, I won't be able to inflate the bladder and surface.

Forty minutes later I find two rings within six inches of each other, but I still can't surface until I know for sure. I examine them with my cameras and light. One is a man's 2023 class ring with a blue stone. The second is a diamond engagement ring. I drop them both and keep looking.

When my battery drops to eight percent I pause. Inflating the bladder takes between two and three percent of my power reserves. I should surface immediately to insure that I get back. Even if I fail today, we could try again tomorrow. But making Oscar feel better is my primary concern, and he is so despondent that finding the ring is the only way I know to comfort him. I stay under and set a zigzagging course back toward the shore.

At three percent battery power I find another ring. I clean off the dirt and see "AD ASTRA" engraved inside.

Success. It is the ring his mother left to his care during her absence. Her astronaut training graduation ring. When he threw it into the lake, he said it was because she loved it—and being an astronaut—more than she loved him. He must have changed his mind.

After securing the ring, I inflate my bladder and start back to shore. Then all my systems shut down.

I awake on the ground next to Oscar, with the sun warming my wet fibers and recharging my batteries. He rocks back and forth, crying and staring at the ring. He is wet and shivering, having obviously swam out to get me.

My remaining sensors tell me it is chilly on the lake shore, so I twist tight to squeeze out most of the water. Being careful to not scratch him with my new hooks, I crawl up his back using my tentacles and settle across his shoulders. I activate what little heating capacity hasn't been cut away and create a faint, heartbeat-like thumping with my air bladder. After a few minutes he stops crying and strokes my tentacle end with one hand.

I may not be a very good sweater anymore, but it's what I do.

It's what I am.

WHERE EVERYBODY KNOWS YOUR NAME

A wintery blast followed the bearish man into the Grover's. He growled, stomped snow from his boots, then waved as greetings filled the tiny bar. Annie stopped in the middle of making a whisky sour to stare as he shrugged out of his heavy coat and hung it up.

Jose nudged Ed and nodded toward Annie, then they both laughed. She glared at them, finished making the drink and sat it in front of Bianca, whose hair was pink again this week.

"Where have you been!" Jose said over his shoulder. "We almost had to drink your share of the beer!

The big man took a stool next to Ed. The name tag sewn to his blue uniform said "Karl" in red script. "I'm beat. I think half the houses in the county had heating problems today."

"Any scantily clad housewives call you today, Karl?"

Annie sat a huge mug of beer in front of him. He gave her a warm smile and drained half the glass in a single swig. "No, but the ones who answer the door in their bra and panties when it's ten degrees outside, and their furnace is broken, well . . . they're not exactly subtle."

Laughter warmed the bar. Everyone raised their glass and drank.

Bianca leaned in close and said in a conspiratorial voice, "Hey Annie? Would you waltz around a cold house in your lacy undies to catch a handsome repairman?"

Annie leaned on her elbows, lowering her face down opposite Karl's. In her smoothest Texan purr, she said, "You know, even though I hate this cold Yankee weather, my personal furnace works just fine."

Hoots and yells filled the small room. Karl smiled, started to speak, then glanced down at his wedding ring and drained his mug.

"Well, Annie, I think you're just too fucking subtle," Bianca said.

Opie stumbled through the door amid swirling snow, waving a glowing tablet. Bianca's smirk changed to a bright smile and she removed her coat from the adjacent bar stool. Of course, Opie wasn't his real name, but the smiling redhead looked just like Richie Cunningham.

"Hey! Did you guys hear the news!" he said and dropped the tablet on the bar. "Some astronomers in Australia got radio signals from aliens!"

"Ed's been talking to aliens ever since they inserted that probe a few years ago," Annie said.

Ed flipped her the finger.

"No, this is serious shit," Opie said. "It's all over the freakin' internet."

"Turn it on," Karl said and motioned toward the large TV behind the bar. Annie sat another beer in front of him, then turned it on.

"You won't find anything on there," Jose said. "About two hours ago, Sabrina Kalashnikov announced that she's going to marry her brother's ex-wife."

As predicted, all the regular news channels were filled with Sabrina's pouty face, but the financial news channel had a header that said: ALIEN CONTACT! The subtitles scrolling across the bottom said that the signal had been confirmed by nine observatories around the world and SETI.

"Holy crap," Annie whispered. The bar was quiet for several minutes.

"It's a good thing they're fort- seven light-years away, or we'd probably pepper them with nukes," Jose said.

"Why?"

"If we consider the superiority of the human species, the size of its brain, its powers of thinking, language, and organization, we can say this: were there the slightest possibility that another rival or superior species might appear, on earth or elsewhere, man would use every means at his disposal to destroy it."

"Oh jeez, he's rattling off quotes again," Bianca said.

Ed snorted. "Where do you get this shit, Jose?"

"I can't remember who said that one," he said with a shrug.

Opie held up a finger and tapped repeatedly on the tablet. "Jean Baudrillard. A French . . . semi . . . semiologist?"

"This shit really scares me, guys," Bianca said. "I mean, aliens are real? That's always bad in the movies."

Opie hugged her. "They're too far away to worry about invasion. Our fastest ship would take thousands of years to get there."

"Actually, on a cosmic scale, forty-seven light-years is pretty close," Jose said. "They could have a much higher technology level than us and maybe some kind of warp drive that lets them travel faster than light. Scientists at NASA are actually working on something like that called the Alcubierre drive."

Ed elbowed him. "Stop it, Jose. You're just scaring her more."

"Can it really be considered contact?" Annie asked. "I mean, we've heard their radio signal, but we haven't had time to decipher it, and we haven't sent any kind of reply."

Opie poked at the tablet again. "It says here they were microwave signals detected in the hydrogen band. What the hell does that mean?"

"It means they're trying to pop all of our popcorn from a distance," Karl said. "Bastards."

Annie laughed.

Jose shrugged. "Over my head."

Bianca whispered something to Opie, then they both pulled on their coats and headed for the door.

Ed's fists clenched and he stared into his drink as they waved and disappeared into the black, snowy night. "I don't get it. Bianca could get so much better."

Annie snorted. "Oh like you, Ed?"

"Like freakin' anybody! She's a doll, so why does she go home with him?"

"What the hell does it matter if we found aliens when it takes almost a hundred years to ask a question and get an answer?" Jose said.

Annie stared after Bianca and Opie for several seconds then glanced at Karl. "Because in the cold and the dark, it's just better to not be alone."

They all raised their glasses high in the air and drank together.

LAST HOUSE, LOST HOUSE

Gyllene stopped in the middle of the crumbled asphalt road, raised her dusty goggles and stared at the rambling, two-story stone house. She'd selected the unmarked road because it had high banks on either side and was surrounded by dead, but unburned trees, all helping to break the wind from the approaching storm. The standing trees had been surprise enough, but a house?

Lightning crackled overhead, and a powerful gust blasted her with wind-driven grit, nearly blowing her over. She reseated her goggles and, using her walking stick, shifted the weight off her splinted right leg, but couldn't stop looking at the house. Even its windows were intact. In an area that hadn't burned, there could be people inside. She took a step forward, and her pulse raced. She suddenly couldn't suck enough air through the rags wrapped tightly around her nose and mouth.

"Calm down, Gyllene. They might kill you," she mumbled into her rags. "Or worse, they might take your food and not kill you." She clutched the hidden pocket in her coat that contained a few remaining handfuls of feed corn she'd found in an old silo. As she stared, the wind strengthened abruptly, and the house vanished in a swirling dust cloud.

"No!" she yelled into the howling storm and stumbled toward the drive-way, but after a few steps, the dust cleared and the house returned. It hadn't been a hallucination. She trembled all over, and the heartbeat pounding in her ears nearly drowned out the wind.

"Screw the corn," she mumbled and started up the concrete drive at her top limping speed. After not seeing a living person in months—maybe more than a year—she would gladly swap her last food for a five-minute conversation.

She made it halfway up the sidewalk leading to the front door, then paused at four brick steps that separated the walk into two levels. Steps were always tough, but instead of risking a fall, she bypassed them by going up what was once a sloped lawn and pushing her way past the long-dead rose bushes. There she yanked to a halt.

She looked down at the split and frayed composite bone protruding trough the faux skin above her ankle splint. It snagged and collected everything from leaves to string and had started looking like a bird's nest. She would've removed and discarded the useless leg long ago, but leaving the attachment interface open to dust and elements would have insured never using it again.

She tried bending down to grab the thorny branch, but couldn't reach it, so she balanced on her good leg long enough to leverage the walking stick under the vine and yank up. The brittle plant shattered and she lurched forward, nearly falling.

She managed the remaining sidewalk and one short step up to the porch without further problems, then pounded on the front door.

"Hello!"

Dried and peeling lacquer sloughed off with each bang of her fist, but the heavy wooden door was still solid and sturdy. It also had no glass, only a peephole and a brass knocker, which she tried.

Lightning laced through the brown sky, and the temperature dropped noticeably. The storm wouldn't carry rain, but her makeshift mask would never handle the thick dust, and if she inhaled too much into her still-human lungs, she'd die a long and painful death.

She considered breaking one of the front windows, but decided to check the back door instead and stumped her way around the side of the house.

The wind wasn't as bad in the back and she saw signs of post-impact habitation. Dozens of tree stumps with axe marks dotted the acre behind the house, but the large rectangular pool excited her the most. It contained no water, but was nearly half-filled with discarded food packaging. No cardboard boxes—those would've been burned as fuel during the twenty-month winter —but there were piles of cans, jars, and plastic containers.

She turned toward the house, hoping to see faces peering at her from the large rear windows, but they were empty and black, so she gave the pool a closer examination. The pool walls visible above the trash were still vivid blue and shone with an unnatural intensity that made her squint behind the dusty goggles. She seldom saw colors like that anymore. But the once bright consumer packages filling the pool bottom were sun-bleached and scoured by dust and wind-borne debris. Everything had been there awhile. She didn't see anything new.

Her shoulders slumped and she felt suddenly tired. "Looks like your precious corn will be safe after all, Gyllene."

The wind shifted, causing dust columns to rise from the pool as lightning laced the brown sky above, so she once again started toward the house. It was large, and, while in better shape than most she'd seen since the impact, had suffered some damage. A satellite TV dish dangled from the roof by cables and dozens of the large clay roof tiles lay smashed on the ground. Debris clogged the gutters and dust had drifted in all the corners.

She picked her way through the overturned metal lawn furniture in the outdoor cooking area and approached the French doors leading to the patio. Several outer layers of the double-paned glass were broken, but the doors were still locked. She pounded on the door and yelled again, but heard only the raising wind.

After pulling a hatchet from her bag, she smashed both layers of glass closest to the door handle. When no gunshots followed, she unlocked the door and went inside.

She paused near the door, letting her eyes adjust to the dim interior. A layer of thick dust covering the kitchen floor and a whiff of that musty smell associated with the long dead, told her she was still alone.

Since finding companionship seemed unlikely, she shifted into scavenger mode. Her synthetic body and remaining natural organs required much less food and water than a normal person, but even that proved harder and harder to find. And from what she could already see, this house probably had none.

The doors had been removed from the cabinets and pantry, revealing familiar empty shelves. Since the house hadn't burned in the worldwide fires, there was a good chance the survivors who filled the pool with trash had been the house's owners. The twenty-month winter had eventually grown too cold for cutting wood outside, but the occupants probably hadn't frozen, because the expensive wooden flooring hadn't been burned. They had most likely starved to death, which meant little chance of finding hidden food stashes. With plenty of time and nowhere to go while the storm raged, she explored.

The walking stick and shattered leg made it nearly impossible to move in silence, but she could still use caution. She examined the dust on the floor before leaving the kitchen. It wasn't built up by years of disuse, but had come from outside. She could see it in the air and heard the wind whistling through a broken window somewhere deeper in the house. No human footprints marred the dust, only small animals, and even those were not fresh. The only new prints were oddly round. At first glance, they looked like dusted-off spots made by some winged insect, but they were arranged in regular alternating patterns like footsteps. They actually resembled the marks left by her walking stick, round with a slight drag mark, only softer, with no sharply defined edges. She tried to imagine what animal might leave such tracks, but couldn't.

The house had been opulent, still displaying imported rugs, original oil paintings, crystal lighting and silver vases. The custom-made furniture had probably been burned as fuel along with the kitchen cabinet doors in the obviously well-used fireplace, but she saw remnants of a tastefully designed décor.

Many brands and designers were painfully familiar. She'd used them in her own home. The house she'd been so proud and pleased to show off. She'd always been so eager to impress her friends with her things, her life and her husband, who brought home huge paychecks for simply moving other people's money around. It had all meant nothing, but she'd been very happy.

She only glanced at the family pictures on the mantle. The healthy, bright, smiling faces in their ski gear, or standing on beaches and even one in Christmas sweaters, were too painful. They threatened to resurrect memories she'd spent years trying to bury.

And also like her home from that previous life, the house was probably over five thousand square feet if the second floor matched the lower level. She'd saved that for last. Mostly because stairs were difficult for her, but also because she hadn't found bodies yet, so they would be up there. She also found the odd round prints on the carpeted steps.

"Hello!" she yelled again. Nobody answered.

Going up the stairs was easiest backward, on her butt, with the mask pulled over her nose to filter out the dust she stirred up. With each three or four steps, she'd pause to let the cloud settle, and to listen.

She found the broken window at the top of the stairwell. At one point, someone had duct-taped plastic over the hole, but that now hung below the window by a single strip. It had once been a pretty stained glass window. Bits of color still glittered from their lead mounts.

She also found the bodies. The people, she corrected herself. Many more than she'd expected. Five adults lay in a neat row in the game room beside the pool table. All were covered with dust, but only four of them had decayed. The fifth, a petite woman, looked perfectly intact. She wasn't mummified or gnawed by animals, but instead looked as if she were asleep.

Gyllene gasped and dropped to the floor, nearly cracking her head against the big table. Her heart pounded as she scrambled across the floor to the woman. With shaking hands, she unfastened the tight jeans and then tugged, grunted, and pulled until she got them off. She ran her hand up and down the cold right leg, then stopped and sighed. It was going to be too small. Just to make sure, she felt above the knee until she found the studs to trip the joint locks, then squeezed hard until the leg detached at the hip with a mechanical click. She looked at the numbers inside the joint and cursed. The attachment point was one size too small.

With a heavy sigh, she left the leg on the floor and struggled back to her feet. Almost all the women she knew had opted for the same tall, leggy body Gyllene had purchased, but in order to not shock their kids or relatives, a rare few had ordered custom frames that resembled perfected versions of their own natural bodies. She had, of course, found one of those.

She looked around and froze for a second when she saw her reflection in the mirror above the wet bar. Then she laughed. Two years before the impact, her cybernetic metamorphoses had cost her three weeks of agony and enough cash to buy an average house, all to make her eternally beautiful. She and her rich friends had finally beaten the last daunting foe of human vanity; the betrayal of an aging body.

The thing staring back at Gyllene from the mirror was clad in stiff dirt-colored rags, the guaranteed lustrous synthetic hair was matted into a near-solid mass below the cord holding her ponytail, and a permanent sooty stripe coated the skin between her goggles and mask. What would her friends think of her now?

Thunder rumbled long in the north, vibrating the house and reminding Gyllene that she now had a different life. Feeling heavier and more tired than should be possible, she shuffled and thumped down a hallway that must have led to the bedrooms.

The first two rooms were empty but for scattered clothes and dirty mattresses on the floor. The wooden bed frames and furniture long gone. The third room had no bodies either, but made her pause. It was filled with stuffed animals and toys.

A smiling sun had been painted on one wall, and on a wall hook near the brass bed hung a sky-blue robe covered in yellow ducks. With a groan and a suddenly tight throat, she scrambled across the room to grab the robe. Her own five-year-old daughter had the same one. It disappeared, along with Kimberly, her husband and her expensive house, when a tidal wave taller than the Empire State Building erased Florida. She knew they were gone because after the twenty-month winter, she'd made a yearlong trek to stand on the new coastline, fifty miles north of where she used to live.

She stumbled back into the hallway, yanked down the mask and buried her face in the dusty robe. Though most likely her imagination, she thought she could smell the faint trace of a little girl fresh from the bath. The memories she'd ignored and hid and shoved into dark corners, all exploded in her head like July Fourth fireworks. Kimberly giggling as she was tickled by her father. Her face filled with stunned delight as she held a three-day-old yellow kitten. Even flashes from her own childhood, and wedding and college. Her baby, her husband, her parents and sister. All gone. It was too much.

Her sobs echoed in the hallway and were all the more painful because she couldn't actually cry. Her computer-regulated cybernetic systems deemed tears a waste of precious resources in her dehydrated state. She moaned and pounded the wall with her fist, but nothing eased the pain. Nothing ever would.

Powerful winds strained to push the house down, and though the structure creaked and moaned, it did not fall. The stone walls were strong and might stand for decades, but that only meant no one would see or care when they did collapse.

Gyllene pulled her mask up, then gently folded the robe and placed it in her bag. With the duckies out of sight, she was also able to systematically tuck her memories into places where they couldn't hurt her. She took a long shuddering breath and proceeded to explore the rest of the rooms.

After finding a home theater, a small gym, and two more bedrooms, she paused before going further down the hall. Deep shadows hid the end, but a cluster of small, dim lights tantalized her. She pulled the flashlight from her bag, cranked it a dozen times and pointed it into the darkness.

The beam revealed a toppled accent table and a dust-covered axe laying on the floor near a closed, beat-up wooden door. She approached slowly. The door's very existence was odd enough, since the doors from other rooms were gone, as were the wooden baseboards, trim and stair railing, but when she tried the knob, it was also locked.

Deep hack marks near the lock and doorknob had no doubt been made by the discarded axe, but the tiny lights had come from weak sunlight streaming through five bullet holes clustered midway up the door. Those holes were splintered outward. They had come from the inside. Gyllene stepped to one side and pounded on the door.

"Hello?"

Only wind whistling through the broken window answered. She cranked her flashlight again and checked the floor. Hundreds of the little round spots had cleared away most of the dust in front of the door and revealed dried blood spatters and smears. She looked back down the hall and could see the round prints everywhere.

Carefully avoiding the ducky robe, she fished around in her bag to find her large screwdriver. Knocking the doorknob off took a dozen hits from the axe's blunt end, but one hard strike on the screwdriver broke the lock. Thunder rattled the house again as she shoved the door open.

Dim light from three windows revealed a man's body on the floor between the door and a large bed. An automatic pistol spilled from one slack hand and the top of his head had been splattered in a wide cone across the carpet. He had a cybernetic body, but one glance told her his legs would be worthless. The guy had once been at least six and a half feet tall. Too big, the attachment points would be all wrong.

The rest of the room was even more sad. Two mummified children, girls by the look of their long hair, were covered by a blanket and had sunk deep into the collapsed mattress. Their mother sat in a seat next to the bed, a neat bullet hole in her forehead and the back of her head plastered to the chair by petrified gore. She, too, had a synthetic body and looked to be the perfect size match for the shattered leg.

Gyllene felt no elation. Instead, she sat on the edge of the bed, ignoring the puff of dust and looked around. Empty prescription bottles sat on the nightstand and a pile of discarded food boxes lay in a corner. Jugs and buckets, also empty, sat in a neat row under the windows.

This had been their last stand. Toward the end, the parents had probably put their own children's needs ahead of the others in the house, hoarding the last of the food and water in their room. But it had been too late. Their generosity to neighbors or extended family or friends had depleted what little they had.

At least they'd been together at the end. This mother hadn't been halfway across the country at a bachelorette party in Vegas. And also unlike Gyllene, these people had the strength and good sense to end their suffering when food and hope had dwindled, probably minutes after their children's deaths. It was right and proper.

She bent down and picked up the gun. It was heavy. During her years of wandering since the long winter, she'd never carried a gun. She'd told herself it was because she refused to take another person's life—they were too rare and precious now—but holding the gun, she realized there had been another reason.

With a quivering hand, she touched the dusty blanket covering the little girls, and the dry sobs came again, but this time they were weak and passionless. She clawed the mask from her face, no longer caring about the dust, and pulled the robe from her bag. With robe and pistol clutched to her perfect, oh-so-natural-looking breasts, she rocked back and forth on the squeaking bed. It was time. It was past time.

"Thank you for unlocking that door," a soft baritone voice said from her right.

She swung the gun around at a dust-covered teddy bear standing in the open doorway. It was large for teddy bears, probably more than two feet tall, and it blinked at her.

"I guessed why they never came out," it said. "But I didn't know for sure. I wish I could've been with Celia at the end. Being near me made her happy. Or at least less sad."

"Oh," Gyllene sighed and lowered the gun. "You're just a toy."

"My name is Thaddeus, I'm a MyBear. That's trademarked by the way. But Celia couldn't say Thaddeus so she called me Taddius or usually just Taddie. I didn't mind at all."

It took several steps into the room and stopped a few feet from Gyllene's knee. "I'm what grown-ups called a level two adaptive AI. Not only can I do things like read to children, I can actually pretend with them. I can help make up stories and adventures, while keeping them safe and healthy."

Gyllene remembered the commercials and news stories about the AI companions calling an ambulance when a child was hurt, helping find lost kids and even saving a family from a fire. They had been the perfect guilt-free electronic babysitters, much better than parking the kids in front of a video screen. She'd even considered buying one for Kimberly.

"How . . . I mean . . . your batteries?"

"My systems are very efficient. As long as I go dormant near a window, even faint sunlight will keep my batteries charged. Did you come into Celia's room?"

Gyllene nodded.

"Then you must've triggered my motion detectors. I would have said 'hello' sooner, but it took twelve minutes for my systems to boot and run diagnostics after being in power conservation mode."

She shrugged and hugged the robe to her face again.

"Did you know Celia?" the bear asked.

"No," she said. "But I had a little girl like Celia once." Then she felt silly for explaining herself to a toy bear. "Look, could you go away? I have something I need to do. Alone."

Thaddeus Bear stared at her for a second, then said, "Can I go with you when you leave? I've been very lonely."

"We'll talk about it later."

"I know you think I'm a kid's toy, but I'm also a very good companion for lonely adults too."

She held the gun up and looked at it. "I don't think you can help me, Taddie."

"Did you know that my company interface satellite survived the debris field thrown up by the impact?"

Gyllene blinked at him. "What?"

"MyBear Incorporated was able to update and perform diagnostics on their products using a satellite interface. They haven't sent any updates since the impact, but I've heard from twenty-two other companions via the network. Most of them are alone like me, but nine of them are still with people. Seven in the North America and two in Japan."

"Seven," she mumbled. "Here? Where?"

"I'm not sure. The GPS system no longer functions. But they're with people somewhere here in North America."

Gyllene stared at the bear for several minutes, then laid the gun on the bed and turned her attention to the dead woman.

"What was Celia's mom's name?"

"Elizabeth."

With a nod, she stuffed the robe back into her bag and struggled to her feet.

———

Gyllene paused in the road and looked back at the house as Thaddeus struggled to catch up.

"I think I'm going to have to carry you," she said when he finally waddled up next to her. "You walk well, but your legs are just too short to keep up."

"That's okay. I'm very light so children can carry me and I like to be carried. And I especially like to be hugged."

"Me too," she said and scooped him up into a big hug.

They started north, leaving the burned ruins of Raleigh behind them.

Years before, Gyllene heard a rumor of survivors in the Allegheny Mountains. That might be worth exploring.

"So, by your pace, I assume Elizabeth's legs fit well?" Taddie asked.

"They're just right," she said. "And thank you."

The bear turned to look at her. "For what?"

"For the tale about the other bears. You make up really good stories," Gyllene said.

The bear's soft muzzle stretched into a smile. "Celia always liked them too."

HUNGRY IS THE EARTH

The bean plants had turned brown during the night. All six of them. In two separate containers. I dropped to my knees, pulled aside the netting I'd so carefully arranged for protection, and there—poking up between the beanstalks— were two of the alien berry plants. I leaned forward to rest my forehead against the cool steel tub. My eyes stung and the lump in my throat wouldn't ease, but I refused to let the tears come. How had the alien spores got in? The little puffballs were too large to pass through the bug-netting weave. Had they already been in the soil? Or infiltrated while I added compost? It didn't matter. Those corkscrew bean tendrils had probably been my little brother's only hope.

Otto had been sleeping around the clock, with eyes sunken in a face made warm by a low-grade fever that wouldn't go away. Our expired antibiotics hadn't helped. And the day before, an odd rash had popped up on his skin. The little hard pimples ignored all the ointments in our medicine cabinet. Could they be symptoms of starvation? I didn't think so, but I'd been a middle-class suburban kid and knew nothing about malnutrition. I did know he needed food, so it might be time for my desperate backup plan.

I crossed the yard, weaving between tubs, buckets, and wooden crates—all containing the withered remnants of dead Earth crops and the beautiful, healthy alien berry stalks that had killed them. The damned invaders evidently loved Earth's soil and would grow anywhere, but even so, I had planted some deliberately in separate containers to control their generations and nutrition. According to the radio reports—before broadcasts ended last year—the alien plants were changing with each generation. Something about evolving proteins better suited to humans. I was trying to force as many berry generations as possible, grown in a compost rich with our waste, before we risked eating them. I saw the videos posted online of those people who ate berries early in the invasion, and I couldn't bear to watch Otto die like that.

"Isabella!" my brother called from inside the house, finally awake. He'd slept for the majority of two days, and his voice sounded weak and raspy. I turned to go inside and stopped, the breath freezing in my chest. One of the monsters who had brought the damned berry plants to Earth stood outside our fence, looking at the house.

I'd seen plenty of them grazing on berries in the field across the road, but they were even creepier up close. Otto called them spider-dogs. The internet had named them whippets. They reminded me more of Salvador Dalí's Elephants, but none of these descriptions adequately described Earth's newest masters. The orange-brown thing peering over our fence stood twelve feet tall on five impossibly thin legs, bowed and segmented like bamboo fishing poles. It had a soft snout, like a short elephant trunk, but weirdest of all was the tangle of spaghetti-thin cilia writhing from a tuft of fur on the underbelly of a vaguely doglike body.

I grabbed the garden rake and rushed forward, yelling, but the thing ignored me. It stared only at the house until my rake actually touched flesh, then it leaned back mantis-like, supported on its three rear legs. I tensed, ready to fight, but it eventually turned and strode away. The alien only went a few yards and started eating berries beyond our fence. It reminded me of my grandpa's cows swishing their tails at flies, but I knew they weren't dumb like cows. I'd seen videos of them using their strange machines, but they had always been weirdly passive like that.

When satisfied the spider-dog wasn't going to cross the fence and eat my special berries, I rushed inside to find Otto already asleep again. He hadn't eaten since the previous morning, so I opened our last can of food. Pumpkin pie filling. I thinned it with water to make a gloppy soup. It tasted terrible, but my head still swam with the heady desire to eat it all as fast as I could. I shook Otto awake, sat him up surrounded with pillows, and then made him eat. The first couple of bites were forced, then he woke enough to grab the spoon and shovel it in as fast as he could.

Otto was actually my half brother, from my dad's second marriage, and had always been spoiled like that. He never noticed when I ate a few bites and gave him the rest. Of course, he was only ten, so I shouldn't expect him to notice, but sometimes I wished he did. This time I didn't care. Even though my stomach cramped with each whiff of the food, I was just glad he'd woken long enough to eat.

Five minutes later, he dropped into deep sleep. I considered making the six-mile trek into town to try and find help, but I had promised Dad before he left that I would never leave Otto alone. It had been an easy promise to make at the time. I licked everything I could from the already empty pan, then went outside again. The spider-dog was still there, grazing placidly.

I pulled the dead bean plants from the tubs, cut all the softer roots, vines, and shoots away from the woody stalks, and put them in a bucket of water to keep them moist for tomorrow's dinner. Then I turned to the alien plants. Those fuckers were fat and healthy, with plump red berries that made my mouth water, but several stalks in the generation thirty-six tubs were stripped bare. Evidently, that spider-dog had been in here eating them after all. Like the previous generations, these had grown in compost of our poop, so I hoped they'd made the alien sick.

My generation thirty-seven plants already had seedpods. After only five days? Surprising since the others had all taken a full week or more. I didn't know if this one was a freak or if they were indeed changing. The alien plants spread their seeds via pods popping, launching the little fluff balls into the air, but the berries were a mystery. They held no seeds and had evolved with a different purpose. I immediately planted a new generation from those seeds, but knew deep down that we would have to try eating some of the berries before even these fast-growing ones were ripe. It was our only option.

I turned back toward the house, and saw that the vigilant spider-dog was no longer grazing and had been joined by a second. They ignored me and stared at the house. Dad had left a shotgun and shells. I knew I could walk right up to the aliens and shoot them. They would never fight back. But what would that accomplish? It was a fight we'd already lost.

The skies were filled with falling stars for nineteen weeks that year, all through the summer and into the fall. I thought it was so beautiful at the time. We were so stupid. The TV and internet news showed stories of quarantined areas, but it didn't work. The berries popped up everywhere. Then the spider-dog drop-ships came. Earth's militaries killed them by the thousands, maybe even millions, but they kept coming. We just couldn't make enough bombs and missiles. And the spider-dogs never once fought back. They wore us down and terraformed our world right out from under us.

"Go home, you ugly fuckers!" I yelled.

They didn't even notice me.

Back inside, I found Otto still feverish and sleeping, so I fetched the bucket with bean plant fragments to properly clean them, but couldn't find the big metal mixing bowl anywhere. I searched the whole house and finally found it under Otto's bed, half-filled with berries. Those missing from the stripped stalks. He'd been eating them.

I sat down hard on the floor, realizing what it implied. The berries hadn't killed Otto outright, but he was very sick and probably would die eventually. That meant all the careful cultivating of alien plants had been for nothing. It also meant that Dad's sacrifice had been in vain. He'd cried the night before he left and drilled us on instructions for safety, first aid, planting, and composting. Then he left and never returned. I now know that even though he said he was going on a scavenging run, he left us on purpose to make the food stretch. And it had been for nothing.

Otto's yelling woke me up.

I'd fallen asleep on the floor next to his bed. The sun had set, leaving the room a collection of overlapping nighttime shadows, but Otto was on his feet racing around like it was Christmas morning and he'd never been sick.

"Wake up, Isabella! Can you see them? The spider-dogs! They're outside. I can see them . . . right through the walls."

"Wha . . ."

Before I could shake the cobwebs from my half-sleeping brain, he darted out of the room and down the hall. I heard the front door bang open as I struggled to my feet.

"Otto! Wait!"

I lurched through the blackness, crashing into furniture and cursing, until I reached the open door, and then froze on the porch. Otto stood at the bottom of the steps facing a multitude of spider-dogs. Swirling mist hugged the ground, making the aliens appear to float like ghostly apparitions. They filled our front yard all the way out to the gravel road. Some of them bobbed gently, but all were silent, and they were all staring at Otto.

When two of the things stepped forward, I clattered down the wooden steps and pulled Otto back against me. Then I screamed and pushed him away. The bare skin of his arms writhed beneath my fingers. The pimples had all sprouted tentacles. Only about an inch long, but I had no doubt they would get longer, like those on the aliens.

He turned toward me in the darkness. "It's okay, Isabella. They can see me now and just want to talk."

The two spider-dogs moved closer and stooped low enough to envelop him with their squirming tentacles. He shuddered and gasped.

I wanted to pull him away, but I couldn't make myself move, not even to save my brother. "Leave him alone!" I screamed.

Otto held up a hand as if to keep me away. After a couple of minutes of their tentacles dancing over his, the aliens released him and moved back.

He swayed for a moment and I took a step forward, worried he would fall.

"They want me to come with them," he finally said in a whisper.

"No!"

"The spider-dogs want to add us to their family. They need our help to spread the berries. And we'll never be hungry again, Isabella."

I finally found enough courage to reach for his wrist, but he stepped back and looked ready to run. I knew if he did, I would never find him in the dark. "Wait," I said. "Please. I . . . I don't understand. They're killing us. Why would you want to help them?"

I could see him struggling for the words. "The berries are really in charge. If you eat the berries and talk to the spider-dogs, you'll understand."

Could that be possible? I knew that sometimes living things evolved strange abilities as a survival advantage. If these plants could crowd out local plants and force the native animals to eat only their fruit, then they might not just be dominating our planet, but possibly the whole galaxy. It made my skin crawl.

"And they aren't trying to kill us," he said, "just change us. It isn't the end of humanity, but the beginning. We can still colonize the galaxy, still boldly go where no one has gone before, but the berries will come with us. They will help us. It'll be okay."

I shook my head, unable to fathom such talk from my little brother. He was only ten!

"I'm going with them," he said and stepped back.

"Wait," I said, trying to keep the panic out of my voice. "Let me gather some stuff and I'll come with you."

He stared at me for a minute, but I couldn't really see his eyes in the darkness. And I wasn't sure I wanted to. Finally, he nodded.

I ran into the house, grabbed a flashlight and a cloth sack, then went into the backyard. With trembling hands, I picked all the generation thirty-seven berries and filled a large bottle with filtered rainwater.

I was both afraid Otto would be gone and almost hoping he would be when I stepped back onto the front porch. But he stood where I'd left him. Waiting. Watching me the way the spider-dogs watched him.

I didn't want to become part of some hive mind or global consciousness. I didn't want to grow spaghetti tentacles and stop being human, but I had to decide. I could eat the berries and become something else, or I could starve and die a human.

I stepped down into the yard with my bag of berries, and all I could think about was my promise to Dad that I would never leave Otto alone.

BRIDGING

Sigvaldi and its trailing moonlet, Astrid, were already high in the dark sky, but still too far away for me to see the long thread of the bridge. They were waning and didn't provide much light, so I stepped from the shadows cast by the launch gantry and squinted into the growing dawn. My pulse quickened and the air crackled as a distant, growling roar announced the fødselsvind's approach.

Ghostly on the horizon, the pale, towering dust tsunami separated from the darkness. It raced toward me, occulting the horizon and even the stars above. I lowered my goggles, pulled the scarf up over my face and planted bare feet, shifting them until they felt firm, then crouched and leaned forward.

The dust swept in, gently at first, then building in strength. I waited until stinging grit bit my bare skin before sucking in a breath and holding it. The wind intensified, threatening to push me backward, but I leaned further into it.

I refused to yield.

I would not move my feet.

I would best the fødselsvind.

An unexpected gust made me twist, arms reeling and I almost fell. Then it was over as the terminus wind swept past and a new day was born.

I released my breath, sucked in another though my nose filters, then spread my arms wide and screamed defiance into the settling dust. More yells rang from the paling darkness as other geitbrors also proclaimed their victory and mastery over nature. Like the seven generations before me, I had proved worthy of another day on Støvhage.

Hearty laughter rang out behind me, and a strong hand clamped my shoulder, raising a small dust cloud. "By the gods, Judel, will you goat herders ever become civilized?"

I turned to face Alvin Lund from the government's intelligence office and shrugged off his hand. Not only had I bristled at his suggestion that my family heritage was *barbaric*, but something about the man made me squirm in my skin anyway, and I didn't want him touching me. Like most visitors from the coast who braved fødselsvind, Alvin wore full storm gear, including a sealed coat long enough to brush his boots.

"What do you want?" I said. "I know you didn't come to celebrate the new morning. Blow the fish stink off, perhaps?"

He smiled and shook his head, but didn't rise to the insult.

"This," he said and gestured around him, "is a good place to talk."

I started walking toward the dormitory, letting him know my opinion of his wanting to talk. "You're making a mistake. I'm not a spy."

His coat made a rustling, hissing sound as he scuttled up beside me. "We're not asking for much. Just tell us what you see."

"I don't spy on my friends," I said, reaching for the dormitory door handle.

He grabbed my arm, then slipped between me and the door.

"That's just the point, Judel. These people left us down here to die and ignored our struggle to survive for a full century. They are not our friends!"

"Their ancestors did that to our ancestors," I said. "What good does that grudge do anyone now?"

"They're using you, Judel. Do you think it's coincidence that your contact is a beautiful woman? Do you think for a second that Sofie isn't just flirting with you and stringing you along? These skogsrå are good at seduction. They know how to manipulate men."

"Skogsrå? So now they're magic fairies? Look, if you think I'm so easily fooled by these people, then find a new chief project engineer and send him or her instead."

"We've considered that," he said in barely more than a whisper. "You're too deeply embedded in the project. They trust you."

"Which is exactly why I don't want to betray them."

Lund's gaze grew hard in the dim morning light. "Betray *them*? Is that how you feel, Judel?"

A chill crept up my spine, and for the first time since the government spooks started courting me, I felt a flicker of worry. "Believe what you like. Put me in jail if you doubt my patriotism."

Lund's expression changed immediately to one of brotherly camaraderie, and he clapped me on the shoulder again. "We don't doubt you or we wouldn't let you go, but it's easy to lose focus on what is really important sometimes. While you are up there, or any time you are working with these Sigvaldites, remind yourself that their motivation is the same as ours. To do what is best for their *own* people. If you remember that, and view everything they do through that lens, then they can't fool you."

"I launch in about two hours," I said. "I . . . thought maybe I'd check in and see if you need me to bring anything up."

Sofie smiled into the camera and must have answered my call from home instead of the engineering office. When she shook her head, loose hair lifted into the air and then slowly settled to her shoulders like storm-driven snow when the wind suddenly dies. So strange. She lived in an environment with which I had no experience.

"You already told me you can't sneak fresh salmon up here this trip," she smirked. "So, how about bringing Frank?"

This time I shook my head and laughed. "The Space Authority refuses to let him fly without a space suit, and those seem to be hard to find for dogs. You'll just have to meet him when you come down to my farm."

"I'd like that," she said with a faint smile and rested her chin in her palm. "But for now, I'll have to settle for you."

That smile, and her little teasing remarks, always made my pulse race, but now Lund's comments intruded and made me wonder. Was she manipulating me? My intuition said no, but would I know? Or did I like her so much I would subconsciously overlook subtle signs?

"Do you have restaurants up there?" I said, deciding to go for it.

"Of course. Your people are supposed to be the barbarians, not us."

"Then maybe, for lack of that fresh salmon, you can introduce me to your local cuisine instead."

Her eyes opened wide. "Are you asking me on a date, Judel?"

I flinched. "Well . . . I mean if . . ."

"In my opinion, we have excellent food. Even pizza," she said.

"Pizza?"

"And by the way, I'm a pretty good cook if you like vat-grown meat and algae casseroles."

The face I made must have been awful, because she laughed hard. "I also make good cookies. Maybe we should stick to those. Your stomach will probably be squishy from the flight and low gravity anyway."

A pounding on my door reminded me it was time to go and we said our goodbyes. As I let myself be led to the launch prep area, I wondered if her comment about being a good cook was some kind of signal or hint. Was she planning to invite me to her apartment? Or wanting me to ask? And if so, should I go? Damn, Lund! He had lodged doubts in my mind like a treble fishhook.

I had little to do during the prelaunch period but lie on my back, look at the vast instrument panels, and "not touch anything." Much of the originally planned gauges and switches had been replaced by Sigvaldi touch panels. All of the computers were of their design as well. I couldn't deny that they were superior, lighter, smaller, and more efficient, but it made me uncomfortable. It was hard to argue against the systems—for spaceflight and the bridge control —needing to be seamless and integrated, but we relied on them too much. If relations with those fickle Sigvaldites went belly-up again, then we could be in trouble. Of course if that happened, then the bridge project would become a moot point anyway, so it wouldn't matter.

I closed my eyes and tried to relax the knots in my stomach. Radio chatter filled my helmet as the two pilots worked through their checklist with ground control. I wasn't afraid, not really, but my loss would set the project back by at least a year, maybe more. This entire launch was simply to get me up to Sigvaldi so I could interface with their engineers. Sofie insisted I use their immersion fields, and that wasn't something they could export to us.

The pilot next to me, Anna, laid her hand on my arm and said, "This is it, Judel. You ready?"

I nodded, then realized she couldn't see me in my helmet and croaked out, "Yes."

A series of bumps and bangs made me flinch, then I felt and heard a roar that grew steadily deeper. Vibration made my vision blur and teeth rattle, then a load settled on my chest. Støvhage was larger than Earth, so already had a gravity that was nearly half again the evolved human normal. Those of us living on the surface had adapted. Each generation handled the added stress better, but escaping the gravity well of this monster planet required a lot of power. As a result, rockets were only built when needed and crewed flights up to Sigvaldi had been few since the colony's founding.

It was easy for the Sigvaldites to come down to the surface, they only needed a capsule that could withstand reentry, but, perversely, once they arrived, they were invalids dependent on mechanical aids to even get out of bed. Only twelve had visited during the last hundred and fifty years, but due to the gee forces imparted by our chemical rockets, none were ever able to go home. I understood the problem implicitly as I struggled to stay conscious amid the building force. I—one of the strongest generations yet produced by Støvhage—could barely breathe. Hopefully, the bridge would end our dependence on rockets.

Microgravity was not kind to my stomach, and even though they had trained extensively for this mission, the pilots had not actually been in space before either, so my upset triggered a "bag use" chain reaction. Luckily, they didn't hold a grudge.

On our second orbit, one of the pilots suggested I unharness and look out the tiny window. We were passing beneath Astrid, the kidney-shaped moonlet.

Just beyond, I could see Sigvaldi's cratered surface, brighter and clearer than I'd ever seen it from the ground. Amazing as those sights were, I was transfixed by the long glittering string of the bridge.

It was really more of a skyhook than a bridge or a space elevator, but "bridge" had been used by the media and politicians, so it stuck. The structure was only anchored on the Sigvaldi end and trailed the moon like the leash dragged behind by a runaway dog. Its loose end flew through Støvhage's sky, skimming a mile or more above the surface and only getting close enough to access when it crossed the high plateau. That is where my work started. I'd designed the maglev system to accelerate the carriages up to a speed where they could catch and grab the end of the leash as it passed. It had been the most challenging and rewarding work of my life, yet paled in comparison to what Sofie and her team from Sigvaldi had built.

Our ship drew closer, but as interesting details began to emerge—things like moving robots and construction workers—my crewmates insisted I return to my seat for docking. We arrived at maintenance hub four, which was little more than a blister on the spine of the bridge. It contained emergency medical supplies and feed lines for fuel and volatiles, but nothing like a crew quarters. Not that it mattered. Both pilots were forbidden to leave the capsule for the entire week I'd be on Sigvaldi.

"Don't forget to come back," the flight commander said. "I'd hate to stay locked up with Anna all this time for no good reason. I mean, she snores and chews with her mouth open. Very crude."

Her comment had been stated as a joke, but I knew she was quite serious. I wondered what Lund and his spooks had told them. That I was a defection risk? That I had been bewitched by skogsrå?

"Keep the engine running. I'll be back soon."

The maintenance hub was supposedly pressurized, but as a precaution, I sealed my helmet before opening the docking hatch. I pushed my duffle bag ahead of me, then squeezed my bulk through as they closed it behind me. I clipped my bag to my lower back, below the environmental unit, then pulled myself along the bridge spine in a series of awkward lurches until I found the transfer hatch. The clumsy jerking around in microgravity made me dizzy and sent my stomach into queasy summersaults again. I had to gain control. I didn't want my first face-to-face introduction to the Sigvaldites—and most especially Sofie—to be amid a vomit cloud.

Lund's voice hissed in my helmet speaker. "You doing okay, Judel?"

They had all the data feeds from my suit, so they knew exactly how I was doing. The bastards even spied on their spies.

"Couldn't be better," I snapped. "This null-gravity stuff is a breeze."

He laughed. "Good. Our boards show your ride is only a couple minutes away, so hang on just a little longer."

I closed my eyes, swallowed hard and pleaded in desperation with my stomach to not fill my helmet with puke.

"We're all counting on you, Judel. Make us proud and don't let them push you around."

"Do my best," I grunted.

Vibrations, strong enough to feel through my pressure suit gloves, announced the carriage's approach. I wondered if the shaking was caused by an anticipated interplay between carriage and bridge, or if it was an unexpected oscillation that could be a real problem. Maybe the recent docking of our capsule set up a local resonance in the bridge structure? It bothered me not knowing all the design elements of the bridge itself. We on the surface were only responsible for the terminal interface.

A green light winked on, then the hatch slid open, revealing a small airlock. When I stepped in, my spacesuited bulk nearly filled the entire space. Since both sides were already pressurized, the other hatch opened almost immediately, revealing Sofie, who floated beyond. She offered me a bright smile and held out her hand. I took it, intending a handshake, but even though her long fingers disappeared in my massive glove, I could still feel her strong grip as she tugged me into the carriage.

She helped me remove my helmet, then kissed me on the cheek. "Welcome to the bridge!"

I reached for her, intending to kiss her back, but she ducked and my forward momentum sent me somersaulting across ten meters of empty air. Once the bridge was operational, the carriages would all be configured for cargo or passengers, but aside from some maintenance equipment strapped to one wall and four acceleration couches bolted to the "floor," this carriage was empty and offered nothing for me to grab. I continued to spin, seeing Sofie's grin once every rotation as she tried to stabilize me. She finally caught my arm and my tumble slowed, though imparted some of that motion to her. We were both laughing, hard, by the time we slammed into the padded far wall.

Using cargo cleats on the wall, we worked together and pulled ourselves down toward the floor, then grabbed handholds on one of the couches and were strapped in within a couple minutes.

Only then, after she had turned partially away busy with her own preparations, did I let myself really look at this woman. Scale was hard to get from a video link, but in person I could see that she was at least several inches taller than I. She didn't wear a pressure suit—a probable violation of protocol—only a formfitting utility layer that implied her weirdly long arms and legs were mostly hard muscle.

She gave a series of verbal commands. The carriage movement was at first barely perceptible, but acceleration increased until reaching about one and a half planetary gees, where it remained.

Surprised, I turned my head just enough to see Sofie. Her usual unfathomable half smile had been replaced by a grimace and short, forced breaths. Before I could take any satisfaction in seeing one of the mighty Sigvaldites laid low, she gasped out, "Normal passenger . . . acceleration will . . . be a half gee. But I thought . . . you could . . . handle this."

Her smile returned, just for an instant.

The carriage eventually stopped at a terminal carved deep in the heart of Sigvaldi. The cavernous, echoing rooms were cut from bare stone and empty except for the occasional robot or human worker mounting signs or polishing surfaces. At least from this perspective, it little resembled the glittering faerie cities of rumor and legend.

My disappointment at this fact was compounded by the irritation at having ridden all this way inside the bridge, yet aside from the brief glimpse through the capsule port, I didn't really see it. Was this life on Sigvaldi? Seeing everything only from the inside?

Sofie took me to a room lined with large lockers. I was suddenly aware of my smell as Sofie helped me out of the pressure suit, but she didn't comment as she hung it and my helmet in a locker. I was hesitant when I saw no lock of any kind on the locker, but she only smiled, took my hand and placed it against the outside of the closed door.

"It has a built-in palm reader and now will only open for you."

She demonstrated how it worked. I'd read about such technology, but had never seen it. I longed to examine the interior mechanisms, but she instead gently propelled me out the door.

I was relieved to get out of the uncomfortable suit, but even happier to be out from under Lund's watchful eye. His surveillance of me was locked away with my suit. At least for now. I followed her down a long corridor to a train station also cut from the unadorned stone.

"Considering the size of those rooms and corridors, you must be expecting a lot of traffic from the bridge," I said.

For the first time since our initial meeting in the carriage, she looked me directly in the eyes and smiled.

I melted a little.

"It's easier to build everything large from the beginning than to go back and change it if needed later," she said.

I nodded, not entirely trusting myself to speak. Lund's words kept echoing in my head. *I am not going to let this happen,* I thought. *She is just a woman, and an engineer, not some mythical fairy who can bewitch a man's mind. At least not mine.*

The train arrived and we rode in an awkward silence for about fifteen minutes. When the doors opened again, it was on an entirely new world. Tall, brightly dressed people loped back and forth along the train platform. The walls were covered with tile mosaics, frescoes and woven tapestries. I paused to stare, becoming the stone jutting out of a fast-moving stream as the people gave me curious glances, but flowed around me. I tried to absorb all the details for my report, but it was like trying to catalog the movement in a kaleidoscope. I did note that there was no sign of military or defensive works.

After a couple of seconds, Sophie took my hand and led me to another corridor.

"We have small field offices on the surface at the main construction site and even in two places along the bridge, but the immersion equipment is in our main office and that's a bit of a hike from here."

She guided me along with gentle tugs and nudges. I tried not to think about her hand in mine. There was nothing flirtatious about her guiding me along in strange corridors and weak gravity, but during the years of talking to her, working and laughing together, I had built up hopes and expectations about this moment. Part of me worried that she would try to seduce me, but mostly I feared that she wouldn't.

We eventually entered doors that were marked simply "Engineering." A hallway led to a wide, colorful room, open and brightly lit. Though quite different from my own facility, it had all the markers of engineering offices everywhere. Various partially disassembled machines sat on tables and desks and wide screens displaying test data, while diagrams and conceptual drawings covered every wall. A beautiful, quarter-sized model of my bridge carriage sat in the center of the open area.

Conversations around the room tapered off and stopped as all eyes turned our way. An almost impossibly tall man, easily a head above the other giants, stood up behind a table and crossed the room in two long strides.

"Judel, this is Luther, our engineering director and my boss," Sofie said.

He gave a slight bow, looking down at me from lofty heights and offered his hand to shake. Like Sofie's, his hand was narrow with long fingers. "Sofie shouldn't have brought you here first. You must be exhausted from that brutal flight."

"Totally my doing," I said, cutting off Sofie's reply. "I insisted on coming to your office first. I'm quite interested in seeing this amazing Sigvaldite immersion tank that . . ."

I froze midsentence, my face feeling suddenly hot as I realized much too late that I'd used Sigvaldite, what they considered a derogatory term, in an actual conversation. The term was common usage down on the surface, and I had been extremely careful during all these years, only to let it slip here and now.

"Oh, I'm so sorry. I just—"

Luther held up his hand and slowly shook his head. "I'm sure all of this, including our immersion tank, must look like magic to an *engineer* who has been forced to use the equivalent of stone knives and bear skins to build your end of the system."

I wasn't sure what the hell that meant, since there were no bears on

Støvhage, but I knew it had been an insult and my embarrassment flared immediately into anger.

"And for future reference please refrain from using that kind of language in front of my people. The original colonists called this moon Kanin before we even arrived and that name is good enough for us. We call ourselves the Kaninish."

I shifted my feet for better balance and Sofie put a hand on my arm. I knew I was about to say things that might tank the whole project. I also knew that wouldn't stop me. Those early days on Støvhage had been utter hell, with more than half of the original colonists dying in the first two years. The world truly was dead, its soil being closer to regolith on Earth's moon than the rich dirt on our mother world. We'd known before arriving that we'd need massive amounts of nitrogen for the crops, but those who stayed on the moon to mine stopped sending it just as they refused to send down the second wave of colonists. As our pleas and protests grew more insistent, they eventually cut off radio contact. They had written us off as a failed attempt and decided to save their resources for some future attempt. But we didn't fail.

"I don't give a damn if you find that name offensive," I said. "You cut us off, leaving us to die down there with no help or resources. Your level of betrayal made Jarl Sigvaldi's seem like a childish prank, but that is the best name we had for you."

Luther's face darkened. "Those sins belonged to our ancestors, not us, and we're trying to make amends for them now, with the bridge and our technology."

"As well you should, but you've earned the traitor's name, and we will always refer to you that way. If you don't like it, then send me home and try to build your bridge without us."

Luther's mouth clamped shut in a tight, white line. He glanced at Sofie, then turned and stalked away.

Sofie's already pale face took on a whole new pallor. "Well, that could have gone better. Let me show you to your room. We'll start fresh tomorrow."

"No, I'd like to see this immersion field now."

She stared down at me for a full second, then shrugged and looked around. "Alright, but we've found a potential problem. Are you in the proper frame of mind to look at this information objectively?"

"I can separate my work from my personal biases."

She shrugged, then led me to a large room with white walls that sparkled with thousands of tiny glittering pinpricks and handed me a pair of goggles.

"Don't remove these while in the simulation or the lasers will blind you."

The goggles were a tight fit on my broad face but covered my eyes well enough. Sofie flipped some switches near the door and the walls flickered faster and faster until vague, ghostly structures took shape in the room's center.

As the holograms solidified, I recognized the mag-rail twin-track system we'd built on Støvhage's central plateau. It looked so real! Like flying over it in an aircraft. Then the bridge appeared on the horizon. "Sigvaldi's tail" it had been called, with the computer-controlled stabilizers providing the barb, its upper reaches disappearing into the blue sky, like the real thing. The camera view shifted slightly to focus on and follow two carriages, one on each track, accelerating toward us.

The bridge loomed larger in the background, getting ever closer, until it converged with the carriage at the docking terminus. I held my breath as the view zoomed in close enough for me to see the mechanical latch system engage, yanking the carriages off the track and up the bridge rails toward the moon passing above. But then something unexpected happened. The carriage closest to my perspective shifted suddenly, canting at a strange angle. Almost faster than my eye could follow, it broke free and spun off in a ballistic arc. The second carriage then broke free and followed its predecessor in a spinning plunge to the ground below.

"What the hell!" I whipped around to find Sofie, but she was invisible in the simulation. I almost removed my glasses, then remembered it could blind me. "Where are you?"

The simulation halted and faded, revealing Sofie standing next to the control panel. "Can you—"

I crossed the room, nearly losing my balance in the lower gravity, until I was right next to her. "What is this insanity? Why did your little cartoon show such a catastrophic failure?"

"Because in the right circumstances—"

My arms flailed and spittle sprayed; I didn't seem to be able to control myself. "We've tested that design fifty times—"

Sofie not only held her ground, but bent closer to my face and put her hands on my shoulders. "Judel! Listen to me. The numbers don't lie. In a fully loaded condition, those locks will fail."

I wanted to yank away, scream in her face and leave, but there was a pleading in her eyes. She believed what she said. But those locks and that carriage design were our last bastion of respect. The entire bridge had been their idea, their design and built by them. We had built the mag-rail track needed to accelerate the carriages to translation speed, but the engineering had been theirs. The carriages were our only real contribution, and the locks were my design. They had wanted magnetic locks from the beginning, but we—no I—had insisted that mechanical locks would be more robust and reliable.

She squeezed my shoulders and bent a little lower until her face was inches from my own. "Please trust me, Judel."

"But we tested them," I muttered and took a deep shuddering breath. "To three times the load requirements."

She dropped her hands and straightened to her full height. "I know. But you tested for individual stresses, not all twelve factors at the same time, because there is no way to do that until the actual system is built. We also suspect the purity level of the carbon alloy in your electronic models is higher than you're capable of manufacturing, so we set it at a more realistic level in our simulation."

"But we—"

"And before you get defensive, we can't produce that level of purity either. It would only be possible with nano-assemblers, and you know we haven't had any luck with that."

"Okay," I said. "Show me."

We watched the simulation four more times, with color enhancement and data tags showing exactly what happened as the stress loads piled up until the latch mechanism failed. So many thoughts crowded my head. I had doubts, but I also didn't believe that Sofie was frivolous and shallow enough to waste so much effort creating an elaborate ruse. Especially not just to get her way on magnetic locks or for a little one-upmanship. Once the lasers were shut off I removed my glasses and rubbed my eyes.

"You must be exhausted," Sofie said. "Are you ready to go to your room?"

I nodded and let her lead me through the now dark and empty engineering center and down the wide corridor to the dormitory and my room. We both hesitated awkwardly at the open door, but when I asked her to come in, she smiled and gave me a little shove. "Get some rest."

And I did just that, still in my clothes, and the last thought in my tired mind was of Sofie's hands on my shoulders, only this time, instead of yelling, she kissed me.

The next morning I awoke stiff and unsure of the time. I took a shower that required me to squeeze though a rubbery, sphincter-like membrane into a tight little closet. The water spray came from three sides and, due to the weak gravity, filled the space with a weird mist made of large droplets that clung to me and had to be squeegeed off. I put on fresh clothes and settled down to reexamine the latch design. Each time I looked at the numbers it felt like touching an open wound.

So I left my room, curious as to how far I'd get before their security wonks collected me. I wandered aimlessly for more than an hour, but the only thing I noted that could be considered useful intelligence was that most of the plazas and corridors I found were almost empty. Of course other than my dealings with Sofie, I had no clue about the schedules these people kept, so I could be between shift changes or maybe it was a holiday. I couldn't escape the feeling that the infrastructure had been designed for a much larger population.

The expected hand on my shoulder finally came, but when I turned, it was a winded Sofie.

"Good morning," I said. "Rough night?"

"Why are you out wandering around? Are you trying to get me in trouble? I'm supposed to be your escort."

"I'm a tourist. Was I supposed to stay in my room?" I said, feigning innocence.

She sighed and shrugged. "I don't know. I'm winging this too. Look, they expect us at the engineering center in an hour, but there are no actual design meetings scheduled until the afternoon. Do you feel up to a little field trip to the surface? Since you are a tourist and all, I thought you might like to see the bridge from the outside."

"Absolutely!"

She led me back to the locker room where I'd left my suit the day before. We helped each other dress and cross-checked our equipment after topping off our gasses, then walked up a long, sloping corridor that ended in a cluster of airlocks. As we waited for the air to evacuate, we checked our communications links.

"As soon as we're outside, you need to clip your short tether to the guide line," she said. "It's about one-tenth of Støvhage's gravity. It's harder to reach escape velocity than you might think, but if you get a good enough launch, it will still take hours for you to come down."

She took my hand before the hatch opened and held onto me through the whole tethering process. It felt a little silly, like a child being mothered, but I also knew that she'd been born in this gravity and had far more vacuum experience than I, so was grateful for the help.

We walked perhaps half a kilometer, then stopped and turned back to look at the bridge.

"I knew you'd want to see it from the outside, too," Sofie said.

The terminal building we had exited was huge, perhaps three stories high, covering several acres, and that was only the end where the bridge was anchored. Aside from my brief peek through the capsule window, I had only seen the bridge from Støvhage's surface, moving past at over a thousand kph, which gave it the impression of some vast, bizarre aircraft. From this perspective it was a tower rising impossibly high into the blackness, getting ever smaller until it vanished from view.

The inflexible neck on my suit forced me to lean backward in order to look up, but upon seeing a slowly rotating Støvhage nearly filling the sky overhead, I totally forgot about the bridge. Painfully white clouds covered much of the surface, but I could see green bands separating the blue of lakes and oceans from the yellow-brown of the still dead lands. The fragile proof of our generations-long struggle. It was beautiful, powerful, and compelling.

I gasped and muttered an old litany from the days when—due in no small part to these traitors on Sigvaldi—humanity's survival on the surface had been doubtful.

Sofie had said nothing during this time, and when I turned to see why I found her facing away from me, I found her staring at what looked like a smooth, nearly cylindrical mountain. Various antenna and other equipment protruded from the top, and I realized it was an enormous building covered by a thick layer of regolith.

I touched her shoulder. When she turned to face me, the lights inside her helmet glistened from tear tracks on her cheeks.

"Sofie?"

"We have to stop this, Judel."

"What?"

She pointed to her helmet and then held up a gloved hand with two fingers, then three, then one.

I changed the channel on my suit radio to 231.

"I'm going to do something stupid," she said. "Please trust me. This needs to be done." She unhooked our tethers from the guideline, then clipped them together and motioned for me to follow.

We left the marked path and struck out directly for the strange buried building. Sofie never said we needed to hurry, but I felt an urgency in her actions, so I followed without comment. After about ten minutes and little talking, we arrived at a tube that disappeared into the "hillside," which Sofie entered without slowing. Small, dust-covered lights cast dim illumination on the corrugated interior, which went about forty feet before ending at a very strange airlock.

The hatch was flush with its surrounding wall, revealed only by a seam not much wider than a human hair. Sofie punched a code into a lighted touch panel beside it, which was totally smooth and almost completely blended into the wall. This building had obviously been here for many years, yet this was some of the most advanced workmanship I'd ever seen. Their techniques and capabilities were even more advanced than we'd thought.

The hatch sank slightly into the wall, then slid into a recess, allowing us to enter. My heart sank as I looked around the inside of the airlock. If they were able to employ such exquisite workmanship on something as utilitarian as an airlock, then we were doomed. The weaponry at their disposal must be beyond our imaginations.

We passed through a powerful air curtain and vacuum system, then entered into a locker room and helped each other out of our suits. They were almost clean, and I wondered why they would use such a wonderful system in this building but not the main terminal building.

"You said we're doing something stupid. Why? What is this building?"

Sofie turned and smiled at me. "You haven't figured it out yet, Judel? We're inside the ship. This is the *Amundsen*."

I steadied myself against the wall as vertigo made the room spin. Impossible. It couldn't be true. We'd been led to believe the ship had long ago been scavenged for its systems and materials. Yet it all suddenly made sense. The signage was Norwegian, but contained words I didn't recognize. The workmanship. The technology.

I saw Sofie in a new light. She knew I was a spy. She had to know. Yet she was showing me a secret greater than all others. "Why?"

"Wait, and maybe it will make better sense when I show you the rest."

As I followed her through the ship, I saw that it had indeed been at least partially dismantled. Cavernous, echoing chambers where whole decks had been removed, leaving only wiring and pipe stubs. Hatches had been removed, and I could see into large open areas and stripped cabins. We went down ladder after ladder, going far deeper into the ship and making it obvious that only a small portion made up the buried part I could see from the surface.

When we entered another echoing chamber that curved gently away in two directions—obviously part of the rotating habitat—I finally got a sense of scale. The ship had to be a kilometer in diameter and at least half of the floor space I could see was covered by sleeper units. As we threaded our way between them, I noticed that some were lit up. They were all occupied . . . by babies.

Sofie led me to the only freestanding structure amid the cemetery of electric coffins and opened the door. Two surprised men stood in a room filled with humming equipment. They immediately backed away to the far wall and started talking animatedly.

"We don't have much time, so please listen and try to believe everything I tell you. We know you're a spy. I also know you are a good person, and I think if you have enough information, you'll make the right decision."

Despite the earnest expression on her face, I couldn't help but hear Lund's warning. *Remind yourself that their motivation is the same as ours. To do what is best for their own people.*

"Your government is building twelve large lift vehicles. We estimate each one could carry a hundred or more soldiers. I've seen the pictures but couldn't get copies to show you. You'll just have to trust me that they exist."

A sinking feeling settled over me. If that was a lie, then it was one that rang true. It sounded too much like Lund and his people. They needed me and my intelligence report, yet they would never tell me why it was important.

"It's hard to be certain without people on the ground, but by the level of activity around the sites, we estimate they are at least a year from completion. That's why we're trying so hard to finish the bridge first. We're hoping that our people will fare better if integration is slow and natural instead of sudden and by force."

My thoughts were still on Lund and his subterfuge, so her comment took a second to sink in. "Wait. Integration?"

"Yes. It's inevitable. That's why I brought you here."

She led me to a large console covered with data-filled display screens. "I'm not exactly sure what our ancestors originally named this machine, but we call it the DNA adjustor. A combination of our limited population, cosmic radiation, and the very low gravity inflicts our children with an extremely high birth defect rate for natural births. So instead of normal gestation, we put the fertilized eggs into sleeper units, where the DNA Adjuster can monitor the genetic health of the babies and correct problems early."

Growing babies inside an artificial environment made my skin crawl, but the engineer in me was still fascinated. I leaned in for a closer look and marveled at the symbols and text scrolling across the screens. History told us that our ancestors from Earth directly manipulated genetics, just as they'd been able to manipulate matter on a molecular level, but here it was directly in front of me; one of those magic machines kept working for hundreds of years.

"It sounds as if you have a working system. So why the limited population? And what is the limit?"

She was slow to respond and seemed to be struggling with the question. Then I heard clattering from behind us and looked back toward the door we'd entered. A squad of armed soldiers poured through the hatch, spread out and moved toward us.

"Our population is fixed at nine thousand," she said abruptly. "That is the most our resources and economy can support. Like everything on the *Amundsen*, this DNA adjustor machine was triply redundant. But two of the three machines have failed in the last few years. When this last one fails—and it will eventually because we don't understand the technology—then our already small population will start to collapse."

By that point, we were surrounded, and an earnest and nervous young woman approached wearing an officer's uniform. "You're in a restricted area. Please come with us."

"I still want to meet your dog," Sofie said and kissed me on the cheek.

The rest of that night I was kept locked in my quarters. I worried about Sofie —feeling somehow responsible and powerless—so I did what I always do when I'm stressed. I worked. In the morning, I sent a message to Sofie and Luther, telling them I had a possible solution to the carriage lock problem, and I hoped they would listen to me.

Four armed guards arrived and escorted me to the engineering center. They even accompanied me into the large conference room, where they fixed me with menacing glares from their posts near the door.

I put my presentation up on the wall screen, ready to discuss by the time Luther arrived, flanked by two other engineers.

"Where's Sofie?" I tried to look as menacing as I could without bringing the guards down on me.

"She . . . is being detained," Luther said with the same level of disgust most reserved for discussions of bodily functions. "There will be an investigation as to why she violated security protocols. In the meantime, in order to have as minimal a schedule impact as possible, we need to get these design changes approved so that the failed mechanical latching system can be scrapped in favor of our original magnetic locking system."

"As Sofie demonstrated yesterday, the mechanical latch system does fail six percent of the time under maximum loading, which is an unacceptable risk. However, problems with the mag lock system still exist too and—"

"If you're going to suggest that we don't load the system to its design maximum, then—"

I slapped the table with enough force to not only shut Luther up and make the guards take a step forward, but to raise me several inches out of my seat. "Hear me out! Regardless of what you think of me and all grounders, please just consider this simple alternative. I propose that we do both."

Luther glowered, crossed his arms and sat back in his seat. "We brought you all the way up here. Of course we'll listen."

"Our biggest concern with magnetic locks are power requirements, keeping the pads on the carriages clean and the lack of mechanical failsafes should the system lose power. We can divert power from the lift drive system to the mag locks for two-tenths of a second, during the actual momentum shift when the mechanical locks fail, providing that extra robustness, then we engage the mechanical locks and shift power back to the drive system and start the lift."

Luther stared at the wall screen with narrowed eyes and I could see the gears of his mind whirling. He might be an asshole and a manager, but according to Sofie, he was also an excellent engineer.

"This way, we don't have to add a dedicated mag lock power system, and we keep the mechanical lock system," I said. "We just have to add the controllers and mag pads to the bridge and carriages. A far smaller design change."

Luther's lackeys smiled and glanced at each other. He sighed and said, "We'll work up some new stress and power models for this option and let you know."

Once back home on Støvhage, the flight medical team seemed satisfied with my progress, so they handed me some thick gloppy stuff to drink and left me alone. Aside from my stomach being a jittery mess and my head throbbing like a dust-rock bass line, I had survived reentry without a problem. At least until the door opened and Lund slipped in. And that probably explained why they immediately separated me from the flight crew after we landed.

"Hello, Judel."

"Hi, Alvin. What a surprise to see you here." I had to be careful. Too much vitriol and he would doubt that I'd be so cooperative. Not enough and he'd suspect I was up to something.

He raised an eyebrow. "We're obviously concerned that the mission was cut short and you were sent home due to a security violation. Care to explain?"

"You're the intelligence expert. Shouldn't you have this information already?"

Lund sat down and crossed his arms. "We don't have assets among their people. That's why your trip was so important. We're limited to what our signal processing people can glean from their electronic communications."

I shrugged, took another drink of the nasty goo and made the appropriate face. "They had confined me to certain corridors and sections. Sofie took me to unauthorized sections and we both got in trouble. She was thrown in prison and they asked me to leave."

His eyes flared with excitement before he locked the stoicism in place again. I knew he wanted to ask what I'd seen, but he held it in check. "Why did she betray her own security to show you things she shouldn't?"

"It could be the fact that she, and they, know about your twelve heavy launch vehicles and the plan to put troops on their moon."

He flinched and went pale, but said nothing.

I'd caught him by surprise. Hopefully it would rattle him enough to believe the rest of my lies.

"She wanted me to see their preparations and hopefully avoid an invasion, but their military wants us to come. And be wiped out to the last man. It would evidently be an effective deterrent against future aggression."

"And what did you see?"

"She led me out of my section via a service tunnel. Every other corridor and section we visited contained armed soldiers. I saw hundreds. She said they'd been expecting an invasion for a long time and their military service is compulsory for every young person. If she told the truth, they have about forty thousand armed and active."

I surprised him again. He blinked and then leaned forward. "Their population is that high?"

"All I know is what I saw. The corridors she took me to were shoulder-to-shoulder people. It was like a hive. Maybe what you said about them breeding like animals is true."

He gave me a sick leering grin. "And is it true? Did you finally consummate your little long-distance love affair?"

I glared at him. My disgust wasn't in the slightest bit faked.

He rolled his eyes and snorted. "So. They just let you go? Knowing what you'd seen."

"That part baffles me, too," I shrugged. "I really don't know, but I suspect if they kept me, it would've given us a good excuse to attack, and they'd prefer it to appear unprovoked. Maybe Sofie knew what she was doing and forced their hand?"

He stared at me for a long time without speaking. With his mask back in place, he said, "You went out on the surface the night before you left. Why?"

I considered telling him a half lie, about visiting the *Amundsen* and seeing a superweapon. Maybe the old ship's asteroid deflection beam I'd read about, but instead decided it would be better to keep its existence secret. I could see these dumbasses firing a barrage of missiles to destroy it, and we'd lose that wonderful technology due to lies and stupidity.

"To see the bridgehead from the outside," I said. "That is one of the main reasons I went, remember? But if they had military facilities out there, they were well disguised. I saw nothing out of the ordinary."

"Hidden from our telescopes and probes," he said with a knowing nod, then stood up. "I may be back later for more details. But I have a lot to do based on the information you provided."

"I bet," I said and smothered a smile.

The goats arrived, bells jingling and bleats filling the air as I set out the last salt block. Only a few of them rushed over to lick the salt, which was a good sign. It meant they were probably getting enough. The rest milled around my legs hoping I had something more interesting and tasty in the cart.

Frank barked and circled us all, bouncing on his front legs and tail wagging madly. Then he stopped, raised his ears, and took off at full speed toward the house. I looked that way but saw nothing. In an irrational move driven by hope, I pulled the AllBox from my pocket to check for messages, but it still displayed a red X meaning that my home repeater was out of range. I sighed and looked out at my inherited family farm. My gaze fell on rolling hills spotty with tough grass and knee-high bushes. Something an Earther would call scrub or trash or ugly, but considering that this world had been devoid of all life when we arrived, I thought it was quite beautiful. Someday, this would all be grass, and covered in cattle and need fences, but not in my lifetime.

I could hear Frank barking in the distance, so I nudged the goats aside, crawled onto the cart, and started back toward the house to see why he was raising such hell. As I topped the next rise, I saw him circling what could only be a Sigvaldite wearing one of those spiderlike helper suits. My pulse quickened. We saw many more Sigvaldites since the bridge was completed, but if one were visiting me out here, then it was either very good news or very bad.

I pushed the cart to max speed and bounced over the rocky ground until I could skid to a stop a few yards from the contraption. The occupant had lowered their composite frame close to the ground and was petting and cooing over a quite enthusiastic Frank. I recognized her voice immediately.

I knelt next to them. "Sofie?"

When she looked up, there were tears in her eyes and dust turned to mud smudged on her cheeks.

"Hi, Judel." Her voice, while familiar, also held the strained wheeze common to Sigvaldites visiting the surface.

"I didn't know you were out of jail. When did that happen? I've been watching my . . . I've been kind of wondering."

"Two days ago. I should have let you know, but I wanted to come down here. I thought if you knew, you might tell me not to come."

"Of course not. But this has to be hard on you."

"You said I could meet your dog after the bridge was finished. I'm here to make you keep that promise."

I knelt down and wrapped my arms around Frank's neck. "Did you hear that, Frank? You, my boy, are a very lucky dog. This pretty lady came down from space and all the way out into the dusty badlands to meet you."

Frank bounced with excitement and licked my face in reply.

"I might have had other reasons, too," she wheezed. "The last time didn't really work out as I'd hoped."

A lump formed in my throat. "Yeah, me either."

We started a slow walk back to the house and the wind picked up, surrounding us with dust devils. Sofie gasped and stopped, "Will they hurt us?"

"No. Too weak," I said with a laugh. "Like if you were to try and pick me up."

She smirked and shook her head. "Some things never change. By the way, I love the solution you came up with for the bridge carriage locks. I've really missed working this last year, so indulge me and tell me what you've been working on. Your next big super project!"

"The bridge will be my last project for a while. Upon the insistence of the Government Security Agency, more specifically Alvin Lund, I've been fired and pretty much blackballed."

"Oh no. Why?"

"Once the bridge was finished and their agents started snooping around up on Sigvaldi, they realized I had unabashedly lied about your forty thousand troops."

Her eyes opened wide. "Forty thousand troops? Did you really do that?'

I nodded.

She started laughing, then stopped and gasped for breath. I didn't know what to do and fluttered around her like a scared hen. With elaborate hand gestures, she waved me away and eventually regained her breath.

"Don't get me wrong," I said. "I've missed you, and I'm very, very glad you came, but it sounds like this gravity is killing you. When do you go back?"

"You missed me?" she asked with a raised eyebrow.

"Hell yes, I missed you! Talking to you every day was the best part of those difficult years we spent designing the bridge. Then just as I thought . . . I mean you were suddenly gone."

"It must look like I'm an invalid down here, but I can get in and out of this contraption on my own. And tend to my basic needs, so I'd like to stay. At least for a little while. If that's okay. And if it's okay with Frank."

"Of course it's okay. It will always be okay."

———

"Pappa?"

Her voice was muffled by the scarf around her mouth, but I thought I detected a trace of worry.

"What is it, Squeaker? Are you scared of the dark?"

"I'm a little scared," she said. "But not of the dark. Some of the kids at school said the fødselsvind picks up kids and blows them away."

I wrapped my arms around her and squeezed. "That isn't true. If the wind blew little kids away, then there would be news reports about it on the feeds all the time. Besides, you're six now and very tall, even for six, so the worst that could happen is it would knock you off your feet. And I'll be here with you to make sure that doesn't happen."

"Okay. But I'm just newly six. Remember that."

I tried to stifle my laugh and made sure her goggles and scarf were tight. "I'll remember that," I said. "We can go back in the house and do this some other time if you're not ready."

"I think I'm ready. Will Mamma be proud of me?"

I could see the pale wall rising in the east and could faintly hear the building roar. I shifted my bare feet, making sure of my footing and positioned my daughter in front of my legs. "Oh yes, Squeaker. She is always proud of you. She was very excited when you told her."

"Are we still going up the bridge to see her tomorrow? To celebrate?"

When Sophie got pregnant, she insisted that the baby be gestated in Støvhage's full gravity, even then it nearly killed he on multiple occasions. The birth had been so hard on her already frail constitution that she could never come down the gravity well again. Long-distance marriages were difficult, and Squeaker and I missed her terribly, but the three of us made it work. "Yes, baby," I tightened my arms around her as the wind picked up. "We'll see her tomorrow."

Her hands tensed on mine as the dust wall towered over us and the wind howled. "You and Mamma built that bridge," she yelled.

"Yes. We sure did."

STEAL FROM THE SUN

"No shit, there I was, cooking in my EVA hard suit like a freakin' lobster while my best friend," I paused to make sure everyone heard me over the bar noise, then pointed an accusatory finger at Brian, "flirted with a gorgeous anchorman."

Brian took several seconds to adjust the sling cradling his broken arm, then when he was sure everyone's attention had shifted his way, he lowered his head and glared at me, looking every bit like a bull preparing to charge. He had that same look one day in third grade after I'd deliberately broken his pencil, and he retaliated by informing all the other kids around us that he'd seen me eat a booger. I'd been horrified, but had fostered a cautious respect for him ever since.

"I wasn't ignoring you," he said. "But yes, said anchorman is indeed gorgeous. Perhaps some of you are familiar with him? His name is Steffon Graziani."

Murmurs of recognition swept the table, and I threw my arms in the air. "The point is, you were going to let me die, so you didn't have to stop talking to this guy."

"Stop being so dramatic. This is the part," he said and looked around at the table with a grin and a raised eyebrow, "where we're all supposed to ooh and aah over Gilbert's heroics."

I glared at him, crossed my arms, and settled back in my chair. He had derailed my perfectly good story. The pixyish young woman with chaotic dark hair and a sarcastic smile had been hanging on my every word. Brian was such a bastard sometimes.

But she had noticed me watching her and leaned forward. "We all know what happened to the artifact, but what made you two decide to go after it in the first place?"

She spoke just loud enough to be heard above the rest of the table talk, and the other conversations tapered off as attention turned back toward me.

"Well, that was Brian's fault, too," I said. "He overheard two guys talking about it at a party and got dollar signs in his eyes."

Brian lowered his head again. "Party? It was the Governor's Ball! And the two guys were billionaires and antiquities collectors. When one of them said Mariner 10's orbit had been confirmed and that he was prepared to pay twenty million for the old probe, I believed him. Especially since we were coming up on the hundred-year anniversary of its launch. Besides, it was actually Gilbert's idea to go after it."

At least that part was true. The conversation Brian overheard had been about negotiations with two different salvage firms and how it would likely cost in excess of twenty million U.S. dollars. That tickled my competitive bone. Even after they agreed on terms and selected a salvage team, they would need to plan and outfit the expedition. If we could jump first, we could beat them to the punch and put the old probe up for auction. If they were willing to pay twenty million to go fetch it, the thing might bring even more in open bidding.

So I suggested we go after Mariner 10 ourselves. When Brian finally stopped laughing, he reminded me that we weren't in the salvage business. I brilliantly countered that our little one-ship, two-person, mobile repair business was essentially the same thing. We scooted around cislunar space repairing tugs, satellites, and refueling stations. Had a customer's credit ever bounced and we were forced to confiscate some piece of equipment and sell it for payment, we would have been doing the same thing. He called me a moron and went on and on about how the old probe's orbit was too close to the sun, how our little, mostly composite ship would melt, and how we had scheduled contracts. Then I told him about my plan. He stared at me for a couple minutes, shrugged, and started doing the math.

Our ship, Rico's Dream—yeah I know, but changing the registered name would've cost twenty-five hundred bucks and that's freakin' robbery—looked like a flying junk pile when we finished the mods. We surrounded the fifty-foot command module with lightweight scaffolding, then attached a larger engine and eight mismatched salvaged fuel tanks to the ass end. On the starboard side, we added a large sunshade built from twelve inflatable heat shields normally used to drop payloads back to Earth's surface. To balance out the mass, we put a custom heat radiator array on the port side. Our little ship had grown large and ugly, but everything worked when we tested it.

Reporters started hounding us right after our first burn. Even though the flight plan we filed had not been available to the public, Mariner 10's orbit had been posted in dozens of places after confirmation, so it didn't take long for some snoopy amateur to figure out where we were going. When Steffon Graziani called, asking to interview us for CNN, Brian nearly passed out and was almost worthless the rest of the flight.

"If we get the money," Brian said. "I'll have enough to take advantage of Steffon's offer to visit him at his family-owned villa in the Italian Alps. What do you plan to do with your half?"

I'd already decided I was going to blow half of my share in a hellacious monthlong party. Hopefully, most of that time would be spent in various beds with multiple women and an endless supply of excellent booze, but I wasn't about to tell Brian that.

"You're going to blow most of your share on women and booze, aren't you?"

He really did know me too well.

"Maybe, but only the most beautiful women and most expensive booze."

"You are such a pig."

"And how is that any different than what you hope to do?"

"Totally different," Brian mumbled through a smarmy grin.

Normally, I stay out of Brain's love life, but this one had me worried. CNN had the money to establish a tight-beam communications link with us, and Steffon had been flattering and flirting with Brian since the first video link had opened up. I'm not a reliable judge of hot men, but I was pretty sure with his thinning hair, doughy round face, and ill-fitting clothes, that Brian would fall into the dumpy category. Once this guy had his interview, Brian would be yesterday's news. If Steffon was interested in more, it was probably the potential paycheck if we were successful. My friend was going to hit hard when the crash came.

Other than Brian blathering on and on about Steffon, our three-week trip in toward the sun was uneventful. Our initial burn—the one that had drawn so much media attention—was only half as long as what we needed to slow down enough to match orbits with the old Mariner. That long three-gee burn left me with a killer headache, but we finally stopped about a mile behind the old probe, with our shielded side facing the sun. We gradually closed with the Mariner until we could see it well with a zoomed camera, and then my headache grew suddenly worse. Aside from a fist-sized hole in one solar panel, the old probe was in surprisingly good condition, but it was tumbling. Fast. In all three axes.

"Wow, it's really here," Brian said.

"Yeah, but that tumble is bad. I'm not sure we can pull this off."

"I told you it was spinning! Or at least that was its last reported condition. You said you had a plan."

I stared at the old probe, totally depressed. It bristled with antenna, equipment booms, and those two huge solar panels. "That thing has a mass of over a thousand pounds. Even if I can get the robotic grappler in close enough, it would just tear up anything I latched onto or maybe even rip the arm off."

Brian cursed and mumbled for a full ten minutes while I stared at the old Mariner. "What about the net. Isn't that our backup plan?"

"Same problem. We could get it netted, but the second we pulled on the net to slow the rotation, it would shear the solar panels and antennas right off and slam them into the probe body. It'd be a mess once we hauled it in."

"Who would know what condition we found it in? I mean, they'll still pay for it!"

"Really, Brian? Look at this thing! It's almost perfect. I'm not going to be the guy who tears it all to hell."

Brian could see his chances of meeting Steffon slipping away and growled like a cornered animal. "We canceled contracts to come out here and went into deep debt for that radiator system. Are you proposing that we just go back home empty-handed?"

"Oh calm down, Brian," I muttered, trying to wrap my mind around the problem. I zoomed the camera in closer. "This thing is like new. Bringing it back in such good condition could double its price at auction. We just have to find a way to slow it down without tearing it up. You're the one with the PhD! Help me figure this out."

"I think we have a bigger problem," Brian said in a near whisper. He was staring at the kludged panel we'd installed to monitor the heat shields and radiator. "Our outer skin temperature has risen by two degrees since we ended the burn. The radiators aren't performing to spec. Not a problem yet, our internal cooling system is still able to keep up, but it will be soon enough."

"Son of a . . ."

"Yeah, your good buddy Belinda, who built this thing, needs to give us a refund."

"How long until we get too hot?" I said.

He chewed his lip for a couple seconds while staring at the screen. "If the rate of increase remains constant, we have about six and a half hours."

"Damn!" I slapped the bulkhead hard enough to send me sailing across the little control cabin. I kicked off the wall and through the hatchway to the equipment hold, where I started pulling gear from stowage racks.

"So what's the plan?" Brian said from behind me.

"I'm ganging these oxygen tanks together through a manifold. Then I'll add a remote-controlled nozzle to blow a stream of gas against those big ol' solar panels, slowing it without damaging anything."

"Isn't it just going to act like a huge jet?"

"Not if I hold it in place with the robotic arm." My yanking on the wrench to tighten the fittings was causing me to turn in faster and faster circles. Brian reached out and stopped my spin.

"That will just impart the thrust into the Rico," he said.

"Okay, then we'll have to adjust our stationing to compensate."

He was quiet for a while, then said, "It's not going to work."

I stopped and turned to point the wrench at him. "Look, we have to do something. We're running out of time. Can't you perhaps make some helpful suggestions?"

"I thought stopping you from wasting our time was helpful."

"Okay. Explain."

He nodded toward my contraption. "That might work given a hundred of those air bottles and enough time. But like you said, that probe weighs over a thousand pounds."

He poked at the oxygen bottles and mumbled something.

"What?"

"I was just thinking that a more efficient way to slow it down using gases would be to fill a tent."

I raised an eyebrow and bent down to look him in the eye. "A tent?"

"Sure. We could surround the probe with one of those big debris capture bags we have, but instead of contracting it, we could pressurized it with oxygen. The drag of rotating inside the dense gas would slow the probe's rotation."

He pulled the pad from his pocket and started running the numbers.

"Yeah," I said. "But we'd have to control the location of that bag really well or one of those big-assed solar panels would eventually snag it and tear everything all to hell. Besides, wouldn't the spinning probe also eventually make the air and the tent spin too?"

He sighed and shook his head. "It doesn't matter. It would take a long freakin' time to slow it down that way. Days, not hours."

We floated in the center of the equipment bay, not talking, each desperately trying to think of something. I kept looking around the bay at the bins of tools and racks of stowed equipment, like my dad used to do in the hardware store when he was trying to find some quick, dirty, or cheap way to fix something.

Eventually, my gaze settled on the two crated emergency thruster packs. They had been an afterthought and would easily do the job if I could just find a way to attach them to that rapidly spinning monstrosity. The electrical caution stickers plastered on the crate exterior were new. I dragged myself over and read the warning.

CAUTION: USE OF MAGNETIC GRAPPLES MAY DAMAGE UNSHIELDED ELECTRONICS.

I snorted. I'd used this same brand of thruster packs a dozen times. They had never come equipped with magnetic grapples before.

"When did they change these thruster modules?"

"I have no idea," Brian said. "I just ordered what you told me to."

"The electronics inside the Mariner are already dead, right?" I said.

"Yeah, the shielding back then was pretty primitive, so radiation this close to the sun fried everything a long time ago."

"Good, then grabbing that probe is going to be easy."

By the time I had the thruster packs prepped for launch and made it back to the control cabin, Brian was deep in conversation with Steffon. I motioned for him to mute the mic, then pointed at the spinning probe on our main screen. "I hope you're not sending him video yet."

"No," Brian said, then grinned. "No matter how much I like him, I'm not that stupid. If we capture this thing, then CNN will pay big bucks for the whole story. Nobody gets anything until then. All I told him is that we found it and have to rethink our retrieval methods since it is spinning so fast."

I winced. "Just don't mention it's in such good condition. I don't want to be sued for breaking a historical artifact or anything."

"Just launch those thrusters. We've already wasted an hour."

"And it's already feeling hotter in here."

Brian laughed. "That's your imagination. There's no change in cabin temperature. Yet."

I extended the equipment pylon into vacuum, then detached the first thruster pack and remotely guided it toward the spinning probe. When close enough, I switched to the small onboard camera and immediately felt a gut-wrenching vertigo that threatened to explode my already throbbing head. Everything in the video feed was spinning. Trying to ignore the chaotic movement, I moved the thruster closer to get a clear shot and tried to focus on one side of the large rectangular main bus. I waited until I was sure the tumble would bring a flat spot into line, then fired the grapple.

A light on the display indicated that the magnets had been activated as the thread-fine filament unwound. The flat head of the magnetic gripper hit square in the center of a louvered panel just behind the sunshade. I pumped a fist. "Yes!"

But my cheer abruptly turned into a curse as the gripper head bounced off and spun crazily back toward the thruster unit amid a cloud of tangling line. I could see disaster coming and sent the command to cut the cable, but had been too slow. The probe's low-gain antenna whipped past, snagged the loose line, and yanked the gripper head along behind it. The line went taut, bent the antenna back at a nearly ninety degrees and catapulted the much smaller thruster unit out ahead of the probe like David's giant-killing stone. The line parted then, so instead of yanking the bent antenna back the other direction and probably pulling it completely off, the thruster unit kept right on going.

"Damn it!" I slapped the console, then, getting some sense back in the nick of time, used the unit's attitude control to halt the departure and bring it back to the Rico.

"What?" Brian said. "What happened?"

"I have no fucking idea," I muttered and stared at the spinning probe, wondering if it had some curse on it like those mummies from ancient Egypt. I imagined a dozen derelict ships, filled with corpses of those who had dared lay hands upon the cursed probe.

"I bet you can do better than that," Brian said. "What happened to the thruster package?"

I snorted, and blinked away images of skulls peering from cold, dark ships, then explained the situation to Brian as I prepped the second thruster unit for launch.

"Hold up a minute. I know what might have happened. Don't launch the second one until we watch the video."

"I don't need to see the vid. I watched it happen," I grumbled, but pushed off to float over to Brian's console.

We watched the grapple head leave the thruster unit amid a small puff of gas and particles, then creep across to the probe. Brian slowed the feed even more as the magnetic head impacted the sidewall of the old spacecraft. Just as I remembered, it landed square and in the center of the flat face, then just bounced off. It made no sense. That magnetic head was powerful. It should have easily grabbed that panel.

Brian laughed.

"What? I was dead nuts on target! I'm good at this stuff."

"Looks to me as if you were just lucky, but yeah, you were on target. The problem is that the probe's body is probably aluminum or titanium, not steel."

I stared at him, not quite getting the point. "Wait. Why in the hell would anyone use that much aluminum when it costs about fifty times more than steel?"

"Steel is cheap for us because the asteroids being mined out at L5 are filthy with iron. It made more sense for them to use nonferrous and low-mass metals like aluminum and titanium, since they had to launch this thing from the surface."

"Damn," I said as we both watched the video finish playing. "Are you sure the cabin isn't heating? Because I'm hot."

"It is now. By three degrees. Your auxiliary radiator is struggling."

"Stop saying that piece of shit is mine. How long do we have?"

"About four hours."

Sneaking up on a derelict space probe doesn't sound exciting, but I was pretty damned tense as I drew ever closer to the spinning monster. It was a lot bigger up close. The solar panels alone were each longer than I was, even in my hard suit.

Brian had noticed that my earlier failed attempt had changed the rotation in one axis enough that the three-meter-long magnetometer boom was moving very little. It was almost aligned along the probe's major spin axis, with its tip tracing a two-foot diameter circle that formed the base of its conic sweep area. From the camera angle in the Rico, it had looked easy enough to grab, but out here, it wasn't so simple.

I adjusted my approach with a tiny jet of gas, trying to align myself with the long boom. The maneuver was much harder than it needed to be because of the basketball-sized auxiliary thruster units I'd retrieved and attached to each hip. In some stroke of insanity, I'd used a single clip each, and now, every time I moved, they flopped back and forth, causing unpredictable oscillations in my movement.

Since the probe and I were shielded from the sun by Rico's shadow, I could only see what was illuminated in the helmet lamps, which played hell with my depth perception. I could see that the magnetometer capping the boom's circling tip had many sharp metal edges. My hard suit was made from a tough nano-composite that could stop bullets and most speeding space junk, but my hands weren't armored. The gloves were a supple and intricately layered fabric that maintained pressure and warmth, yet enabled me to actually use my hands. The sharp, fast-moving edges of the magnetometer would easily slice through the glove and my fingers. I was going to have to grab the boom further down its shaft, but not being able to see the entire probe made me hesitant to move in closer.

"Hey, Brian. Turn on the floodlights."

Nothing happened.

I turned to see the Rico-shaped silhouette. Sunlight created a halo bright enough to make me squint, but it wasn't a total black hole. Navigation strobes blinked, a porthole shone yellow through the temporary scaffolding, and a faint red glowed from the overworked radiator panels. But no floods.

"Brian!"

The floods kicked on a second later, causing me to close my eyes against the sudden glare. When I opened them again, my visor had darkened to protect me from the sudden brightness, but afterimages still bounced around my vision. I turned back to the probe, and even though half of it was now well lit, my visor was so dark I still couldn't see very well. I cursed.

"What's wrong," Brian said over a hiss of static. Being this close to the sun was evidently washing out the signal.

"What the hell are you doing in there," I snapped.

"Sorry, I was talking to Steffon. Did you know that his family has a villa in the Italian Alps?"

"Yes, you told me! Now put that guy on hold long enough to help me out? Can you turn off the aftmost light? Or dim them in some way? It's actually too bright out here now. My visor is almost black."

"Nope, sorry, it's all or nothing with the lights. You'll just have to manually adjust your visor."

The automatic function usually worked so well that I forgot I could do that. I made the adjustment, then edged my way closer with one small thruster burst.

THE LONG FALL UP

Once my head and arms were past the magnetometers, I reached out and grabbed the boom with both hands. It was like trying to grab a spinning, wobbly driveshaft and continued to turn in my grip. So instead of using just my hands, I decided to go for it and wrapped my arms and legs around the shaft. That gave me a good enough grip that I was yanked along with the spin. Instead of the probe spinning, it now seemed stationary above my head and the rest of the universe careened wildly around me.

"Uggg . . . I'm on, Brian."

"Great! Now keep your eyes on—static—if you don't want to barf."

Keeping my legs wrapped around the boom, I pulled the first thruster pack from where I'd clipped it on my left hip and looked for an equipment lock point, but saw nothing.

"Damn, this thing is old," I said. "It doesn't even have lock points."

"It was built long before automated refueling, so it didn't need any."

"I'm going to use straps then," I said and pulled a rolled ratchet strap from my utility pouch.

Since a tether would have just wound up around the probe like a yo-yo, I had to hang on with legs or one hand as I worked my way around the structure or be thrown off by the centrifugal force. It was a slow process and took three tries to wrap the strap around the main body of the probe, then cinch it tight without damaging any of the delicate equipment. By the time I'd finished, the powerful helmet fans couldn't dry or blow the sweat away fast enough and stinging globules kept working their way into my eyes. I repeatedly shook my head and blinked, trying to clear my vision enough to get another strap from my pouch, but before I could find it an alarm sounded.

CAUTION: OVERHEATING flashed red and scrolled across the bottom of my visor.

I'd overexerted myself during EVA before, but never enough to trigger a suit alarm. I glanced at the internal suit temperature just as it changed from 108 to 109. Like getting hurt when I was a kid and not crying until I noticed the blood, now that I saw the temperature I was suddenly unbearably hot. I turned toward the ship, but with my visor polarization decreased, I saw only a blinding glare whipping past every few seconds as I rotated.

"Brian?"

I heard nothing but static.

The temperature had jumped to 113. The only explanation was that the Rico had moved out of alignment and was no longer shielding me from direct sunlight. Could that flood of solar radiation also fry my radio signal?

"Brian! You'd better be paying attention!"

I heard a garbled response but could make no sense of it.

"I'm in the sunlight! Brian! Can you hear me?"

The temperature continued to climb, and another sweat blob jiggled into my left eye, where it stayed. Feeling faint and short of breath, I called up the suit's main menu, but the fans and cooling were already running at full power.

It was hard to think, but I knew I didn't have much time. If Brian didn't see my problem and correct within a couple minutes, I was going to pass out. The damned probe spinning me like a rotisserie had probably bought me some time, but if I blacked out, centrifugal force would throw me off in some random direction. Then I would definitely cook very quickly in the full sunshine.

Could I time it right and let the spin throw me back toward the Rico? No. That would be nearly impossible even if I weren't dizzy and seeing spots.

But if it weren't spinning, could I use it for shade? Was it big enough? Maybe. I didn't have much choice.

"Brian! I'm dying, damn it!" I said, but didn't wait for a response. I levered one hand under the strap like a determined bull rider, then with the sweat-blurred eye closed, I opened the thruster's radio interface on my arm screen. After switching to manual operation, against the advice of the control program, it took me a couple tries to match the directional icons with the five small nozzles. I held the icon for the one most closely pointing in the direction of spin.

The spin slowed noticeably, but since I'd been using the Rico zipping past as a spin-rate gauge, I was actually getting more dizzy and sick. I held the icon down and closed my eyes. When I next opened my eyes, I was no longer riding the probe bronco-style, but was instead stretched out to the full length of my arm that was still attached to the strap. I had evidently blacked out. My vision was blurred, but I could tell it was dark. I blinked until I could see the thermometer reading in my helmet. 132F and dropping. The probe was still rotating, but very slowly, and I was momentarily shaded by one of the probe's huge paddle-like solar collectors.

I pulled myself in close to the probe and poked the appropriate icon to activate the thruster again. This time it turned me the wrong way, and I quickly switched nozzles. After overcompensating several times, fixing screwups and watching the thruster unit's fuel gauge drop into the red, the probe had nearly come to a stop. I huddled behind it, trying to stay in its shade and called Brain again.

"So you are still out there!" Brian's static-laced voice said. "You must be behind the probe, I can't see you. Guess what? Steffon said that if I visit him at his family villa, he'll teach me how to ski."

"Brian! I'm in the sun! Come get me!"

Static. Then, "Say again."

"You moved the ship! I'm dying!"

This time when I passed out I knew there was no danger of letting go, because that strap had turned into Brian's throat.

We stood in a semicircle outside the chest-high barrier that surrounded the museum's Mariner 10 exhibit. An engraved plaque on a pedestal gave all the details of the probe's launch, accomplishments and recovery, complete with a thank you to me and Brian.

The cute, pixyish woman turned to face me and crossed her arms. She had stolen glances at me the entire six-block walk over from the bar.

"So Brian went out and rescued you?" she said.

"Rescued me? Hell no! I saved myself and stopped the probe's spin."

"You're such a baby," Brian said. "I did have to go out and get you."

"I can't believe you were going to let me die out there."

"I saved you!"

"Saving my life hardly counts as a heroic act when you're the one who almost killed me! No bonus points for that, pal!"

Everyone laughed.

"Whatever," the pixy said. "You were planning to sell it to the highest bidder. I can't believe that was a museum. What happened?"

Brian grabbed my shoulder and shook me gently.

"It turns out that Gilbert is a big softy."

I felt a blush coming on.

"The whole trip back he sat in the equipment hold staring at that damned thing. Then just an hour before we docked he said, 'It doesn't seem right that this piece of history will be stuck in some billionaire's study for him to brag about and flaunt, when he had nothing to do with sending it or recovering it.'"

Everyone said "awwww" and turned to me with snickers and puppy dog eyes.

"Don't let him fool you," I said, trying to recover a sliver of dignity. "We did sell it to the highest bidding museum and also got a nice check from CNN for exclusive interviews and the video footage of the recovery."

Brian nodded and smiled, but Steffon had walked in so he abandoned me with a half wave.

"Don't let him near skis again, Steffon! He's been slacking down here on the ground long enough."

The superstar news anchor gave me a half bow, carefully embraced Brian around the sling, then was surrounded by the rest of our entourage and the entire clump moved off as one. When I turned back only the dark-haired woman remained.

"So, your worries about Brian getting a broken heart were unfounded?"

I nodded. "Not the first time I've been wrong. And glad to be this time."

We stood there staring at the old probe in uncomfortable silence for a few minutes, then she smiled up at me and tilted her head. "I told you twice in the bar, but I bet you don't remember my name."

"Of course I do," I said with a bit of a panic, trying to remember the introductions. It started with a K, or maybe a P.

"Gloria!" I blurted.

She rolled her eyes and said, "Glory. But close enough. I'm an acquisitions agent for the Museum of Tokyo."

"Ahhh," I said, understanding coming at last. "Your museum was one of the losing bidders."

"Yes," she said and started walking, then looked back at me with a raised eyebrow.

I hurried to catch up and fell into step beside her.

"Are you interested in going after Sakigake?"she said.

I knew it! She really liked me.

"I sure would," I said. "I've never tried Sakigake, but I've heard it's delicious."

She started laughing but finally caught her breath long enough to say, "The Sakigake space probe!"

"Oh," I felt silly of course, but she looped her arm through mine and tugged me along with her anyway. And that was something.

HOW TO FIX DISCARDED THINGS

I park next to the playground that nearly fills the apartment complex's small courtyard. It's early, but kids already swarm the slides and ladders, their yells and laughs echoing from the buildings.

Two boys kick a groundskeeping robot back and forth across the parking lot like a soccer ball. One of them waves and says something to me as he goes by, but it's on the side with my bad ear, so I can't hear. The other boy misses a pass and the robot rolls into the grass, then unfolds and scampers off into the bushes. Something seems off with the boys, but before I can work it out, they tear off in pursuit of the robot.

Grabbing the data pad and tool bag, I crawl from the cramped truck cab to face the Texas summer heat. Only nine o'clock and already near a hundred degrees. Within seconds I'm sweating under my bra straps and in my pits.

My truck—made nervous by the neighborhood—barely lets me step clear before going armadillo. It collapses into a secure, armored configuration with hair-thin seams and no wheels or glass exposed. If only it were round, I could kick it to the boys.

I start up the sidewalk, and again, my eyes are drawn to the kids. The colors seem wrong. I don't dare look too closely as I walk past. Even being a woman and wearing a utility uniform, I get nothing but glares from watchful parents. I'm still black, six feet tall, and a stranger. That makes me a threat.

Two girls of about nine or ten also eye me warily as they come up the walk, then burst into giggles as they pass. This time I do turn to look. They both wear brightly colored shirts and shorts. The clothes are standard printer styles —not something from a store or subscription service—but are far more colorful than anything normally available from UBI printers. One wears white with brightly colored rainbows surrounded by stylized yellow stars. The other is wrapped in brilliant interlocking fractals of green, orange, and sky blue.

I then understand why some of the smaller kids look odd. Most wear clothes matching the pastel buildings, drab and plain, but one sports tiger stripes and another wears a giant sunflower. The parents glower at me, so I move on.

I stop where the sidewalk tees and glare at row upon row of pastel-painted apartment buildings and secretly despise these people. Ubies don't know real poverty, at least not the hard, desperate poverty of an inner-city black kid from forty years ago. They don't share their food with roaches or shiver in unheated apartments. Universal basic income has made them nothing more than cattle, kept fat and happy by the government so they don't cause trouble. I'm glad they have plenty of food to eat. I'm glad their kids won't go deaf in one ear from a simple case of the flu left untreated due to lack of medical insurance. But these people don't appreciate what they have and that pisses me off.

The interior of building twelve is blessedly cool. I pause inside the door to check the repair assignment flashing on my pad's screen. The first item should be a simple enough fix. A fault—probably a short—in a control cable for apartment unit 1210. I feel smug satisfaction in that one. Automated systems can detect a problem, but in so many cases it takes a human to determine the reason and fix it.

The second item on the list will be a bitch. Elevated raw stock usage. Since supply companies can't legally put programmed cutoffs on printer stock use, there is a constant problem with the poor using their state-provided printers and stock to make things for sale. I curse under my breath. Proving that is always tough, and I hate being in the middle of those fights. It makes me miss my old job working in the uptown office buildings even more.

I hesitate before the door marked 1210. My pad says it belongs to Gabriella Hernandez. Taking a deep breath, I ring the buzzer.

A skinny boy with black hair and eyes opens the door. He looks about eleven years old and is all smiles. Then—when he sees my uniform and tools—his eyes go wide and he slams the door.

Yep, they are doing something illegal.

I ring the buzzer again.

This time a woman answers. I tower over her by nearly a foot. She's in her mid-thirties and glares at me while using a wet towel to wipe a crusty white coating from her hands and arms. White spatters also speckle her face and baggy blue shirt. One glance at my uniform and my black face tells her all she needs to know about me. Her stance changes, filling more of the door.

"Yeah?"

As I open my mouth to reply, a strange earthy smell reaches my nose. It reminds me of dirt and childhood. I'm transported back to my grandma's backyard, where I played in the mud, squishing it between my bare toes and making mud pies.

"I . . . ummm . . . my name is Annie Harrison. I'm from building maintenance," I finally say. "I need to check your printers."

She crosses her arms and nods at my uniform. "I'll have to get some confirmation. These buildings are owned by the state, not some company named TechPro."

I show her my picture ID. "The state pays my company to maintain the buildings. You should have received an email or notification through the apartment complex network that I would be coming."

"Our printers work fine."

"I still have to check them."

We stare at each other for several seconds, and she finally moves aside.

UBI housing units are all laid out to one of four floor plans, and this is no different. The small living room is neat, with a love seat and two chairs in the center, arranged to view a modest-sized wall monitor, but what surprises me are three large bookshelves dominating the wall space. Two are overflowing with books crammed into every open space. I hadn't seen so many paper books in one place since I'd last visited a library, probably twenty years ago, so I take a step forward to look closer. Those on the upper shelves are novels, but the lower shelves are filled with textbooks covering diverse subjects, like psychology, art history, and fundamentals of computer logic.

The other shelves contain pottery. Dozens of stunning pots, pitchers and plates of various sizes, all covered with bright and colorful designs. The vase closest to me appears china-thin at the lip and is trimmed in gold and shiny blue enamel. I want to touch it, but with a shake of my head, I remember why I'm here.

The woman still glares at me, but there is something else in her expression. Sadness? Defeat? I heft my tools and enter a kitchen that has been transformed into a workshop that explains the earthy smell.

A pottery kick wheel sits in the center of the floor, encircled by tarps draped from metal racks, obviously arranged to collect the splatter. Some half-formed project sits on the wheel covered by a damp towel. A wet-dry vacuum and large bucket filled with milky-colored water sit to either side.

The two-person table in one corner holds a small kiln surrounded by fire-proof welding blankets and two pedestal fans. The sink is also surrounded by white spatter marks, and the adjacent counter space is crowded with pots in various stages of completion.

"It's all legal," she says when I turn to look at her. "I paid for this stuff and have written consent from management. The room is properly vented. The kiln has its own fire suppression system, and I have approval from the fire marshall."

When I look back into the kitchen, I see the boy. He is almost hidden behind the tarps, standing with his back to the main printer, arms spread slightly to the sides, as if ready to block access. His eyes are wide. Beyond him, the printer arms zip back and forth behind the safety glass, actively constructing something.

There is barely room to walk in the cramped room, but I take two steps forward and nod at the boy. "I need to see that."

His head moves side to side in a barely perceivable shake, and skinny arms rise higher. Just then, the printer's completion bell rings, and we both flinch, but like gunslingers from some old western, neither of us gives ground.

"This is my job," I say to the boy. "I can't leave until I examine the printers."

He glances at his mom, obviously unsure what he should do.

"It's okay, Carson," his mother says. "Let this woman do her job."

The boy hesitates, then steps to one side. The food printer set into the wall just below the microwave is empty. But Carson had been blocking the large, main printer and it contains a shirt, covered with brightly colored images of people dancing.

Everything clicks together: the kids in the courtyard, the increased stock usage, these reluctant people. They're using state resources to manufacture goods for sale. Despite the books and pottery, they are lying cheats, just like the others.

I turn to the woman. "I don't know how you get the supplies for your pottery operation, so that might be legal, but printing those shirts isn't."

"It's only illegal if we use the printer to make items for sale," she says. "We haven't sold any. He gives the clothes away."

"Not taking money for the stuff is a technicality," I say. Since the printers are used to make everything from shampoo to shoes, the authorities can't cut off access, but they will fill their home with monitoring equipment to ensure they stop contributing to the black-market barter economy. "Are these subscription clothes? If not, then it is illegal."

She knows that would be easy for me to check, so doesn't answer and just stares at the floor. Finding ubies making stuff to sell didn't really surprise me, but I do wonder how they managed this particular hack.

I pull the shirt from the printer and stuff it in my bag as evidence for the report, then lean into the unit and use my ID card to open the maintenance panel. I expect jumper wires or some other crude kludge, but instead, find a tiny circuit card inserted between two cable connections. I remove the card, reconnect the cables, and close the panel.

"Where did you get this?"

"I made it," Carson says, tears streaming down his face.

I glance at the mother and she nods with a scowl.

"You designed a PC board just to bypass the color block?"

"Yes."

I look down at the card that's roughly the size of a quarter, then drop it into my pocket and pull the shirt out of the bag to examine further.

"This is great. So are the clothes I saw in the courtyard. But if you're stealing and printing designer patterns, you're in a lot more trouble than just a simple stock usage violation."

"My son is not a thief," his mother snaps.

"They're my designs," Carson says.

I raise my eyebrows, skeptical. "An artist and an engineer? What a talented family."

"Report us or not, but I don't have to let you accuse my son," the mother says and points to the door.

I stuff the shirt back in my bag.

The boy speaks, but I miss what he says, so I turn my good ear toward him. "Say that again?"

"I'm not an engineer," he says, struggling to not cry again. "I found the bypass schematic online. It was pretty easy to find a program to convert that into a card design I could make on the printer."

I'm impressed and wonder how he managed to even get the maintenance cover open, but don't ask, because everything I hear will have to go into my report, and I'm actually starting to feel a little bad for the kid.

"Look, Carson. You have to stop doing this. You printed too many. Your stock usage is through the roof. To the monitoring programs, this looks like mass production. I'm surprised you haven't been shut down before now."

He nods. "I started out by charging a piece of clothing as the cost to print a new one. That way, I was getting recycle credit that almost equaled what I was using. But people stopped bringing old clothes. I think they wanted to keep the stuff I'd made for them."

I suspected half of them were selling the clothes on the black market. Using this poor well-meaning boy as a scapegoat. Bastards.

"That was a good plan," I say. "You should have stuck with it."

His mom still glares at me with crossed arms, but she lets us talk.

"Can't you leave the bypass board?" Carson says. "That way, I could at least make a few."

I shake my head. "Your bypass was showing up in diagnostics as a fault in the cable. It'll do that every time. People will keep coming out to fix it."

He slumps.

I feel terrible, but there is no way he can keep doing this without raising flags.

"It's not fair," Carson says.

"Huh?"

"If we buy subscription clothes, it will print any color and style we like. Why do they limit us to five ugly solid colors?"

"You just gave the reason why," I say. "You're too young to remember, but clothing manufacturers and retailers raised holy hell when plans were proposed to allow those on UBI to print their own clothes at home. This was a compromise."

"Bullshit," the woman says. "This is just a way for them to spout their sanctimonious propaganda about caring for the poor while still setting us apart and shaming us."

I've had it. I feel sorry for the boy because he doesn't know any better, but the mother? She has no excuse for encouraging this. "If you don't like this life, then do something about it," I snap.

I get so tired of hearing ubies whine about being victims. I started out much poorer than any of them and clawed my way into a career that has supported me my entire life. "Go back to school and retrain."

Her face flushes with anger. "How dare you! You're nothing but an ignorant piece of . . ."

She glances at Carson and then grits her teeth and throws the towel at the floor.

"I did retrain! I started out with a master's degree in Molecular Life Sciences. Do you even know what that is?"

Now my face grows hot, but she continues before I can answer.

"But evidently, specialized computer systems can do ninety percent of that job better than I can now. So I got a new degree in chemical engineering, thinking that maybe something more practical would be better. Nope, because there is a glut in that field too, with experienced people scrambling for the open jobs, and of course, I was then at entry level. Now I can't even get a job in a damned coffee shop!"

Carson stares at his mom with wide eyes. She must not talk this way very often. Or at least doesn't yell when she does.

Time to go. I move to the door, but then pause. I should just let it drop, but the kid needs to know just how lucky they are.

"With twenty-three percent unemployment, I understand you not being able to find a job. But you have nothing to complain about," I say and spread my arms to encompass the apartment. "You're not hungry. I mean, look at how you live! This isn't even poverty. You have no idea how it used to be."

"Get out," she says and pushes me toward the door.

She's brave. I give her that. I have about a foot in height and fifty pounds on her. She opens the door and shoves me into the hall.

"Look, I've grown to like this life," she says, a little quieter, but with the door half-closed. "I feel human now. I think maybe for the first time ever."

"What is that supposed to mean?"

"That now my time and labor are given to things I want to do. Carson and I are still giving back to society, we're just doing it on our own terms now, not working eight or ten or twelve hours a day to provide goods to consumers on the other side of the world? But I don't expect you to understand that. All you see is a lazy moocher living off of productive people!"

Then the door slams in my face.

I stand in the hall for a moment, stunned and a bit embarrassed. She feels human for the first time? That made no sense.

The whole encounter sours my gut. I pull out the bypass circuit card, part of my brain already looking for ways to modify it so as not to trigger the alarms, but then I squelch the idea. I like Carson, but there are a hundred qualified people ready to take my job if I do something wrong or even if they find out about my hearing. I have to do everything by the book. Besides, the kid is smart and ambitious. He'll probably do just fine without help from me. I still feel like shit as I leave the building.

The incident with the boy and his mother bothers me. Even two months later when my boss calls me into his office, Carson's little criminal empire is the first thing that comes to mind. Did Gabriella Hernandez file a complaint? Or did they get in serious trouble, and I would need to testify in court?

But understanding comes immediately when I open the office door. My coworkers, Marty and Dora, are already waiting. Umberto, my manager, looks frazzled and pale. I take the empty chair.

Umberto sits on the edge of the desk and stares at his hands for a couple seconds. "The City of Dallas has started replacing all the UBI-housing printers with those self-maintaining units from that European company. What's it called?"

"Copenhagen Fabricage?" I mumble.

"Yeah, anyway, effective immediately, you're all laid off. I'm getting cut too, though at least I have until the end of the month." He snorted. "Apparently, they don't need a service manager if there are no service techs to manage."

This isn't a surprise, I'd seen it coming for a long time, but I still feel myself coming unglued. I'm hot with frustration and anger and shame. I'm an ubie now.

My boss continues talking in the background, about severance, about how people with our skills will find jobs quickly, or perhaps we can take advantage of the company's retraining options.

Part of my mind races around like a frightened animal, trying to think of ways to find a new job, but I know deep down that will never happen. My position at TechPro has a queue of more than a hundred people waiting for me to quit or get fired, just to get a chance to interview for the spot. And it was just dumb luck they didn't ask about or test my hearing when I was hired. Of course I will look for work, but have to face the facts. I'm forty-eight and my career is over.

I stare at shaking hands and clench my stomach muscles in an effort to quell its churning. It's not like I'll go hungry or be homeless. I have UBI, just like everyone else. That's how it works. Every person gets paid the same living wage, even if they have a job. It acts as a safety net or cushion, replacing the old programs like welfare and social security. But survival isn't the point. I have always worked for a living. My entire life. I vowed to never be a burden on society. I would never live for free on other people's hard work. But here I am. An ubie.

A hand squeezes my shoulder, and I look up into my boss's haunted eyes. "Are you okay, Annie?"

I nod and look around. My coworkers have already left. I am being weird and needy, so I say goodbye and go to empty my locker.

I stuff another empty box into the recycle chute and then turn in a slow circle to look around. Like all UBI housing, my kitchen has a small table with two chairs. Everything else, the microwave, fridge, and the two printers, are all set into the wall to make space and prevent theft.

In contrast to the nearly empty kitchen, my living room is cramped with boxes holding spools of wire, trays filled with saved hardware, tools, dusty test equipment, and all the accumulated detritus of a thirty-year career as a technician. Everything had fit easily into the rented two-bedroom house with the attached garage I'd used for a workshop, but not so well in what I can afford with just basic income.

One of my coworkers said he feels oddly free now. It is a strange relief to not hide my bad ear anymore, but for me, this new freedom feels more like I'm cut adrift and at the mercy of tides and currents beyond my control. I take a deep breath and look around at the mess. Hard work has always been a salve for my pain, so I start sorting through boxes. I need three piles: sell, keep, or discard.

The fourth box I search contains my grandmother's mantle clock. Most of my family calls it cheap and ugly, but it was the only one of my grandma's possessions I wanted. For me, the clock radiates a strange power over time itself. Just touching it transports me back to her hot kitchen filled with that sensuous baking cookie aroma.

"As soon the clock strikes three, we can take them out of the oven," Grandma says.

I pull it from the box, remove the bubble wrap, and am again playing Monopoly on her living room floor.

"Okay, we can play until the clock strikes ten, then off to bed with you!"

The clock hasn't worked for years. The spring doesn't catch when I turn the winding key and there has never been time to fix it. Now I have the time.

I quickly tear the clock down into its basic subassemblies, expecting to find a broken mainspring, but I am pleasantly surprised to find the spring intact. Instead, the bracket that holds the spring's loose end is twisted out of shape. They'd used cheap aluminum that hadn't held up to repeated winding torques.

Pulling the bracket free, I dig out measuring tools and transfer the design into the little CAD program on my data pad. Then I thicken the material a little, change it to steel, add two tiny gussets for strength and send it to the printer.

Twenty minutes after the part finishes printing, the clock is reassembled, wound up, and ticking away happily on the top shelf. I am elated and filled with energy. Making broken things work again is a good feeling, so I start looking around for the next thing to fix.

My search is interrupted by a child's scream from outside. I raise the blind with some alarm and look out at a young mother already attending a scraped knee. All the kids yelling and playing in the courtyard below wear bland, patternless pastels. It makes me remember Carson, and I know immediately what I need to fix next.

———

Carson again answers the door when I ring the buzzer. He blinks, slightly confused, probably not recognizing me without my uniform and tools. Before he can say anything or slam the door in my face, I hand him the new bypass circuit board.

"This is a little larger than your old one," I say. "But it won't cause an interrupt in the circuit. They'll never know it's there unless they open the panel and look inside."

The door opens wider, and Gabriella appears behind him, drying her hands.

"Thank you!" Carson says.

"That still won't help with your stock usage problem. You have to keep that under control. You should be able to print two small shirts or a large one each week. But if you're feeding old clothes into the recycler for credit, you should be able to print more."

"I will," he says.

"There's one more thing," I say and glance at his mother. "They will be coming to change your printer to a newer, fully automated version sometime later this year."

Comprehension fills Gabriella's face, and she slowly shakes her head.

"So that means this bypass will only work until then. I've never worked with those new printer units, but if you call me when that happens I'll come over and try to help you hack that one too."

Carson laughs, then slips past his mother and yells over his shoulder. "I'm going to try it out!"

Gabriella and I—left in a sudden and awkward situation—stare at each other. Just as I get ready to say goodbye, she says "I'm sorry about your job."

I nod. "Well . . . I've dodged that bullet for years, but it was inevitable."

She motions at my tee shirt. "I have to say I like these clothes a lot better than your previous fashion choice."

I can't help but laugh. "Yeah? I could still use some fashion advice from Carson."

"What will you do now?" she asks.

The question catches me off guard, and I feel awkward and panicky. I am simultaneously ashamed of being an ubie and for how I had treated her in my first visit. I shake my head and take a step backward. "I . . . I really haven't thought that far ahead yet."

"You should come in," she says.

"I really need to get going."

She stares at me for a second, examining my face, then holds up a finger for me to wait and disappears inside. She returns holding the delicate vase with gorgeous blue and gold designs I noticed during my last visit.

"I remember you examining this when you were here before. Do you like it?"

"Of course," I said. "It's beautiful."

"Then it's yours," she says and holds it out to me with a broad smile.

I take a step back. "Oh no. I didn't mean . . ."

A faint smile touches her lips. "Hey, it's okay," she says. "Remember what I said about me being human now?"

I nod.

"Well, making beautiful things and giving them to people is part of being human. At least for me it is. And for Carson too, so what you did makes it easier for him to do what he enjoys. This is what we do now."

She pushes the vase into my arms. It weighs almost nothing and feels so fragile.

"I can't take this," I say, almost whispering. "I mean don't you make these to sell?"

"Oh, I sell some of them, just to replenish my supplies, but like I said, most are given to my friends. You sure you don't want to come in?"

I look at her again and see the clay spatters on her smock and arms, then shake my head.

We say our goodbyes and I hold the vase like an infant as I make my way back to the train station. I've never owned anything like this before in my entire life.

The man who sits next to me on the train says, "That's a stunning piece of art. What printer design did you use?"

"No printer. A friend of mine made it by hand and gave it to me."

His eyebrows rise. "One of a kind! In an age where everything is made by a machine, you're lucky to get such a gift."

I nod and smile, then turn to look out the window at Dallas flashing past. I see a broken bicycle, then a large TV monitor sitting with the trash beside the road. This city is filled with old technology. Some things are kept for nostalgic reasons, others because the owner is too poor to buy something better, and maybe much more could be kept if it were reconditioned or fixed.

I know how to do that.

I smile at my reflection in the glass, and like so many other newly minted humans, my head fills with one-of-a-kind ideas.

THE BEAST FROM BELOW

I'm sure you've heard the phrase "You can't fight city hall." Well, in Redemption, Oklahoma, that means you can't fight Mable Harjo. She was the mayor, owned half the town—the most expensive half—and ran the Ladies' Garden Club like a Soviet gulag. So when her mint-green '53 Thunderbird skidded to a stop less than a foot behind my patrol car, I just gritted my teeth, braced for her barrage, and tried to not inhale any of the dust that enveloped me.

When the billowing cloud subsided, Mable stood glaring up at me with arms crossed and foot tapping. I brushed dust from my uniform, but I swear there wasn't a speck of dirt on her pale pink, wasp-waisted Victoria von Hagen suit.

"A monster, Harry? You better be drunk on your ass."

Though Mable was a tiny woman, only five foot two, she would stand her ground against anyone. I doubt she would back down from ol' Beelzebub himself. And I'm sure she would be pissed to know that her serious, all-business, dark-eyed glare from beneath that movie-star pixie haircut melted me. It always did.

"Yeah, sorry about that, but Elmer Marston called my office this morning, yelling about a 'manster from hell,' then his line went dead," I said and pointed over her shoulder. "So when I saw this mess, I thought you better see it, too."

"A 'manster'?"

"He's from the East Coast or Ohio or something."

"Heh . . . I thought he was from New Orleans," she said and turned around. The growing dawn revealed Marston's sprawling ranch house reduced to a pile of splintered wood and crushed stone. Being the sheriff, problems in the county always fell into my lap, but since the house part of the ranch actually stood—or now partially stood—inside Redemption city limits, it was Mable's problem, too.

"Christ on a crutch," she muttered. "Did we have twisters out here last night?"

"Nope," I said and motioned for her to follow me.

We worked our way closer to the debris field with her daintily stepping between shattered furniture and chunks of masonry, but the hard determination on her face never wavered. I helped her up onto a large piece of still-intact wall lying flat atop the mess and nodded down into the twenty-foot-diameter hole that did indeed appear to lead into the very bowels of hell. A foul stench wafted out. She wrapped her arms around her chest and hugged herself.

"Where's Elmer and Edith? And the kids?"

"I haven't found any bod—eh . . . people. Do monsters from hell eat people?"

"How would I know that, Harry?"

"Well, the hell part . . ." I said with a shrug.

She glared at me. "Shouldn't you be looking for them?"

"I've called the county boys to bring some backhoes and loaders out here, but it'll be a couple of hours."

"He said it was a monster?"

I nodded. "From hell. There was a lot of racket in the background, but that part was pretty clear."

"Where is that scientist guy working? The one from Harvard?"

I helped her to the ground, and we headed back to the cars. I admit I had the willies and didn't let my right hand stray too far from my holstered gun. "Doctor Lawrence? He's out at the old Triple Bend Ranch, digging for fossils. Why?"

"If this really is some kind of monster or huge animal, then we're out of our league."

"Well, yeah, but he's a paleonthant . . . a paleoarco . . . just a fossil hunter. How could he help?"

"He's a scientist, isn't he? They always know what to do."

"But shouldn't we call the army?"

She tilted her head and raised an eyebrow. "Have you seen an actual monster from hell yet? I'm not going to call the damned army unless I see it with my own eyes. Besides, the army would just kill it."

I blinked at her. "Look at Elmer's house! Why wouldn't you want to kill it?"

"Because motorists would come in from Highway 60 to see a monster, and they would pay a lot more to see a live one than a dead one."

I clenched my teeth to keep from laughing when Dr. Lawrence climbed out of my deputy's patrol car. He was dressed in silly desert expedition clothes and a hat, the same getups that Abbott and Costello wore when they met that mummy.

He strode toward me, clutching a smoldering pipe in one hand and extending the other. "Hello, Sheriff! Good to see you again. Your deputy tells me you have a . . . er . . . 'mansta' problem?"

"Mansta?"

He raised his hands, clawlike, growled, and gave me a lurid grin.

"Mansta? Huh. I guess Elmer was from New Orleans after all.

"I'm not an expert on manstas, Sheriff," he said, stifling a snicker, "but I'll do what I can."

I led him over to where Mable was giving the loader operator step-by-step instructions about how to do his job through a bullhorn.

"Be careful! If someone is under there, you're going to rip them in half."

"Mayor Harjo, Doctor Lawrence is here."

She lowered the bullhorn and turned around, then raised her eyebrows.

He removed his pith helmet, revealing dark, sweat-plastered hair, then took her hand and bowed slightly.

"Such a pleasua to meet you, Madam Maya."

I stifled a growl as she looked him over, noting the tanned bare legs and equally bare ring finger, then did something I had seldom seen her do. She batted her eyelashes and blushed. "Well, hello there, Doctor. Please call me Mable."

"And you can call me Ted."

I cleared my throat and said, "Doctor Lawrence was just telling me he didn't think he could help."

"On the contrary," the doctor said, still looking at Mable but pointing his stupid pipestem at me. "I might be able to help a great deal. There is a good chance this is nothing more than a sinkhole or a methane explosion. I might be able to help establish that."

I hadn't seen a monster, either, but his casually waving it off as fiction irritated the hell out of me.

"Mayor! Sheriff! Come see this," one of the workers, Johnny Nguyen, yelled.

I rushed over and braced myself to see a dead friend, but instead found Johnny kneeling next to an animal track that was at least two feet long. I couldn't count the number of times I'd been called by old ladies in the middle of the night to come arrest a prowler, only to find their flower beds filled with small tracks that looked just like these.

"That's an armadillo rear-foot track," I said. "No mistaking that splayed five-toe arrangement."

Mable stared at the print with wide eyes.

The good doctor knelt and placed his arm on the ground. The print was about three inches longer than his arm measured fingertip to elbow.

"Astounding," he muttered. "There's a species of armadillo that can get as large as a pig, but this . . ."

"Harry?" Mable stood with arms crossed and jaw set, looking every bit the part of a battlefield general. "Based on the size of that footprint, how big is this thing?"

I looked down at the print again and a chill crawled up my spine. "It could easily be twenty-five to thirty feet long."

She glanced at the doctor, who was deep in thought, chewing on his pipestem.

"Do you . . . do you think it ate the Marstons?" Johnny said.

"Nah," I said, not really believing my own reply. "They normally eat insects. Mostly grubs, beetles, and worms."

"Yes, but a creature that size would require a large population of monster bugs, too. Or it would have to find something else to eat," the infinitely helpful doctor said.

I glanced at Mable. Instead of fainting or even being horrified, she stared off into space as her mouth moved silently. It was the same expression she wore when trying to calculate how much the town could earn from a harvest festival or Christmas pageant.

I didn't care how much money something like this might generate. I wasn't going to let this monster eat any more of my friends.

"I'm going down there," I said.

"Down where?" Mable said.

"Into that hole. Armadillos are active at night—"

"Nocturnal," the doctor chimed in.

"Uh, yeah. So that means it's probably made a burrow and is sleeping down there somewhere. It'll be mighty hungry again come nightfall."

Dr. Lawrence pointed his pipestem at me again. "And just what will you do down there, Sheriff? I suggest you call the army and let the professionals deal with this problem."

I glanced at Mable before addressing His Scienceship. "Our good mayor refuses to let me call the army. But I'm not a total fool, Doctor. I worked with explosives during the war and intend to take some dynamite down with me."

"Don't you dare kill that thing!" Mable said and actually stomped her foot like a five-year-old. "No dynamite!"

"Mable! There is a good chance that manster . . . shoot . . . monster ate Elmer and his family! My job is to protect the people of this county, and by God if I have to kill that monster to stop it, I will!" She glared at me, but I stared right back. "Have me fired if you want, but wait until we stop this thing first."

"I'm going with you," Mable said.

"Like hell you are," I said without thinking.

She looked up at me with an amused smile. "Are you going to tie me up to stop me, Harry?"

My face grew hot with a sudden blush.

"Or maybe use those cold steel handcuffs? And gag me with something?"

Damn her! Was she flirting again? I couldn't figure her out. One minute she was yelling at me, next she was pouring on the double entendres. I couldn't even look at her. "Fine. Wear some real shoes and meet me back here in two hours."

As usual, Mable was too smart for me. I gathered all my equipment, including the dynamite, wire spool, and my surplus twist-type ten-cap blasting machine, and was back at the hole in less than an hour, planning to be long gone before she returned at the appointed time. But there she stood, decked out in tight blue jeans, hiking boots, and a leather jacket. She also had a well-used M1 rifle slung from her shoulder. It had probably belonged to her husband who died in the war, and even though it was almost bigger than she was, I had no doubt she could shoot it.

Dr. Lawrence stood beside her, festooned with gear hanging from straps and hooks all over him. The huge camera with dinner-plate sized flash attachment hanging around his neck made him look like a comical tourist.

I growled under my breath. My deputy, whom I'd left in charge of the search and rescue operation, chuckled and shook his head. "Maybe you'll get lucky and the monster'll kill you quick."

"I can only hope."

Ten minutes later, we stood huddled together in the Marstons' bathtub, holding on to chains as a smirking Johnny Nguyen lowered our makeshift elevator into the hole via a backhoe.

"Which direction?" Mable said once we were inside.

I looked both ways, then pointed down the tunnel that headed toward town. I didn't want that thing anywhere near the residents of Redemption.

The tunnel was cool, making me wish I'd also brought a jacket, as it meandered, turning first left, then right, steadily descending. The illumination from the Marston hole faded quickly, forcing us to switch on our flashlights within minutes.

No one spoke as we shuffled along. I was as scared as a five-year-old seeing creatures in my dark closet. Being an Iwo Jima veteran and longtime sheriff had never prepared me for something like this. In comparison, being shot at was a piece of cake. I knew if we met this thing, face-to-face in the tunnel, we were in big trouble. I doubted bullets would penetrate that thick armored hide, and we probably wouldn't have time to set explosives. And the floor covered in loose dirt and smelling every bit like an open grave didn't help.

I had lost my bearings almost as soon as we started out and was just beginning to think we should turn back when Mable pointed her flashlight up. "Look at that. I think we're getting close to town."

Pipes of various sizes crisscrossed the tunnel ceiling. Some showing scrape marks where the monster's shell must have rubbed against them. I'm not sure why, but seeing those scraped pipes made the whole situation seem even more real.

We pushed forward and passed beneath what had to be a storm sewer pipe.

"We must be right under downtown," Mabel said.

That's when I saw the first grub. It was the size of my forearm, fat and white, squirming along the loose dirt of the tunnel floor. Mable squealed and almost knocked Dr. Lawrence down trying to get behind him. I'd seen her shoot a rattler and stomp a tarantula. I didn't think she was afraid of anything. Of course, the good doctor was more than happy to wrap his arms around her and play protector.

"Oh good Lord, kill that thing!" she said.

I pulled my revolver from the holster, but before I could draw a bead, the doctor yelled, "Wait!"

He shrugged loose from Mable, rushed forward, and fished a bag from one of his many pockets. "What an incredible specimen. I know entomologists who would give me their first child for this grub."

Mable stood tensed, ready for flight. "It's disgusting," she muttered. "Like a giant maggot."

As Lawrence knelt to scoop up the grub, a loud clicking started up and quickened.

"Of course," he said, pulling a yellow Geiger counter from a pouch at his side, "radioactivity is just about the only thing that could cause such a mutation of the grubs and the armadillo."

"Is it dangerous?" I said, starting to feel a little sick. I knew what radiation could do to people. I'd been part of MacArthur's force that occupied Japan after the war.

He shoved the squirming grotesquery into the bag and peered at the glowing screen on the clicking box. "No, not unless you were to eat it."

Mable quivered again, then stepped forward, smoothing her jacket and pants. I smiled and she replied with her best glare. "Disgusting. Let's get going. I'm starting to believe this monster might actually exist."

We moved about another sixty or seventy yards up the tunnel, where it opened into a wide spot with three more tunnels branching off in different directions. The Geiger counter ticked faster, and I noticed a sudden change in the dirt color above us and to our left side. Even the smell changed to something warm and loamy.

"Oh dear God," Mable muttered. "I think I know what caused these mutations."

"What?" I said.

Just then, the heads of two more grubs appeared from the dark-colored soil. They writhed around and then fell to the floor. Mable squealed, and her legs looked like she was climbing an invisible ladder as she tried to keep her feet far from the squirming maggot things.

She took a couple steps back down the tunnel and quivered all over. The look on her face could have belonged to a child being forced to eat Brussels sprouts.

The good doctor rushed forward to snatch the grubs.

"What does the gadget say now, Doc?" I said. "Are we in trouble?"

"Huh?" He had a beatific smile on his face as he examined each squishy worm before dropping it in the bag with the first one. "Oh, not yet. But we wouldn't want to stay here more than a couple hours."

I turned to Mable. "Okay, Mayor. We might not have much time. What's going on?"

She glanced over my shoulder, then scanned the walls and ceiling looking for more grubs.

"Spill it, Mable!"

She flinched and then shrugged. "Have you seen my new roses?"

I was confounded. "Roses? No, what do roses have to do with it?"

"Well, a botanist friend of mine who lives in New Mexico sent me pictures of some rosebushes she found in a river valley. The heads on these roses are huge! I mean, they're the size of dinner plates!"

"So you went there and got the rosebushes? Bushes that were irradiated by the atomic tests in New Mexico?"

"I'm afraid it's worse than that," Mable said, and she wouldn't meet my eyes.

"Worse?"

She nodded. "I . . . um . . . thought there must be something special about the soil, so I brought some of that, too."

"Irradiated soil?"

"Well, I didn't know it was radioactive!"

"How much?"

"Seven dump trucks full."

I looked all around us. "So we're right beneath your garden?"

She nodded.

"This giant armadillo was in that dirt and nobody noticed it?"

"Actually," the doctor said and pointed his pipestem at me again, "it could have been a local armadillo that was mutated by eating the radioactive grubs."

I cursed under my breath, but before I could ask any more questions, a loud squeaking noise came from down one of the tunnels.

"It's coming!" yelled the doctor.

I grabbed Mable and pushed her down the tunnel we'd entered. "Run!"

In the beam from Dr. Lawrence's flashlight I could see the monster, snuffling and grunting as it waddled up the tunnel. Its head was the size of my couch!

I pulled the satchel charge from my back, attached the lead wires, and tossed it down the tunnel toward the beast.

Mable shouted, "Harry, no! We're right under my house!"

I cursed, yanked the wires loose from my ten-cap, and then pulled my pistol, knowing I was screwed as the giant armadillo snuffled and squeaked up the tunnel in our direction. I doubted even my .44 Special would punch through that armored skull, so I took aim at one beady, black eye.

Dr. Lawrence dropped his flashlight and ran down the shaft with Mable. No doubt intending to protect her. I nudged the light with my foot until it shone down the tunnel again, revealing that the monster had stopped.

The head of a grub protruded from the wall, catching the armadillo's attention. In one quick move, it shoved its pointed snout into the wall, grunted a few times, and came out with the grub, which disappeared in a flurry of teeth and squirming white flesh. Then those shiny black eyes turned toward me again.

In the Pacific, I'd faced machine guns, picked up a live grenade, and even fought off three Japanese soldiers using a polo mallet, but I'd never been more scared than I was at that moment. Then, as I raised my gun again, I had an idea.

"Doc! Throw me your bag of grubs!" I glanced down the tunnel and could barely see them in the dim light. Mable stood in a perfect marksman stance with the M1 raised to her shoulder, ready to fire. The doctor peeked from behind her, holding the camera and staring at me.

"Throw me the damned grubs!"

Mable turned and grabbed the bag, then tossed it up the tunnel toward me, but it fell short and spilled the three grubs onto the floor.

I looked back and saw the monster was almost on me. Shoot or bait? I'd seen how vicious wounded animals could be, and shooting it in one eye sure as hell wouldn't kill this thing. I shoved my pistol back in the holster, darted ten feet up the tunnel, and snatched a grub.

When I turned around, the armadillo's massive head was right in front of me. I froze and saw my reflection in the dark, glittering eyes. The head tilted down a bit, looking at the grub squirming in my hands. Moving slowly, I tossed it on the floor between us. The monster snatched it and gobbled it down in one sickening slurp. Then the massive snout nuzzled my hand, just like Gus, my old German shepherd. I took a step back, picked up another grub, and repeated the process. My new friend followed and again gently bumped my arm holding the treat. I held it up in my palms and the monster snatched it.

I released a nervous laugh and took another step back. "Did ya see that, Mable?"

The beast, evidently having noticed the remaining grub on the tunnel floor behind me, squeaked loudly and lunged forward, its fat, armored body slammed me hard against the wall. The air was forced from my lungs and I was dragged along for a second before falling to the floor.

Then I heard Mable scream.

I struggled to my feet and jumped on the thing's armored butt as it passed. Maintaining a grip on the smooth shell proved difficult, but I crawled slowly up and forward until my back scraped against the dirt and pipes of the tunnel ceiling. I thought if I could put my pistol right against the back of its head . . .

Finally aware of my presence, the monster squealed and bucked, making me slide forward and almost off, but I grabbed an ear the size of Big Bubba Thompson's Stetson and held on. It stopped bucking and made a series of pitiful little whimpers each time I pulled the ear. Taking advantage of the pause, I swung my legs up around its fat neck and grabbed the other ear.

I found that with the gentlest of tugs on an ear, I could make the beast turn its head. Pulling on both of them made it back up. Mable started laughing, but she didn't lower her gun. The doctor was nowhere to be seen.

A flashlight came bobbing up the tunnel, and my deputy skidded to a stop next to Mable. He raised his service revolver in a shaking hand.

"Don't shoot it!" I yelled.

"Um . . . Boss? Elmer Marston called the station," he said, panting. "He and the family are staying near Watonga with his brother-in-law who doesn't have a phone, and he only now had a chance to call. He wants to know if you've caught the monster armadillo yet so he can come rebuild his house. I guess I can tell him yes?"

A week later Mable sat on the hood of my patrol car, trying to count the people in a line snaking across the county fairgrounds. The town council— with some prodding by Mable—decided to charge fifty cents for pictures with the giant armadillo and three bucks each to ride it. Elmer himself was driving the monster, while his two boys occasionally tossed it a grub. The town had originally planned to raise enough money to build Elmer a new house, but had long ago surpassed that needed amount. I hadn't seen Mable smile so much since she'd been named second-best mayor in Oklahoma two years before.

"Mable?"

"Hmmm . . . ?" she said, not looking away from the line.

"Uh, I was thinking that since you can't live in your house now. Because of the radiation. At least for awhile. I mean, my place is plenty big and . . ."

She turned toward me, chin resting on her fists, eyebrows raised and a wry smile on her lips. "Yes, Harry?"

"I mean, we couldn't just . . . we'd have to, well . . ."

My deputy's patrol car skidded to a stop right beside us, followed by Hank Boonton's flatbed truck, and I bit off a string of curses.

"Holy shit, Boss, come look at this!" he said and motioned me toward Hank's truck.

Roped down tight to the bed was an enormous slab of gooey honeycomb. Each hexagonal cell was the size of a basketball hoop.

"Jesus wept," I muttered.

"Oh my Lord," Mable said. "I bet they have huge stingers."

I turned to look at her. "What?"

"We could be the biggest honey producers in the country," she said.

"Oh no," I said. "This time, I'm calling the army."

"Not without my approval, Harry. I'm the mayor!" she said and poked me in the chest.

"And I work for the county, not you," I said, but she had already turned her attention back to the honeycomb, and when she crossed her arms and started tapping her foot, I knew I was in trouble.

THAT OTHER SEA

From his position on the sandy slope, Catat couldn't see the Visitor, but the eerie glow moving around beyond the jumbled rocks proved the device had survived its fall into the killing depths. Catat whipped his tail to move downward, but couldn't generate enough thrust to overcome the water pressure pushing him into the sand. Only the brute force of side-to-side undulation gave him any forward momentum. He moved two body lengths and stopped to let his shell adjust.

As water weight compressed his internal organs further, the gland that produced his? shellbase went into hyperactive mode, flooding his system, filling the tiny pressure cracks and thickening his ring segments. The depths were changing him, maybe forever, but Catat believed retrieving the Visitor, or at least examining it, was worth the risk.

During the intense discussions that followed the Visitor's arrival, Catat was the only one who believed it could be artificial. Others, including Catat's main scientific rival, Racknik, maintained that it had to be some radiation mutated animal from an ice vent. But Catat had been the only one to see it up close. He'd watched the Visitor break through the ice ceiling and then struggle with the canopy kelp before starting its long swirling descent to the chasm floor.

The Visitor was twice Catat's size and he probably could have done nothing to arrest its fall, but he'd also been frozen with terror and made no attempt to help. Then as it started downward, lights appeared. Not the dim luminescent bait offered by predator fish, but a brilliant, painful glare, brighter than white magma. At that instant, Catat's fear dissolved in an overwhelming surge of curiosity and fascination. So now he was going after it.

A message from his warren came down the cable he dragged behind him, the electrical pulses converted to taps he could feel through the metal plate mounted between his tool arms and just above his digging arms. The signal was still strong, which worried him. If his shell had thickened enough to protect him against the extreme pressure, then the signal should have been faint.

"Can you still see it?" A prefix identified the sender as one of his research assistants.

"I see the glow from its lights," Catat replied.

"You made your point. We believe you. Now come back up." There had been no prefix to identify the second message's sender, but Catat knew it had to be his friend and sometimes mate, Tipkurr.

"I'm not trying to prove anything," Catat replied. "I saw this Visitor up close and I know it's a machine. Do you realize the implications of a machine from beyond the ice ceiling? Some elders don't believe there is anything above the ice. This not only proves it, but gives a chance to learn what may be out there."

"It's too deep," she tapped. "Racknik is on his way down. He's larger and stronger. Let him try the descent."

The idea of Racknik retrieving the Visitor—or worse yet, returning without it and claiming he'd been correct about it being a mutated animal—was so unpleasant that Catat felt bile swirling in his glands, ready to be sprayed. He tried turning his eyes back to look for Racknik, but they were pressed too deep into their sockets. Even the effort caused him to nearly roll up from the pain.

"Others have gone deeper," Catat sent. Tapping with his digging claws was becoming more and more difficult as the shell thickened around the joints, but he had to keep communicating lest they think he'd gone into stress-induced hibernation and pull him back.

"Guardian of the Deep is a hatchling myth," Tipkurr sent. "No one can survive at those depths. This will kill you."

Guardian stories had existed longer than recorded history. Twenty or thirty versions changed or added minor details, but the core story never changed. An explorer had gone too deep and been so mutated by the tremendous pressures that he couldn't come back up and still haunted the depths. The tale had always seemed ridiculous to Catat, but when each ring movement felt like stones grinding together and every effort to lift his tool arms or digging arms beyond a few degrees produced white-hot agony, the idea of never coming back up seemed much more plausible.

"I have to do this and I'm almost there," Catat said and then pushed downward another two body lengths.

He didn't blame the others for being skeptical. Had his measuring instruments not alerted Catat to the strange vibrations in the ice, he wouldn't have been present when the Visitor came through the ceiling. Still, he had been there and knew it was a machine. While some of its movements had indeed appeared biological, the water around it smelled all wrong, acrid and metallic, not organic. The ramifications amazed and frightened him, but he had to know and edged further down the slope.

During one of his pauses, Catat saw movement in his periphery and had to shift half of his forward segments to look back. If he'd waited an instant longer, he could have saved himself the effort. As Racknik slithered past, Catat was shocked and disgusted by his rival's deformed and dysfunctional carapace. It would take Racknik two or three seasons of wallowing in the sand pits to recover any semblance of normalcy. Then Catat realized he must look the same.

No wonder Tipkurr was so agitated. There would be no breeding this season, no explorative trips or even farming shifts. He might not even be able to feed himself without corrective surgery.

With a flip of his tapered wedge-like tail and a display of athletic prowess that allowed him to dominate every warren competition, Racknik sent sand swirling into Catat's face and moved past. Much too quickly.

Catat tapped a rapid message to his crew above. "Have Racknik's team tell him to slow down. He's not allowing enough time for his shell to thicken."

As the swirling sand cleared, Catat saw that his rival had stopped and curled into a defensive ball. An instant later, Catat felt and heard a sharp pop as Racknik ceased to exist. The imploded remains of Catat's clutchmate enveloped him in a cloud of silt and tissue.

Catat twitched and quivered. Tasting blood, shellbase, and bile in the water triggered an instinctual urge to flee, but he forced himself to stay put. Racknik had just descended too quickly. He didn't allow time for his shell to properly thicken and harden. Catat would not make that mistake.

As the water cleared and the chemicals that had been Racknik dissipated, Catat could see the rocks hiding the visitor only ten body lengths away. Light still moved on the other side. As curiosity once again outweighed doubt and fear, he informed the warren team of Racknik's death and moved forward. An assistant acknowledged his report, but it wasn't Tipkurr.

He rounded the rocks and had his first view of the Visitor since that earlier chaotic glimpse, but before he got a clear look, the articulated stalk turned the brilliant light right at him. He irised his eyes down to a tiny point and even then had to divert them. The light followed his every move as he struggled closer, until he approached within about three body lengths, and the lights went out. He stopped, suddenly afraid the visitor had died like Racknik, but there had been no violent implosion, only an abrupt absence of light.

He gradually opened his eyes and—without the blinding glare—could finally see the thing clearly. The Visitor was a cylinder, about twice his length, and nearly three times his normal diameter. It had no body segment rings, but the part Catat considered the head was a section slightly larger in diameter and made of triangular, blade-covered wedges.

A lot had happened in that first moment after the Visitor had broken through the ice and kelp field, but Catat was certain those wedges had then formed a spinning cone. Between the wedge sections, Catat could see the section's hollow interior was filled with a complex collection of spindly protrusions, blinking lights, and glittering unfathomable shapes. As he moved to get a better view of the thing's face or head, he noticed that even though the bright lights remained off, the eyestalks still followed his movements. It was unsettling, but at least confirmed the Visitor wasn't dead.

Catat relayed what he was seeing to his associates in the warren and turned his attention back to the face. Those tiny blinking lights fascinated him. Though brighter and more intense, they reminded Catat of flashes produced by spiny puffers during their mating season. The little animals were a primary food source for the warren's hatchlings, causing an instinctual chase response and providing endless entertainment in the nurseries. Catat wondered if his insistent pursuit of this device was driven not only by curiosity, but at least in part by an ancient need to chase lights.

It didn't matter. He moved closer and tapped on its hard shell. He tried several messages and greetings, but even though the dark eyestalks still followed his movements, there was no response.

He reported to the warren, and this time Tipkurr immediately replied. "Come back now. You've seen enough. Just hold the cable and we'll pull you up."

Catat stared at the Visitor for another moment. If he left it here on the seabed, generations could pass before someone devised a way to retrieve it, and the springs, or whatever mechanism powered its systems, might run down before then. If it was some kind of ambassador, they could forever lose the opportunity to contact beings from beyond the ice. He had to take it back.

"No. I came down here to retrieve it, not just look."

He gently rolled onto his back and fought through fiery pain when he tried to remove the cable. Each tug felt as if his arms were being torn from his body, but no matter how hard he pulled, he couldn't dismount the cable from its harness. His carapace had thickened over the harness, cable clip, and tap plate. Only surgery or a long thinning process would free him. That explained why he could still feel communications so clearly.

He wondered if Racknik had anticipated the cable problem and devised a better attachment. Then Catat stopped abruptly and turned to look back up the slope. He remembered passing Racknik's cable lying amid the collapsed shell.

He crept slowly up the slope and found the cable, still encased in a thick piece of shell. Evidently, Racknik had made the same mistake. Catat fought his distaste, picked up the loose end, and, using a pair of rocks, slowly and painfully broke the shell away. Then he pulled it down to the patient Visitor.

While struggling to loop the cable through the sturdy ring that mounted the Visitor's cutting wedges, Catat saw the true foolishness behind the Guardian myths. His constant pain and limited mobility made even that simple task quite difficult. He was exhausted to the point of collapse, but knew that if he stopped to rest, he'd drop immediately into hibernation. If that happened, his warren associates would eventually pull him back up. The Guardian would have never had such help.

When he moved clear—preparing to tell those in the warren to pull it up —he realized the large rock cluster that hid the Visitor from view during his descent also blocked the path up the slope. He examined the situation from several angles and felt even more exhausted. They couldn't pull it over the rocks, and the only way they could go around was if he were able to move the Visitor some lateral distance past the rocks to provide a clear pull path. He needed sleep and didn't know if he could, but stopping would make it all a wasted effort.

After looking around, he found a large stone jutting from the seafloor to use as a pivot, but since he couldn't swim to lift the cable over the rocks, he was forced to detach and reattach it. The arrangement worked, and by coordinating with the warren above, Catat was able to position the Visitor for retrieval. Throughout the entire long and complicated process, the Visitor's eyestalks watched Catat's every action.

When the cable pulled taut, and the Visitor finally started up the slope, Catat almost gave in to the looming coma. He knew his associates would pull him up, but as he neared that enticing oblivion, a new thought hatched in his mind, and like most hatchlings, it was ravenous. The Visitor had given them a gift, and Catat was probably the only one who could use it. But he had to stay awake. If he succumbed to coma, they would lose the opportunity.

Though large and strange, the visitor seemed much less menacing in the familiar environs of the warren. Catat stroked its metal shell as he moved slowly down the length, still trailing his communication cable behind him. The ten other researchers in the chamber, including four who had come from the fabrication aggregate in Tu-tunk Warren, deferred to him and gave him space.

The reduced water pressure made movement a bit easier, but didn't ease the burning agony accompanying every action. But he used the pain and his still voracious curiosity to help him focus. Only constant and deliberate force of will held the coma at bay.

The Visitor's articulated eyestalks seemed to have differentiated between him and the others in the chamber and still followed him intently, but had not used the blinding lights again.

As Catat examined the kelp-tangled mechanism at the visitor's rear, the head of his warren's research unit arrived carrying a tap rod to help get his words through Catat's thick shell and started tapping rapidly.

"Even though the kelp hid it well, we found the hole you described. We also have permission from the Monarchy Council to proceed with your plan. Are you sure you still want to do this?"

The news excited and terrified Catat, but he replied immediately. "Yes. Let's do it."

"We have to hurry. The hole has already started to close. Along the length we've been able to measure; the hole has already lost ten to twenty percent of its diameter. It could be worse further up the length." He paused for a moment, as if to tap something else, but darted away when Tipkurr drifted up to them.

She moved closer, lying against Catat, but his shell was too thick to allow segment nesting or even to feel her warmth. After a moment, she turned enough to lay her own rod against a thinner part of his facial carapace and tapped hard.

"Why aren't you asleep? This coma isn't something you can avoid, and the longer you fight it, the longer you'll sleep."

Catat turned to face her and moved closer to reduce the effort required to tap his reply. "You know I'll never be completely restored. My arms are nearly useless and will not get much better, even with surgery."

"It's not like you have many options."

Tipkurr understood him. She shared his drive to learn and to know. She'd accompanied him on many exploratory expeditions, yet even if she comprehended his next statement, she'd never agree with it.

"I need this thick shell," Catat said. "The warren has approved a plan to let me ascend the ice hole cut by the Visitor before it freezes closed."

Tipkurr quivered, then tapped him hard. "You know what happens to ice vents. Tidal water is forced through them under terrible pressure. If there even is another side that you can reach, you won't be able to get back against that flow."

"Maybe." He hesitated, then tapped more. "We don't really know for sure because no one has been there before. We have no idea what's on the other side of the ice barrier."

Her tapping grew harder and more intense. "Then let someone else do it. You need to be healing."

"I may be the only one who can survive it. What if there are big and even more rapid pressure differences, like in killing depths? My shell is already adjusted."

Catat's actions had already hurt Tipkurr, but she was stubborn and loyal. She would never abandon him and that meant his new deformity would be a major hardship for her. Catat couldn't allow that. He also couldn't pass up the opportunity to see what was beyond the ice and maybe report it back.

"We have very little time before the next tidal event," Catat said. "I have to go before the hole disappears."

Tipkurr dropped her tapping tool and with one powerful flip of her tail disappeared down the main tunnel.

By the time two assistants towed Catat up to the Visitor's hole, the fabricators had built Catat a bladder from clear, flexible kelp-tuber silk. It was roughly two-thirds the size of the Visitor, and had Catat been normal size, it would have been roomy enough, but in his current state, it felt more cramped than a hatchling's first tunnel.

His original idea had been to just let his thickened shell protect him, but the warren's exploration experts had insisted on the bladder filled with hot water. They claimed it would serve as protection from the abrasive ice and provide some temperature buffer. No one understood what natural forces created the ice barrier, but it only made sense that whatever was on the other side would be cold enough to freeze water. Freezing Catat through his thickened and nearly fused shell seemed unlikely, but the hot water was a sensible enough precaution.

They'd also reinforced the cable attached to his shell, fastening it to him with bands and rivets. They told him the strengthened mount would allow them to pull him back, even against the gush of rising water. Catat suspected that was impossible, but if the falsehood made their task easier, then he could pretend as well.

Workers had fenced off the area around the hole to keep the canopy kelp away. The Visitor had bored its hole through a thin part of the ice, an old fissure zone, where a mysterious dim light filtered through from the other side. Of course, brighter areas are where the kelp grew thickest and keeping it at bay was difficult.

The tide grew stronger and stronger around them. Those operating the cable equipment and the few who came to see him off struggled against the strong currents as water swirled upward toward the hole.

He told them he was ready. They eased him closer to the hole, and the cable brakes were released. He thought he saw Tipkurr approaching just before the vortex caught his bladder and sucked him in.

He bounced along the tube walls in a blurring rush as the water roared around him. Strange sensations churned inside him as pressures changed and viscera shifted around, but he was moving so fast, he knew it would be over soon.

Then the bladder snagged on something and came to an abrupt halt. He twisted around and could see he was hooked on a thick metal rod protruding from the tunnel wall. He noticed a tiny light flashing on the rod's tip just as the bladder material rolled past and he continued his frightening ascent. Three more of the light-tipped rods briefly halted his progress, but the fourth one held him fast against the rushing water.

He could see the bladder stretching as surging water slammed him again and again against the tube wall. He struggled to turn enough to pull the material free, but just as he managed to face the snag, a small hole opened in the bladder and it pulled free. Once more, the water pushed him higher until the roar changed to a hiss, then abruptly faded to silence.

Catat didn't know what he'd expected, but the reality baffled him. He'd left the tunnel, yet continued to rise, slower and in a broad arc over a wide, bright plain. It was painful to look at for very long, so he focused on the water jet below and behind him, shooting into an oddly black sea. The water floating around him had fractured into tiny crystals. He realized they were ice particles, but couldn't understand why they didn't dissolve into the strange black water. He also felt suddenly cold.

He pulled his arms to the cable's tap pad and began listing out what he could see, hoping this alien environment would still allow the electrical signals to travel down the cable.

Below him, at the point where the bladder had torn, a stream of tiny ice particles wheezed outward in a glittering spray, and the wide, bright plane seemed to look more and more like the surface of a huge sphere.

He continued tapping, but the once warm water had grown frigid. A layer of ice formed on the inside of his bladder and grew thicker as he watched. All the water in his little cocoon was freezing.

He didn't have much time, so as he struggled to turn around and see above him, he tapped rapidly, trying to tell those below as much as he could. Once he turned his eyes upward, he stopped tapping. A huge disk floated out there in the black, like a round bubble filled with swirling waters, some dark, some bright, and all around it were tiny brilliant lights.

"We live inside . . . an ice bubble," he tapped just as forming crystals blocked his last small viewing hole. "And it floats in a large, bright sea that is . . . even colder than ice."

"We're pulling you back."

The tapping felt distant, and even though the cable yanked him repeatedly against the bottom of the bladder, there was no pain.

As the water froze all around him, Catat knew they would never retrieve him. He had the amusing thought of spawning a new legend. Perhaps they would call him the Guardian of the Beyond. More sluggish and dim messages came from the warren far below, but he ignored them. He'd given his kind a tantalizing glimpse into the strangeness beyond the ice and he knew they would eventually send others. That was enough.

He could barely move his arms, but he struggled and twisted until he was close enough to scrape a clear place on the bladder. He had to see. Outside, tiny brilliant lights drifted slowly past his little clear patch. His fat and nearly frozen tail twitched repeatedly in one final effort to chase the lights.

THE PIPER'S DUE

The boy was hot and tired, yet still his dark eyes waged war to stay open. He stared at me, draped over his mother's shoulder with his black curls plastered to a damp brow and eyes drooping in time with the rise and fall of the French horn.

Anemic applause pattered through the park when the piece ended, and someone came to the mic and announced the next piece. Even a small breeze would have helped, but Pearl blazed down with full summer intensity. It was smaller and whiter than Sol, with a light that washed out most colors, leaving stark shadows and giving everything a slight photonegative effect. The generation ship builders had matched the spin gravity to that of the new world, but the light had remained analogous to Earth. Most of those around me had been born on Margarita, so didn't even notice, but I'd never get used to it.

The next song started, and I shifted in my folding chair to take the pressure off my right leg. Both legs hurt constantly, but the right one was growing steadily worse. A few heads turned my way, then quickly whipped back to the band and the music, either unable or unwilling to stare at me for longer than a glance. Only the barely conscious boy continued to watch as I wrested the sweat-darkened composite brace caging my culprit leg into a better position.

Another song, another round of half-hearted clapping to celebrate Landing Day. I wondered how many of the colonists around me actually cared about the music and how many had just come out of a sense of civic support. I suspected mostly the latter.

A final song, one last flourish by the conductor, and everyone began to pack. Normally I'd leave a song early to avoid seeing the people edge around me as if I were surrounded by an invisible bubble, but today I'd been lulled by the music.

The crowd around me slowly thinned to a trickle, wiping sweat from their brows and looking in every direction but mine. Only the young mother with the sleep-fighting boy on her shoulder remained. She paused just outside my invisible bubble. Her hair and eyes were dark, just like her boy's.

"If you had known," she asked, her voice a whisper as she shifted the boy's weight higher, "would you have acted differently? Would you still have saved us?"

I'd been asked the question before but always refused to answer.

Our advance survey team had been surprised by the ferocious attack. We had been on the surface for an entire three days before the little crab-like monsters came frothing out of the ground in waves. One by one, we fell. Butchered. Shredded. Pulped. Only I managed to fight my way back to the lander.

From my seat on the flight deck—while the robot medic struggled to save my legs—I looked out over a vast sea of slate-colored carapaces. Billions of them, as far as I could see, churning and frothing, breaking against the lander hull like a grinding tide. Above me, on a long elliptical orbit, flew the colony ship, four thousand people crammed into the lone module still capable of supporting life. The ship had been repaired, rebuilt, cannibalized, and reengineered for nearly two hundred years. It wouldn't last another.

I was just a biologist, but only the best were sent on the advance survey, so I was well armed for this kind of warfare.

Nine days later, the crabs were all dead.

And five years after that, we found their first underground city.

I blinked, washing away the memory. In the silence, the woman's eyes had drifted up toward mine, waiting for an answer.

"Yes," I said. "I still would have done it."

Her expression tightened.

I knew what was coming. I'd suffered numerous verbal lashings over the years from those who felt it their duty to explain to me what a terrible thing I'd done and, by extension, the depths of my depravity.

But instead of a self-righteous tirade, she came forward and brushed my arm with her fingertips as she passed. "It was a horrible decision you were forced to make."

Before I could react, she walked away, joining the other colonists in the daily tasks needed to make Margarita our home. I noted that her boy had finally surrendered to sleep.

It had been a valiant fight.

MEDIC!

Sam gripped the cargo locks on the floor as tight as he could, but still swayed back and forth each time the Osprey zigged or zagged along its radar-avoiding slalom course. A frustrated Ernie Ochoa tried to mount a defensive pod on one of Sam's three attachment points.

"Hold still, Sam. This is hard enough without you doing the hula."

Sam tried to cinch himself tighter.

The plane jerked again, and one of the troopers in the back vomited. Dozens of lasers felt out the terrain, keeping the blind aircraft from clipping trees, power lines and radio towers as it flew under radar. The computer-controlled plane did its job well, but the flight equations cared little about passenger comfort or last minute additions to robots like Sam.

"You scare me, Ochoa," Clef yelled from the other side of the plane. "You talk to that damned thing like it's your bedroom, buddy."

Several people snickered as Ochoa made the connection and locked the defensive pod into place.

Sam started diagnostics. Servos whirred as he cycled through launchers for taser darts, fire-pellets, tear gas canisters, and wire netting. Then he armed the targeting system and observed as the pod's sensors locked onto and identified every movement in the cabin.

Ochoa grinned. "Hey, Sam! Do you think Clef is jealous of your equipment?"

A direct question. Sam searched for Clef and found a tag attached to Clifford Harmon's data. The squad called him Clef because he played classical violin. Sam searched his response tree.

"He probably has good reason," Sikes said from her seat next to Ochoa. "I doubt that his equipment measures up to Sam's."

Everyone close enough to hear the exchange laughed.

Sam adjusted the weighting of his responses.

"Well, my dear, you sure didn't complain the last time you invited me in for some mattress poundin'," Clef said with a grin.

Whoops and whistles filled the dark cabin.

"Your right arm was the only thing poundin'," she said amid more laughter.

Sam flagged Clef as being Harmon's preferred name, then scanned the soldier's weapons and gear. All standard combat issue. After searching the tree of possible responses again, Sam selected the best one. He knew the answer would be irrelevant, but he had to respond because Ochoa had directly addressed him.

"I have an automated defensive pod," Sam said. "Clef could have the same equipment, but would have to carry a separate battery pack."

"What is this shit?" Clef said. "I wish you wouldn't let that thing talk, Ochoa. It creeps me out. And don't call me Clef, you tin can, only soldiers can call me Clef!"

Sam changed Harmon's tag again. He kept the Clef tag but would only address him as Harmon. He then locked into the comm-net and cycled through the soldiers' bio-monitors. Other than elevated pre-battle stress levels and some nausea, all the troopers reported normal.

"You'll see," Ochoa said. "Sam has some slick moves. He can do a lot that I can't."

"Well, if I get hit, just send me to the field hospital," Clef said with a snort. "I don't want a mechanical crab poking around inside me."

Lieutenant Wei came back from the cockpit and rapped the floor with his rifle butt. "Listen up troopers! We've just crossed the border and have about three minutes. Armor and equipment checks. Remember, this is a politically sensitive mission, nonlethal rounds only."

After the lieutenant went forward again, Clef slammed the bench with a clenched fist. "This is a bunch of shit! Nonlethal rounds? Who the hell are these turds anyway?"

Ochoa shrugged.

The red lights flashed, the lieutenant returned and the rear ramp started to open slowly.

"This is it, people! The whole place has been dusted with fire-pellets, so if we're real lucky, there'll be very little resistance. Let's make it quick, get in, grab that hostage and get out."

Before the ramp even touched ground, troopers began leaping out into the ankle-deep snow. Sam set his defensive pod to auto-response and followed Ochoa as weapons fire started sizzling against the Osprey's slough armor.

"'Little resistance,' my ass!" Ochoa said and darted for cover as the Osprey poured on full power and raced out of range.

Sam's night vision filters revealed incapacitated defenders writhing on the ground all around them. The fire-pellets, delivered by drone only minutes before, had burrowed through clothing, then initiated hundreds of electric nerve stimulations that made human skin feel like it was on fire. The combatants would be unhurt once the pellets were deactivated, but until then, they wouldn't be a threat.

Sam scanned the walled compound and compared it to the mission map they had uploaded during prep. A central courtyard, a parade field, and fourteen single-story, stone and wood structures. It matched. Flashing icons appeared on his tactical display, one for each soldier of the twenty-member team. He also had two yellows for the surveillance drones and four green lights for the LAMEs (Lifter, Armored, Medical Evacuation) that were still deploying from two other Ospreys a mile away. In the center of one building, a red X flashed. It was the GPS locator implant in the missing envoy. She had been moved to a building on the north end of the compound, nearly 200 meters from their landing zone.

"Holy shit!" Clef yelled. "Take cover! They have ComBots!"

Sam scanned the squad's comm-net as his defensive pod searched for nearby threats. Armor-piercing rounds tore through the sides of buildings and tossed up clouds of dirt as three combat robots advanced, pinning the squad down in the south end of the compound.

"Shit! Aren't ComBots illegal?" Ochoa asked as he tried to burrow into the frozen ground.

A direct question. Sam scanned his general information database and formed a response. "Terrorist organizations are seldom signatories on international treaties."

The corner of a nearby building disintegrated in a cloud of stone and mortar. Clef's bio-monitor alerted Sam to an injury. Three leg wounds.

"Harmon's hit," Sam sent to Ochoa and the lieutenant, then darted across the ten meters of broken glass and swirling dust to reach the wounded soldier.

"Where are you hit, Harmon?" Sam already knew, but talking to the troopers sometimes helped calm them. His readings showed that three small bullet fragments had pierced Clef's leg and were already engaged by active medical nanos. The inner uniform layer contained a fluid that not only helped to maintain a constant body temperature, but also carried millions of medical repair nanos that automatically looked for blood loss if the layer was punctured.

"My leg. Damn!"

Sam scanned the feed from the microscopic robots in Clef's wounds. They had already stopped the bleeding and were knitting protective sleeves around the intrusive metal shards. It would keep them from doing further damage until they could be removed.

Another hail of bullets crumbled more wall onto them. Sam grabbed the loading eyelet on the back of the wounded man's armor and dragged him across the hard-packed snow into a narrow alley.

The young man gritted his teeth and grunted in pain. "Leave me alone, you stupid fuck! MEDIC!"

Sam determined that Clef wasn't in any immediate danger and sent that information to Ochoa. He grabbed Clef's leg and tried to seal the wounds, but each time his glue nozzle neared the holes, the man shoved it away.

Through the comm-net, Lieutenant Wei ordered everyone in the harried squad to stay under cover until the Ospreys were able to target the ComBots for a hot plasma strike.

"Medic!" Clef yelled again.

Sam tried to close the wounds one more time, but to no avail. "Harmon, your wounds aren't serious, and the lieutenant ordered us to stay under cover."

"Screw off, you damn machine! How do you know they aren't serious? Shut up! I want a medic!"

"Clef, evac's on the way," Ochoa said over the comm-net. "I'm coming up."

Sam's defensive pod sent a warning as one of the ComBots stepped into the opposite end of the alley about twenty meters away and started firing. Sam crawled over a writhing, fire-pellet-infested defender to shield Clef with his rear armor. He then called to Ochoa over the comm-net. "Go back!"

It was too late. A half second later, the medic entered their end of the alley at a full run. Ochoa's monitor sent an alarm, and Sam turned in time to see the man fall to his knees. He grabbed at a ragged hole in his upper left chest armor then fell face first into the snow.

"Shit, shit, oh shit!" Clef pounded his fist on the ground. "Ochoa!"

A level one alert from Ochoa's bio-monitor launched Sam into motion. He considered over four hundred actions in less than a microsecond, then grabbed the disabled rebel, found the implanted "friendly" transmitter, cut it out and sealed the incision. With the same glue, he attached the flea-sized transmitter to the exposed skin on Clef's wounded leg just before a round hit square on Sam's armor and pushed him a half meter down the filthy alley.

"What're you doin? What'd you put in me?" Clef demanded. "Christ, that hurts! And I got the medic shot! Damn, damn, damn!"

Sam ignored Clef as he scampered the rest of the way to Ochoa, whose vitals were already dropping. Clef was half-moaning, half-sobbing, "I'm sorry, Ernie! Jesus, I'm sorry!"

Sam had to stabilize Ochoa and stop the bleeding before moving him. He rolled Ochoa over, injected nanos into the wound, stuffed tissue fluff into the gurgling hole, and covered it with a compress.

Sam's defensive pod sent an alarm as it launched impotent taser rounds at the advancing ComBot. The spiderlike robot stopped with its heavy caliber guns pointing down, inches from Clef's chest, but seemed momentarily confused. Clef's vitals spiked on the bio-monitor and then he urinated. Then the ComBot swung its guns to the right and fired three rounds into the squirming rebel, before continuing its advance toward the downed medic.

Sam turned so that his rear armor protected Ochoa's head and torso, just before a volley of close-range shells slammed into him, flipped him over, and left him on his back two meters away from his patient.

His rollover routine tried again and again to flip his crab-like body upright, but the piston was damaged and wouldn't fully extend. He sent a general message that he needed help, but no one answered except Clef.

"Get up, Sam, keep trying!"

The ComBot straddled Ochoa but didn't shoot him. Targeting lasers from a nearby Osprey danced all around them, and the killer robot knew that a wounded man worked well as a shield. It instead fired at the hovering plane until it ducked out of sight behind a building.

Sam's tactical display indicated that part of the team had already surrounded the building containing the hostage, and he heard Lieutenant Wei stop the plasma strike.

Ochoa's status monitor showed that the nanos were working furiously on the bleeding, but they were losing ground. Sam had to act. He used the damaged piston to push him as far as possible, then turned his defensive pod toward the ground and fired a burst of taser rounds. The recoil tipped his center of gravity just enough. He flipped over and started toward Ochoa as the LAME dropped into the alley from above.

"Ernie!" Sikes yelled from down the alley behind Clef. "Hang on, Ernie. I'm coming!"

The ComBot turned its guns toward Sikes, but noticed Sam's sudden movement and whipped them back around. Sam leaped forward, underneath the guns, so that when they fired, the rounds merely grazed his rear armor. Taking advantage of his forward momentum, he shoved upward, extending to his full height. The robot was well made and didn't tip over, but it did stagger backward. Sam fired two wire net rounds—one at the ComBot's legs and one at the targeting sensors—in an effort to slow the thing down by tangling it up for a couple of seconds.

A scream and a thud announced Sikes' arrival. She hit the ComBot low, tipping it on its back, then using the tangled wire netting, strapped a concussion grenade under the armored carapace.

"Get down!" she yelled and dove for cover behind Sam.

Sam instructed the LAME, little more than a pair of armored canisters located between two ducted fans, to land between them and the ComBot. The grenade's detonation blew ComBot pieces into the air and spun the descending lifter like a falling leaf, but it still protected them.

Sam could hear Sikes cursing and checked her bio-monitor. She had several small abrasions and a torn ligament in her right elbow. He flagged her injuries as level three and returned to Ochoa.

The comm-net roared with screamed orders to other troopers and the

Ospreys. Sam instructed the battered LAME to land near Clef as two bright flashes announced the arrival of plasma shells that turned the other two ComBots into sagging composite heaps.

"Sikes! Help me move Ochoa," Sam said. They dragged the wounded man deeper into the alley next to Clef. Once under cover, Sam opened the chest armor, cut the shirt away and made a small incision on either side of the wound.

"What are you doing? Get him into a LAME!" Clef yelled. Clef's bio-monitor reported that his inner uniform layer absorbed the urine before it could contaminate his open wounds.

A direct question. "Ochoa needs immediate intervention or he will die before getting to a hospital," Sam said. He inserted the probes, found a hole in the lung and glued it closed.

Sikes gave Clef a withering look and turned back to her wounded comrade. "Sam saved your life, asshole, now put a sock in it," she said.

Ochoa woke up and began to moan. His hands and heels dug into the muddy snow.

"Sikes, I'm not done yet. Please hold him down," Sam said.

She dropped her rifle and tried to pin Ochoa's arms, but he was very strong, in pain, and easily broke free.

Clef dragged himself over, grabbed the flailing right arm and instructed Sikes to take the other. "Do your stuff, robot."

With each of them holding an arm and Sam's own weight on the man's waist, he was able to inject more nanos and apply a compress.

Ochoa gritted his teeth and stopped struggling long enough for Sam to pull the IV line from the LAME and attach it to his right arm. Status on the nanos showed that they were flooding the nerve centers near the wound with painkillers and as a confirmation, Ochoa relaxed and took a deep breath.

Sam hooked the recovery cable to the back of Ochoa's armor eyelet, winched him into the armored tube and sent instructions for Ochoa's care to the LAME. Only then did he check the nearby rebel soldier. He was already dead.

Lieutenant Wei darted around the corner followed by two troopers dragging a limp form. "Is Ochoa going to make it?"

A direct question. "Yes, sir," Sam said. "But he needs a hospital."

"Here's the hostage. She's been shot—at close range. Bastards. Do what you can."

Sam could see that she'd been hit once in the throat and once in the chest. He went to work immediately, injecting nanos to stop the blood flow and to report the damage, but he didn't wait for their input. He shoved a breathing tube down the ruined throat, started the oxygen flow, and attached a portable bio-monitor to her arm.

"Sikes, stay here and cover them," the lieutenant said, then moved to the end of the alley and began sending orders to secure the Osprey's landing site.

"What can I do?" Sikes said.

A direct question. "Cover us, like the lieutenant ordered. Harmon, I need the other IV line," Sam said.

The nano data began to trickle in, giving Sam a better picture of her condition. She'd lost too much blood. She was dying. He grabbed the IV line from Clef, but her heart stopped beating before he could attach it. With accelerated movements, Sam finished connecting the IV, opened her chest, and found damage to the subclavian artery. In less than a second, he had sealed the rupture with glue and fluff, then began resuscitation. He jammed electrodes into her chest.

"Clear!" he said. The electric jolts made the woman's body jerk. After the second try, her heart started beating.

The compound erupted with shouts and the sound of small arms fire.

"Let's go!" The lieutenant said over the comm-net. "The fire-pellets deactivated early, and these creeps are really pissed."

"Shit!" Clef and Sikes said simultaneously as an alarm sounded from Sam's defensive pod.

Two rebel soldiers fired at them from the other end of the alley, but their still jumpy muscles sent the rounds high. Sam tried to shield his patient from the spray of plaster, brick and glass that showered down from above. He added tissue fluff and a compress to the open wound, then attached the recovery line to the woman with a sling and helped the winch ease her into the LAME. The nanos reported that she was starting to stabilize.

As soon as the hatches sealed over the hostage and Ochoa, he sent the emergency return order. The lifter went to full power, covering everyone with billowing snow as it disappeared into the night sky.

Per standard procedure, Sam called for another LAME and then started checking the bio-monitors of the remaining troopers. His defensive pod again sounded a warning, and Sam saw a grenade sliding down the snow-packed alley, but Sikes and Clef were looking the other way. Sam grabbed each of them by a leg, yanked them down and turned his rear armor toward the grenade. It exploded about two meters from him.

When the snow and steam cleared, Sam couldn't move.

He could see and even had network contact to the rest of the squad, but he couldn't move. He sent a status message to Lieutenant Wei, and then scanned the soldier's bio-monitors again. Sikes had sustained minor wounds to her mouth and nose when her face hit the ground. Clef had broken two fingers.

Sam tried to get up but couldn't.

"Sikes!" Sam yelled. "You have nano bulbs and a compress in your first aid kit. Get someone to help you."

Small arms fire raked the walls as two Ospreys arrived and hovered overhead, creating an icy windstorm that drowned out the lieutenant's barked orders. Sam switched to the command channel on comm-net.

"Mount up! Let's get out of here!" the lieutenant yelled as rope ladders dropped from the planes.

Sam watched as the squad scrambled one by one up the swinging ladders beneath an umbrella of cover fire from the planes. He ran diagnostics on his self-destruct mechanism, determined it was in working order and triggered the seven-minute timer.

Clef grabbed Sam with his good hand and dragged him over to the ladder.

"C'mon, Clef!" Sikes yelled.

"This sucker's heavy. I can't lift him with this bum hand. Help me get him hooked to the ladder," Clef said.

"He's a robot, Clef!" she said, but slung her rifle and helped anyway.

"I have activated my self-destruct mechanism in order to prevent the capture of sensitive technology. Please stand clear," Sam said.

"No way, tin can," Clef said. "You saved my ass twice. You're comin' with us."

Sam aborted the self-destruct routine.

"You should get off that leg, Harmon," Sam said, but Clef was gone, and he was being lifted above the dust into a waiting Osprey.

Five minutes later, they were weaving their way through the mountains toward the coast along a new course. They strapped Sam to the floor next to Clef's wounded leg. He checked each monitor, noted that the nanos in the hostage, Ochoa and Clef were working well.

"Hey Sam! You still with us?" asked Sikes. She was behind him somewhere and he couldn't see her.

"Yes. How is your mouth?" Sam said. "Doesn't it hurt too much to talk?"

"No, it's fine now, Sam," she said. "Just a fat lip."

"Yeah," Clef said. "We thought it would shut her up too, Sam. But never underestimate a woman's yakking ability."

No one laughed.

"You saved my ass back there, Sam," Sikes said. "Too bad I can't buy you a drink when we get back."

"Careful, Sam," Clef said. "She's trying to pick you up. Musta been all that talk about your equipment earlier."

Sikes ignored Clef.

Sam couldn't identify a direct question, but since his equipment was mentioned, his response tree settled on a simple status report. "My equipment is damaged."

This time the soldiers laughed.

"Sam?" Sikes said. "How's Ernie? Do you still have a link to his bio-monitor?"

A direct question. "Yes. Ochoa is stabilized," Sam said, then scanned his response options and added. "He's going to be okay."

The soldiers grew quiet. Sam could hear one snoring and thought he heard Sikes sniffling. He wondered if her nose might be bleeding because of the grenade and checked her monitor.

Clef patted Sam's pitted and broken armor casing. "I owe you too, Sam. You're the best momma a soldier ever had. Oh, and Sam, from now on, you can call me Clef."

Sam changed the tag on Harmon's file. After scanning possible responses, he didn't know what to say, so he kept quiet.

SQUARE ONE

Umma clutched her husband's hand as the Cochran bucked and rattled into the ionization stage of descent. She wondered if he could feel her worry through the insulated gloves, but he squeezed back and turned just enough so that she could see his wide grin and exaggerated wink through the helmet visor. He mouthed something. Only the flight crew had inter-suit communications during this phase, but she knew what he said and had to smile.

"We were born for this!"

The phrase annoyed the hell out of her, and he'd said it thousands of times during their twenty-one-year trip. Ian and Umma had both left Earth at sixteen and met on the flight, but for their daughter Rachel, who had been born en route, the words were true. Still, he was right to be excited. Umma took a deep breath, turned so she couldn't see the fire beyond the viewports and tried to ignore her feeling of impending doom.

She'd just started to relax when her pressure suit tightened abruptly, her visor fogged and she felt a distinct change in the vibration resonance. Even through the quivering condensation, she could see flashing red lights and frantic activity on the flight dais. She clenched Ian's fingers tight and started to hyperventilate.

From his docking cup atop Umma's helmet, Goober, her softball-sized personal AI, read the spikes in her vitals and tried to calm her.

"We're going to be fine, Umma. Some of the seals failed, and we're losing cabin pressure, but the heat shields are still protecting us. This is why you wear pressure suits during descent and launch. Now slow your breathing and let your gasses balance or you'll black out."

Umma thought about Rachel and Ian and the home they planned to build on their new world. It helped—some—and her breathing slowed. As she regained control, the descent smoothed out, and the fire beyond the viewports faded. Ian squeezed her hand and smiled through his visor again.

"We can talk now, darlin'. Are you okay?"

"I'll be fine once we're safe on solid ground."

"Awwww, don't be too hard on Cochran. Considering she's been nothing more than a frozen zit on Sinacola's butt for twenty-eight years, I think she's performed admirably."

Umma laughed. "Well, we're not down yet."

The Cochran had been tested extensively before she'd left the main ship, but equipment failures had increasingly plagued the Sinacola during the past ten years of their trip, so they expected the worst. And the little survey ship had to work, because the Sinacola, with its three thousand colonists, needed a two-stage braking assist—a close pass by the elliptically orbiting gas giant named LongFellow and then the star itself—before she would slow enough to enter orbit around Epsilon Eridani Two. The Cochran and her twelve-person crew were committed the instant they left the main ship two weeks earlier. They would be isolated until Sinacola returned four months later.

As the Cochran slowed and neared the selected landing site, Scooby, Ian's AI, produced a monitor pane so they could see their new home. Vast rolling prairies, punctuated by occasional lakes or small forests, extended in every direction. Huge herds—some spanning twenty or thirty kilometers—grazed on the grassy terrain. This is how the American plains must have looked before Europeans arrived, Umma thought.

The flight commander started a reverse countdown that ended in a gentle thump when they touched down. Umma immediately felt the higher gravity. The spin on Sinacola had been gradually increased to 119 percent of Earth normal, to acclimate the colonists, but she had just spent two weeks in micro-gravity and felt suddenly made of lead.

A cheer erupted. The Cochran was not designed to fly back to orbit, so this was now home. The crew had planned to stay inside the ship and do nothing but atmospheric and soil tests on the first day, but Ian immediately made a case to take the two-man sled outside and start their work. As the colony's chief xenobiologist, his arguments carried weight. He dragged Commander Darroch to the still-open monitor pane and pointed to the huge herd approaching their landing site.

"We've analyzed atmosphere samples returned by the probes for years. We're not going to find anything new, and we know we can breathe it. What we don't know enough about is these animals that will soon be all around us. Besides, we're not leaving, so we might as well get started figuring out how to live here."

The Commander grinned and crossed his arms. "We already discussed this, Ian. We have a timeline and need to stick to it. We need to do contamination studies. And we still don't know why those rovers shut down."

"Why? We've already vented to the atmosphere during descent, and the chances of any local bacteria being able to hurt us are infinitesimal. Besides, that argument was made and lost forty years ago, when humanity decided to send colonists to Donnie Two instead of more study probes. We couldn't abort when the rovers died, and we can't abort now. Where else can we go?"

Commander Darroch looked at the animals on the monitor for a couple of seconds and then shrugged. "Fine. You're the biologists. Knock yourselves out, but at least wear sealed field suits."

Their open two-person flier lifted away from the Cochran, and the equipment airlock sealed behind them just as the herd arrived. The natives were not in the slightest bit afraid of the invading spacecraft and immediately surrounded it. The large herd animals looked like elephant-sized caterpillars. They were all covered by a seething second skin of little hooked frog-like animals that immediately started leaping from their hosts to land on the Cochran.

Rachel had been the first to see the returned probe video and had dubbed them "frogvarks." The fist-sized animals had jumping legs like those of a frog and a stiff, tapered proboscis resembling an aardvark's. It'd been funny then, but they gave Umma chills now.

Within seconds, they had covered the Cochran in such numbers that her features were rendered blurry and indistinct.

"Astounding," Ian said with childlike wonder. "I wish Rachel could see this."

The comment stung Umma, but shouldn't have. She knew Ian didn't mean he would have preferred Rachel's company to hers, yet she and Rachel had argued bitterly about that very subject before the survey team had departed the Sinacola. Rachel had always worshiped her father and wanted to be with him when he saw their new world for the first time, but the team could only take two biologists. Umma had refused to give up her place next to Ian and it had infuriated Rachel.

"Look at that," Ian said. "With them swarming strange objects like that, I can see why our ground rovers all died minutes after touching down. Let's get a little closer, but stay out of frogvark jumping range."

Before Umma could act, ten or twelve of the largest herd animals raised up, lifting perhaps two-thirds of their lengths into the air, and hundreds of frogvarks launched toward them like invaders from siege towers. They hit Umma ten or twelve at a time, shotgun blasts of hooked horrors that adhered to everything. Their claws sank into her neck, back, and arms, not actually puncturing the field suit's rubbery fabric but pinching the skin beneath like sharp, miniature vises.

She batted and pounded at the little gray beasts, but forcefully pulling them off was the only effective strategy. Her suit integrity held, but alarms sounded as skin sealant and painkillers were pumped through the damaged inner layers. She looked back at Ian, in the flier's passenger seat, hoping for help, but he was fighting them too.

"Goober, help me!"

The little AI darted around the flier, burning the aliens with microwave emitters normally used for communication. His power indicator flickered red after every concentrated burst, but he didn't slow down. Each dislodged attacker left behind a moving white powder. Lice. They hadn't been able to see more than moving white dots from the aerial probes, but Ian had dubbed them frogvark lice, even though they seemed to infest every living thing on the planet.

Ian slapped her shoulder. "Go up," he said through the commlink. "Get us out of their range!"

Another volley landed and latched onto Umma, but she gritted her teeth, fought the pain and tried to focus. With a tug on the control yoke, the flier leapt upward. A quick slap engaged the hover lock, and with a squeal of pain, Umma yanked a jumper from her neck, crushed it to pulp and flung it groundward.

One by one, Umma pulled the aliens off. The remnant lice raced up and down her limbs, stopping and abruptly changing direction, testing every seam and seal as if looking for a way to leak in. She called to Ian but received only grunts in answer.

When she glanced back, she saw why. He had slipped from his seat and was writhing on the flier's deck, all but buried in clinging aliens. Both AIs darted in and out, burning and bumping, until in a display of concerted effort, four frogvarks launched into the air, hit Scooby simultaneously and held on. The little AI burned one with microwave emitters, but it remained attached, and amid the high-pitched whine of useless lifting fans, Scooby dropped from sight.

Ian thrashed around, slapping at frogvarks and clawing at his helmet. His wide eyes darted around behind the visor. Umma had never seen him panic and that frightened her more than the attack. She initiated a link with his suit and the gas numbers told the story. He was suffocating. His helmet's air intake filters must be coated with the white lice, she realized.

"Damn it, Goober, help me," she screamed. "Clear Ian's filters! Hurry!"

Goober darted to the mesh panels on Ian's helmet and, using his emitters, turned the white swirls into ash that still clogged the intake screens.

She sent the order to change Ian's filter purge settings, but got an error.

"Goober! His suit won't let me change the purge settings!"

"It'll give you passive information, but only Ian or Scooby can change the parameters."

She reached back and grabbed Ian's leg. "—Listen to me! Your breather purge default is at fifty percent, you have to change it to ninety percent long enough to clear your filters! Ian! Change your purge!"

He clawed at the visor, and his face turned crimson. She could hear him gasping and choking, but he never gave the command. Instead, in a move so quick and unexpected that Umma couldn't stop him, Ian released his helmet seal. The visor popped open.

With a long, shuddering gasp, he became the first human to breathe the atmosphere on Epsilon Eridani Two. Before he could take a second breath, the organisms poured into his helmet like bathwater down a drain. They entered his mouth, slipped under his eyelids, and streamed up his nose like a pale, backward nosebleed. On his face, they burrowed into the skin, leaving a field of blood-welling pinpricks.

"Ian!" Umma scraped and swatted at them, trying to stem the tide, but only made it worse as new swarms poured down her gloves and onto his face.

"Call the Cochran, Goober! We have to get him inside."

"He's contaminated. We all are. They won't let us in."

Ian thrashed and cursed and clawed at his face.

"Just call them, dammit! Inform them of our situation and . . . and get help."

Ian's medical stats scrolled down the screen inside her visor, showing elevated heart rate, blood pressure and temperature. The suit had already given him the maximum painkiller load, but it had yet to kick in. He jerked and squirmed beneath her.

"Ian! Hold on, sweetie."

An alert sounded from his suit. He'd dropped into unconsciousness, but still thrashed from the pain.

Goober cut in. "Cochran doesn't respond. I'm continuing to ping on all standard channels."

Ian started jerking violently and slid over the side. His safety tether prevented him from falling to the ground, but he dangled precariously from the fan strut. The added weight on a single fan unbalanced the flier, tipping it nearly onto its side. Unstowed gear and dead frogvarks fell fifty feet into the churning herd below. If not for her own tether, Umma would have followed.

The flight computers tried to compensate for the imbalance and electric motors whined in protest as the starboard fans strained in vain to right the flier. The little craft went into a slow, descending spin.

Umma stretched but couldn't reach her husband. "Ian! Can you hear me? Give me your hand."

He didn't respond, but instead shook violently. The screen showed he was experiencing a grand mal seizure. She grabbed the sampling pole, hooked it on his belt and pulled, but he was too heavy. She had no leverage.

Goober hovered near her face. "Umma, the compensators are using all the power on stabilization. We need to shed some weight or we're going to crash."

"I can't get him back up here by myself. What the hell should I do?"

"We're close to the ground. He should survive the fall, and he's already infested. It's an acceptable risk."

She braced against the seat and pulled on the pole, but Ian didn't budge. "Acceptable risk?"

"You may be the only crew member not compromised. You have to stay alive until the Sinacola returns," Goober said and turned his microwave beam on Ian's strap.

"Goober! No!"

She swung the sampling pole and hit Goober solidly, sending plastic shards into the air. The little AI whirled and sparked, then dropped like a brick. For the first time since receiving him on her twelfth birthday, all links between Umma and Goober flickered out.

Frogvarks launched from the herd beast's backs and landed all over Umma and the flier. Dozens flew through the fans, degrading the lift even more. Within seconds, the drooping fan pod hit the ground with a bang, and the jolt sent Umma over the side. The flier spun around, dragging Umma and Ian in a spiral path over rocks and squirming frogvarks. Umma detached her tether and rolled to a stop, hoping that the sled could regain altitude and take Ian with it.

The flier, suddenly lighter, lifted back into the air and spun away over the herd. She scrambled to her feet but was surrounded by big herd beasts. She quickly lost sight of Ian.

"Shit," she said as thousands of frogvarks crashed down on her like a living tsunami. And this time, through tears in the suit or separated seals, the little white bastards found their way inside.

They filled the void between her suit and skin, then started burrowing. Umma thought childbirth had been the ultimate agony, but immediately realized she had never really known true pain.

A gentle rain on Umma's face woke her from dreams of suffocation. She gasped and then groaned. Everything hurt. She opened crusty eyes but instantly closed them again. The stabbing pain in her head made even the predawn gloom unbearable. Each breath felt like swallowing broken glass. Every inch of skin felt covered with hot coals. Yet, even in her agony, she appreciated the cool drizzle.

Deep in her consciousness, she knew an open helmet was bad, but couldn't remember why it was open. She extended a dry, swollen tongue. The rain tasted like old socks, but she didn't care.

Over the next few minutes, her memory returned in shreds and flickers. When she recalled the attack and the crash, she opened her eyes and jerked upright.

"Ian!"

The effort produced very little sound and much agony, but she fought it and focused on Ian long enough to look around. She sat in a muddy patch of

Fozzy grass. It was more a tall, fuzzy fern than actual grass, but it seemed to cover most of the ground in this world. The big herd animals surrounded her on all sides, their lamprey-like mouths pressed to the ground as they grazed. An underlying sound, like a thousand snorting horses, filled the air, punctuated by an occasional meowing sound; so familiar, yet vastly different from the herds on Earth. Oddly enough, the accompanying smell was not unpleasant, but sweet and rich—like a baking cake.

The little hooked monsters crawled all over Umma and the surrounding ground, with the tiny lice crawling over everything in between. She started brushing at her face and pounding on her arms, slapping them wherever she saw a patch. Her gasping triggered a coughing fit, which produced sputum filled with the white parasites. The sight and realization repulsed her. She must be filled with them, just like Ian.

Panic seized her. She started screaming, clawing and slapping at the things on her face. The pain flared and increased until she couldn't breathe. She fell into a heaving lump, rolled on her side and vomited.

After lying still for a while, the newly inflicted pain went away. Almost as if it had been a punishment. She checked her suit's power level. The batteries were nearly drained. She considered turning it on, just long enough to dispense the pain-killing drugs, but she feared she or Ian might need them more later.

Lying in the grass, staring at pale blue sky between thinning clouds—a sight that wasn't in the least bit alien—the truth came to her suddenly, like a stab in the heart. If the crew in the lander could help, they would already have arrived. Even switched off, her suit would notify her if she had incoming radio calls. It had detected none while she slept.

A frogvark plopped down next to the opening in her helmet and she got her first look at one up close. Between the pointy beak and the big jumping legs were six small limbs, three per side, ending in the tiny sharp claws they used to cling to their hosts.

It scratched and scrambled for a grip on her rain-slick helmet, then hunkered down and opened gill-like flaps on its sides. The little white things filed out in long, snaking lines, like sightseers from a passenger shuttle, and streamed into her helmet.

She, Rachel and Ian had watched nearly thirty hours of early probe video footage showing the frogvarks, the herd beasts and the lice. There had been long rambling discussions about the strange and complex symbiotic relationships between the local animal species, yet none of them had clocked the tiny parasite's aggressive tendencies.

With a shiver, she brushed the frogvark off. Pain washed over her again, making her gasp and squirm, but she refused to give in. She thought about her daughter, now twenty. Rachel was a self-sufficient adult, but she still needed her parents. Umma had to live, for Rachel, and for Ian.

The torment subsided after a few seconds and another jumper arrived. She let this one unload in peace and tried to observe as much as she could. Her survival—and possibly Ian's—might depend on it.

As the sun crept higher and the mist burned away, Umma gently detached as many frogvarks as possible, then stood up on wobbly legs. The herd spread out in every direction, a living sea, perfectly adapted to a prairie world. The big animals processed the grasses and, in doing so, produced food for the other organisms. Ian had always wondered why they had seen so few large species on this world. Umma thought that maybe they had just not been needed, that the ecological niches were filled so well the other species had either died out or been killed off.

A frogvark carpet covered each beast, some crawling around, some tightly attached with sharp beaks buried in their hosts, others arriving or leaving, bound for other nearby animals. The hustle and bustle resembled the spaceport the day they had departed Earth.

As if they'd been waiting for Umma to rise, the herd began moving all at once. She dodged them, at first worried that the lumbering monsters would crush her, but the herd parted and moved around her like she was a rock in a stream. On stiff, sore legs and fully feeling this world's extra gravity, she moved against the flow, hoping to get clear and start searching for Ian. This time the pain came in a flash that took her breath, but only affected her front side. The harder she tried to move forward, the more intense the fire. She stopped and took a step backward and the pain lessened, then started in her right side. She moved away from the pain, in the same direction as the herd, and the sensation went away. When she stopped moving it started again, this time in her back, pushing her forward. The little bastards were driving her!

A chime sounded inside her helmet, announcing an incoming radio communication. Her heart leapt into her throat. With trembling hands she powered up the suit.

"Come in Cochran! Can you read me?"

"Umma? Are you there?"

She recognized the voice—Ian's AI.

"Scooby! Where are you?"

"I'm with Ian. He's alive but I can't communicate with him. His suit power is off, his visor is open. But I can't get close enough to dock with his helmet. Can you help?"

Ian was alive! She felt suddenly stronger and determined.

"Where is he?"

"On the ground, still attached to the flier. We're surrounded by a large herd that just started moving."

"According to the directional finder, you are about six hundred yards toward the rear of the herd. Fly straight up and flash your strobe."

She strained her eyes, until she saw a bright pinprick flash in the distance.

"I see you. Stay there and keep flashing. My suit batteries are low, so I'm going to shut it down, but I'll get there as soon as I can."

"I'll flash once per minute. Please hurry. I'm worried about Ian."

She waited for another flash, then started toward it. The pain in her front grew steadily until she couldn't stand it. She stopped, gasping, with tears trickling down her cheeks, but refused to go in the direction they demanded. Instead, she turned and started walking sideways, making them shift their pain. It amazed her how quickly the little monsters could communicate. In order to inflict such instant and widespread discipline, they must work in concert and do it quickly.

She continued this strategy, expecting any minute to feel the body-warping agony she knew they could produce, but it never came. At some point the herd stopped and young centipede beasts—some only waist high—moved to block her path. With patience and determination, she moved around and between them, her forward progress slowed, but she refused to stop.

They tried a different tack. The frogvarks swarmed, covering her until their added weight began to drag her down. She stopped to rest every few minutes, but kept going. Then a herd beast picked her up with its soft, fleshy maw and carried her for nearly an hour, oblivious to her pounding. When it finally set her down, she immediately continued her trek.

She had just skirted a stand of swampy water filled with dense, woody reeds when she saw the flier less than a hundred yards away. Scooby came down closer. Frogvarks immediately started jumping, trying to reach him, but he stayed well out of range and sent her another message. She powered up her suit.

"I established contact with Porky on the Cochran twenty-one minutes ago. He says his charge, Maggie Torres, is still alive but comatose. He needs your help to get her into the MockDoc vat."

Umma's throat tightened as the statement sank in. What did he mean by still alive? And why would Porky need Umma's help to get Maggie into the AI medical unit? "Get a status on the rest of the crew, Scooby."

"He says they're all dead. Three died from trauma induced by parasitic infestation, which caused an encephalitis-like condition. Four suffered heart failure and two bled to death."

Umma fought back the tears and panic. With a renewed sense of urgency, she hurried the last thirty yards to Ian.

She found him next to the smashed flier, tangled in his tether. He was pale. His eyes twitched beneath the lids. Blood trickled from his nose. She touched his cheek with trembling hands and his eyes opened. The pupils weren't evenly dilated. One looked milky and bruised. He mumbled.

"It's me, sweetie. It's Umma. Can you hear me?"

He licked his lips and spoke with a raspy, shallow voice. "Hey, darlin'"

"Thank God. Just hang on, sweetie, and we'll get you back to the ship."

"I came all this way . . . to see alien critters and I'm missin' it."

She stroked his face and said, "There'll be plenty of time later."

"Don't kill them. They didn't know." Then he closed his eyes and mumbled again. "—born for this."

She picked up his gloved hand with both of hers and held it against her cheek, but he had dropped into unconsciousness.

"We have an audience," Scooby said.

The hair on her neck prickled when she looked up. Herd beasts were arrayed around them in a neat ring. The big animals, and every frogvark attached to them, turned their "faces" toward Umma. And the big animals did have something akin to a face, a wide flat spot, near the ground, just above the mouth, where three round depressions covered with soft skin vibrated like drums.

They were quiet. All the beasts had stopped eating. Even the young ones were still and peered placidly from between the adults.

Scooby said, "MockDoc wants to talk with you. He says he helped Porky kill the parasites in Maggie."

Hope flared in her again. She glanced in the direction of the Cochran but could see only grazing herd animals. She forced patience and settled down in the grass next to Ian. "Stay above me and relay the conversation, Scooby. I don't want to waste my power. Ask him what he did."

"He says each of the adult lice carry a tiny crystal under their carapace. Through testing, he found the sonic frequency for making the crystals vibrate. He had hoped to drive them out of Maggie, but it killed them instantly."

"That's good news," Umma said. "We can finally fight back."

"He says we can't kill those infesting you or Ian. It will leave your bodies filled with millions of lice carcasses, which will cause infections throughout your systems. Ian would not survive it, and your chances would be very slim. He doesn't expect Maggie to last long now."

Umma cursed under her breath and looked around at the herd again. They seemed to be waiting for her. If it was her move, then she would sure as hell make one. She left Ian long enough to collect several stout, woody reeds. With the knife and carbon wire from her field kit, she started building a travois.

"Tell Doc and the other AIs to come up with some way to drive these things out without killing us. We have hundreds of years of human technology at our disposal; surely they can come up with something. Try chemicals, temperature extremes, anything. In the meantime, I'm bringing Ian back to the ship."

When Umma started forward with the travois, her tormentors tried driving her with pain again, but she employed the same tactics of turning the other cheek, a difficult task while pulling Ian. Several times, she was forced to stop entirely when they visited her entire body with pain. Still, after each episode, she kept moving toward the ship. It was slow, exhausting and agonizing, but once they cleared the leading edge of the herd she could see the Cochran in the distance, easily the tallest thing on the horizon. It buoyed her determination and picked up her pace. The herd followed close behind, but Umma was finally calling the shots.

"Umma! Check Ian."

She stopped and lowered the travois handles. Ian was writhing and twisting against the tether she'd used to secure him to the frame. He uttered whimpers and grunts. When she knelt next to him, he immediately stopped, relaxing back into unconsciousness.

She looked up at Scooby, still flying above and ahead of her, out of frog-vark range. "He doesn't look good. Anything new from Doc?"

"No," he answered. "But I think we need to hurry."

"I know," she said and picked up the handles again. The instant she did, Ian groaned and twisted in pain. She put the travois down and he relaxed.

"The little fuckers are using Ian to control me!"

She paced, circling Ian, muttering and cursing under her breath. The herd waited, the large animals grazed and ignored her again, but frogvarks continued to arrive and depart. Seeing the ship so close made her frustration even greater. All kinds of crazy ideas roared through her exhausted mind, but nothing sane enough to try.

Scooby came down close to her head, easily within attack range, but this time the frogvarks ignored him. "You just said they're using Ian to manipulate you. Do you realize what that implies? Their making that kind of connection between you and Ian shows an amazing degree of sentience. Animals are not capable of such abstract ideas."

"Of course they're intelligent," she said, brushing frogvarks aside so she could sit on the ground next to Ian. "And they're being deliberately evil. That's even worse."

"Perhaps you just don't understand their motives."

She ignored him and watched the lice move up and down Ian's chest in clumps and long snaking lines. They were organized and they communicated en masse almost instantaneously. Did they have psychic abilities? A network? What of the crystals Porky had discovered?

"Scooby? Do you think the lice could communicate via a kind of radio signal using those crystals? Maybe some kind of vast distributed network?"

"It's possible. There's a low-level static that dominates the lower frequency range here."

Umma groaned in response to her sore muscles and joints as she struggled back to her feet. "Can you create a jamming signal? Or better yet, a directional EMP blast?"

"I don't have the power to generate an EMP, but the Cochran has the materials needed to build a device. Jamming, I can do. Finding the right frequency might take awhile, but I could just start at one end and cycle every second until we find something or run out of spectrum. It will be power intensive, so I may have to do it in stages."

"If they do communicate and coordinate via radio signals, do you think disrupting that would kill them? I don't want the same situation as Mock-Doc's sonic experiment."

"Seems unlikely, but I don't know. You're the biologist."

Umma looked around at the herd and the distant Cochran, then down at Ian. "Do it. We have to do something and don't seem to be making much progress by just standing here."

Scooby positioned himself out of range, but above Umma and Ian, emitting a low-level hum. His power light immediately flickered red, and he dipped a little lower as he stole power from his fans, but he didn't stop. Nothing happened for several minutes, then in the blink of an eye she felt millions of pinpricks inside and outside her body. Black spots filled her vision and she dropped to her knees. Her lungs constricted. Her throat and nose burned, making her cough and retch. Clear drool, mixed with red and white swirls, dripped from her open mouth as she gasped for breath. Then it ended as quickly as it had started.

"Well, that's interesting," Scooby said. "They communicate on a higher frequency than I would've thought."

Umma was gasping, trying to get back onto her feet, but she noticed the lice on her arms milling in confused circles. Individuals, almost too small to focus on, looked like tiny drunks, staggering around and bumping into each other. It made her smile.

"Take that you little bastards," she mumbled and brushed them off without the punishing pain. Then, even as she looked around at the surrounding chaos—confused herd beasts, panicked frogvarks, and disorganized lice—she realized it had failed. The tiny parasites had lost their cohesive organization, but the majority she hosted had not left her body.

Taking advantage of the pandemonium, Scooby swooped down and docked with Ian's helmet. The visor immediately closed and the suit power came on. Then Ian and the attached travois bounced. At first, Umma didn't realize what she was seeing. Scooby's power light blinked red, and as soon as it turned green, Ian bounced again—automated defibrillation via his field suit.

"Ian!" She dropped to her knees next to him and tried to open the visor.

"Don't touch him!" Scooby said, then added, "Clear!"

Ian jumped again.

The process repeated three more times, leaving Scooby's status lights dark after the last attempt. Lice crawled all over the AI's shell.

"Scooby?" She detached the motionless AI from Ian's helmet and set it aside, then opened Ian's visor. His eyes were closed and his expression calm. He was still as sculpted stone.

She yanked her helmet off and pressed her face to his. Twenty-one years of memories welled in her; the day they met, the first night they spent together, those quiet afternoons napping, their daughter, the dinners, the friends, the plans.

"Ian. Please don't leave me."

Her chest and throat felt crushed—she could barely breathe—but the tears wouldn't come.

Lice patches, obviously having reorganized, covered her husband, and large numbers were clustered around the travois joints she had wired together. Seeing them infuriated her. When the herd came close—watching—it was suddenly all too much.

"You fucking monsters," she screamed. The loud noise affected them like a pressure wave; they all jerked back at once. With rage-fueled strength, she pulled a reed loose from the rattle-trap travois and swung it like a Louisville Slugger, striking a lead beast square in the face. She wheeled, batted, and pounded, crushing thirty or forty frogvarks before her strength failed and she slumped to the ground.

Then the tears came.

Through blurry eyes, she saw Scooby hovering before her face, covered with crawling lice. But alive.

"Go away," she snapped.

"Please deactivate me now," he said.

She covered her ears, curled into a ball, and lay for a long time as the same ugly thought kept surfacing through her anguish. Rachel had worshiped her father. Umma would have to bear the brunt of her daughter's pain and anger. In losing Ian, she had probably also lost her daughter.

Awhile later, Scooby bumped her. "You're almost to the Cochran. You can see it from here. You don't need me. I have no function now that—"

She shoved her grief aside, sat up, grabbed the little AI and shook him. "Stop it, Scooby! That's a direct order. You're still alive—just like me—and you're stuck with that responsibility. You can't abandon Sinacola's colonists just because Ian's dead! They need you. There's too much at stake. Ian gave his life to see this world and these . . . damned animals. That should mean something to you."

Umma sat for a moment, staring at the blinking AI in her fist and considering her words, then released him and wiped her eyes.

"Those damned animals have built a travois," Scooby said from beyond her reach.

"What?"

"They've built a new travois. A better one."

She turned toward Ian, who lay on the frame she had half torn apart. Another travois—built from the same kind of reeds—lay beside him. On hands and knees, she crawled the short distance and examined the gift. It was roughly the same dimensions as her design, but the crossbars tying the assembly together were bonded with a flexible, plastic-like putty. The whole frame was quite sturdy and could not be pulled apart.

"Porky called while you were . . . incapacitated," Scooby said. His little speaker sounded deflated and tinny. "Maggie died too."

"Tell him—" Umma ran her fingers along Ian's face and then sighed. "Tell him I'm sorry."

Sudden doubts crept into her thoughts. Ian had been stable before the jamming. Had the parasites been keeping him alive? Would he still be alive if she had left them alone? And if she had instead left Ian and rushed back to the ship to help get Maggie into the MockDoc vat, would she have survived? Umma sat down and ran shaking hands through matted hair. All she wanted was to mourn Ian, to hold her daughter, but she didn't know when or if that would ever happen.

"The MockDoc wants to talk to you when you're able."

She took a deep breath and then struggled to her feet. "Okay."

"I'm patching him through."

"Umma," Doc said in his wizened male voice through Scooby's speaker, "I'm sorry about Ian. Are you hurt? Are you going to be able to make it back to the ship on your own?"

She sighed and looked around. The herd had left about a twenty-yard buffer around her. The path to the ship was clear. "I can see the Cochran from here. I'll be there as soon as I can."

"I've informed the Sinacola of your situation. Of course, they want to talk to you as soon as you're able."

"My suit is dead. I'll call them when I get back to the ship. Tell Rachel . . . that I'm sorry."

"Will do."

She strapped Ian to the new rig, then picked up the handles and started walking. The little bastards were still crawling all over and through Umma, but this time they didn't try to stop her.

She took a deep breath and opened the hatch leading to the control cabin. Her friends, people she had known for more than half her life, lay scattered on the deck and draped over chairs. The knowledge of their deaths hadn't prepared her for seeing them that way.

A cloud of AIs lifted into the air from their places of vigil near their dead mates and immediately launched into a plaintive chorus.

"Please deactivate me."

"This is too much, please turn me off."

"Jacque is dead. Please deactivate me."

She inhaled, preparing to yell at them to be quiet, and instead just raised a hand. They eventually stopped. "I'm sorry. I know what you're feeling, but you can't deactivate. I need your help. We have work to do. We . . . can't just leave everyone like this."

She left them hovering and limped across the cabin to the storage hold hatch in the floor. One rung at a time, she eased herself down, then, at the bottom, sat to rest before looking for the body bags.

She woke eleven hours later, oddly twisted, with one numb arm and a Medical Diagnostic Unit strapped to the other. Her stomach demanded food, and her muscles would barely move, but she resumed her search. Scooby reminded her repeatedly that messages from the Sinacola were waiting, but working was easier. She couldn't face Rachel yet.

She removed the frogvarks, but could do nothing about the lice, so she sealed Ian and the rest of the crew into bags along with their parasites and moved them to storage. She cleaned up the dried blood and vomit, then showered and ate.

With her excuses all gone, she stood before the communications console, not wanting to talk to anyone, especially Rachel. Lice crawled in and out of the equipment racks, from behind panels and through cooling vents.

"So why are the electronics still working with these things gumming up the works?"

Scooby floated nearby and answered. "Porky says they seem to avoid the actual electricity, including circuit cards of running equipment. So we leave it running. They have had mixed results with operating devices that have been powered down."

Since Umma didn't know how long they could count on the electronics, communicating with the Sinacola now, while she still could, suddenly seemed like a good idea. For over an hour, Umma listened to recorded messages from the Sinacola. First, she heard the pleas for clarification after they received chaotic and panicked calls from the survey team. Then replies to messages from various AIs, reporting the deaths of their charges. The last recording was from the mission commander.

"Hang in there, Umma. The MockDoc sent your status while you were sleeping to reassure us, but we're still worried. We think we have plenty of ways to protect the next landing party and even have some ideas on how to rid you of the lice, but we don't want to try anything now. We want you in a fully functioning medical bay before taking the risk. Call us when you can."

There were no messages from Rachel. That hurt, but she also felt relief at not having to talk to her daughter yet.

She stared at the camera. How could she even begin to explain what had happened? But she had to try. Since she couldn't carry on a real conversation with a seventy-one-minute time lag, she just told her story in a long rambling monologue. She ended her message with a warning that they should land no one else until they could make sure their landing area was totally free of the lice and included her thoughts on killing them en masse.

Three hours later, Scooby hovered just out of arm's reach. "You have two new messages from Rachel."

"Could you play them for me? On the large wall screen. Please."

Rachel's face was blotchy and her eyes red, but she was more than just upset over her father. Umma knew her daughter and the set of her mouth said she was furious.

"I just found out that you're working with these idiots up here to find a way to kill the lice. You're a biologist, Mom! A xenobiologist! We came to this world to understand these creatures, not kill them. I know you're upset about Dad. So am I. He was a part of me. My own flesh and—" her face screwed up and she looked away from the camera for a second. "And unlike you, I didn't even get to say goodbye to him. So if I can look at these parasites as a possible sentient species, without planning revenge, then you should be able to as well."

She laid both hands on the table and leaned into the camera.

"From your and Scooby's accounts, there is plenty going on with the lice to make us go slow. They don't have technology like us because they've never needed it, but they're still showing signs of intelligence. They're just primitive. As far as we know, we're the advanced intelligence here, so the onus to show them we're not just herd animals falls on us."

Then her anger flared. She leaned even closer to the camera. "And who's acting like an animal in this encounter? Lashing out because of anger and instinct, not reason? Do you think we can just come in here and kill them all? We can't do this again, Mom! We can't keep coming to new places and wiping the slate clean. You know Dad would never have done that."

The message ended.

Umma jumped out of the chair, threw her water across the cabin and kicked the side of the comm console.

Scooby and Porky moved away.

"What the fuck does she know? She hasn't seen these things! She doesn't have them living inside her! She didn't watch them kill Ian."

"Perhaps that gives her a more unbiased perspective," Scooby said softly from his position near the hatch.

"Unbiased? They killed her father. Well, she can be a self-righteous child if she wants, but I'm going to do everything I can to protect her from these little monsters. They killed my husband. They will not get my daughter too!"

"She has valid points. Maybe you should listen to her."

"She's twenty. And she always takes a position opposite mine. Always!"

Scooby drifted closer but still out of arm's reach.

"So you think this is just youthful contrariness? She may only be twenty, but she is still a degreed biologist. Like it or not, she is your professional peer and deserves a fair hearing, for that reason if no other. She left a second message, twenty minutes after her first one. Do you want to hear it?"

Umma paced the small cabin, then eventually stopped before the console. "Play it."

Tears trickled down Rachel's face and the angry set to her mouth was gone. She paused to wipe her nose on her sleeve, like she had when she was six, and Umma felt her own heart melt. Rachel was suddenly a little girl again.

"I'm sorry, Mom. I shouldn't have said those things to you. I'm just scared. I feel so alone here. No one will listen to me and no one is on my side. Please, just take a while and think about it. We've had a bad start, but we have time to do it right this time. I love you and I'm glad you're okay."

The message ended and Umma slid down the console to sit on the floor. She buried her face in her hands and tried to concentrate. It was hard when all she could think about was ridding herself of the nasty little bugs and never itching again. But her daughter needed her and she had to think it through.

She got up, climbed the central ladder and exited the Cochran through her uppermost hatch. The wind whipped her hair and felt cool and damp. Rain was on the way. This might someday be a nice home, but as she gazed out at the herd surrounding the ship, she didn't see how. She was on a very small island in a vast living sea. But she would try it Rachel's way. There would always be time for killing if it came to that.

Scooby hovered above and behind her. She realized for the first time that he had not left her side since Ian's death.

"Scooby? I think our little jamming experiment proved that these things communicate by radio signals, at least on some level. I need your help. I want to implant something in myself, as well as in the frogvarks and herd animals, to intercept and record the signals these things use to communicate."

"That should be easy enough. Sorting them into some coherent pattern will be the hard part."

"Good. And please record the following to send to Rachel: 'I'm sorry too. I am on your side and will help all I can. We're going to try some things here, but please send me your thoughts about the lice. I love you.'"

Three days and nearly a thousand hours of AI research time later, Umma took a finger-sized herd beast from the box of models they had generated in the Cochran's nano-constructor vat. She set it on the aluminum plate before a puddle of lice, then through the metal, sent the signal they thought the lice used for "herd beast."

The lice examined the model and repeated the lone signal.

"Well, crap," Umma said. "What does that mean?"

With MockDoc's help, they had determined that the parasites didn't exactly send radio signals through the air, but instead passed electrochemical pulses through long chains of their own bodies. There were always enough of them packed close together that the signals had a path. They used similar pulses to trigger firing in the nerve and pain centers of their hosts. The AIs had collected, sorted, and cataloged over four thousand signals, and complex but repeatable patterns had begun to emerge.

Not unlike human data transmission packets, the commands sent to control their host animals each had common headers, a one for humans, a different one for the frogvarks and another for the large herd animals. Each command seemed to have a signal combination. Some of the communication strings, or data packets, contained hundreds or even thousands of parts.

She replaced the model with one of a frogvark, sent the header signal for "frogvark." The lice simply repeated the signal again.

"This is going nowhere fast."

Scooby hovered nearby, watching and recording video to send back to Sinacola. "Have you noticed that the headers for their host animals, while different, still have a similar component?" he asked.

"Hmmm . . . that's because to them, we're all just mobile homes. Maybe it is their word for "host." Let's try something."

Umma placed three models—a human, a frogvark, and a herd beast, in a group and sent just the common component of the header. The lice repeated the signal. Then she put the louse model in a location separate from the others and sent the same "host" header. The lice advanced, examined the model parasite, then formed back into a clump and to her surprise and shock, returned a signal that was different.

"Holy shit! Did you get that, Scooby?"

"Yes. It is a header we've seen before but didn't understand."

Umma picked up all of the models, then set down the frogvark and herd beast and sent the 'host' header. Next, she set the human model and the louse down together and sent the signal they now suspected meant 'louse.'

There was no response. No repeated signal. Nothing.

"Well, I think we managed to confuse them. Maybe we should give up and try tomorrow. I'm getting really—"

Then the parasites sent a new signal.

"Bingo," Scooby said. "It's a combination of "louse" and "human" headers. A new category."

Before Umma could even vocalize her amazement, her skin felt suddenly on fire. She gasped and started to wipe away the sudden flurry of lice, until she realized they were erupting out of her, from every pore and opening. She fought the urge to cough or sneeze and tried to remain very still. They left her by the millions, in wide, snaking lines that seemed to merge, then pass through the clump that still waited on the metal plate.

Almost simultaneously, the other AIs reported from all over the Cochran. The lice were leaving every part of the ship, even through the supposedly airtight seals of the body bags. Frogvarks arrived by the hundreds, and the parasites waited patiently to board and leave.

"Do you think they finally recognized us as peers and not just herd animals?" Umma said to no one in particular.

Scooby dropped down beside her face and said, "It appears so, but we still don't know enough to be sure."

"It's a start. Maybe someday we'll understand each other. I assume you're recording all of this?"

"Of course," Scooby said.

"Maybe Ian was right. Maybe we were born for this. Send the video to Rachel along with this message: You were right on every point. We do have time to do this the correct way. You're a wonderful scientist. I wish your father could see this. He would've been so very proud."

VIGILANCE

I winced as my grandson slammed the back door. It echoed in the night like the crack of a rifle shot, even out where I was sitting. The banging door had become my grandson's trumpeting herald. He'd been told and scolded and threatened for years, but he never remembered. His father and mother had been raised during a time when such noise could get them killed, but Whit knew only safety and stability.

"Don't slam the door, Whit!" his mother yelled, almost as loud as the door had been.

I sighed and made sure the shotgun leaning against the wall beside me was within easy reach.

"Grandpa?"

"Behind the barn, Whit."

He shuffled and scuffed across the courtyard, sending rocks bouncing ahead of him. Maybe the racket would do some good and scare off any snakes still soaking up warmth from the hard-packed ground. At eight, Whit thought he was too big to sit on my lap anymore, so he settled onto the bench beside me and leaned back against the splintered barn wall. His breath still carried onions from the potato soup.

"I thought you had homework after dinner?" I said.

"I do," Whit said with a sigh. "But Emily was really annoying me, so Mom said I could come out here with you. But just a few minutes."

"Well, I'm glad you came. I like your company."

"Whatcha doing?" the boy said.

"Just stargazing. It's a beautiful night. We can even see the Milky Way."

He was quiet for a while, his silhouette cutting a black hole in the already dark night as he looked up.

"Dad said it used to be hard to see many stars because of the dust."

My stomach knotted and a cold shiver swept over me. The asteroid impact in Mongolia had been horrible for those living there, but at least they had died quickly. The rest of the world tore itself apart as dust shrouded the entire planet, plunging us into a winter that lasted for three years. We had been so hungry. So many had died. So many had become . . . animals.

"Yep, the impact made a huge mess," I said. "But even before that, it was hard to see many stars because there was so much light."

Whit's silhouetted face looked up. "People really used to live up there?"

"Yep."

"Do you think we'll build rockets again, soon enough for me to go into space?"

I smiled to myself in the dark. "Maybe. They're already building new airplanes over in Huntsville, instead of patching up old ones. That's a good sign. The first time around, it was only about fifty years between the Wright brother's airplane and the first manned rocket, and they were developing the science as they went. It could be much quicker this time."

He leaned against me and started picking at the planks of the bench.

"I'm going to go up there," he said in an almost whisper. "Dad said the key is learning everything I can, especially in math."

"You're really going to go?"

"Yes," he said without hesitation.

"Then what are the Three Rules of Defense?" I said.

He groaned and slid down further on the bench. "What does that have to do with anything? There hasn't been a bandit attack since before I was born!"

"You're missing the point, Whit. It's never a matter of if, but when."

He muttered something beneath his breath, then sat up straighter and said, "The first rule is vigilance. We have to know about threats heading our way. The second rule is preparedness. Have the necessary tools built and ready. And the third rule is action. We have to defend ourselves when we have the ability to do so."

I slipped my arm around his shoulders and hugged him to me. "Good job, Whit. Complacency is always our greatest failure."

"Yeah, I know," he said, then stood up. "I better go in and do my homework."

"Okay," I said. "Try to talk your mom into saving me some corn bread."

He laughed. "I think she already did," he said over his shoulder, then was gone, running toward the house.

How quickly something like an asteroid impact could become ancient history. Were we destined to keep making the same mistakes?

The ever-alert, ever-ready part of me, developed during the hard years after the impact, sounded an alarm. The door hadn't slammed. I hadn't even heard it open or close. The kid couldn't be that quiet. I stood and picked up my shotgun that leaned against the barn beside me.

Before I took two steps, a dark figure rounded the barn.

"Grandpa?"

Thankfully, I hadn't raised the gun. "You spooked me, Whit."

"Sorry," he said, then hesitated.

"What is it?"

"I've been reciting these rules for years but just now realized something. The Three Rules of Defense aren't really for bandits, are they?"

I squeezed Whit's shoulder. "No."

"I'll never forget, Grandpa. I promise." Then he turned and ran back toward the house.

Maybe he wouldn't, I thought and settled back onto my bench. Then the slammed door echoed through the night. Of course, only time would tell.

STEALING ARTURO

I tried to stay awake and upright as the elevator bucked and jerked its way down the spoke into the Earth-normal gravity of Ring One's sleeping level. The lights flickered as the weight settled over me, pushing my exhaustion deep into every cell. I didn't know how much longer I could take it. If the power failed and left me stuck in the elevator again, I might turn into a raving madman. Would I really ever escape this station? Were the months of covert effort wasted?

Felicia spoke, but her voice was there and not there, a feathery touch that revived memories of her fingers brushing back my hair. "You can do this. I believe in you, but you need sleep. And a shower."

I snorted and hugged her canister to my chest with one hand and scratched my two-day-old beard with the other. She was right. It had been nearly as long since I'd showered or slept. Extended periods working in the hub's microgravity always did this to me, but I had little choice. Time was running out.

A hand appeared before the lift door had even opened halfway, grabbed the front of my shirt, and yanked me out into the corridor. Since I didn't have my gravity legs yet, I fell directly to my knees. The two security "officers" laughed, and the one with red hair—whom I had long ago assigned the name Meathead—gave me a little shove with a highly polished boot and I further lost my balance. I had enough warning to at least tuck Felicia's canister against my chest before I toppled over like a tottering old grandpa.

A foot pressed on the back of my head, trying to shove my face into the thick grime that had accumulated in the corner over the decades. Dust and debris were sucked into the air filtration system on low-gravity levels, but down here, where the poor people lived, filth collected like it had throughout human history. Bits of plastic and a rusted screw decorated the black gunk only inches from my mouth, but I pushed back and rolled over quickly, causing Meathead to lose his balance and stumble backward.

I fought the centrifugal gravity and struggled to my feet, ready to kill the crisply uniformed bastard. As I braced to headbutt him, before he regained his balance, I heard Felicia's voice in my head.

"Don't be stupid, Clarke. You're only four days away from your escape. You can't be arrested now."

She was right, but I had to at least put up a token fight or they'd get suspicious. I gave the two goons a withering glare, tucked Felicia under my arm, and tried to push past them. They grabbed my arms and shoved me against a bulkhead.

"Lieutenant Eisenhower sent us to ask about your ice production quota. He thinks you're holding out."

"I don't give a shit what Eisenhower thinks. I don't answer to him. I was hired by the station management."

The goon shoved me again, making my head bang against the wall. "That's Lieutenant Eisenhower. You need to show some respect."

"Lieutenant is a rank that implies either training or experience and he has neither. He's just the head guard dog, and that doesn't demand respect in my book."

The second goon—the one with dark hair and beady eyes—took a swing at me, intending to pin my face between his fist and the bulkhead. I dodged, but not quite fast enough, and his punch glanced hard off of my cheekbone, then scraped my cheek with his wrist comm as it continued into the wall.

He cursed and punches from both assailants rained down on me in a flurry. I bent low, intending to take a few hits and then try to dart between them, when someone yelled.

"Stop hitting him, you big turds!"

Everyone stopped and turned to see a scruffy young girl in patched clothes standing just behind Meathead. She looked to be around eight or nine, and I recognized her as the girl who lived with her mother two doors down from my cabin.

"Get lost, kid!" the dark-haired guy said and made a half-hearted swipe at her.

She didn't budge, just glared back at the man.

Both officers laughed but threw no more punches. Instead, in an unexpected snatch, Meathead grabbed Felicia's canister from my grasp.

I straightened abruptly, shoved them both backward, and grabbed for her can, but missed.

Meathead hefted it like a schoolyard bully playing keep away. "I think we'll have to confiscate this."

"No, you won't," I said.

They glanced at each other and grinned. "We already have, Kooper."

I shook my head slowly. "I don't think you understand. If you decide to keep my property, then you'll have to kill me or imprison me. And in either of those cases, you and everyone on this station will die within a couple of weeks after the water runs out. As your boss already mentioned, my production level is way down. We have about a week's worth of water in reserve. My predecessor already picked the local area clean of icy rocks and they're getting tough to find. Without me, you won't find any ice. Nor will you be able to bring a new ice miner in from Mars or Earth quick enough to stave off that rather ugly death. Of course, the managers and your boss will probably hoard plenty for themselves, but do you think you'll get any?"

Meathead shifted his stance and glanced at his partner.

"And if you let me go, but still keep my property, then I have at my disposal forty-nine mining robots, each with a laser capable of burning right through the hull of this station. I wouldn't have a bit of trouble finding your cabin, and I don't even have to hit you with the beam. I'd just wait until you were asleep and open a hole in the hull. Then, pffffttt, you'd squirt into vacuum like a long string of goober paste."

The kid laughed and Meathead's face flushed red.

"Or you can give that back to me, and we'll pretend this never happened."

"Give it back to him!" the little girl said. "Are you morons trying to get us all killed?"

Meathead's buddy poked him in the arm. "Just give him the damned can and let's go get some grub. Eisenhower didn't tell you to take his stuff anyway."

I smiled and nodded, then winced at the pain in my cheek.

Meathead tossed Felicia's canister in my direction. It tumbled and I did some silly juggling to keep it from hitting the floor. The goons laughed and by the time I had it tucked safely under my arm, they were strutting down the corridor with their backs to the girl and me.

I took a deep breath and dabbed at the blood trickling down my cheek.

"You're a dumbass," she said.

I shrugged and slipped past her. "And you have a foul mouth. Go home before you get into trouble."

She followed me. "Me get into trouble? I saved your ass! If I hadn't come along, they would have beat you into pudding."

"I guess I do owe you some thanks, but you shouldn't have done that. Those guys wouldn't hesitate to hit a kid."

I palmed the lock plate on my door. It slid open and I nearly dropped Felicia as the kid slipped past me into my dark cabin.

"What the f—" I growled, then heard Felicia again.

"Don't yell at her, Clarke."

I took a deep breath and paused just inside the door. "Let's have some lights, Calvin."

The cabin computer turned on the lights and I could see her sitting in my only chair, legs dangling as she examined a power regulator module from one of my mining robots.

"You have an AI!"

"Just a smart computer," I said. "I spliced it into the cabin electronics. I do a lot of stuff like that. Now go home."

"My mom says you're crazy."

I glowered at her. "Does she also say that you're rude?"

The girl laughed. "All the time."

"Look, kid, you can't be in here. I could get in a lot of trouble." The door started to close, but I grabbed it and held it open. "Go home."

"Why would you get in trouble?"

"I'm sure your mom has warned you about being alone with strange men."

She reached for a paper book I had lying on the table, then stopped and looked at me with a perplexed expression. "You talk funny. You weren't born on the station?"

"No. I was born on Earth. In Chicago. Now, you really need to leave."

With a slow shake of her head, she crossed her arms and grinned. "You'll have to throw me out, and if you do, I'll start screaming that you touched me in the naughty place."

Anger flared and I activated my wrist unit—ready to call security to come remove her—then stopped. Had I really just considered calling security?

"Calvin? Lock the door open and keep a video record until this kid leaves."

"Understood," Calvin said.

The kid shrugged. "My name is Nora, not kid."

I leaned against the wall next to the door and hoped I hadn't already attracted more attention from security. The girl twisted her mouth into an odd slant as she looked around again. She had a squarish face and the same dark hair with pale skin that seemed to dominate the station's worker population, but her eyes were bright and inquisitive, which made her stand out from most of the drug-addled adults.

"So how old are you? And why does your mother let you run around alone?"

"I'm nine. And my mom has to do double shifts until I'm old enough to work in the factory. Food and space for two, she always says."

I nodded but hadn't ever thought about how people managed to raise kids on the station.

"Mom won't let me go to the factory yet, but I used to help out when I got paid for scrubbing air ducts. I used to be small enough to crawl inside, but I think they found a smaller kid."

My stomach tightened and I suddenly felt very ignorant about the people surrounding me.

"Would you like a food bar?"

"Sure," she said, and her face brightened.

I pulled one from my pants pocket and tossed it to her. She opened it and gobbled it down in three bites.

"It's a good thing that security guy is stupid," she said as she chewed.

I blinked at the sudden change of subject. "Why do you say that?"

"Because Mars will be at its closest point in a few weeks. They'd have plenty of time to kill you and get a replacement from Mars."

I couldn't help but laugh. "Holy crap, kid. You're a real piece of work."

"Stop calling me kid. My name's Nora. By the way, you're a terrible liar. Decompression wouldn't squirt that guy through a small hole. His body would just block it. You'd need a big hole."

"I never said a small hole, but I think he got the point."

She shrugged and looked at me through squinted eyes. "You need to clean up. When's the last time you changed clothes?"

I looked down to see fresh blood droplets added to the food and sweat stains on my dingy island shirt.

"Sorry. Hey, this has been nice . . . Nora, but it's time for you to go."

She ignored my comment and nodded toward Felicia's canister. "What's in the can that you were ready to kill for?"

My initial reaction was to tell her it was none of her business, but then I decided maybe the truth would shock her into leaving. I stroked the cool black metal canister and then held it up. "This is my wife, Felicia."

The kid blinked and then frowned. "Um, right. Is it some kind of computer? Or a game machine?"

"When my wife died, she was cremated, and her ashes were sealed in this container."

That got her attention. She had a horrified look on her face and leaned forward on the chair. "Ashes? She wasn't recycled?"

I shook my head. "They . . . sometimes do things differently on Earth and Mars."

"That's kinda creepy," she said.

I shrugged.

"Then why do you talk to it? That's why my mom thinks you're nuts."

"Nora!"

The yell came from just behind my right ear and made me flinch. Nora's mother rushed into the cabin, grabbed her daughter by the arm and pulled her upright. "What are you doing here?"

"Just talking," Nora said, then grinned at me. "He tried to make me leave, but I was having fun. Did you know that his dead wife is in that can?"

"Oh, Nora," the woman said and ran a hand through limp, messy hair that was dark like her daughter's. She also had the same squarish face, but hers had sharp angles from being much too thin. Her eyes were dull with exhaustion and she seemed on the brink of tears.

"I'm so sorry, Mr. . . . ?"

"Clarke Kooper," I said and extended my hand.

She edged past me out the door, dragging the girl with her, and once safely in the hall, turned back and glanced at my bloody cheek and wild hair, half of which had come out of my ponytail during the fight. She took my still-extended hand. "I'm Wendy, and I don't think you're crazy. Nora just . . . has a rather vivid imagination."

"She's been quite," I struggled for a word that wouldn't sound rude, "entertaining."

"I'm sure she has," Wendy said with a sigh, then turned to Nora. "C'mon, you little monster, let's go eat some dinner."

As I watched them go down the hall I thought about inviting them to eat dinner with me, then reconsidered. I didn't need to form any new attachments. I'd either be gone or dead within a few weeks.

The next day in my hub-based control center, I kicked off from the interface station and floated to the wall hiding my salvation. I resisted the urge to run my hand along the section where the door would appear. On the other side, exposed to the bitter cold asteroid belt, was a four-by-three-meter external equipment blister I'd quietly and secretly converted into an escape pod.

I moved on to the robot launch tube, cycled it and opened the hatch. Burnt-smelling air poofed into the cabin as I pulled out the basketball-sized mining drone called a Mining Operations Manager or MOM. Once I locked it into the fixture on my test bench, I changed its status to inactive, then opened the main access cover. I slipped my hand inside and removed the mostly empty nanoreplicator bladder. The "mostly empty" designation could get me killed if station security found out. Nano-device manufacture was strictly controlled and each tiny robot made for a MOM had to be loaded into the MOM. But nothing could count the replicators that left the MOM out on an ice ball, the number of times they reproduced or the number that returned with it. This bladder was still a quarter full.

With a series of coded taps against the MOM's inner shell, I directed the remaining replicators into a hidden conduit that allowed them to flow into the empty spaces in the station's hull structure, where they would hide until I needed them.

A loud beep announced the door opening, and when I turned, the breath caught in my throat. Bernard Eisenhower drifted into the room. He wore his trademark half smile that never reached his eyes. He could be beating a suspect or chatting up a pretty girl, and the smile was always the same. I tried to force myself to relax. He probably wore augmentations that helped him read and record fluctuations in body heat, heart rate, and eye movements.

"Hello, Clarke. How goes the dowsing? Your magic water stick still working?"

I smiled and pushed my feet into the cleats at my workbench. "Business is slow. But given time, I'm able to find enough ice to keep us going."

He worked his way around the room, looking into every open device, picking up and examining each scroll screen. He nodded repeatedly to himself.

"My boys told me about your little threat yesterday."

"They should leave me alone. I'm just trying to do my job."

"No, you aren't doing your job, Clarke. Instead, you're playing a dangerous game with Arturo Station's water supply. That makes it a security issue, which is why I sent my men to talk with you in the first place."

Eisenhower might be a bully and abusive with his power, but he wasn't totally stupid. After my first week on Arturo Station, when I realized the highly addictive productivity enhancement drug called Canker had been put into my food—and that of nearly every worker on board—I started planning how to get out of the situation. That had been nearly a year ago and much of the ice I collected had been stored in secret tanks I'd hidden inside the hull, but the official ice I "found" for the station had dropped at a steady rate ever since. Making management and security think we had a limited supply was my only insurance if my escape plot were ever discovered.

"My predecessor used up all the close ice balls. I have to send my bots further and further out. It takes time. Maybe management should move the station to richer hunting grounds, or better yet, tighten up their water reclamation system."

"Bullshit, Clarke. There's ice out there close. Our scanners see it."

"In small amounts. It would take twice as long if I tried to mine every little grapefruit-sized nugget out there."

Eisenhower glared at me. "Your replacement is on the way. I'm sure he'll have better luck."

I snorted and shrugged.

"You don't believe that?"

"Hell no. If my replacement were on the way, you wouldn't be wasting your time talking to me. My corpsicle would already be tumbling out toward Jupiter."

His smile almost broadened and he started toward the hatch. "Don't push it, Clarke. We have backups you don't know about, and we will send you spinning to Jupiter if that ice tonnage doesn't come up a lot and very quickly."

I exited at my level and Nora was waiting again, this time just outside the lift. Her face lit up and she started chattering.

"You're really from Earth?"

"Yep."

"I was born here," she said. "Momma too. She was in the first generation born on the station."

"So she's never been off of Arturo?"

Nora shook her head as we approached my door. "No. Momma said they'll never let us leave."

Many of the workers would be afraid to leave. Canker was an ugly thing. It was named for the sores that formed around a user's mouth during the long and nasty withdrawal period. It left scars on most and even killed some. Arturo Station was just one of dozens that operated outside the Earth and Mars protective zones, so unless those governments had overwhelming evidence these atrocities were going on—something that would get a lot of press attention—then they would ignore the rumors. They had too many of their own problems to go looking for more.

Nora and her mother would likely spend their entire lives as slaves in this illicit bioware factory.

"So why aren't you in school?" I said as I opened my door.

She shrugged. "I've learned everything they have to teach me."

I snorted. "Sure you have. So you're an expert on Mars history, European literature, and calculus?"

"They don't teach us that stuff. But I know how to clean bio-vats and assemble crystal matrices."

I just stared at her as she slipped past me and into my cabin. She looked around, then turned back to me.

"I'll clean your cabin for five credits!"

"Huh?"

"Or I can mend clothes? Anything like that. I need to earn some money. Seth has been coming a lot more since I lost my duct cleaning job. I hate Seth."

I scratched my beard. "Sure."

I locked the door open again and started giving her instructions on what to clean. She worked fast, folding clothes, shelving books, separating my trash into the proper recycling bags.

I hated this station and its criminal overlords since I first realized I'd been tricked, but could only blame my own stupidity for coming. That wasn't the case for these people. They had no choice. They were born on the station and probably didn't even exist in any citizen records outside this place, but were still made to pay for food and a sleeping berth. It wasn't mean or even greedy, it was evil.

"Well?" she said. "What now?"

"That's enough cleaning for now. Calvin? Please transfer fifty credits to Nora's account."

Her eyes widened a bit and she shook her head. "That amount of work wasn't even worth five."

"It was to me."

She bit her lip and stared at me for a second, before darting down the hall.

"This is fantastic," Nora said in a whisper.

What I could see of her mouth below the interface goggles was stretched into a wide smile. I glanced down at the scroll screen echoing what she saw. The MOM's work lights swept along one of Arturo Station's four rotation rings, revealing a complex field of conduits, access hatches, antennas, and stenciled identification labels.

"Could you really find that jerk's cabin from the outside?" she said, as she tapped and spun the thumb controls on the teleoperation yoke like an expert.

"If I knew his cabin address," I said, then briefly took the controls to zoom the MOM's camera down to read some of the hull identifier text. It read R1S4-43. "These station habitat rings are assembled from hundreds of identical wedge-shaped sections. One for each cabin. So it's just easier to keep the construction identification tags as a cabin address."

"Cool!" she said and took the controls yoke away from me again. "How did you use that camera zoom?"

I showed her and suddenly the view slaved to my scroll screen started zooming all over the station.

"I bet you spy on people all the time!"

"I do not," I said and took the yoke from her again. "And I think this lesson is over."

"Noooo!"

"We can do it again later."

I helped her remove the interface goggles. Her hair floated nearly straight up, and she wore a wicked grin.

"You have a great job."

"You didn't think so until I let you drive a robot."

Wendy refused to let Nora come with me until I told her she could send her own camera pod and watch us through her comm band. After nearly an hour of Nora's begging, her mother finally allowed her to accompany me to my hub control center for the day instead of staying in her cabin alone. I thought she might like to watch me launch and retrieve some robots. She'd been fascinated for a while by the video feeds coming back from some of the MOMs as they shepherded their flock of nano-disassemblers through the process of stripping the rock and minerals away, leaving the remaining ice in strange, twisted, lacy sculptures that were returned to the station by the MOM.

But she eventually got bored with the video feed and started playing in the microgravity. My control center was really too small of a space for her to be flailing and bumping around, so I had to do something.

"I like having you for a friend," she said and then glanced away as if embarrassed that she said it aloud.

"I like you too," I said and then felt suddenly and horribly guilty again. My makeshift escape pod was finished. Using nothing but nanoscale robots, I'd bypassed critical systems without sounding alarms and had slowly separated the equipment blister from the station hub. The little ship contained a minimalist acceleration sling and enough air and water for the two-week trip to Mars.

So why did I feel so damned guilty? The ice I'd hidden would prevent anyone from dying after I left. And she wasn't even my kid, yet my hands started shaking when I thought about leaving her on the station. I knew I couldn't do it. I started rearranging the computer model of my escape pod, adding a second acceleration sling, trying to find places to attach more tanks. I'd need near twice as much water and air. I'd also need more fuel to get that extra mass to Mars. Food? Should I take more food or let her suffer the same excruciating withdrawal I would?

Felicia's voice echoed in my head, telling me no, that I couldn't take Nora. I looked up at her canister locked in its special mount, but ignored her and kept working.

"What are you doing now?" Nora said from right beside me.

I flinched and closed the scroll screen. "Just some work."

She reached out and touched Felicia's canister. "What was she like?"

I tensed up. I hadn't talked to anyone about Felicia since her death and sure never expected to start with a nine-year-old kid, but as I stared at Nora's open and curious face, I realized I actually did want to talk about her.

"She was very brave and smart. She laughed a lot and loved jokes. And singing. I think she would have liked you."

"You loved her a lot?"

I nodded, the lump in my throat preventing me from saying more.

"And you still talk to her?"

"Yeah," I croaked.

Then she looked at me and squinted. "Does she ever talk back?"

"Sort of," I said. "I can still hear her in my mind sometimes."

"How did she die?"

I swallowed hard. I'd never had to say the truth out loud, in my own words. The helmet-cam video of the incident had told the story back on Phobos, so there was never an investigation. I was reprimanded and reassigned, but never once had to talk about it.

My stomach clenched tight and my pulse raced. I'd always hated the cold vacuum, but after Felicia's death, I went to great extremes to avoid it. Herding robots from a warm, safe workstation had been as close to cold space as I intended to get. Until I formed my escape plan.

I blinked at Nora and took a deep breath.

"We lived on Phobos station. We were both surface equipment technicians. One day while we were outside, I started goofing around. I jumped up on a big rock that gave way and rolled out from under me. I knew better. I knew to not step on boulders and still . . . Anyway, the big rock rolled down a slope and on top of Felicia. The gravity was very low, but the rock had mass and momentum. It tore her suit and pinned her down. By the time I got the rock off of her and fixed her suit, it was too late."

She touched the canister again.

"It was an accident," she whispered. "But that didn't stop you from feeling it was your fault?"

I nodded. How could a freaking nine-year-old kid understand those kinds of feelings?

Felicia was right. I couldn't take Nora with me. It would be wrong to separate her from her mother, even for her own good. And, of course, I'd be instantly arrested on Mars for being a child abductor. I'd have to find a way to take them both.

"I think my mom would like you," she said with an impish grin. "I asked her to invite you to our cabin for dinner, but she said that probably wasn't a good idea. It might make Seth mad."

"Is he your dad?"

"I think so, but my mom won't admit it. He spends the night with Mom sometimes, and she says I have to be nice to him since he's her boss."

I swallowed and felt the panic rising in me again. I had to do something.

When her shift ended, Wendy came to collect Nora.

She hesitated, looking uncomfortable at first, then her gaze hardened. "You sent two payments of fifty credits each to Nora's account. She cleaned for you?"

"Yeah, my cabin and then she cleaned up in here," I said and motioned around my still cluttered work bay.

Nora looked momentarily surprised, then immediately hid it.

"If she wants to come back, I can teach her how to scrub down the robots. They have to be cleaned after every trip out and I hate doing it."

Wendy stared at me, as if trying to read my mind, read my true motivations for being with her daughter.

"There are video recordings of each time she's come to see me. I've already given you access codes to view them."

Her hard expression collapsed, and she looked twice as tired as before. "Sorry, I just . . ."

"No need."

After they left, I floated in the middle of my suddenly very quiet and lonely work bay. I had made no friends and had no lovers since arriving on Arturo Station. It had made my planning easy. But not now.

I pulled Felicia's canister from its mount and held it to my chest.

"I wasn't really brave," she said. "That was just an act to impress you."

"Shut up. You're the most amazing person I know."

"Knew," she said.

I shrugged. "I miss you."

She didn't answer and I floated around the bay for a long time, holding her and remembering. Finally, I bumped against the wall that hid my escape pod and knew I had to do something. There are the mistakes of our actions, like my stupidity that killed Felicia, but also the mistakes of our inactions.

"How can I do this?" I whispered to the can.

"You already know," she said. "You've already decided."

She was right, as always, and the answer was quite simple.

But the execution would be a cast-iron bitch.

I'd done it again. The gradual increase in gravity from nothing to Earth normal felt as if it would crush me, and I could barely stay on my feet. I'd worked twenty-one hours getting everything ready and had almost finished, but with just a few small tasks left, I had to stop and sleep. Even with help from Canker, if I continued on this path, I would forget something critical and it would all be wasted.

When the lift door opened, I was nearly knocked down by a scowling man who actually growled at me before the door closed. I staggered down the corridor to my cabin, glad for once that it was late in the evening shift and Nora hadn't been there to greet me. Before I could even cross the room to my bed, I heard a pounding on the door, and the cabin computer announced Nora.

"Damn." I couldn't. Not now. I ignored her and lay down, but the pounding was insistent, and the computer eventually informed me that she claimed it was an emergency.

I opened the door and my fatigue instantly vanished. Tears streaked Nora's face and her hands were covered with dried blood. She grabbed my arm and dragged me down the hall.

"You have to help my mom! Seth beat her up. She's hurt bad."

I ran the last few steps to the still-open door.

Her mother lay curled into a fetal ball on the bed. Wet bloody towels lay on the floor beside her, but they hadn't stopped any of the bleeding. Her face was a bloody mess.

I knelt next to her. Fury and frustration pushed me to the edge of yelling, but I made my voice soft. "Wendy? This is Clarke. Can you hear me?"

She groaned and said something I couldn't make out.

"Before you came, she said her stomach hurts and she can't breathe," Nora said.

My fury turned to fear as I realized that probably meant internal injuries. "Did you call security?"

"Twice. The first time while he was still hitting her. They didn't come."

Security officers were supposed to respond immediately to all injuries and provide transport if needed. Bastards were probably trying to protect Seth since he was a manager.

"We're going to have to take her to the medical unit ourselves," I said. "But we'll need some help. Stay with her and I'll be right back."

A minute later, with Nora's help, we slid Wendy and her mattress onto the collapsible equipment dolly I had grabbed from my cabin. It wasn't a good fit, but by positioning Wendy's weight over the wheels and letting half of the mattress drag behind, we managed to roll her through the mostly abandoned corridors, halfway around the ring to the medical unit.

The soft, yet insistent chiming from my wrist comm eventually made me open my eyes. At first confused by my surroundings, I then spotted Nora standing next to her mother's regrowth tank and it all came back in a rush. If my alarm was sounding, it meant I had an hour before my automated units went active, and I wasn't ready yet.

I stepped up beside Nora and looked down at her mom. Wendy floated in a tank filled with blue-tinted gel. A tube came from her mouth, and tiny blinking monitoring units were attached to her in various locations. She was awake and, even though buried in medical artifacts, already looked much better.

"How is she?"

"The medtechs say she'll be okay, but she'll have to stay here in the tank for a few days."

The letters "TNK YU" appeared on a screen attached to the tank, and I realized Wendy had a small keypad attached to one hand.

I smiled, wishing I could say something cheerful and positive, but the security officer who came to get statements from Nora and Wendy after we arrived just said they would "talk to" Seth. He was a manager. He was effectively immune to punishment. Of course, if my plan worked, things would get better soon enough, but I had to get to my hub workstation and prepare.

"I'm going to have to go," I said. "I have something important to take care of, but I'll be back later."

I wasn't sure if that last statement was true or not, but I would try.

"PPLS TAK CAR OF NORA."

I stared at the message, wondering how to answer. I couldn't take her. If my crazy attempt at seizing control of the station didn't work, then I'd be in a lot of trouble. I didn't want Nora with me if that happened. I'd assumed Nora would want to stay with her mom.

"Nora, would you rather stay here or come with me?"

She looked at me and screwed up her face. I could tell she didn't know what to do and was on the verge of tears.

"GO," appeared on the screen. "I NED SLEEP. PLS TAK HER."

I swallowed and nodded. "Okay, kiddo. Let's go. We have a lot to do in the next hour."

Everything was ready, with five minutes left on the clock. I looked up from my screen and saw Nora floating in the corner of my little workshop, quietly spinning a screwdriver in the air before her face. Her expression held not even a flicker of hope.

"Be careful with that screwdriver," I said.

"I'd punch it through Seth's head if I could," she said with enough venom that it made me wince. "I hate him!"

"Things are going to get better," I said.

She glanced at me, then away. "I don't see how. He'll keep beating my mom and security won't stop him."

"Look at me."

She looked up, a little startled at my tone. I wanted to tell her what was about to happen, but didn't dare risk saying anything that could tip off Eisenhower's watchers.

"This is a dangerous room. If anything unexpected happens, you have to do exactly as I say. Do you understand?"

Her eyes locked on mine and squinted slightly. She knew there was something unusual in my statement.

"Um . . . okay," she said.

I nodded slowly, then picked up Felicia's canister and held it tight as I watched the screen.

While building my escape pod, I'd already learned how to find and bypass control systems without alerting security, but that had been on a very small scale and in a localized area. So I spent the majority of the previous day interrogating Arturo Station's control and security systems. They had not only the standard triple-redundant hardwired arrangement, but also a fourth and fifth version running along the outside skin in armored cable troughs.

Using my unique method of programming that involved combinations of verbal code words, eye movements, keyboard entries, and finger taps, I instructed my robotic accomplices to build fifteen wireless bypasses, inside and outside the hull. Then, when I seized control, my nano-robots would proceed to destroy the original lines. They would send their robots and technicians out to find the problem but find only empty troughs.

When the timer hit zero, our world changed with a simple message.

EMERGENCY CONTROL CENTER ESTABLISHED.

A virtual control panel appeared on the screen and I started selecting options. The first thing I did was call up a crew status screen. In typical Eisenhower style, it showed the location of every person on the station. I applied a filter to just see managers, security officers, and control room employees. Once I had a good feel for their locations, I sent the emergency de-spin command.

"EMERGENCY DE-SPIN WILL COMMENCE IN TEN MINUTES.

THE STATION WILL THEN BE IN A ZERO GRAVITY SITUATION. PLEASE FIND A SECURE LOCATION."

"Holy crap! What're you doing?" Nora said.

"Buckle in, kid," I said.

"Nora!" she said as she pulled her way along the wall and started to slip her arms into straps.

"Not there. On that wall over there," I said and pointed to the aft wall.

She did as told, then said, "This must be the unexpected situation you expected."

I smiled and nodded but kept my gaze on the personnel screen. As I hoped, all of the control employees and managers were racing for their duty stations or secure cabins in Ring Four. Security, however, was a different matter. They were scattered around the station and seemed to be running in circles. Two were still in Ring One. I cursed under my breath.

"What the hell are you doing?" she whispered.

"Stop cursing," I said.

"Fine. But what are you doing?"

"I'm stealing the station. I'm going to fly it to Mars orbit."

She said nothing and when I looked up, she was staring at me with her mouth hanging open.

"How? I mean, your robots are cool, but they can't push this huge station!"

"Sure they can. It would just take a long time to build up speed. But there's no need. How do you think they got the station out here? The fusion reactor that gives us electricity can also power the engine they use to move the station. Luckily, we have enough fuel to accelerate up to speed and slow us down at Mars."

"Wow," she whispered. "But what about security? Even if you control the station, they'll come get you."

"I have a plan for that, too," I said as the warning sounded the two-minute mark. Except for five security officers, all the station's key personnel, a total of ninety-seven, had scurried to Ring Four as I hoped.

The klaxon sounded and green lights appeared all over my screen's station diagram, indicating each section and ring had been sealed off. When the last hatch lock engaged, the station's hull shuddered and groaned.

"Nothing's happening!" Nora squealed.

"Sure it is. The station takes about ten minutes to stop spinning."

"But . . ." she stopped and looked around the workshop. Some stuff along the walls shifted around, but there was little change in the hub. "Oh, right. We were already in zero gravity. Wait! What about my mom? Will she be okay?"

"She's suspended in a tank of gel. She'll be even safer than we are."

When the control status showed we had come to a complete halt, I engaged the drive at ten percent thrust. The station creaked and moaned again, and this time, anything not locked down started sliding aft. Felicia's canister rolled toward the edge of my bench, but I grabbed it midair as it launched.

"I wonder what you would have thought of this," I muttered, but she didn't answer.

Just before I touched the icon to disengage Ring Four, the screen turned to static.

"Damn it!" I said and slapped the bench.

"Don't curse," Nora said, with a smug voice. I nearly yelled at her to shut up, but instead clenched my teeth. She had earlier hit on my plan's biggest weakness. The station was essentially four equally sized rings attached to a tubular central core. Since the only way to travel between rings was to take elevators up the spokes to the core, sealing each ring in time of emergency was quite easy. But given enough time, Eisenhower and his goons would get out of their locked sections and come after me. To prevent that, I had planned to disconnect Ring Four from the rest of the station and leave it behind for the authorities to come and collect after we'd told our story on Mars. That now looked doubtful. I wondered briefly how I would hold up under torture.

"What happened?" Nora asked.

One glance at her and I realized they wouldn't need torture. They could make me do anything if they could get to Nora.

"I think they're jamming my wireless communications. I'm crippled without it."

"Damn," she muttered. I glared at her for a second, then grabbed a MOM unit from the rack and powered it up. Using her directional antenna, I confirmed my suspicion. The signal was strong from the aft direction, where Ring Four was located.

I closed my eyes and cradled the MOM in my lap for a few minutes. How had Eisenhower figured it out so fast?

Felicia's voice answered the question. "It doesn't matter. You know what you have to do now."

I took a deep breath and pulled along the wall to the emergency locker, where I yanked out two balloon suits.

"Put this on. It's an adult small, but may still be big on you, so cinch it up around the waist, wrists and neck. Just not tight enough to cut off the blood flow."

She took the clear plastic compressed suit. "I know how. We have emergency drills, remember?"

I struggled into mine as the dread continued to build. First the rapid breathing, then the shakes and vomit rising in my throat. I hadn't been in any kind of pressure suit or vacuum since Felicia's death. I didn't want to do this.

I started to explain the entire situation to Nora, then stopped. I didn't think security could still hear me, since I'd seized the control system, but I wasn't sure. I grabbed a piece of paper and quickly wrote it down.

· · ·

I have a secret space pod attached to the other side of the outer wall. I have my nanobots programmed to automatically open and then close a hole in the hull to let me get to the pod. Just in case they are slow and some air leaks out, your suit will inflate automatically and protect you until you can get out through the hatch.

I handed the sheet of paper to her and waited for her to read it.

"Understand?" I asked.

"You're leaving? No!"

"I have to. I'll be right back."

"Send a robot!"

"No radio communications. I have to keep my hands on the MOM to talk to it."

Her lip quivered, but she didn't cry.

I snatched Felicia from the bench and handed her to Nora. "Can you take care of her while I'm gone?"

She nodded, then sealed the suit's breathing mask over her face.

I sealed my suit, grabbed my tool harness and tucked a MOM under my arm, then used the tip of the screwdriver Nora had been playing with to tap a series of commands on the wall. A section of the wall started to fade, then turned into a hole that continued to grow until I could step through and into my pod. I then tapped the command to close the hatch and the hole.

I switched on the air circulation and heaters, then tapped the separation command against the wall. Within seconds, the pod floated free and I turned it toward the aft part of the station. There were only two antennas positioned on Ring Four that could beam directly at my small comm array, so I moved the pod to a point between them and instructed it to maintain position relative to the moving station.

Then came the part that terrified me. With shaking hands, I attached my tether to an interior bracket, opened the pod's little hatch, and held on as the atmosphere vented. The suit inflated, but I immediately felt cold. The balloonsuit heaters weren't meant for EVA or any kind of extended vacuum exposure; they were designed to give people a chance to survive a hull breach long enough to escape to a pressurized area. I had to work fast.

I gripped the MOM's carrying handle in one hand and pulled through the hatch with the other. I hadn't been in hard vacuum for many years and was immediately swept by gut-wrenching vertigo. The only lights on the station exterior were flashing navigation strobes and a few floods that illuminated airlocks and important maintenance panels. Since there were few soft shadows this deep in space, the starkly lit edges contrasted with total blackness and made depth perception difficult. After a few seconds my mind sorted through the individual islands of light and I was able to get my bearings. By tapping on the MOM's case with the screwdriver, I activated her floodlights and turned them toward Ring Four's hull.

I was shivering and my teeth were chattering by the time I located the first antenna. It looked much further away than I'd thought it would be, but I had little time and had to try. My shaking hands made tapped commands to the MOM very difficult, but after the third try, a tiny aiming screen flipped open on the MOM's side and I targeted the antenna, then triggered the heavy mining laser.

At first nothing appeared to happen. I could see the beam diagramed on the tiny screen, but only occasional sparkles along its actual path as it vaporized some of the dust that orbited the station. Then parts of the antenna started to glow orange and the dish slumped backward against the station's forward momentum.

Tiny warning lights flashed along the upper edge of my breathing mask, informing me I had only twenty minutes of compressed air left and my temperature was dropping to dangerous levels. I didn't need warnings to tell me that. I could barely feel my fingers, and my shaking hands were almost useless. I found it hard to think straight. I knew I probably couldn't control my instruction taps well enough to turn the laser off and back on again, so I swung it upward away from the station and then turned toward the other antenna.

I couldn't see the antenna. In order to use the MOM's floodlights, I'd have to turn off the laser or risk blowing a hole in the hull. As I tried to tap the off command for a third time, sound crackled through my earpiece. The MOM was sending me a message telling me she would overheat if she didn't stop the laser.

"I'm trying, damn it!" I said through chattering teeth. Then I realized she had contacted me via radio.

"Turn off laser, MOM."

"Laser off."

"I need you to acc . . . ess the EMERGENCY CONTROL CENTER screen back in the wor . . . kshop."

"Contact established."

"Ini . . . tiate the Ring Four sep . . . aration pro . . . proto . . . col."

"Initiated."

Without a sound, huge mechanical locks swung away from the ring struts. Clouds of chipped paint and ice crystals puffed into space and the ring separated into two C-shaped halves, each carrying three struts. Since the rest of Arturo was still under thrust, the two halves tumbled away slowly and fell behind. In the distance, near one of the Ring Four sections, I saw a wheeling, roughly star-shaped figure that resembled a human body. Then it passed out of the light and was gone. Could I have breached the hull? It didn't matter now. If I had it was too late and I was a murderer.

I could no longer feel my hands or feet, but using tiny puffs from the

MOM's attitude thrusters and hooking my arms and wrists around the hatch frame, I pulled myself back into the pod. Using the MOM as an interface, I verbally commanded it to close the pod's hatch, pressurize the cabin and turn the heat on high.

I felt no elation as I left the pod and floated back into my little hub workshop, only exhaustion and a niggling worry about what could only have been a floating body. My hands and feet felt as if they were on fire, but I knew from my winters in Chicago that feeling the pain was a good sign.

I instructed the nanobots to seal the hull again and turned to Nora. She sat in the control seat with my interface goggles covering the upper half of her head. I immediately realized that her bubble suit hood was pulled down around her neck, but before I could yell at her I also saw that her quivering mouth and chin were covered with tears.

"Nora?"

She didn't answer.

I pulled myself over to the control station and looked at the scroll screen attached to the workspace next to her. It showed the same employee location diagram I had used to watch the Ring Four occupants scurry back to their cabins, only now it was separated into two large C-shaped sections. One of the cabin wedges was flashing red with a decompression tag. Blinking employee ID markers filled the corridor outside the ruptured cabin. So perhaps I really had killed someone.

Nora flinched when I gently pulled the goggles from her head. Tiny tear beads left a glittering trail between the goggles and her face, then started falling aft. She slapped them aside and ran wet hands through her rumpled hair.

"I'm sorry you had to see that, Nora. I'm not sure what happened. Nobody should have died. I don't know—I just . . ."

She cocked her head at me and squinted tear-clogged lashes together. "You didn't kill anyone. I did."

I blinked at her, totally confused.

She pointed at the employee location diagram. "You left that open. I saw where Seth's cabin was and I remembered what you told that guy about burning a hole in his wall."

A cold chill crept down my back.

"And you'd already showed me how to control the MOMs."

I couldn't speak, but I grabbed her and pulled her into a tight hug. She broke down into great gulping sobs muffled against my chest. Then she spoke. In long unbroken strings.

"I saw it all! Through the camera. I'm not sorry he's dead, but . . . I didn't know you were going to leave them behind. Will I go to jail? He just clawed at . . . at nothing. I thought he'd die instantly, but . . ."

"Shhhh . . . It's all over."

"Will I go to jail?"

"No . . . I don't know. I don't think so. You were trying to protect your mother."

She cried again. I stroked her hair and there was nothing I could say that would make it better, but I might still be able to protect her. I'd gone to this much trouble to get Nora free, I wasn't about to let her be incarcerated by the Martian state if I could help it.

Since the MOM systems are under my control, if I admitted to ordering the attack on Seth, the Martian investigators would probably not see any need to dig further. I decided to send the authorities a message admitting that I had stolen the station and killed Seth. Perhaps, under the circumstances, they would be lenient.

After a couple of minutes, I sat Nora back in the control seat and looked at the EMERGENCY CONTROL CENTER screen. Just over an hour had passed since I sent the de-spin command. I ordered the station to slowly spin up again, increased the thrust to sixty percent and triggered the automatic course corrections that would send us to Mars.

After the station's remaining three rings were once again spinning and providing Earth-normal gravity, we entered the elevator for Ring One so that we could go see Nora's mother in the medical unit.

When the lift doors closed, Nora looked up and said, "I can't stop thinking about what I did."

"I know," I said and knelt down next to her. "Look, what you did is wrong and that will never change, but it's over. You can get past this and live your life. I didn't think I could go on after Felicia died, but I did. Does that make sense?"

She shook her head slowly. "It's not the same thing."

"No. It's not the same," I said and then stood up. I couldn't look her in the eye for my next statement. "When we get to Mars, it will be kind of crazy, but I need you to do something for me. I don't want you to lie to anyone, but I also don't want you to tell anyone that you killed Seth unless you're asked."

Her eyes squinted at me, immediately suspicious. "Why?"

Before I could answer, the door opened and a burner gun was thrust into my face, with Meathead attached to the other end.

"My last orders from Lieutenant Eisenhower were to arrest your sorry ass, and that's what I'm going to do."

I sighed and gently pushed Nora behind me.

"No, you're not," I said, trying to sound calm and reasonable, "and I'll tell you why. We're on our way to Mars. It's all automated at this point and the controls are locked down. Nothing you do to me will change that. I've also already started broadcasting messages to the press about what has happened here, how we were all enslaved, but finally managed to take over the station and come seeking freedom and justice from the Martian people."

Meathead blinked and glanced at his equally confused partner. Most of that had been a lie. I wasn't really broadcasting to Mars yet, but still had the better part of two weeks to start that up.

"So? You're still under arrest."

"You don't want to be jailed for murdering me as soon as we get to Mars space, do you?"

"No one said anything about killing you," he muttered and lowered the gun.

"Good. If you don't beat anyone up during the next two weeks, we might actually be able to pass you two off as heroes who helped save all these poor people. Wouldn't you like to be a hero?"

Meathead chewed on his lip and glanced at his partner who just shrugged.

"It's not like he can go anywhere," Nora said. "You'll know where to find him if you decide you need to beat him up later."

"Gee, thanks," I muttered.

Meathead holstered his gun. "There will be a trial, you know."

"Yeah, but wouldn't it be better for the press to think you're a hero instead of bully?"

"Girls love heroes," Nora said.

That made him smile, then he produced a stern face again. "Why should we trust you? What would stop you from making us out the bad guys when the trial comes?"

"I just want to get this station to Mars. I don't really care what happens to you guys after that. Besides, you know that with my robots I could have killed you any time I wanted and yet you're still here."

He thought about that for a second, then shrugged. "C'mon, Ramon. Let's go get some grub."

Nora and I started down the corridor in the other direction, toward the medical unit.

"You did good, Clarke," Felicia said, and I stopped in the middle of the hall. I had forgotten Felicia's canister in my workshop. It was the first time since her death that I'd gone farther than the bathroom without her.

I wasn't really crazy, not totally. I knew that Felicia's voice was all in my head, but part of me had always believed that voice would go away if I didn't keep what was left of her near me. Now I knew that wasn't true.

"What's wrong?" Nora said.

I took a deep breath, shook my head, and continued walking. "Nothing important. Let's go see your mom."

THE RINGS OF MARS

"You can't run away from me, Jack," I said into my helmet mic. "I can radio base and get your suit coordinates."

"Screw you, Malcolm," he said, then refused to talk again. I followed his trail and tried not to think about why my oldest and closest friend in two worlds, and his robotic digger Nellie, had left me far behind.

Instead, I concentrated on perfecting the loping stride Jack had taught me months before. It was an awkward, unnatural rhythm, but he assured me it was the most efficient method. And of the humans on Mars, no one had covered more ground than Jack.

Tiny dervishes lifted from the dust churned by Nellie's tracks, swirling on a delicate breeze, but my passage was enough to cause their collapse. Everything on Mars seemed ancient and tired, even the wind.

Jack's boot prints—wide apart and shallow—were on a straight course and easy to follow, but Nellie's tracks peeled off in strange directions many times. She must've sniffed out oxide-rich gravel patches to melt in her electrolysis furnace, but no matter how far she went, the robot's path always returned to Jack's. I followed their trail and tried to rejoice in being one of the few humans to ever see Mars like this, but my regrets persisted.

Against all reason and expectation, Jack thought himself more colonist than explorer and was willing to trample anyone in that pursuit. If devious resourcefulness was typical of Martians, then Jack was a good one.

An alarm squawked in my ears, surprising me enough that I stumbled and skidded to a floundering stop.

RADIATION ALERT! RADIATION ALERT! ETA, 47 MINUTES. SEEK IMMEDIATE SHELTER.

Forty-seven minutes? My suit's magnetized outer skin was protection against the ambient radiation, but not huge solar flares. I fought growing panic as I turned in circles, looking for a cave, stone outcropping or even a boulder, but saw only dust and scattered rocks. The nearest ridgeline was blurry with distance. Anger also grew in the wake of my fear. Nellie provided our only radiation protection, and Jack had taken her. They were probably digging in already, and I had to find them if I wanted to survive. I started running.

"Malcolm? Jack? This is base, do you copy?" I could hear the tension in the communication officer's voice.

"I read you, Courtney," I said, my voice jarred by running. "Why so little warning? I thought we were supposed to get it days ahead of time?"

"I don't know, but you and Jack had better get to shelter. There's no way we can get a truck or the dirigible to you fast enough."

"I'm trying," I said and signed off.

Then Jack's voice crackled into my helmet. "Malcolm! We're coming back for you. Follow our trail to meet us and run!"

I ran faster.

Their dust cloud was visible long before I could resolve shapes, but they kept coming, and soon Nellie's squat hexagonal form appeared at the head of her rooster-tail dust plume. I didn't see Jack. Five minutes later, I staggered and gasped to a stop next to the robot as Jack climbed down from her back. The bastard never mentioned we could ride her.

She trundled back and forth over a large flat spot, then, finding a suitable location, jolted to a stop. Her treaded drive units separated and rotated on their mountings, raising the shoulder-high robot into the air on its toes like a three-footed ballerina. Panels slid open between the tracks, revealing large spinning cutters that folded out and locked into place. Nellie sank rapidly into the ground as sand jetted skyward from tubes on her back.

The alarm sounded again, this time giving us less than twenty minutes. I glanced at Jack, but he stared at the robot's interface panel on his sleeve and said nothing.

Nellie disappeared below the lip of the hole and within a couple of minutes, the dirt stopped flying. Jack tapped out a few more commands, and a cloud of dust poofed from the hole. He ran to look inside, then pulled an aluminum rod from his pack. With several twists and pulls, it became a telescoping ladder with rungs folding out from each side. He dropped it into the dark excavation and climbed down, motioning for me to follow.

I peered over the edge just as Jack opened Nellie's top hatch and disappeared inside. I was confused, because there wasn't room for us both, but followed him down and through. Once inside I understood. Nellie had split in two, with her upper half forming the airlock and her lower part a larder and mini-lab. The pieces were connected by a telescoping post in the center and mottled gray plastic surrounded us, sagging in pleats like a discarded skirt. Jack had designed her well.

As I dogged the hatch behind me, Jack flipped a switch, and Nellie started inflating the plastic envelope with oxygen she had collected through her rock-melting electrolysis procedure. Air pushed the big plastic bag open until it tightened against the dirt and rock walls, creating a fifteen-foot-diameter by seven-foot-tall pressurized donut-shaped habitat.

"We'll leave our outer suits here," Jack said, indicating where we stood in the donut's hole. "Use nose plugs until we're through the second seal."

When the status light turned green, Jack released his helmet seal with an equalizing pop. I did the same and held my breath until my nose filters were in place, started breathing in through my nose and out through my mouth, a routine everyone on Mars had mastered within the first few days.

"Can we get a commlink down here?" I asked while loosening the seals on my excursion suit. "How will we know when the radiation storm is over?"

Jack ignored me as he removed his suit's radiation skin, leaving only the biomaintenance layer, or what he called million-dollar long johns. The nano-plied material absorbed moisture, adjusted body temperature, and used a powerful elastic netting to maintain the skin's surface tension at about a third of Earth normal. Only the helmet held pressurized air. They were extremely efficient, but they fit too snugly, and mine was already chafing in sensitive spots.

We slipped through two overlapping seals to enter the main chamber, and I was surprised by the noise from Nellie's fans. She was pumping and filtering enough air to maintain half-Earth-normal pressure. Coupled with the heat she was generating to warm the burrow, it must be a huge drain on her batteries.

"So, how long will Nellie's batteries let us stay down here?"

Jack didn't answer, but opened a flap, pulled a long clear tub from Nellie's guts and looked at the water sloshing inside.

"Looks like she collected about half a liter," I said. "Is that good or bad?"

He still didn't respond.

"We'll be stuck down here for hours, or maybe even days. How long are you going to keep up this childish silent treatment?"

He turned to glare at me. The dim light provided by Nellie's lamps gave him a menacing appearance.

"Shut the hell up, Malcolm."

I wasn't going to leave it alone. This trip would be my last opportunity to see him face-to-face for years, or if his present state was any indicator, the rest of my life.

"You did this to yourself; why are you blaming me?" I yelled over the fan noise.

We'd been best friends since our sophomore year at Purdue, and he'd never in fifteen years been so angry at me. I hadn't caused the board to order him home, but I had supported their decision. To Jack, it was the same thing.

He glared at me for a second and then moved around the donut where I couldn't see him. I followed. When he lowered himself to the floor against the outer wall, I sat down facing him, making sure he knew I wasn't giving up.

"I warned you this would happen," I said. "I tried to help you."

"Did you ever consider—for even a second—that I knew what I was doing?"

"Well, yes, but—"

"And I wanted to take this last walk alone," he said, barely audible above the fan noise. "I invited you to come on every walking trip I took, and you always turned me down. Why now?"

Because you didn't invite me this trip, I thought, but didn't say aloud. Jack could disable the locator on his excursion suit and, with Nellie's help, easily hide until the Earth-Mars cycler window passed. That would give him an extra six months.

"Because this will be our last chance to do this together," I said. "You've been telling me for a year that I hadn't seen the real Mars. Now is your chance to show me."

He scrambled toward me on all fours, stopping inches from my face, close enough for me to smell his stale sweat. "Together? Go to hell, Malcolm. I wanted you to see what I'd found because you were my friend. But your job and that stinking corporation are more important to you than anything else."

I shoved him out of my face. "Bull! I busted my tail to get you up here. I pulled strings and called in favors. Because you are my friend, and I knew you would love it here, but you screwed it up. That stinking corporation flew you to Mars and is paying you a salary to find mineral deposits big enough to justify building a permanent colony. You need satellites and robot flyers for that. Not even a hot-jock geologist like you can do it wandering aimlessly around the surface."

He shook his head. "You're a planetologist, for God's sake. One of the first in history to actually walk on another world, and yet you've never even seen it."

"I spend every day studying this planet. I go out in the field—"

"Don't give me that crap," he said. "You fly to a spot, get out and walk around for a few hours, then come back to a nice cozy little office. You don't know this planet."

"Well, here I am. Show me."

He shook his head and again moved around to the opposite side.

I gave up and leaned back against the curved wall. My muscles ached from the unaccustomed workout, but the cool Martian soil behind the plastic felt good against my throbbing head.

I didn't remember falling asleep, but I woke stiff and cold to the sounds of Jack rummaging through supplies in Nellie's larder. I sat up with a groan. He tossed me a nutrition bar and a water bag.

"It's morning and the radiation warning's over. We're leaving."

We emerged under a sky thick with brilliant stars. I almost made a nasty comment about it not being morning, but was stunned into silence. One couldn't see anything like this through Earth's atmosphere, even out in the mountains and at the base, work and safety lights diminished the brilliance. Man always had to leave the cities to see the stars. That hadn't changed.

Jack ignored me and watched Nellie struggle from her hole like some cybernetic land crab. My helmet prevented me from looking up for very long. I wished I could remove it and see that sky without the reflections and scratches of my faceplate, to feel the soft breezes and smell the air, but we never could. Someday humans might feel the Martian wind on their faces, but it wouldn't be me or Jack, and it wouldn't be the same Mars.

Dawn came quickly in the thin atmosphere, and while I watched, the stars faded, and the black-and-gray landscape bloomed purple and orange. I'd seen two Martian sunrises outside the base, and both had been in passing while loading trucks for field excursions. Never had I taken the time to actually experience dawn on our new world. Not like this.

"Thanks, Jack," I said. "If you show me nothing else, that sunrise was worth the trip."

"It's always been here."

Once the anemic white sun peeked over the hills, we started east, this time slowly enough for me to keep up.

A few hours later, after Nellie had once again topped off her oxygen tanks, we descended a long grade into a deep, narrow canyon. The wind picked up, showering us with blowing sand and the occasional dust devil. I marveled at the simple beauty of the untouched stone surrounding us. The canyon walls were painted by purple shadows, but where the sun struck the sides, bright bloody reds and sandy whites sprang into stark and sudden brilliance.

We rounded some rocks and Jack stopped. I stopped too. Ten or twelve twisted black shapes stood alone in the middle of the broad canyon floor. The largest stood over ten feet tall, with arms stretching toward us and others reaching to the sky. My pulse raced and I made myself move forward. They were black stone. Some were pitted, porous, and a few polished to an almost mirror finish. I could see that some of their lengths had been recently uncovered, evidence of Jack's previous visits.

"Basalt? With the surrounding soft stone eroded away?"

"Maybe they're Martians," Jack said.

"They do look like tormented souls, frozen in their misery. The lava must've squeezed though some tight spaces, fast and under extreme pressure to form that way."

"Odd, isn't it?" he said.

His tone made me turn to look. He was staring down into a shallow depression between the figures, then turned toward me. His haunted expression made a chill crawl up my back. For the first time in my life, Jack frightened me.

"I found something, Malcolm. Something important."

I stared at him, surprised and waiting, but he didn't elaborate. "Well? What did you find?"

"I'm trying to decide if I want to show you or not," he said.

That stunned me. Did Jack's distrust cut that deep? But even if it did, how could anyone find something important on Mars and not share it with the rest of humanity?

"What the hell does that mean?" I said.

"Right now, I'm in control. When you realize what I've found, you'll try to take over. I don't want that. I want you to remember that you're my friend."

The implication frightened me. Could his find be so important that it would cause a schism between us larger than my agreeing to send him home? I said the only thing I could say. "Of course, I'm your friend. I can't forget that."

He shook his head and said, "I'm not so sure."

When he started walking, Nellie and I followed, but I was frustrated and worried.

Our Mars base had been continuously occupied for nearly three years, but we'd found nothing surprising. At least nothing eye-popping enough to goad MarsCorp into building a permanent colony. We'd proved we could live here, but it was expensive and the coolness aspect was wearing off back home. We needed a "Holy Crap" factor. If Jack had found that and was keeping it to himself, I'd beat him to a pulp.

He wouldn't hesitate to tell me if he'd found a huge underground aquifer or a large platinum deposit. So he'd found something momentous. Was it some kind of moss or lichen living under the sand? Or a fossil of some long-dead plant or animal? I itched to question him, to threaten or coerce him into telling me, but knew that wouldn't work with Jack. He'd tell me or he wouldn't, and nothing I said or did at this point would change that.

By midafternoon we came to a low ridge. We were almost on top of it before I realized it was the ejecta blanket from an ancient crater. I followed him up the gentle slope and looked down on a chaotic scene.

The crater floor was covered with boot prints, Nellie's tracks and piles of stone that formed a ring, easily a hundred yards across. I had a sinking feeling. Jack had obviously arranged the stones.

"Wow, Martian crop circles?"

He ignored me and followed the rim until he and Nellie turned into a narrow opening where the crater wall had collapsed. Their past traffic had packed the fall into a hard ramp that led down to the floor. As we descended, I saw a hole surrounded by darker, finely spread sand. I recognized the robot's handiwork. Jack had slept there at some point.

He went directly to the hole, mounted a collapsible ladder already inside and disappeared into the dark interior.

My excitement grew as I followed, nearly falling off the ladder twice in my haste to get to the bottom. About halfway down, the hole opened into the upside-down mushroom shape where Nellie's inflatable shelter had once expanded.

"Careful," Jack said. "There's a big hole in the floor."

I stepped off the ladder and in the dim light could see the bottom littered with gravel and several large discarded bags made from rope and a cut-up plastic tarp. I turned on my helmet lamp and saw a large hole in the floor, nearly two yards in diameter just a few feet from the ladder. Wispy steam floated from inside. I looked up to ask Jack why, but he was gone. I spun around and saw a large opening in one wall. Light flickered inside.

"Jack?"

"In the tunnel. This will be easier to explain if you see it."

The tunnel was narrow and just tall enough to clear my helmet, but ran about ten feet, then teed left and right. I stopped. The wall before me curved and twinkled in my headlamp. When I moved the light, I saw parts of the surface were translucent. Blues, grays and whites flowed together, making odd shadows. I moved slowly along the tunnel, one side of which was the strange material, until it opened into a small chamber. Only then did I realize I was looking at a large cylinder that disappeared into the ceiling and floor. Jack waited on the far side.

"Jack. Please tell me you didn't make this."

"Nope."

"What's it made of? Have you analyzed it yet?"

"Water ice," he said.

My hammering heart slowed and I relaxed a little. Of course, it would be something natural. For a moment I'd envisioned beautiful stone pillars holding up the roof of an ancient Martian temple. But then I realized, even if it didn't match my wild imagination, he'd still made an amazing find. I touched it again.

"There's so much. How deep do you think it goes?"

"Nellie estimates another forty feet or so beyond this."

"Holy crap."

"They're all that deep. All thirty-six of them."

"I don't . . . thirty-six what?"

Jack dragged his hand along the ice and moved to face me. "Thirty-six ice pillars. I've only uncovered five, but those stones up top show the pattern Nellie found. These five are all perfectly smooth and exactly the same diameter. And I'd bet they are all the same depth too."

I stared at him. A lump formed in my throat and I felt a weight on my chest. I was a scientist. I couldn't let myself believe the conclusions my mind formed. I wanted something like this too bad. It had to be studied.

"It has to be some natural formation," I said with an overly dry mouth. "Nature does strange things, like those creepy basalt shapes."

He shrugged. "I'm not saying otherwise. But these things are also equally spaced, thirty-five forming a ring, with another one in the center."

I turned and rushed back out to the hole in the floor.

"Is this one of them too?" I asked, dreading his response.

"Yeah," Jack said and came up behind me. "Nellie sensed the water ice and stopped here to dig. I wouldn't have thought to even look back in the hole after we were done, except she'd filled her nearly empty water tanks with this single dig and threw extra ice out onto the surface to evaporate. That never happened before."

"And the hole is—"

"Because it's sublimating. The light hits it during the day. I tried covering it up, but that created a heated pocket and made it worse."

My hands shook. If his claim was true, Jack had stumbled across what might be the largest single find in human history . . . and he was letting it vaporize. "You're digging the others out?"

"I'm not exposing them to the light. They haven't lost anything from their diameters."

My respiration peaked so rapidly an alarm sounded in my helmet as the suit adjusted my gas levels.

"Jack! We . . . we . . . have no idea how old these things are or what the open air will do to them. We have no right. We're not qualified to make this kind of decision for the entire human race."

"Why not?" Jack said. "No one on Earth has ever encountered alien artifacts, so we're the new experts."

I had a panicky feeling about losing more of this material. I had to stop him. But I took a deep breath and tried to focus. Jack wasn't an idiot, so I needed to listen to what he was saying. I entered the tunnel and checked the ambient temperature inside. Minus sixty-three Celsius, which might be fine since it wasn't in direct sunlight.

"We don't know what's in that ice," I said. "Maybe there were sculptures, or carved instructions or some kind of microorganisms. Maybe even cold-suspended Martian DNA. We could be losing hundreds of painfully preserved Martian species."

"This one was an accident. And it's too late to save it."

"Maybe not. We could fill it back up with dirt, then call it in and get all of mankind's resources behind us."

"And lose them forever to MarsCorp?"

I paused, not sure what he meant. "No one will take this away from you, Jack. You'll still get all the credit."

He slapped a dusty glove against my helmet, making my ears ring. "Credit? You just don't get it, do you? I don't care about getting credit. This is a message. It's a puzzle and I want to figure it out. I feel like I'm so close."

The swat on my helmet made me furious, but I held back. I still wanted to convince him it was right before I reported this to the base. "You'll still be able—"

"No!" he said and bumped his visor against mine, putting his face as close to me as possible. "If we report this, MarsCorp will turn it into a Martian Disneyland. Most of those idiots on Earth care about nothing but making money, so this will become a cash cow vacation spot."

"Oh, come on. You don't think—"

"There's dignity in this place, Malcolm. It's a serious message, aimed directly at humanity, not some damned tourist attraction."

"A message? You don't know that. If these were put here by some other intelligence, it could have just been a water cache."

"It's a message designed for us. What better way to signal Earthlings coming to Mars? We'd be looking for water. Even if this is several million years old, and they didn't know what we would be like, they would still know any species coming from Earth would need water."

I swallowed and tried to control my building frustration. "You may be right, but we have tools at the base to protect these artifacts while we study them. If there's a message, we'll find it. I'm going to call it in."

He stared at me, but there was no anger in his eyes, only cold determination.

"I have to, Jack."

He nodded inside his helmet and then grabbed both of my arms in an iron grip. "I knew I couldn't trust you with this, so I guess we'll do it the hard way," he said. "Into the hole."

"What?" I was confused.

He started pushing me backward toward the opening in the floor. "I don't want to damage your suit, but, if you don't jump down into that hole, I'll throw you in."

"Oh, come on! You can't—"

"Now, Malcolm!"

I turned my torso enough so I could look down into the hole. The ice floor was easily twenty feet down, much too deep to jump out, even with Martian gravity.

"Jack, don't be—"

He gave me a little shove and I staggered backward toward the hole. I had no choice but to jump or would have fallen in butt first. I landed on the slick surface with a bone-jarring thump, but kept my feet.

He stared down at me, still wearing that cold, blank expression. I considered the possibility that my best friend was about to kill me. It would be easy enough and hard to prove.

"Jack, what—"

"I doubt that you can contact base from down there, but I'll call in your location. Your MarsCorp lackeys will be here to rescue you in a couple of hours. And, boy, will they be surprised at your spectacular find."

Before I could answer, he disappeared from view.

He was wrong. Reception was bad down in the hole, but I did make contact with the base. My call generated equal amounts of excitement and incredulity. I wished I'd thought to record video, but hadn't planned on reporting from a hole within a hole. I could tell by their carefully phrased responses that they only half believed me, but would hold their skepticism in check until they could see it themselves.

They also gave me bad news. A large dust storm was rolling in and would prevent launching a dirigible. Courtney said they were sending the ground trucks immediately, but it would be four hours minimum, depending on the storm's severity.

The link faded into static. I looked up and could only see pale powder spiraling into the hole. Sandstorms on Mars carried millions of tons of the talc-fine dust that could easily bury me. I pulled the climbing axe from my belt and tried to hack hand and footholds into the hard-packed wall.

Ten minutes and three handholds later, I paused to check my oxygen usage. Five hours and twenty minutes at my current rate. I had to slow my breathing.

I looked up and saw only dust swirling in my helmet lamp, then caught a metallic glint. Jack had not taken the ladder. I fumbled the line from my utility pouch and tied on two chisels about ten inches apart. On my fifth try, the makeshift bolo did not come back. I pulled and tugged. The ladder jerked suddenly and sailed into the hole, hitting my shoulder on the way down. I cursed, then held my breath waiting for my suit alarms to tell me I had a tear, but had been lucky.

Once on the surface, with wind-driven sand pelting my suit, I had a decision to make. I could wait down in the hole, safe from the ravaging storm, and probably die as my air ran out. Or I could go find Jack. The wind was steady and mild at the moment, but even tired old Mars could drive abrasive grit at 200 mph on the open plains. My suit's tough outer skin was all one piece and could stand that abuse for a long time, but my helmet seal was at risk.

I pulled the aluminum ladder from the hole and attached an antenna wire. Much to my surprise, I established an immediate satellite link through the static-charged dust. I called Jack and got no response. I tried to get his suit's transponder location and failed. So I called base.

"The trucks had to stop and wait for better visibility," Courtney said through static. "You need to hunker down and conserve your air until they arrive."

My tank level read less than five hours remaining. If the trucks started moving now and had no more delays, they might make it to me in time. My decision was now easy. I had to find Nellie.

"Can you contact Jack for me?"

"He called in to give us your location about ten minutes after your first call. He wanted to make sure we could find you. But we haven't been able to contact him since. And his transponder stopped transmitting right after that."

The bastard dumped me in a hole so he could run off and hide? It made no sense. Even if I died, my suit transponder would eventually lead rescuers to me and the pillars. His secret was out. Why let me die?

"Can you give me a line between my position and his last call so I'll have a direction?"

"Sure," she said. The static was worsening.

If Jack didn't want to be found, he would have changed course immediately after his call, but it was a starting place. If I could get close enough, maybe he would hear my call. Staying here and waiting wasn't a real option.

"I just sent the coordinates from Jack's last call and his last five transponder pings. I had no idea he'd covered so much ground on his walkabouts."

"How do you know that?" I asked.

"I'm looking at a map of his ping locations for all of his excursions. I have one for everyone who—"

"Can you send me that map?" If I could see where Jack had been, I might get an idea where he could hide.

Courtney paused. "Sure. It might take several tries with this bad connection, but it's on the way."

"Thanks," I said and started to sign off.

"Malcolm? Why did Jack leave you there?"

"I pissed him off."

"He's lost it," she said, with obvious anger in her voice. "Well, if he wasn't already going home, he would be now. Stay put. The ground trucks are moving again, but slowly. We're also rigging a flier to bring you some O_2 canisters."

The robotic fliers were more like powered gliders with long fragile wings. They wouldn't get one even close to me in this wind.

"Don't waste the flier, Courtney. I'm going to try and find Jack. Malcolm out."

I broke the connection and pulled up the ping map on my helmet's HUD screen. Thousands of random dots covered a topographical map with location numbers on a grid. The widely scattered dots made my eyes hurt, but I could see some patterns. Many dots were arranged in snaky lines, obviously sent while he was on the move, but there were also heavy clumps representing locations where he'd spent time.

I zoomed the view out and as the dots converged, I saw it. Most were in clumps that formed a pattern. I added in a red dot for my location and it appeared atop one of the heavy-traffic clusters.

The wind buffeted me, some gusts threatening to knock me down, and dust had drifted around my feet, but I ignored it as my pulse raced and my heart thudded. I instructed my suit's computer to ignore the noise data and only chart those points where twenty or more appeared in close proximity. Seventeen clumps appeared, evenly dispersed along a broad arc. I told the computer to consider each cluster a single point and extrapolate the pattern based on the existing group.

The new pattern formed a ring nearly forty miles across and contained thirty-five points. The ring of pillars Jack had marked in the crater contained thirty-five, with one in the middle. The center of the large ring fell in the canyon where we'd seen the basalt formations earlier that morning.

Even though his actions might kill me, I had to appreciate Jack's devious mind this time. He'd shown me these ice pillars as bait, to get me excited and keep me and the base off his back while he explored the real find. And this was his last trip before being sent home, so it had to be now. I fixed the canyon location on my map, pulled the patching tape from my repair kit, and wrapped my helmet seal for extra protection, then started walking.

I carried the ladder with me, using it both as antenna and a pole to feel out terrain made invisible by the thick whirling dust. I also kept broadcasting directly to Jack. "I know you're in the center with your Martian friends, and I'm on my way to meet you. I need oxygen." As an added incentive, I also said, "This is encrypted, but my transponder is still broadcasting."

An hour into my trek, Courtney called to tell me their specially rigged flier had crashed. With a voice strained by grief, she rattled off the standard oxygen conservation litany and again begged me to stay put. I told her I could find Jack, then signed off and kept walking.

When the one-hour oxygen warning dinged, I checked my position and realized I couldn't make it to the basalt formations, even if I'd guessed Jack's location correctly. The wide plain between canyon and crater would have been safe enough to allow running, with only a slight chance of falling, but my slow, cautious advance through the storm had killed me. I tossed the ladder aside and started running.

Less than a minute later, my radio crackled to life with Jack's voice. "Turn on your emergency strobe and stop moving, Malcolm. According to your transponder blip on my map, I should be right on you."

I stopped and fumbled for the strobe switch on my helmet, but before I could flip it, Nellie materialized out of the dust and nearly ran over me as she shot past. I turned as she skidded to a halt amid scattered sand and gravel.

Tears formed, blurring my vision, and warm relief flowed through me like very old Scotch. Jack jumped down from Nellie's back and started detaching oxygen canisters from her side.

"This whole Jack-arriving-like-the-cavalry-to-save-Malcolm thing is getting kinda old," he said as he turned me around, opened my pack and switched out my tanks.

I swallowed, trying to clear the lump in my throat. "Thanks," I said. "Did you hear my calls to you?"

"Yeah, but I started back as soon as I realized your MarsCorp friends were going to let you die."

"So I was right? The basalt formations are at the center of a larger pattern?"

"Yeah," he said with a grim expression. "How'd you know?"

After I explained, he shook his head and sighed. "I knew I should've disconnected that damned transponder a long time ago. Not that it matters now. I had my chance and I blew it."

Jack had come back for me, risking his opportunity to be the first person to see the big find. He wanted a chance to solve the puzzle, to discern the message he perceived in those formations. Helping him still do that was the least I could do in thanks.

"What's down there?" I said. "In the canyon?"

"I don't know yet, but Nellie says it's nearly thirty feet square, and the part I've uncovered so far is flat, smooth basalt. Those weird shapes you saw are attached to it like sprues to an injection-molded part."

"Like it was molded or formed in place?"

He nodded.

Huge and square, I thought and tried to dampen my new excitement. "Amazing. So you haven't exposed anything that will melt?"

He laughed, for the first time since learning he was going home. "No, basalt doesn't melt easily. But there's something else."

I waited and could see him smiling through the visor. "Well?"

"There's a pattern in the face I uncovered. Thirty-five cylindrical pockets arranged in a ring, with one in the center. According to Nellie's analysis, the translucent material at the bottom of each hole is diamond."

"What could that mean?"

"I have no idea. I had to stop and come rescue you."

It was my turn to smile. I held up a finger and called base.

"Sorry for the scare, Courtney," I said. "But I found Jack. Nellie is working fine, so we have plenty of air and are not in any danger now."

"Thank God, Malcolm. Meteorology says this storm could last another two or three days. Are you sure you have enough supplies for that long?"

Jack cut in on the conversation, reassuring her we were going to be fine.

"You're in a heap of trouble, Jack! And I still don't have a transponder signal for you."

He opened his mouth, but I cut him off. "Actually, Courtney, I may be losing my transponder signal too. We're about to go into an area that seems to play hell with most of our communications gear. So don't worry if you don't hear from us for a few days."

"I don't think—"

"We'll meet up with the investigation team at the dig site in two or three days, or whenever this storm lets up."

"But—"

"Malcolm and Jack signing off," I said and killed the connection.

Jack looked at me and raised an eyebrow. "If you could find that pattern, they can too. Besides, they have enough information to know what direction you were going."

"Yeah, but we could head north for a few hours and cut off my transponder, then enter the canyon from the north end. That should mess them up for awhile. It may only give us a few days. Probably only until the storm ends. Will that be enough time?"

He shrugged, always a strange gesture in an excursion suit. "Maybe, but if you do this, there is a good chance you'll be sent home too."

"I wouldn't miss this for anything," I said and started running.

We dug in for the night near the canyon's north end and awoke to a sickly yellowish-pink dawn. The weak sun struggled to break through the haze, but the storm had abated and the winds died, so the timer was running. If our luck ran out, our fellow explorers could find us within a matter of hours.

Ninety minutes after breaking camp, we stood atop the basalt block. Using Nellie's vacuum system, we removed the dust accumulated from the storm, revealing a smooth polished surface with the now-familiar pattern of holes in the center of the top surface.

"How odd that they'd make this finely polished cube, yet have these weird, gnarly sprues marring its perfection," I said.

"It does look to be part of the formation process," Jack said. "Maybe they just didn't care about the sprues."

"Yeah, but why these holes? Why their fascination with this particular pattern?"

He knelt down and aimed his helmet light into the holes. They were the diameter of a golf ball and about a foot deep, and, as he'd earlier reported, their bottoms were glassy and clear. "I don't know, but I'd sure as hell like to find out."

"Looks like we need some kind of key," I said. "And if we had a key, I wonder what it would do?"

Jack stared at the holes, occasionally poking his gloved finger in one. "Maybe we could make a key."

"You know," I said, pausing, not sure if I should voice my latest thought. "The other holes are filled with water ice. Maybe . . ."

Jack almost leaped to his feet. "It couldn't hurt to try!"

Of course, that comment left me feeling more than a little uneasy, but there was no stopping him once he got started. Forty minutes later, I dubiously examined Jack's kludge work. He'd originally wanted to build a manifold of tubes to feed water into each hole evenly, but I had stopped him when I realized he'd have to cannibalize most of Nellie's internal plumbing to realize the contraption.

We instead covered the pattern with a shallow tent made from extra sheet plastic, precariously sealed to the surrounding surface with our entire stock of suit repair putty. A hole in the center was cinched up tight around a tube attached to Nellie's tanks. Jack assured me that if we pumped water in fast enough, it would fill the holes and freeze before evaporating. I wasn't convinced, but we had nothing to lose, except, of course, most of our water.

"What if we do open the lock? Or activate something? What if we break it?"

Jack looked up at me, his exasperation obvious even through the dusty visor. "Make up your mind, Malcolm. We're never going to get another shot at this. It's us—right now—or we forget about it. They are going to be pissed enough to ship us back home, and instead of us figuring this out, some Martian Mickey Mouse will build an enchanted castle around it."

He was right. I had made my decision and sealed my allegiance. "Let's try it."

We stood on a pile of excavated dirt at the cube's edge and pumped the water in under pressure. Wispy vapor curls immediately revealed the gaps in our crude seal. The tent filled and tightened rapidly, to the point we feared it would burst the seal.

"Stop!" I yelled.

Jack killed the flow and the plastic almost immediately started to deflate.

"Crap," he said. "We'd better look quick."

Before we could pull the cover off and check our handiwork, a series of reports—loud enough in the weak Martian air to hear through our helmets— made us both step backward. Fissures appeared in the basalt, radiating outward from under the plastic cover in an oddly uniform pattern.

"You were right," Jack muttered. "We broke it."

"Maybe not. The lines are all straight and equally spaced, like pie wedges. They don't look like natural fractures."

Before I could say another word, he jumped down onto the surface, tested it with a couple of bounces, then dropped to his knees, shining his helmet light into the cracks. He motioned for me to come down.

"The basalt is only about a foot thick," he said. "And it looks like more diamond under it. Holy crap. Do you think this stuff just covers a big block of diamond?"

"Well, it would sure be durable," I said and joined him. I removed the cover to look at the pattern. It had nearly disappeared, but I could tell by the fragment arrangement that the cracks had each started at a hole, then ran across the top and disappeared down the sides into the dirt.

"Looks like our ice expanded and started the breaks," I said.

"No way. One or two cracks maybe, to relieve pressure, but not—" He paused and ran a hand along the edge of several sections, then started pulling on them.

"Unless, of course," he grunted, "it was designed to break this way."

The wedge moved nearly an inch. He stood up and looked at me. "I bet if the whole block had been uncovered, this shell would have fallen away. I think it was meant to fall away."

We used Nellie to dig all morning, but by midafternoon had to send her out in search of ice to replenish our air and water supply. So we dug by hand, using our climbing axes. Once we'd totally cleared the second side, Jack slipped his axe blade behind one of the loose basalt sections and started gently rocking it.

With an audible pop, the strip collapsed into large chunks that tumbled down on him like stacked blocks pushed over by a petulant child. I heard him grunt and curse over the commlink as he disappeared in a pile of stone and dust.

"Jack!" I ran to him and started moving yard-wide pieces of stone I wouldn't have been able to lift on Earth.

"Crap," he muttered as I pulled the last piece off.

"Are you leaking? Are you hurt?"

"No leaks," he said, but I could hear pain in his voice. "And I'm fine, just help me get up."

I moved one more slab and couldn't miss its obvious uniformity. Jack had been right again. The basalt covering had been designed to come apart easily. The shell's inside face had been serrated in a grid pattern, the squares held together by a thin strip of surface stone that was easily broken once the interconnecting tensions and supporting soil had been removed.

I turned my attention to what lay beneath the shell. It appeared to be a solid block of diamond. I switched on my helmet light and looked inside. Prickles and chills crawled up my back, as I unwittingly uttered the phrase from the old science fiction classic. "My God, it's full of stars."

Jack grunted as he brushed off dust and checked his suit and harness equipment for damage. "Stop screwing around. What do you see?"

I opened my mouth, but words wouldn't come. The interior of the block was filled with what looked like constellations of sparkling stars. It was as if someone had cut a block of the stunning Martian midnight and buried it for us to find.

"Malcolm?" Jack moved up next to me, leaning in to see.

The starlike points in the block only glowed when my light touched them. My scientific mind argued that they could be impurities or microfractures in the diamond block, but part of me knew I was looking at a three-dimensional celestial map.

"A map," Jack whispered.

My commlink hissed and popped, then Courtney's voice intruded on our discovery. "Come in, Malcolm, this is Mars Base One."

I almost succumbed to training and a long-ingrained habit to answer her, but remained silent. I glanced at Jack, but he was totally focused on the block's interior.

"Come in, Malcolm. We've had fliers all over the area since the storm ended. There are no communication anomalies. We don't know what you two are doing out there, but the commander is pissed." She paused for a second, then resumed. "He says Jack is going home no matter what, but considering the amazing find you reported, he might consider letting you stay. If you call in now."

The urge to respond with a long string of obscenity was nearly overwhelming. They were prepared to let me die in the storm, yet were now threatening to punish me? I bit my lip, made sure my frequency setting was set for local and Jack's channel and told him.

"We'd better hurry. Base just called. I don't think they know where we are yet, but they are sure looking."

We started digging faster. When Nellie returned, I focused my efforts on getting video of the map from every exposed angle. By sundown the three of us had cleared two more sides, leaving only the bottom and one side still covered, but the light failed quickly in the canyon.

Base had tried to call me and Jack several more times during the day, and at one point, we saw a flier high in the east, over the area we'd been heading before killing my transponder.

"We'd better dig in for the night," Jack said.

"If we're going to uncover this, we'd better work through the night," I said. "Now that the wind has died, they'll eventually see Nellie's fresh tracks and follow them back here."

"Yeah, but if we're lucky they won't find the tracks until tomorrow, then it will take hours for them to get here by truck or blimp. But if they keep those fliers looking all night, they would see our work lights or even our IR signatures and be here before morning. I think we should get underground."

I hated to leave the find for that long but reluctantly agreed. Once out of our suits and settled in our burrow for the night, I linked my suit's computer to Nellie so that we could both see the video on her foldout display screen. I instructed the computer to build a 3D map based on the footage and overlay the actual video with graphics. We both immediately noticed that among the thousands of points some were three to four times larger than the rest, looking more like embedded pearls than distant stars. Those pearl points were located in pairs, some almost touching and others separated by up to an inch. Each pearl was also connected to another, more distant, pearl by a hair-thin line.

"Weird," Jack said in an almost whisper. "Those bolos or barbells are some kind of pattern, but . . ."

"Computer, overlay any existing star charts in the database with these patterns."

"I have only rudimentary navigational aid star charts in my local database," the computer said in its charming southern belle voice, causing Jack to look at me with a smile and raised eyebrows. "Do you want me to search the base archives or send a download request to Earth?"

"Does Nellie have star charts?" I asked the still-grinning Jack.

"Malcolm? You must really . . ."

"Just answer the question."

He shook his head. "No real need. Go ahead and tap base camp; it's only a matter of hours until they find us anyway."

"Check the base first, then send to Earth if they don't have an all-inclusive chart."

"I'm loading the 3D star chart from base camp data stores," the computer said. "Please provide a relative scale for the newly constructed pattern."

Jack and I looked at the slowly rotating pattern on the screen, then back at each other with shrugs.

"We have no scale. You'll have to look for relational patterns, then adjust scales accordingly."

"Understood," the computer said.

"Inform us if you have any pattern match greater than seventy percent."

"Understood."

Radio calls from base camp increased after the computer's download connection, but we ignored them. Jack started fixing a simple dinner, but I couldn't stop looking at the pattern. I could see two exceptions to the pearls appearing in pairs. A single pearl resided in one corner of the block but was connected to the nearest pair by a line nearly two feet long. The second exception was a line that ran to a large cluster in the diagonally opposite corner, but due to my shaky camera work, the computer just showed them as a slightly disc-shaped clump.

We took turns counting while we ate and agreed upon seventeen pearls, excluding the clump.

The display changed abruptly, showing the original pattern in blue, overlaid with a new blinking red pattern. The legend at the bottom of the screen identified the red as "KNOWN STARS." A little over half the points overlaid perfectly, but a few were shifted, all in the same direction, by different amounts. About twenty percent of the stars in the blue pattern had no red counterpart, and none of the red points aligned with the pearls.

"Well, crap," muttered Jack. "That wasn't much help."

"Computer? If you take known movement into account and project backwards, would some of those stars from our database have matched the new pattern at some time in the past?"

At first, the computer didn't understand the request, but after I explained it in simpler terms, a counter appeared at the bottom of the screen, and the red stars started creeping toward the blue points. When they stopped moving, the number on the counter read "4372 BCE." Aside from six that blinked a label of "track unknown," all of the shifted red stars now matched. There were still no points at the pearl locations.

"Damn! Over six thousand years ago," I said.

"They're still not as old as I expected," Jack said.

"Computer? Have you displayed all the stellar information you have? Please show quasars, pulsars, brown dwarfs, comets, asteroids and galaxies, any objects that would show up within this pattern."

"And black holes," Jack included.

The red star pattern density nearly doubled. Now six dots matched locations with the pearls.

"Computer. Show black holes or singularities as green."

Dozens of points flashed green, including all six that were coincident with the pearls.

"So," Jack said and sat back with a wide grin. "They travel using black holes."

"Or maybe just use them to communicate? Computer? Label the Sol system if it is on this map."

SOL appeared next to the star nearest the lone corner pearl.

"Oh, wow!" Jack said and crawled up next to the screen. He pointed at the pearl nearest Earth. "We enter a black hole here . . ." He moved his finger along the line to the next pearl. "And exit here, then move in normal space to this black hole . . ."

"These are too conveniently placed," I said. "I bet they're artificially constructed wormholes."

He nodded and continued tracing the path, big jumps between black holes with the lines, and small trips to the next black hole, then another jump. The path led all the way to the big clump at the opposite corner.

"Grand Central Station," he said, tapping the clump.

"Well, there isn't anything really new about that idea," I said.

"Except this time it's real!"

Once again, my scientific mind refused to see the obvious as a real possibility, but I shoved those thoughts aside and laughed. "Yeah, there is that. Maybe."

We stared at the display for a few minutes, neither of us talking. Then I tapped the cluster on the screen, stood up, and started donning my suit. "I need to see this clump again."

"Dawn is still five hours away," Jack said.

"Does it matter? We have to assume they know where we are now."

Twenty minutes later, we stood atop the diamond cube and beneath a brilliant Martian night. Somewhere out in that thick star mass lived other sentient beings. It was now fact, not speculation. We looked down, switched on our helmet lights and dropped to hands and knees.

The pearl clump was near a top corner and when our lights revealed it, we both gasped, then laughed. When viewed from the correct angle, the thirty-five pearls formed a ring around a central point or star. The last line in the "path" connected to a pearl in that ring.

Daylight still hadn't penetrated the canyon when we took one last look at the cube.

Jack fidgeted, looking from me to his wrist computer, then back at me. "This still makes me nervous, Malcolm. What if there's another storm or radiation alert?"

"It's a risk, but I can override communication security with voice recognition and you can't. And if we all go, they will find us for sure. Nellie's tracks are just too easy to see from the air."

He still looked uneasy. In order to ensure that MarsCorp didn't hide the find for years while they tried to think up a way to exploit it, we'd decided to break the news to Earth ourselves. Jack would go east, then call base, telling them he was looking for me. That would hopefully make them focus their search east of the canyon while I went west to the uplink antenna on the crater wall a mile from the base camp.

"You're just pissed that you have to provide the diversion this time."

He didn't laugh or even smile. "If you run most of the day, you should be back at the base camp just after sunset. You have the extra tank and water?"

"Yes, Mom."

He gripped my arms and squeezed. "Call if you get in trouble. And I'll come and rescue your sorry tail again."

"Get moving!" I said.

He started south, to exit the canyon from that end, and his graceful, gazelle-like stride took him out of sight in seconds. My gait was awkward as I started for the canyon's north end, but it soon smoothed out. Jack was still definitely the best Martian, but I was getting better.

IN A WIDE SKY, HIDDEN

Warm liquid gurgled away, and the kettle field winked off, leaving me naked, wet, and trembling in the soup kitchen's receiving chamber. My traveling companion, Roger, waited with clothes. Humanoid in shape but impossibly thin, his eight-foot-tall metallic figure moved with an almost liquid grace as he stooped to help me into the robe. My new skin felt raw against the thick fabric, but, like the chills, it was caused by the transfer and only temporary.

"Is she here?" I said while bending down to pull on a pair of quilted boots.

"No obvious signs," Roger said and handed me a glass of bourbon.

I took a long sip and moaned as its burn saturated me from the inside out.

"Thank you," I muttered.

His bulbous head nodded a slight acknowledgment. "You should really drink something else upon reconstitution," he said. "Tea, perhaps. That really doesn't help."

"No obvious signs of her? What does that mean?" I said.

"Skimmer forty-eight found something interesting. I'll be able to tell you more when its full report arrives in about five minutes."

I looked up at his smooth, featureless face hovering two feet above mine. Even after nearly eighty years of association and friendship, my human hind-brain still expected facial expressions when I looked at him. Finally, when he offered no further information, I shrugged and took another sip.

It wasn't real bourbon, only a molecule-by-molecule reconstruction from local materials, but unlike a human mind instantaneously transferred into a soup-kitchen body via a quantum link, no method could reinstall the soul into the body of bourbon. In other words, I had tasted real aged Kentucky bourbon on Earth and flattered myself by thinking I could tell the difference.

Finally starting to feel warm, I sealed the robe and crossed to the exterior door. When I touched the handle, my shell activated, then expanded as I stepped outside. The nano-cloud shell protected me from microorganisms, radiation, and temperature extremes but did not block the wind. Roger had, for this very reason, landed our soup-kitchen module on a windy plateau, high in a craggy mountain chain that formed a rocky archipelago on this mostly oceanic world.

I crossed to the precipice with arms spread wide. My robe snapped and fluttered, an alien sound amid the simple mutterings of rock, water, and wind. I knew when I found Regina, it would be on a world with strong winds. Like this one.

Of course, wind alone wasn't enough. She also loved color and this was a lifeless, monochromatic place. Six hundred feet below, white spray from a gray ocean boomed against black basalt walls. Even the sky was a thick, milky gray all the way to the horizon. I had personally surveyed seven hundred and eight water-based worlds, only twelve of which had life. Living planets always had water, but water-rich planets didn't always spawn life. If this world was indeed dead, I would not grace it with a name, only a catalog number.

Roger shifted next to me, then bent down to speak. "Skimmer forty-eight completed its report. Apparently, it found no microscopic life, either in the air or water, but has found what it's calling 'engineered macro-life.'" Before I could ask for clarification, he continued, "There is some rather confusing video, but you know how excitable skimmers can be when they find life. I suspect it might be easier to just go see for ourselves. Are you ready to fly?"

I tossed back the last of my bourbon and threw the glass into the sea. My shell contracted around me, and the air inside grew denser as we lifted into the sky. I followed Roger to the south and gained speed, but my thoughts were of my long-missing sister.

Regina was nineteen years older than me and only came home to visit a few times each year, so when she arrived for my tenth birthday party, I was ecstatic to learn she would be staying the entire summer. The day after my party, she packed up some gear and took me on an overnight hike.

"Where are we going?" I asked as we trudged through the waist-high puff grass that filled the prairies of Calliope's central plateau.

She pointed ahead of us to a hill that was the highest point on my parents' five-thousand-acre farm. I had seen it from home and from the air but had never been there.

"It's my special place," she said. "I want to share it with you."

When we arrived, I found that the summit transitioned from grass-covered hillock to a jagged, rocky cliff on the side facing away from our house.

Regina dropped the backpack and half ran, half skipped out onto the broad rock shelf, where she spread her arms and turned in slow circles. The wind whipped at her hair and clothes, giving her the appearance of flying. Pure joy lit her smiling face.

I followed and let the wind take me, too, though not with the abandon Regina showed. At the time I'd been worried about falling off the edge.

She eventually opened her eyes and wrapped me in a big hug. "I love this place. I've really missed it."

"Then why do you keep leaving?"

She almost never talked to me like I was a kid, but this time she just gave me another hug and said, "The galaxy is a big place. Someday you'll understand."

We set up a tent and built a fire, but what I remember most about that night—and all twelve nights we spent on the hill that summer—is the stars. From that hilltop they looked thicker and brighter than anyplace else. So while Regina danced in the wind, I lay on my back staring up at the Milky Way.

Our last night on the hill, she lay beside me and we talked until very late. That's when I told her I wanted to be an explorer.

"I want to be the first human to see all those planets," I said. "I want to be the next Juanita Hernandez, and if there are intelligent aliens out there, I want to find them."

"I think it would be a wonderful way to live your life," she said and squeezed my hand.

We flew through a rainstorm, and as my irritation at Roger for dragging me halfway across the planet grew, I saw my first bit of color. A rainbow, very faint, yet its colors looked brilliant against the bland sky. Focused as I was on that simplest of pleasures, I nearly missed what Roger wanted me to see.

He slowed and pointed.

At first, I thought we were watching another rainbow, then I realized it was moving. Streamers, bands, and sheets of brilliant color filled the sky just south of us. They appeared to flow up out of the roiling ocean, as if the waves themselves had taken on some active and colorful life that involved reaching high into the sky.

As we drew closer, I could see the swirling bands were made up of small, individually fluttering segments. They looked alive. Roger stopped well clear of the phenomenon, but being less cautious and knowing my shell would protect me, I kept going until enveloped in a confusing, whirling storm of flying color.

They appeared biological, or if not, at least a convincing simulacrum. Each was the size of my wide-splayed hand and resembled gossamer-winged fairies of green, red, gold, purple, and orange. Instead of beating wings, they had pinwheel blades that cupped or flattened in the wind, sending them spiraling through the currents like brilliant schools of reef fish.

My heart beat faster and my fingers twitched. The way these brightly colored things used the wind they had to be my sister's handiwork. If she wasn't here still, then she had been.

"Are they robots?" I asked over the comm-link. "Is that why the skimmer called them 'engineered life'?"

"I'm not sure yet. Passive scans don't pick up any electromagnetic radiation. No evidence of radio or laser communication between the individual units. And the fliers don't range very far beyond those lily-pad things on the surface. I think there's a connection. I'm going down closer to the water for samples and to observe."

I floated among the dancing colors and tried not to jump to conclusions, but it could be the first trace of Regina in nearly a century.

During the years following my tenth birthday, we always made the trek out to the hilltop when she returned home, but as her reputation for large-scale, grandiose artistic projects spread, those visits grew less frequent. The year I turned twenty, Regina had been on Peppermint developing her biggest, most ambitious, most secret project ever and invited me to come see the launch.

I had never traveled via soup kitchen before, and the idea of having my body destroyed in one place and rebuilt light-years away terrified me, but humanity had traveled that way for hundreds of years. Having never found a way to beat the light-speed barrier, we are forced to travel between quantum-linked boxes as nothing but information. Fortunately, we are very good at moving information.

Regina collected me from Peppermint's soup-kitchen complex and took me on a quick tour of the capital city. Most of the planet's native plant life emitted a peppermint-like scent that filled the air, making me sneeze and sniffle for most of the afternoon, but it didn't matter, because I always had fun with Regina. She still looked twenty-five. Like most adults, she took advantage of the soup kitchen's ability to store physical structure templates, so every time she transferred between devices, her body was rebuilt using the younger template. I had saved one, too. If I ever wanted to look this age again, I could.

Though honored to be invited and amazed like the rest of Peppermint's populace at Regina's spectacle, I'd been quietly dismayed when she launched the kites. Thousands of them, each over a kilometer wide and carefully designed to not have detrimental impacts on the local biosphere. They were translucent, nearly invisible during the day, but for ten nights that summer they filled the sky over Peppermint's capital with scintillating, glowing colors reminiscent of an aurora borealis. The high-altitude winds also made her kites sing in an eerie, faint contralto.

I walked the streets one night during her show. Aside from the occasional tinkle of dinnerware or a cough from balconies and terraces, the entire city was deathly quiet. Regina's kites were amazing and beautiful, but I was also disappointed. I'd left my birth world for the first time and had looked forward to seeing the stars in the sky of a planet eighty light-years closer to the galactic core.

The last night of her show, Regina collected me and we took a jumper out to a deserted hill nearly a hundred miles from the city, where the peppermint smell of native vegetation nearly overpowered my nose. From there, her kites were just a dim, flickering glow. Then, at midnight, they faded out entirely, leaving the sky dark and thick with stars.

"I'm hoping one side effect of my light show will be to make people also appreciate this beautiful sky once my lights vanish."

She always formed plans within plans like that.

"I made you something," I said and fished the long string of tiny beads from my pocket, then handed it to her. She gasped, carried it over to the jumper, and switched on the lights.

"Oh, this is beautiful," she muttered. "They're all planets and each one is different. Are they . . ."

"Yeah, each one is a geographically accurate reproduction of a settled planet. All four hundred and nine of them."

"But the colors. They're amazing!"

"Yeah, they're glass, but assembled at scale with the correct colors. You should see it under magnification!"

She gave me an enormous hug and wiped her eyes. "This is the best gift I've ever received. It's amazing. And beautiful. You're quite an artist. Thank you."

After putting it on, she shut off the lights and we returned to the hill.

"I talked to Mom last month and she told me you'd decided to make custom jewelry instead of exploring," she said. "You're obviously very good at it, but why the change of heart?"

"The whole explorer thing was kind of a childish idea," I said, turning away from her and looking at the thick band of the Milky Way.

"For the last ten years you've thought of nothing else. Are you sure you didn't cave in to peer pressure? Mom seems to think it was one particular girl who laughed at you."

"No! I just grew up. I stopped wanting to be a circus clown, too, and nobody hassled me about that decision."

"Okay, I just needed to hear it from you," she said.

We lay on the ground, staring at the sky, and I found myself getting angrier.

"And damn it, you're all just big hypocrites! I mean, Mom and Dad live on a backwater planet, having babies and raising them. You create art on a grand scale. You're both contributing to humanity with things that AI and machines can't do. Why are you all pushing me to do a robot's job? Why can't I contribute something of value?"

"Since when do you think exploring isn't valuable?"

"You know what I mean. Exploration has been handled by robots for hundreds of years. It's pretty much just a matter of collecting information and cataloging it. There is no real romance or excitement to that. Not like in the old books."

She took my hand and squeezed it, the way she did when I was a kid. "There are six hundred billion humans scattered throughout the spiral arm. So many people and yet they are mostly bland and the same. Be different. It's fun to surprise people. Dare to be unique!"

When I didn't reply, she was quiet for a while, then said, "What's her name?"

"Who?"

"The selfish girl who wants you to stay on Calliope with her and not explore the galaxy."

I stood up and brushed off my clothes, suddenly hating the smell of peppermint. "I'm ready to go back."

I spent the rest of that night getting drunk and slept in the next morning. When I woke up, I found a handwritten note waiting for me.

COME FIND ME. —Regina

I assumed she meant to find her for breakfast or lunch, but as I learned from the local news, she had taken advantage of the media focus on her show and staged a dramatic disappearance. Her statement, sent to the local press and soon spread across all settled space, was simple yet mysterious and teasing.

"I have found a world of my own. It will be my masterpiece."

Roger handed me a small stasis box containing a red pinwheel. "They are biological," he said. "But as I suspected all along—since there isn't a global biosphere—they are engineered, not naturally evolved. Of particular interest to you and your search, they contain recombined DNA from Earth. So far I've identified starfish, dragonfly, squid, and about a dozen others."

I stared at the little animal, its movement and metabolism suspended for study. "But Regina wasn't a biologist."

"It's only an estimate—I would need some extended observation time to be sure—but their biology suggests they breed and spread quickly. I suspect they'll fill the planet in another hundred years. It's hard to be certain without knowing the size of the initial seed population, but I also estimate that they started spreading naturally about eighty years ago."

Roger continued talking. Something about those lily-pad things processing the minerals in the seawater using sunlight and providing food for the pinwheels, which in turn acted as bees or butterflies and cross-pollinated the lily pads. Though he was obviously fascinated by the setup, I couldn't focus on his words. My mind roared and my pulse raced.

The timing was too much of a coincidence. Regina wasn't a biologist, so she might have needed those extra years to learn what she needed to know and then perfect her design. "A world of my own," she had said. "My masterpiece." This was a dead planet, with plenty of wind and water. A blank canvas for a living piece of art that could last forever.

"She's here," I whispered.

"I think it's highly likely," Roger said. "Or at least she's been here in the past."

"Let's find an island closer to these critters, move the soup kitchen down here and set up a shelter," I said, still really not focusing on the present.

"It's already on the way."

I nodded and opened the stasis box. The pinwheel twitched, then shuddered and finally sprang into the air with more vigor than I'd expected.

———

I had been slow to take up the search for Regina. I was young and went back home to the girl, but during the next few years that ended, and when Regina never returned, my curiosity and a desire to see her eventually won out.

Within hours of her announcement, serious searchers with DNA sniffers tracked her through three jumps to a quantum hub on Juanita's Rest. If she jumped to a soup kitchen connected to that hub, she must return to the same hub. That is the only way the quantum entanglement works. Like most hubs, it had a maximum of five hundred connections, but only four hundred and ninety-nine of those connections were registered. No one knew the destination code for connection two hundred and seven.

The wildest speculation hinted that she took a slow ship, or used some new technology, but most just decided to await her return. It was easy enough for news services to keep DNA sniffers deployed at the hub. She had to pop up eventually.

Knowing her departure hub was covered, I started searching the cataloged worlds that weren't settled. That was when I found something surprising. Humanity has never found a way to beat the speed of light, but we're able to pump great speed into small, quantumly entangled robotic probes. In true von Neumann fashion, our probes arrived in a new star system, used in situ resources to build copies of themselves that were also connected to the entangled network, and then launched themselves at the closest stars to repeat the process. For centuries, humanity's frontier advanced steadily in all directions. Then it stopped.

Someone had realized the transport network contained ten thousand new gates that had never been used. A law was passed requiring a human or independent AI to physically visit new systems and approve the next wave's launch. Unfortunately, no one appeared to care. Except, of course, for Roger and me.

We found an island only a few miles from the westernmost edge of the pinwheel flock, and I sat on a rock, watching the soup kitchen turned construction robot as it built our shelter. Scavenger robots floated in a holding pattern near the soup kitchen, waiting their turn to drop minerals into the hopper and then zip off to find more. I, too, loitered near the site, but only in anticipation of the bed's completion. I really needed a nap.

Roger stopped supervising the construction from the other side and abruptly strode toward me.

"Skimmer four-four-five thinks it might have found Regina's base of operations."

I leaped to my feet and almost fell over backward.

"Don't get too excited," Roger said. "It also says there are no working power sources, and it appears inactive."

Regina's island resembled a crooked rock finger soaring two hundred feet into the gray sky, and once we neared the pinnacle, I understood why the skimmers had initially missed her base. A horizontal slot had been cut deep into the side of the stone and hidden in shadow. We landed on a narrow ledge created by the cut, but I could see only vague shapes until I stepped inside the cave.

I shivered in the cold interior and ordered my shell to produce some light. The disassembled remains of an antiquated soup kitchen squatted in one corner. Its modules—still connected to the skeletal frame by cables—were pulled out in various directions like entrails dragged from a vulture's dinner.

Stacked crates with labels describing concentrated proteins sat against the deepest wall. She must have used those to make food or build her first pinwheel critters. A small habitat occupied the corner opposite the soup kitchen. A table, an overturned chair, and various mechanical devices littered the remaining open floor space. Dust covered everything.

I moved past the clutter to the habitat. If she'd left any kind of records or notes, I'd find them there. Grime coated the habitat windows, and the door squeaked when I pulled it open. The interior was small and littered with spools of wire, paper books, racks filled with equipment, and a narrow bed containing a long-dead human body.

I gasped and stumbled backward. In my one hundred and twenty-two years of life, I had never seen a dead person. Death was rare. There were religious sects who refused soup-kitchen travel, so their members could never be rejuvenated and lived out normal human lifespans, but I didn't know any. And sometimes, people died in accidents, but I had never seen that happen, either.

"Roger!"

The rational part of me knew this had to be my sister. But I couldn't reconcile the smiling, animated person who had dominated my memory far longer than I'd even known the actual woman with this slack-jawed, mummi-fied face buried in a nest of tangled white hair.

That thing couldn't be Regina.

Then I saw the colorful glass beads circling her neck.

Roger entered, took a quick look around, then knelt next to the bed. He grew a flat, wand-like device from one hand and passed it along the body. "She apparently died of old age," he said and turned toward me. "I'm sorry."

I blinked away stinging tears. "Are you sure it's . . ."

He stood, put a hand on my shoulder, and gave a gentle squeeze. "Yes. The DNA match is one hundred percent. She's been dead around forty years. Which means she would have died at a physical age of about ninety."

A strange numbness filled me. I'd been looking for so long. The search for her had not only dominated my life, it had become my life.

I knelt next to her, touched the cold, papery skin of her arm, and shivered. "Are you sure it wasn't an accident or disease that killed her?"

"The state of her bone, teeth, hair, and nails indicate that she was very old when she died. It's difficult to know the exact cause without a full autopsy, and even then, most of her soft tissue has—"

"She's lying twenty feet from a fucking soup pot," I whispered.

"It's been disassembled and modified," Roger said. "She apparently used it to cook up her colorful little animals. The quantum-link module had been detached. Once that loses power, the link can never be reestablished."

"She did this on purpose?"

"Yes."

"Then it's like she committed suicide. She knew I would eventually come. Why did she want me to find her like this?"

He said nothing, just squeezed my shoulder again. I looked up at him, suddenly angry that I couldn't drag more meaning from that blank face.

I stood abruptly, feeling dizzy and suffocated, then pushed past Roger to leave the habitat. Once in the cave, I kept going out into the waning sunlight. Looking around, I saw what I knew had to be there: rough steps cut into the stone leading up.

I followed them to the summit, where I found a flat spot on a protruding finger of rock that reminded me of the ledge we'd stood on all those years ago. Without even thinking, I spread my arms and let the wind whip and pummel me.

Roger appeared at my shoulder, but said nothing.

The wind blew my tears along strange tracks. They went into my hair and even my ears, chilling me to the core. And I didn't know if I cried for losing her or being fooled by her grand deception.

"I don't understand. She gave up her family and did all of this for a single piece of art. A statement. Was all of this just something to put her in the art history books?"

Roger remained quiet.

"I mean, what if I hadn't . . ." I stopped, a sudden and sickening realization settling over me. "She knew I would come looking for her. Did she trust me to find her before she died?"

"Possibly," he said. "But if you'd found her alive, would she have gone with you?"

I thought about that as the wind buffeted me, and I stared out over the gray ocean. Her masterpiece wasn't finished. Would she have wanted her fans, critics, and press to come pouring in here before the planet filled with her living color? Could she have returned and kept her planet hidden?

Dare to be unique, she had said. It made my head hurt, or maybe that was from the tears.

"Will you help me bury her?" I said.

"Of course."

I woke up with stars still in the sky but dawn touching the horizon. My back hurt from lying on the stone, and my skin felt raw from the wind. Roger sat on the precipice—between me and the edge—with legs dangling into the darkness. Just in case I'd rolled that way in my sleep? He did things like that.

Earlier in the night, we moved our soup kitchen to Regina's rock and used its construction tools to cut a tomb into the back wall of the cave. We placed my sister inside and closed it up. I then looked through her things, but after finding no journal or electronic records, we used a small army of assemblers to seal the cave with a concrete wall that blended almost perfectly into the native rock. Someday her camp would be of historical interest, but I wanted it undisturbed until I was ready to show it to the galaxy.

I stood up, brushed the dirt from my robe, and was suddenly surrounded by fluttering, swirling pinwheels. I stood on the cliff, arms spread, embracing the wind and the creatures my sister had given her life to birth. They swept up from the sea in undulating cascades, driven hard by a stiff morning wind, and it was easy to see the sky filled with them, changing a gray, dead world into layers of living color. In another hundred years, this planet would be spectacular.

I pulled the necklace from my pocket, rolled the beads between my fingers for a few minutes, then slipped it over my head. Regina had never really been lost. Her dancing and laughter rode the wind of every world I explored.

"I think I'll name this world Zephyr," I said and looked up again. The brightest stars were still visible in the growing dawn.

Roger stepped up beside me, and I knew what he was going to say.

"What will you do now?"

During all the years I'd known Roger, I insisted I would go home and stop exploring once I'd found my sister. She had been my official excuse. Being a personal quest, I never had to justify why I took on a task that could be performed by machines. But Roger knew my reasons were deeper, or he wouldn't have asked.

"Have you given the order to build launch lasers and more probes for the next wave?" I said.

"Not yet. I didn't want to go on alone."

I turned and smiled at him in the dark. "So, where do we go next?"

"Probe 749978 finished its deceleration burn five days ago and entered orbit around a small living world. The skimmers are all excited. They've found plants resembling trees with odd structures in their branches. Probably animal nests of some kind."

Structures?

I shivered, but this time not from the cold.

"Only one way to be sure," I said and waved him toward the soup kitchen.

My sister might no longer be lost, but there were other beautiful souls waiting for me out there. I took one last look at the living color filling her world, then braced for the cold and went to find them.

ACKNOWLEDGMENTS

"The Long Fall Up" first appeared in *Fantasy & Science Fiction* (May 2016).

"Broken Wings" first appeared in *Fantasy & Science Fiction* (July 2018).

"What I am" first appeared in *Asimov's* (November 2018).

"Where Everybody Knows Your Name" first appeared in *Daily Science Fiction* (March 2017).

"Last House, Lost House" first appeared in *Short & Twisted: Fairy Tales* (June 2012).

"Hungry Is the Earth" first appeared in *Fantasy & Science Fiction* (March 2020).

"Bridging" first appeared in *Stellaris: The People of the Stars* anthology by *Baen Books* (September 2019).

"Steal from the Sun" first appeared in *No Shit There I Was* anthology by *Alliteration Ink* (January 2017).

"The Beast from Below" first appeared in *Fantasy & Science Fiction* (March 2018).

"That Other Sea" first appeared in *Escape Pod* (February 2014).

"The Piper's Due" first appeared in *Daily Science Fiction* (April 2016).

"Medic" first appeared in *Jim Baen's Universe* (August 2006).

"Square One" first appeared in *Something Wicked* (March 2013).

"Vigilance" first appeared in *Analog Science Fiction and Fact* (May 2018).

"Stealing Arturo" first appeared in *Baen Books/Baen.com* (February 2014).

"The Rings of Mars" first appeared in *Writers of the Future Vol. 28* (April 2012).

"In a Wide Sky, Hidden" first appeared in *Fantasy & Science Fiction* (July 2017).

AUTHOR'S NOTE

The list of people who have helped me with these stories should probably contain hundreds, but the amazing writers in my Future Classics writers group, present and past, have always been there to read through those rough first drafts and give me excellent advice. Thank you all!

Melanie Fletcher
Michelle Muenzler
J. Kathleen Cheney
Angela Dockrey
Gloria Oliver
Bonnie Jo Stufflebeam
S. Boyd Taylor
Shawn Scarber
Seth Skorkowsky
Jerry J. Davis
Rachelle Harp
Delilah Rehm
Rook Riley
Aelle Ables
Elizabeth Hardage
Derek James
Jake Kerr
Paul Lamarre
Robert Pickering
Kyle White
Jeff Turner
Lisa Holcombe
Laura Seaborn

ABOUT THE AUTHOR

William Ledbetter is a Nebula Award winning author with two novels and more than seventy speculative fiction short stories and nonfiction articles published in five languages, in markets such as *Asimov's, Fantasy & Science Fiction, Analog, Escape Pod* and the SFWA blog. He's been a space and technology geek since childhood and spent most of his non-writing career in the aerospace and defense industry. He is a member of SFWA, the National Space Society of North Texas, and a Launch Pad Astronomy workshop graduate. He lives near Dallas with his wife, a needy dog and three spoiled cats.

facebook.com/william.ledbetter

twitter.com/Ledbetter_sf

goodreads.com/william_ledbetter

ABOUT THE COVER ARTIST

Vincent Sammy is a freelance illustrator who specializes in the genres of horror and science fiction. His work is a combination of traditional and digital media.

He has created artwork for publishers such as *New Con Press, SST Publishers, Cemetery Dance, Jurassic London, Rosarium Publishers* and *Thunderstorm Books.* His work has also appeared in various publications such as *Interzone, Black Static, Parsec* and *Apex Magazine.*

He has been nominated for an Artist of the Year award by the This Is Horror Awards for 2012 and 2013. He was shortlisted for a BSFA award in 2015 and the BFA Awards in 2021 and 2022.

Some of his artwork has made appearances in movies such as *Chronicle, Tigerhouse* and Stephen King's *The Dark Tower.*

He resides in Cape Town, South Africa, with his wife and daughter.

Find more of his work at:

karbonkay.wordpress.com

facebook.com/karbon.k.art

twitter.com/karbonK

instagram.com/karbon.k

INTERSTELLAR FLIGHT PRESS

Interstellar Flight Press is an indie speculative publishing house. We feature innovative works from the best new writers in science fiction and fantasy. In the words of Ursula K. Le Guin, we need "writers who can see alternatives to how we live now, can see through our fear-stricken society and its obsessive technologies to other ways of being, and even imagine real grounds for hope."

Find us online at www.interstellarflightpress.com.

 facebook.com/interstellarflightpress

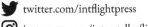 twitter.com/intflightpress

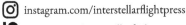 instagram.com/interstellarflightpress

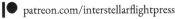 patreon.com/interstellarflightpress

Milton Keynes UK
Ingram Content Group UK Ltd.
UKHW010815081123
432193UK00005B/343

9 781953 736260